Where no men have gone before,
Venture boldly now.
To the blazing sea of stars,
Point the shining prow.

Range the never-ending dark,
Seeking life's undying spark.
On beyond all matter's end,
Bear the race that comes as friend.
Light-years past the last red sun,
Leave the mark of men.
Then turn homeward, toward the day
You go forth again.

—*John Jakes*

John Jakes

was born in 1932 and raised in Chicago, graduating from De Pauw University with an A.B. degree. He also holds an M.A. from Ohio State University. He began to write while still in college and unlike many writers, he had relatively little difficulty in selling his early efforts. Among the editors who aided and encouraged Jakes were Howard Browne, Damon Knight, and Donald A. Wollheim, who was the first to start him writing historical novels (published under the pen-name of "Jay Scotland"). These books were to prove crucial in providing the experience and recognition for Jakes to undertake the bestselling Bicentennial series. His books have appeared in translation all over the world. John Jakes is married, the father of four children, and lists among his organizations the Authors Guild, the Dramatists Guild and the Science Fiction Writers of America.

John Jakes

THE BEST OF JOHN JAKES

Edited and with an introduction by
Martin Harry Greenberg and Joseph D. Olander

DAW BOOKS, INC.
DONALD A. WOLLHEIM, PUBLISHER
1301 Avenue of the Americas
New York, N. Y.　　10019

COPYRIGHT © 1977 BY JOHN JAKES.

All Rights Reserved.

Cover art by Jack Gaughan.

ACKNOWLEDGMENTS

POLITICAL MACHINE, from Amazing Stories, © 1961 by Ziff-Davis Publishing Co. THE HIGHEST FORM OF LIFE, from Amazing Stories, © 1961 by Ziff-Davis Publishing Co. ONE RACE SHOW, from Galaxy, © 1962 by Galaxy Publishing. Corp. LOVE IS A PUNCH IN THE NOSE, from Bizarre Mystery Magazine, © 1966 by Pamar Enterprises, Inc. THERE'S NO VINISM LIKE CHAUVINISM, from Amazing Stories, © 1965 by Ziff-Davis Publishing Co. RECIDIVISM PREFERRED, from Amazing Stories, © 1962 by Ziff-Davis Publishing Co. ON WHEELS, © 1973 by Warner Paperback Library. MACHINE, from Fantasy & Science Fiction, © 1952 by Mercury Press, Inc. THE SELLERS OF THE DREAM, from Galaxy, © 1963 by Galaxy Publishing Corp. HERE IS THY STING, from Orbit 3, © 1968 by Damon Knight.

FIRST PRINTING, JUNE, 1977

1 2 3 4 5 6 7 8 9

PRINTED IN U.S.A.

Contents

Introduction	7
Machine	13
from On Wheels	17
Political Machine	34
The Sellers of the Dream	51
The Highest Form of Life	90
One Race Show	102
Love Is A Punch in the Nose	130
There's No Vinism Like Chauvinism	141
Recidivism Preferred	185
Here Is Thy Sting	198
A John Jakes Bibliography	248

DEDICATION

For Donald A. Wollheim

Introduction

Science fiction is an attractive *genre* for many writers, although relatively few can master its form and themes. It is also something of a closed system, with a relatively small group of men and women controlling the sf marketplace and the apparatus by which young writers can achieve sales and recognition. Indeed, in a number of cases, the same individuals perform both the buying and evaluation functions.

Many writers have failed to achieve recognition in science fiction (as they have in all forms of literature) who deserved it. This absence of appreciation derives from a number of sources. For example, young writers often produce uneven work; if their early novels are not well received, their later, better work may not receive the notice due it—reputations are built early in American culture, and it is difficult (but not impossible) to recover from negative reactions at the beginning of a career. It is also possible that a fine professional writer can be simply overlooked among the hundreds of sf books published each year.

Recently, a number of outstanding sf writers of the Fifties and early Sixties have been "rediscovered" or otherwise rehabilitated. Talented craftsmen like T. L. Sherred, Charles Harness, Margaret St. Clair, Wyman Guin, Daniel F. Galouye, and the late Fredric Brown and Mark Clifton were underevaluated and underappreciated during their most productive years. However, in the last few years, writer/editors like Barry Malzberg and Harlan Ellison have contributed to the reputational resurrection of some of these individuals.

Unfortunately, for science fiction most of these writers are no longer active, either because of death, illness, or disillusionment. A few solid writers of the Fifties and Sixties moved on to more lucrative areas of literature

—three of the most prominent being John D. MacDonald, Michael Shaara, and John Jakes.

John Jakes has been a phenomenally prolific writer in a business characterized by prolificity. At the age of 44 he is the author of over 200 short stories and 50 novels in a variety of fields, not to mention 10 plays and musicals. He has worked in both fiction and non-fiction, concentrating most recently on the historical novel. He is best (at last) known as the author of The American Bicentennial Series; a group of eight novels tracing the evolution of one American family from before the American Revolution to the present day. One hopes that he would consider doing a ninth novel, projecting the Kent family into the future. The first five volumes have enjoyed tremendous success, with total sales of more than 11,000,000 by mid-1976. He is the first writer in history to have four novels (THE FURIES, THE REBELS, THE SEEKERS, and THE TITANS) on the *New York Times Book Review* best-seller list in a single year. Not bad for a man who started out to be an actor.

John Jakes was born in 1932 and raised in Chicago, graduating from DePauw University in Greencastle, Indiana with an A.B. degree. He also holds an M.A. from Ohio State University. He began to write while still in college and unlike many writers, he had relatively little difficulty in selling his early efforts. In fact, Howard Browne, who bought some of his early stories for *Amazing* once remarked that Jakes broke into professional writing more easily than anyone he had ever known. Browne was among the first of a number of editors who aided and encouraged Jakes, including Damon Knight, whose words "Try us again" on a rejection slip renewed his confidence, and Donald Wollheim, then of Ace Books, who bought four historical novels from him. Along with the sale of two historicals to Avon (published under the "Jay Scotland" name) these books were to prove crucial to Jakes' career, since they provided sufficient experience and recognition for him to be invited to write the Bicentennial series for Pyramid.

Jakes sold his first story "Machine" (included in this volume) to the late Anthony Boucher for *The Magazine of Fantasy and Science Fiction* in 1952 while still a student in college. Between 1952 and 1974 he published a total of 75 science fiction and fantasy stories, as well as 20 novels. During examination week of his senior year at DePauw he completed his first book, THE TEXANS RIDE NORTH, a fictionalized account of the post-Civil War cattle drives written for young people. He later wrote a number of young adult books, including the non-fiction FAMOUS FIRSTS IN SPORTS; TIROS: WEATHER EYE IN SPACE; MOHAWK: THE LIFE OF JOSEPH BRANT; and a science fiction novel, TIME GATE, which was a selection of the Junior Literary Guild.

For seventeen years following graduation from college he worked at a variety of occupations, principly in the advertising field. When he became a full-time writer in 1971 he left his job as Creative Director of the Dayton office of Dancer Fitzgerald Sample, one of the largest advertising agencies in the United States. Like Frederik Pohl, his experience in advertising found expression in his science fiction, most notably in the novelettes "The Sellers of the Dream" and "There's No Vinism Like Chauvinism."

Jakes' original ambition to become an actor was not completely frustrated since he continues to act in community theater when time permits, most recently in TOBACCO ROAD. His musical talents have resulted in a number of original works including PARDON ME, IS THIS PLANET TAKEN, one of the very few science fiction musicals ever attempted; DOCTOR, DOCTOR!, a musical comedy adaptation of the Moliere farce; SHEPHERD SONG, a musicalization of the SECOND SHEPHERDS' play; and WIND IN THE WILLOWS, based on the Kenneth Grahame classic.

In science fiction and fantasy, he is perhaps best known as the author of the BRAK THE BARBARIAN books, and while these are solid entertainment they have obscured his more important and serious efforts, for Jakes is a skilled exponent of social commentary and social satire. This is apparant in most of the stories in this book, as well as in a number of his novels, especially BLACK IN TIME (Paperback Library, 1970); SIX-GUN PLANET (Paperback Library, 1970); and ON WHEELS (Warner Paperback Library, 1973).

BLACK IN TIME is one of the few science fiction novels with a Black protagonist and the only one based on the theme of Black history. It is the story of the struggle between Whisk, a white rabble-rouser who uses religion in his battle against the claims and demands of Blacks, and Harold Quigley, a young Black professor who travels back in time studying the history of his people. In brief, the novel revolves around Quigley's efforts to stop Billy Roy Whisk, who wants to change history in order to perpetuate slavery, and Black militant Jomo, head of Brothers United for Revolution Now (BURN) who wants, by murdering Mohammad, to prevent the destruction of the great Black African civilizations and empires that once flourished in Africa. The book, although somewhat dated, is an interesting excursion through Black history, featuring an alternate America where whites are discriminated against by the dominant Black majority.

In SIX-GUN PLANET Jakes develops a society patterned on that of the old American West, complete with gunfighters, pinto ponies and wild Indians. But the planet Missouri has a number of interesting features, not the least of which is the fact that some of the gunfighters, ponies, and Indians are robots. If this all sounds somewhat familiar to you, you are right—the idea was very successfully done in film form by Michael Crichton and called WESTWORLD. Missouri is a planet that made a conscious decision to throw out modern technology and a high standard of living in exchange for an ideal, an attempt to rebuild the present with what the inhabitants believe is the best possible past and the story of what happens to ideals when the truth intrudes. Given the present infatuation in our society with nostalgia, SIX-GUN PLANET can be read as a humorous but grim warning. Jakes' novel is superior social satire, rich in detail and a delight to read. The final shootout between pacifist Zak Randolph and the legendary gunslinger Buffalo Yung is a classic.

Jakes' finest science fiction novel, like the two previously discussed, attracted little or no attention. And that is a shame because ON WHEELS is a superior work that creates a believable, detailed society that lives on America's highways, constantly moving and organized in clans whose family names derive from their environment—the Ramps, the Cloverleafs, the Holidays, the Johnsons (from the motels that dot America—a group that lives in orange-roofed communal vans). Members of this culture do not permit themselves to go below 40 miles per hour—indeed, even to approach that feared figure brings on convulsions. ON WHEELS combines biting social satire with breathtaking action, including some of the most exciting racing scenes available anywhere in fiction. It is an excellent treatment of what the invention of the automobile has meant to America and of America's love-hate relationship with the machine.

Now that their author is one of the best-selling writers in the history of publishing we may yet see these novels back in print. John Jakes is representative of the solid professional who filled the pages of AMAZING, GALAXY, FANTASTIC, IF, COSMOS, and all the other magazines of the Fifties and Sixties, and science fiction will always be in their debt.

—*The Editors*

Machine

This is the first story that John Jakes ever sold. It was purchased by Anthony Boucher (who made a number of suggestions for strengthening the ending) for *The Magazine of Fantasy and Science Fiction,* one of the "big three" of the post-World War II era. It deals with one of the oldest and most honored themes in science fiction—the struggle between man and man's creations.

"Helen, I want you to get rid of that Goddamned toaster!" Charlie shouted, nursing his hand and glaring at the shining silver box buzzing faintly beside the remains of breakfast.

His wife, looking fresh and pretty in her print robe, hurried into the kitchen, pouting a little as she said, "Charlie, I wish you wouldn't shout so. The neighbors will hear you. What's the trouble?"

Charlie sat down and fumbled for a cigarette. He pointed at the toaster and glowered, "I reached out to put another piece of bread in, and the thing jumped and burned my hand."

"Oh, Charlie," Helen cooed, like a mother reproving a naughty boy.

"I swear to God that's what happened," Charlie said earnestly, showing her his hand, with a small area of skin colored a bright pink.

Helen patted his arm. "Aunt Bertha gave us that toaster and it's very useful."

"I burned myself last week, too. I didn't tell you about that."

Helen sank down into a chair.

"I don't know what we're going to do, Charlie. Your

notions about mechanical things are wearing me out." Her voice grew harsh, fingernail-on-blackboard. "Those fixations of yours are . . . well, just plain silly."

Charlie rubbed his pink hand. "OK, I don't feel like arguing. We'll decide tonight."

"But I go to the Women's Club tonight. Some very important man is lecturing on psychiatry . . ."

"Gimme a kiss, I gotta leave."

Petulantly Helen kissed him. She couldn't help hugging him a little, too. She did love him.

He hurried out, smiling just a bit. She looked at his hand as it pulled the doorknob and shut the door. A flash of pink-singed flesh . . .

"He probably bumped against it," she smiled, "the big oaf . . ."

Buzzzz, said the toaster complacently.

Charlie took the streetcar to work. He always rode the trolley because you couldn't trust an automobile. That was part of it.

As the bell jangled and he settled into his seat he thought about Helen, and couldn't see how she could be so blind about the toaster.

I know machines do have souls! he told himself as he had done so many times before. Helen and all the rest laugh, but none of them has ever seen a soul. How can they say a machine doesn't have one, if they don't know what to look for? And then they ignore the evidence that proves—*proves!*—that all mechanical things have souls, some good, some bad, just like men are good and bad. People don't pay any attention to the automobiles that run well for years, or the ones that break down and kill their drivers on the first thousand miles. Those wiring circuits that start fires. Or boilers that explode. Creation —man or machine—is soul! Then there was Rudy Bates, my roommate. Never got beyond his freshman year in college. Always laughing. His bright new automobile— smashed up on a bridge two days after he bought it. Rudy with a broken neck and no more laughter. If you look, you can tell the bad machines. Most people just don't look. The good ones won't hurt you. But the bad ones will . . . kill you. *I* watch, and *I* can see the creations of men go to pieces and kill. The machines with the bad souls . . .

Yeah, Charlie thought as the trolley rumbled, yeah, and that toaster is one of the bad ones. I've got to get rid of it before it does any more damage.

The conductor called his stop and Charlie got off. He could always depend on the trolleys. They were good machines. But the toaster . . .

Walking toward the office building, his mind focused:

Tonight, Helen had said. Tonight was her Women's Club meeting. He'd be home alone . . . to take care of the toaster . . . smash it . . .

He had to smash it before it . . . He couldn't think about it.

Helen left at seven that evening, worried. Charlie had a strange expression on his face. She decided it might be a good thing to come home early from her meeting. Charlie looked tired and several times she caught him staring up at the shelf where the toaster gleamed. It was silly, of course, but she ought to keep an eye on him.

Charlie finished the dishes and pulled down the kitchen blinds.

Walking into the pantry, he took down the chrome-plated machine and set it on the kitchen table. It squatted there, calm, assured.

Charlie got a hammer from a drawer and walked back to the table.

"Now we'll see who's boss," he growled. He slammed the hammer down on the toaster. But the toaster wasn't under it.

It gave a little jump and slid off onto the floor with a bang. It knew he was trying to kill it. Charlie started to sweat.

He mumbled something half groan, half snarl. Then he bent over and picked up the silver box. That was a mistake.

The lights in the room exploded, dimmed, whirled and exploded once more. Charlie felt sick and infinitely weak.

His hands were frozen to the cool metal of the machine . . . he couldn't let go . . . couldn't . . . couldn't . . .

Then he felt something intangible and yet horribly real . . . creeping . . . from the toaster . . . into his hands . . .

creeping . . . taking over . . . making over . . . He didn't even have time to scream.

Helen opened the front door at nine-eighteen. It had been awfully hard to leave such a fascinating lecture. But the speaker's topic, all about people with odd delusions, kept reminding her of her husband.

"Darling?" she called from the living-room.

"Here," a voice said from the kitchen.

Helen didn't like the sound of that voice. She hurried.

Charlie was just going out the kitchen door. Helen saw him toss a mass of something flaccid and sticky into the garbage can. Although curiously lacking in frame and substance, it could have been the toaster.

Charlie carefully replaced the top of the garbage can and came back into the kitchen, watching Helen all the while. "I threw the toaster away," he said.

Helen started for the door. "We're going to bring that right back . . ."

She stopped, wincing. Charlie's hands were fastened on her arms like bands of metal. Charlie had never been very strong . . . and his eyes . . . they looked so strangely . . . bright . . .

"No," he said, and his voice was flat and brassy. "No."

For the first time in her life, Helen actually felt afraid of him. "All right," she murmured.

"Gimme a kiss," he said, smiling then, as if the smile were a repetition of many others, with no emotion in it. But Helen brushed her lips across his, the fear dying away. . . .

Then she stepped back a bit, cocked her head to one side and grinned.

"You look so funny, Charlie. That man who lectured tonight had a word . . . You look . . . unadjusted!"

Charlie shuffled his legs stiffly. "Not any more." He put his arm around her, and his voice held only the slightest shade of remote disinterest. "Not since we got rid of that toaster."

from On Wheels

> This is the opening action in Jakes' finest sf novel. It ranks with the best accounts of an automobile race to be found anywhere in fiction, and has the added bonus of showing the reader a little of the fascinating society upon which the book is created. After you read this excerpt, you will want to start searching for the novel in your nearest second-hand bookstore.

He was drifting along at 85 mph, just drifting, under the fat Nevada moon that iced the distant mountains, when the radiophone blinked.

The tiny red dashlight went on and off, on and off, slowly, like an injured eye. Billy stared at the spot of color a minute, his mouth tightening up and his mind cooling and coiling. God damn that light. God damn it because there weren't many moments like this in a man's life: alone, quiet, in the bucket of a mother with a big i.c. underhood engine bubbling and muttering and blowing out a thin blueness from the dual exhausts.

He wore neither crash helmet nor belts and, because the Twister was old, an authentic machine from the early '80s when his father had been but a young man, there was a sense of challenge in him hard to express but beautiful to feel: here it was just him, just Billy and lightly padded instrument board and shatterable glass and easy-crinkling hoodmetal between him and the eight empty westbound lanes washed by the moon as they rose toward the ten levels of the Calneva Superstack maybe twenty miles ahead, a concrete temple, a lovely thing, set in a notch of a pass in the mountain.

The red light glowed, went out. Glowed, went out. Billy slapped a control, then dialled too far:

"—the President has announced the lightest casualties thus far in the probing activity in the environs of Peking. The White House said there is no truth to the rumor that the 705th Airpack Infantry has belted in to reinforce the—"

Swearing, Billy fiddled till he got the right wavelength, the intercar.

"Somebody want something?"

"Billy?"

"Yeh, Jobe?"

"You keeping watch out behind?"

He hadn't been, but he said, "Sure." He explored the rearvision mirror quickly. Where there had been but two sets of headlamps a while ago, he now saw several; too many to count.

His second cousin, Jobe Spoiler, two years his junior, chose to let the obvious lie pass. "They come on at the last interchange," he said. "Don't think it was anything but chance. Still, they're pulling up quick."

"Recognize them?"

"Ramps."

Even though there was plenty of cool November night air roaring in through the Twister's open windows, Billy's upper lip grew wet. "They're driving mothers, Jobe?"

A second voice, from the second set of headlamps closest behind, came on the link: the lugubrious, always cheering gravel-rasp of old Tal, Colonel Tal, Colonel Talmadge Spoiler, Esq., a hard charger despite his advancing years. Tal was honored in the clan because he'd completed twelve grades of education, and also because nobody knew precisely how he was related to any of them; thus it was presumed that Colonel Tal might be a key, very important, relative of each and every Spoiler, and he was treated accordingly. Colonel Tal answered, "You know them Ramps are too chickenshit to risk an arrest by ever pushin' a mother."

"They're driving their regular turbines," Jobe chimed in. "Oh-oh. There goes the first one past me—"

"Appears like he's heading up your way, Billy boy," said Tal.

"I caught a flash," said Jobe. "I think it's big Lee himself."

"There go the rest of 'em," said Tal. "Two, three—four. I don't recognize a one."

"Except Lee," said Jobe, not happily.

"Yes, right," said Colonel Tal.

Gearing down, sliding through a long banked curve where the eight westbound lanes angled left, and higher, toward the Calneva Superstack, Billy examined the rear mirror again. Suddenly headlights over in one of the eight lanes going the opposite way blinded him. His bowels tightened.

The mammoth turbine van passed, heading into the east on its dozen oversize tires. Commercial vehicle; not a clan hauler. For an instant he'd known the tickle of fear that was part of driving a mother, his own gawdy orange Twister, long after most of the rest of the clan members had gone to sleep in the big lumbering communal vans. There was always the possibility of being hauled in by the Federal Highway Patrol, though not usually this late at night, only a couple of hours before morning; and not usually this far out in Nevada with the finally cooling desert rushing by blank and empty under the piers of the sixteen concrete lanes that headed to the mountains and the Calneva Superstack.

"Chickenshit," Tal said loudly suddenly. Billy flicked eyes to the mirror, saw Tal's mother yaw, veer off to the side one, two, three lanes, nearly impacting the right guardrail before the Colonel corrected. "Those Ramps ain't got an ounce of principle in their bodies."

Billy's eyes got edgy. "He swipe you?"

"Tried. I'm fine. Appears it's you they want. Bad luck you takin' point for our little cruise tonight."

"Never mind," Billy returned, "I've tangled with that Lee before."

"Never raced him, have you?" Jobe said, sounding worried.

"No, never raced him," Billy admitted. "Mostly at clan parties."

Which, on reflection, had never been much fun with any of the Ramps in attendance.

Billy concentrated on the four sets of four headlamps

coming up fast—he was down to 80 mph in one of the two middle lanes of the eight, waiting to see their pleasure and humming the theme of *The Old Rugged Cross* while he waited.

The clans basically trusted each other's essential honor. No communal vans were ever locked—ever. But some clans just naturally got on together especially well, like the Spoilers and the Cloverleafs, while some were so ornery and high-mouthed, nobody cared for them—and the Ramps classified there.

Oh, everyone was always cordial at festive occasions when all the larger vehicles were locked together and rolling alongside. But there was never all-out friendliness toward the Ramps, simply because they most generally looked for trouble. Not sport; trouble. They were always bragging about their reputed blood connection with the Hardchargers, including the terrible, probably legendary demon driver, Big Daddy.

The first of the Ramp turbines pulled up alongside on his left. It was a personal two-seater, the kind a Ramp man and wife would travel in when away from the clan vehicles and out for an evening's festivity. The Ramps favored low, nasty, unadorned turbines with oversize blowholes at the back end and dark metalflake tones for the paint. If this Ramp machine streaking alongside was anything other than black, Billy couldn't tell. He concentrated on steering; the power steering plant in his mother wasn't the best, being antique, and had to be constantly corrected.

That made this current situation ticklish: the Ramp turbine was edging in, edging in, running nearly hub to hub, so close that there couldn't be a hand's width between the caps. Billy licked his upper lip and kept his head more or less straight front. He wouldn't give the other driver any satisfaction at all. But Billy's eyes moved.

The other driver, the Ramp point man, was in fact Lee. His adenoidal voice came across the radiophone connection, barely audible above the mutter of Billy's engine and the turbine powerplant, "Why, that looks like Billy Spoiler over yonder."

"Believe it is," he said. "That you, Lee?"

"Nobody else. You boys breaking the law again?"

"Guess you could call it that."

"Guess! Hell, Billy, any kid who has to get a cheap thrill driving a gasoline engine isn't doing anything else."

"Listen, it's hard work driving a mother," Billy replied. "It's hard to do what I'm doing right now."

"What you doing, Billy?"

"Holding her steady instead of shoving her over and bouncing you off the road."

Lee Ramp's laugh was flat and mean. "You Spoilers are just full of promises. But when it comes to performance—" He said an obscene word with good humor. Or so it sounded.

A pause. The turbine whined. The Twister muttered. Swooping, the eight lanes graded upward more sharply: now the Calneva Superstack couldn't be more than ten miles away, its superhighway radials jutting off from all levels to disappear into tunnels heading through the mountains west, north, and south. Blue lights like ghostly balls floated at the perimeter of every level of the Superstack, which was a glorious big version of the five-level L.A. Stack of decades ago.

Finally Billy said, "What are you boys doing in this part of the woods?"

"Oh, just running and funning some, Billy."

"Thought the Ramps were cruising up in Minnesota."

"You heard the wrong gossip. Listen, this is a lucky thing, us just bumping into you this way. I've got three of my best bunch along tonight." He mentioned three Ramp names, none of which Billy caught because he was suddenly intent on a flare of light on his right: a set of lamps coming up at top speed along a merge-in feeder that would intersect the main lanes in another mile.

Federal? Or just a stopper machine? His whole system was alert, his whole body relating to his mother, to every jounce of the rough old springs and shocks, every instant of hum of the big wide belts he carried on the wheels. The stoppers were far worse than the threat of Ramps; the Ramps at least were competent drivers, clan people, road people. But the unexpected interference of some numbskull from off the highway—some popheaded kid on a high who was accustomed to starting and stopping but unaccustomed to a moonlight run on the California-Nevada border—that was bad news.

Billy kept watching the in-boring lights on the right. "Lucky how, Lee?"

"Why, I was gonna propose a little action."

"Such as?"

Lee Ramp's laugh had that edge again. "Through the Superstack flat out."

"The lanes narrow down in there. To four."

"Why, that right, and there's seven of us. Ought to be a real sport. Or maybe not, being as how those mothers of yours don't keep up so well—"

"I heard that," came Jobe's voice. Jobe had pulled up tight behind Billy, was riding his right rear fender. "We can match you mile for mile. We can match ole Ramps anytime."

Colonel Tal cleared his throat along the connection. "Jobe, you let Billy decide it, he's point man tonight. He'll—" A hair-raising howl of fiberglass wide belts, a clink-*spang* of old metal, and Billy caught a spew of smoke in the mirror. Colonel Tal veered back to the safe side of his lane. The smoke stopped billowing from under his tires. Tal said, "Lee Ramp?"

"Right here, old buddy."

"You tell these snotmouths you're running with that if they swipe me once more before we figure out what sort of sport we aim to have, I'll blister them off with a bagful of dirty tricks and run their tailpipes up their tailbones. You got that now?"

"I got that," Lee chuckled. "Werty, was that you?"

"The ole futz was gettin' too close," said a new voice along the link.

"You ease off till we decide whether we're going to run the Superstack, Werty."

"I don't take the kind of language that ole futz—"

"Werty, I said you ease off."

Billy glanced left for a fraction, through his open window and Lee Ramp's closed one. As they ran hub to hub with just that sliver of airspace between, he saw Ramp's face by the dashlights. Thin. Scrawny, even. He remembered how poor in color Lee Ramp had looked that last time they quarrelled. It had been at a clan get-together. A quarrel in fun, but with nastiness under the crust. They argued over who had claim on the last hot cup of ginger punch left on the table, as Billy recalled.

He despised Lee Ramp even though he could admit the skinny man had a certain kind of doomed good looks that made some girls crazy about him. Also, Lee was a keen, competent driver despite the fact that he lacked the balls to own and operate an illegal internal combustion job on moonlight runs like this.

Like a special effect hurtling at the audience in some telly flicker, a big over-the-lanes sign zoomed up toward Billy's windshield, glaring in sparkly intensity in the headlamps:

CALNEVA SUPERSTACK LEVELS 1—3
RIGHT LANES ONLY
8 MILES

Sadness tugged at Billy. This peaceful, beautiful night-run had been spoiled by encountering the Ramps. There just weren't many times a man could be alone, really alone in the dark on one of the big Federal I-jobs. The minute the daylight peeped, there'd be vehicles by the hundreds, by the thousands, scurry-ratting toward the megs, toward this or that foolish occupation. Perhaps it was just the juicing up of his courage for the about-to-be run, but he felt a complete and lofty contempt for the poor landlocked people who used their wheels to go somewhere; to go, then stop. Billy had been born in a moving vehicle, had never traveled at a speed below 40 mph to his knowledge, and had never once been off the U.S. of A. Interstate Highway system. You had to say this much for the rotten Ramps: neither had they.

Colonel Tal said, "Billy? On your right hand—"

At the same instant, Jobe Spoiler said, "How do you call it, Billy?"

No time to call it; the pophead merging in from the right in a flare of headlamps was merging all the way, peeling in one, two, three lanes. The little electric runabout, white, and being pushed to the full, had smoke coming off its tires as it bulled over to occupy the same highway space Billy himself was occupying. The runabout was hurtling over like a juggernaut.

Billy couldn't veer left or he'd bounce Lee Ramp, and that wouldn't be right, considering the contest challenge already flung. He was in a bind, so he pedaled the brakes and hoped the increased glow of his tails would warn Colonel Tal and Jobe in time.

The popheaded stopper slotted into Billy's space when Billy's brakes grabbed, and the Twister dropped back. Jobe hit him. Brakes screamed. But it was a light smack. Jobe backed off. Billy held onto the wheel, fighting the antique power steering as it recovered from the shock to the frame. It was a minute of terror: Billy checking the rearvision mirror, heartsick as he watched Jobe whipsaw through two lanes, trying to take hold again and avoid slamming Ramp turbines; Billy checking ahead, touching, just caressing the brake with the tip of his half-boot because the runabout driver—crazy girl or woman—her yellow hair burned in the glare, flying and snapping out the left window—kept applying speed, then slacking off, to tease her pursuit. She carried regular state Tin—Nevadas—rather than the Road plates which the government in Washington granted those who lived always moving on the highways.

"You want to get rid of that or shall I?" Lee Ramp said over the radiophone.

"I will," Billy said, shifting up and laying on gas.

He zoomed up behind the runabout, hands tight on the wheel, and gave it a tap from behind, then braked off just enough. The runabout shot ahead as if fired from a cannon. Then suddenly it veered to the right. The right rear tire blew with a loud report. Billy also heard the girl driver shriek as she foolishly went for the brakes.

The runabout did an out-of-control U and came to a shuddering stop with its bonnet crumpled against the right-hand guardrail. Then Billy's Twister was by, and he saw no more.

But he heard another brake-yell, plus some cursing on the radiophone, then more brake-burning, a crash—

Lee Ramp screamed, "Dacey? You all right?"

"This is Werty, Lee. He was runnin' too far to the right. He hit her."

"Drop back, you stupid son of a bitch. Check him."

Headlights in the mirror receded swiftly as the Ramp turbine slowed. Another mammoth over-the-road sign spanning all eight lanes announced the first levels of the Superstack in five miles. The Ramp headlights zoomed up to size again:

"Dacey climbed out. He's walkin'."

"Attaboy, Dacey," Lee breathed, "attaboy, never stop moving, boy. Wasn't your fault—"

And for a moment, Billy could understand. Sympathize. For even if Dacey Ramp were dead, dead in his brains, something in his body would keep him twitching ahead on his feet, then on all fours if need be, because he'd already suffered the supreme humiliation of having his machine slowed to below 40 mph, then stopped; one thing you never did if you were born of the clans was to permit your forward motion to stop.

"You sure bunged that up, Billy," Lee Ramp said, trying to pretend that Dacey's lack of skill hadn't been at fault. Billy stifled a swear word. No point arguing that it was not his skill at fault, but the girl driver's lack of it. And Dacey's; it was worse for a man, the humiliation of coming to a complete halt. No point worrying, either. He had enough on his mind with the nearness of the Superstack—immense, multileveled, built in the vee of slate mountain walls that extended out to the sixteen lanes where Billy was now; the drivers drove down at the bottom between those walls, raising booming echoes.

What about the girl, though?

A stopper, plainly. Joyriding. He hoped he hadn't killed or maimed her. Christ, he hoped he hadn't.

"Billy boy, you cost me one of my good cousins," said Lee Ramp.

"They's only four lanes in the Superstack," said Colonel Tal; he sounded rough; unhappy; and—Billy's palms sweated all at once—none too sure? "What difference does it make?"

"Plenty of difference if you plan to yellow out," Lee returned.

"Did I say we were going to yellow out? Billy exclaimed.

"No, but you didn't say we were running, either."

"There wasn't any time. That silly popheaded—"

"Will you quit making chicken excuses and say yes or no?" Lee yelled.

The radiophone link actually crackled with the noises

of the challenge. Billy flinched, then felt ashamed of the unbidden reaction. Why did these Ramps buffalo him? No reason they should; they were all talk and swagger, lacking real skill; why, Colonel Tal could ram them up the wall.

Couldn't he?

Eight lanes, sharply inclined upward, fled beneath the Twister's glimmering orange hood. Like a carrion-eater, old Lee's low, mean turbine stayed on Billy's left, its metal suddenly rippling and flaring as the drivers swept under the first of the blue lamps that brightened the approaches to the Superstack. Windshields shot off stars of light; it was possible to glimpse Lee's profile hunched above his wheel.

About two miles up the slope they reached the chute, the place where the eight lanes began to funnel down to four. The Superstack seemed to climb to the sky, concrete-white, untended in the fastness of the mountains. Billy tried to remember its layout; a double super corkscrew; you went up and around and around, and if you didn't turn off at any of the radials on the way up—other freeways, leading to other places in the western U.S.—then you hit another corkscrew down, rolling tire-hot off the mountains onto the grade leading down to golden California.

But it was all sort of vague now, lacking crisp detail. Possible injury to the stopper in the runabout had densed his thoughts, slowed his perceptions. The rock walls ran away smeary behind him on both sides of his Twister, which had now developed a strange alarming shimmy in the rear end.

He checked the speedo. Godamighty! 94 mph and he didn't even know it.

"Colonel Tal?" he said to the radiophone. "We're going in."

Colonel Tal cleared his throat, archly. "Why, 'course."

"Jobe? We're going in."

Jobe was small-voiced. "Sure." Billy feared for him.

"Okay," Lee Ramp said with another of those wasp-edged chuckles. He spoke to his own clan, "You lads hear that?" They heard. "Okay, now you drive so Big Daddy would be proud of every one of you."

"Listen, when are you going to stop telling that chickenshit story that you boys are related to the Hardchargers?" Colonel Tal wanted to know.

"You farty old windbag," Lee answered back, "if Big Daddy was here, he'd *prove* it."

"Don't even believe there *is* a Big Daddy." That was Jobe, making himself sound brave so he would be. Billy squirmed to a tense position in his bucket, held the wheel as tightly as he could. "Don't believe there's even a Hardcharger clan—"

"Is," advised Colonel Tal. "Small and piss-mean, but there is. I've met a few."

"Big Daddy wouldn't wipe his grease rags on you," Lee came back. "He's got fatter nuts to tighten. He's gonna see the Big Fifty before he dies and he can't be bothered with people like you Spoilers. He leaves it to his cousins. He leaves wiping up your kind to us."

Across the connection between the speeding machines, Lee Ramp's laugh sounded like icicles that Billy'd heard snapping on a Vermont power line over the turnpike up there. His eyes crawled to the speedo: an ordinary five places; built to accept 99,999 miles before turning completely. Big Daddy Hardcharger was rumored to have eight places on his custom-modified model. Big Daddy was a maniac—*if* he existed. Death-doomed, the road clans said.

Death. Billy knuckled sweat from his eyes; the wind roaring in the window didn't evaporate it fast enough. He wondered whether he'd see the Firebird this morning.

Colonel Tal refused to lose the last point in the badgering game: "If you Ramps—"

Lee cut in, "What say we all kill the mikes and let's get down to some serious driving?" A connection clicked; other clicks followed. The Ramps had shut off. Billy did the same.

The internal combustion machines thundered up the concrete grade. Colonel Tal pulled out to the left of Lee Ramp. Jobe pulled up on Billy's right. The remaining two Ramps flanked the outside.

Hub to hub, the six machines thundered at the chute. The two outside lanes merged out of existence. The drivers were abreast, in six lanes.

Firebird, Billy thought. *What's it look like, that big red monster trailing flame off its wings?*

Would there be the most beautiful, incredible, cream-breasted naked girl riding it, the bird's blazing back between her bare thighs but not burning them? Billy had his own private conception of the girl some said sat astride the harbinger bird. She was a sweet, clean girl of corn-colored hair and radiant blue eyes; his ideal woman, her clean but voluptuous beauty a contrast to the vengeful look of the burning bird.

I believe there's a Firebird.

No I don't either, it's just some old superstition carried over from a long time ago when there was a hightest gas that used it for signs.

But he glanced to the right anyway, up over Jobe's hood past the pearly blue lights; he saw no phantasmal fire-winged thing flying there. He shuddered a little private shudder. He wasn't signed to die just yet.

The way it worked out was, men who were truly men only saw the Firebird the second before the big wheel revolved the last time. As a consequence, nobody in any of the clans had ever actually looked at the hell-red apparition with his own eyes—

A hard bank to the left coming up ahead.

Billy poured on the gas, edging the Twister's bumper out ahead of his flankers. The incline was moderately steep here. The cars streaked into the beginning of the up corkscrew.

Billy was only partially conscious of discrete details: a signboard warning travelers bound for the huge, sprawling Tahoe meg to KEEP RIGHT; another warning to REDUCE SPEED TO 50 MPH. Billy edged the needle up past 95 mph. The Twister began to rattle and yaw in earnest.

Suddenly, on his right, Jobe disappeared.

Quick glance at the rearvision mirror; Jobe was dropping back, his brakelights lighting up the whole tail end of his mother, spilling scarlet along the waxed rear rocker-panels. The highway climbed upward and around to the left, past the radial that shot off through the tunnel to Tahoe. Sound bounced from the high concrete retaining walls. The Ramp car on his right veered over. Instinctively Billy corrected, edged left. He heard his hubs ping Lee Ramp's, corrected again, the steering touchy, slow.

Jobe was out of sight somewhere down in the beginning of the corkscrew behind them. Billy hoped he was all right. He despised Jobe's fear, but he tempered his fury. The kid was only twenty. Billy had two years on him.

Then there wasn't any more time to fret over why Jobe's nerve had gone smash; they were up past the third-level radials; large signs on either side of the lanes zoomed up—

LEFT LANE ENDS   RIGHT LANE ENDS

Fell behind.

Up higher; around, around and up; leftward; force pushed him back against the bucket as he concentrated on steering within the lane markers while his left boot worked the power brake, his right the gas, both helping control his drift in the endless climbing turn. Right and left outside lanes began to narrow, ready to disappear.

Colonel Tal cut it over to the right to scare Lee Ramp. Lee drove steady on, and Colonel Tal looked like he was scared off, whipping back over to his own lane. But he didn't stay there. His purple-flakepainted mother whammed the side of the Ramp on his left; whammed good and hard.

The impact caught the Ramp driver right as his lane ended. He started to put his own squeeze on Tal, trying to edge into Tal's space. But Tal's hit had put him out of control. He went left instead of right, his left front headlamps scraping the concrete retaining wall that angled in where the lanes narrowed.

Sparks and smoke flew. Billy heard tortured metal yammering. The Ramp turbine would bury its nose in the retaining wall unless its driver eased off. He did, with a sudden pound of brakes that dropped him from sight.

So now they were four, roaring in four lanes up past the sixth level where you could glimpse cold stars—if you dared take your eyes off the unreeling twist of concrete. Colonel Tal was on the extreme left; then Lee; then Billy; then the last Ramp. Two and two; an even split.

They held that formation all the way past the Sacramento radial, the LA-Vegas radial, all the rest, to the top.

The four machines burst out along the straightaway at the summit. About one mile of open, guardrailed lanes connected the two corkscrews. The wind whined cold and sharp through the window.

Lee Ramp edged over. Billy wouldn't give. Lee edged back. Billy's speedo read exactly 101 mph. The old mill in the Twister wouldn't take that much punishment for long.

Off on Billy's left, the sky was a steamy orange above the clouds that covered the polluted mountain megs. Dawn; dawn on the great plains. How beautiful.

And how bracing the air. Sweet in the lungs, with just a tang of oil. How fine this feeling, too; this racing toward the down corkscrew with the radials shooting off at all levels, over and under the four main downspiraling lanes —how good, how pure and right it was to be here. There wasn't a sign of a big blazing death-bird keeping pace in the blueblack sky above.

A horn—two horns. Lee's; Colonel Tal's. Billy instinctively turned his head a fraction, saw Colonel Tal inside his mother there beyond Lee's profile. Colonel Tal's old blue-lit face was convulsed with rage.

Billy whipped his head front, suddenly saw the cause of all the horn-blatting. They were roaring into the right-spiraling down incline now. Ahead, showing its tail lamps, was a big, cumbersome wagon bearing Oregon plates. Faces of scared children were pressed to the rear glass. The frantic driver of the wagon couldn't or wouldn't speed fast enough to escape those four thundering machines coming down on his tail, filling all four lanes. The wagon's blinkerlights began to go on and off, *right turn, right turn—*

The wagon slewed into the extreme right lane, trying for the Phoenix radial that led off on the next level below. The wagon almost made it, too; almost. The Ramp turbine on Billy's right clipped its tail end.

Out of control, the wagon skidded down the exit ramp. Instead of following the ramp's curve, the wagon slammed dead ahead into the wall and burst into a fireball whose intensity Billy felt on his bare skin long after they were corkscrewing on down past.

God damn Ramps, he thought, braking, accelerating, working down through the gears when he could afford his brake foot free an instant. *Should of eased off and let that stopper live; poor damn stopper who probably figured he'd beat the monumental dayside traffic by traveling at night.* Out the corner of his right eye, Billy glimpsed the young Ramp whose turbine had done the damage. His mind seethed with foul words. No matter how much honor was up for grabs, Spoilers didn't countenance that kind of blood. But the Ramp—a beaky nose, not much chin—actually looked happy.

They zoomed down past the fifth level. Billy banged over and handed the Ramp kid a good stiff rap. Give him credit—the youngster held on tight. Billy wobbled back into his own lane, fighting for control. Damn power steering never had been any good. Always needed over-correcting—

Lee Ramp recognized the signs of Billy's distress, and took advantage. He wrenched to the right, pasted Billy's Twister a hard one in the side. As if it were a pre-arranged strategy, the Ramp on Billy's right dropped back suddenly. He steered into Billy's lane, directly behind the Twister, as if he knew something would happen to Billy's machine—

It did; it started to skid to the right. The rear end started flipping around out of control.

Lee Ramp rushed on by and down around out of sight. The retaining wall loomed dead ahead. Billy twisted the wheel left just as his machine started to rise on its left side. She wouldn't come around fast enough.

His right fender hit the wall, scraped, peeled completely off. He heard the yell of metal. Suddenly his correcting worked. The Twister pulled away from the wall; its left tires came down, bam, but didn't blow. Then Billy was weaving on down through the corkscrew.

He still had trouble steering. When he turned the wheel too far, the right front tire whined. Obviously part of the body metal was crimped in dangerously close to the tire.

Cutting it? Slashing it?

His eyes fell on the speedo. 65 mph. Falling. *Never below 40 mph!* Sweet God! A man wasn't a man who let that happen!

He geared, got it wrong, threw it in properly an instant after the tire-whine, and continued on down the corkscrew. The others—two Ramps, Colonel Tal—were long gone ahead.

All at once Billy grew conscious of a gumminess in his

right eyesocket. He swiped his eye with his right hand, examined his fingers. In the blue roadway lights they shone stickyblack.

How'd he been banged that way? When had it happened? In the frozen seconds in which he'd skated away from the wall? He hadn't even felt an impact.

Driving cautiously, he made it down past the first level and into the plum shadows of the western grade leading to California.

About a mile ahead he saw Colonel Tal's red tails. The Colonel's mother was going list-and-bump, list-and-bump, the left rear tire in ribbons. But the old hard charger was driving a good minimum 45 mph nonetheless.

Farther on down the grade, two other sets of tails receded quite fast. Billy's throat filled with bile.

He caught up with Colonel Tal, dodging in and out among a convoy of bullet-shaped milk freighters to do it. He pulled up alongside the Colonel's mother. The Interstate was seven lanes each way now. He flipped on the radiophone.

"Lose a tire, Colonel?"

"Yes, sir, I did, and that's when they lost me. You all right?"

"Got a fenderwell about to rip through a tire, but if I keep her bearing ever so little left I think I can make it."

Colonel Tal made a phlegmy sound. "Lee let me have the middle finger nice and proper before they barreled away."

"That bastard." Hot-faced, Billy searched the shadows far down the grade. But the Ramp lights had disappeared.

"I think they killed that poor stopper in the Superstack," he said.

"They're really a chickenshit bunch," Colonel Tal agreed. "Ought to be stopped in place one of these days, every last one."

"Lee will be. Nobody beats me more than once."

The phlegmy sound again. "Hope you remember that."

Billy chewed his lip. "How'd they take us?"

"I reckon it was bad driving on our part and orneriness on theirs."

"Spoilers don't suffer that kind of hurrah, Colonel Tal."

from On Wheels

"Stop saying it, Billy. Just remember it silent. Inside."
Rebuked, Billy shut up.

Turbine and electric cars from the meg fringe towns at the foot of the grade began to fill the superhighway. They came in at cautious speed from the right-hand feeders. Already the groves to either side of the great elevated road were tinged with light off the mountains. Well, Billy wouldn't forget. Billy'd remember, yes indeed he would. He'd meet up with Lee Ramp again, too. It was inevitable. There weren't that many clans on the highways.

The clans represented about ten percent of the total U.S. population, so the government said. They met on regular occasions—at holidays like Christmas—and when Billy saw Lee Ramp again, he vowed he'd smile and hide the knife till the right moment.

" 'Spose we better head back and hunt for Jobe," Colonel Tal suggested. "He was moving, but not very fas— holy waters of Jordan!"

So excited was Tal that Billy automatically looked left. He saw the Colonel staring at him in the new-breaking daylight across the space that separated their mothers. Billy was acutely conscious of being on policed roadway in a wholly illegal, unsafe, air-polluting internal combustion machine, and that fear gnawed him when he spotted Colonel Tal's gap-jawed expression.

"What's wrong, Colonel?"

Political Machine

Science fiction stories about political elections tend to be of two types—the frightening and the humorous. Stories like Isaac Asimov's "Evidence," Michael Shaara's "2066: Election Day," Stanley Schmidt's "May the Best Man Win," and the late Miriam Allen deFord's "The 1980 President" were all one or the other. Here John Jakes combines a terrifying premise with considerable humor in a story about a political system in which everyone and everything is manipulated.

Five in the morning, EDT, with a spongy-wet tidewater wind pushing at the limp draperies of the Illinois Suite. In the flaccid gloom a bell rang and a lucite square turned pearl on one wall.

The Populist Custodian from Illinois, the Honorable Elwood Everett Swigg sat up in bed like a mechanical man. His eyes flew open. Jagged streaks flashed across the lucite screen. Custodian Swigg staggered to his feet. His flannelette nightshirt clung sweatily to his body. Locks of silver-gray hair fell across his impressive forehead. With groggy grandeur he raised a finger in the air.

"Perils beset us on every hand," he said to the chest of drawers. "All around, we are ringed by encircling enemies. Therefore, friends and neighbors, I say that this is no time to reward faith with a lack of faith, to repay dutiful service with a kick in the hindquarters, as my uncle Elmer used to say on the farm down in—"

"God damn it, operator," said a floating face on the lucite screen, "I said no *bells*."

The face focused: egg-like in its absence of hair, but deeply lined, as though dipped in acid over a long period. Which, in a way, it had been. From behind his glasses, Buster Poole, so-called hatchet man of the Illinois Populists, peered into the Washington dawn from his atomic hideaway at Starved Rock, hundreds of miles distant.

"Elwood, where are you? Come over here. God damn these operators any—"

"I am terribly sorree, sir, terribly sorree, and I promise—"

"—so when it's time to make your decision in November, folks, remember—"

In exasperation Buster Poole said: "The quick brown fox."

Elwood Everett Swigg blinked, lowered his finger. "You call me, Buster?"

"You bet your sweet cells I did. Get over here where I can see you."

"I was having a most peculiar dream."

"That operator's going to have a few when I report her."

Elwood fumbled with a humidor, lit an expensive cigar and rolled his shoulders back. He was a tall figure, slightly stooped, with a craggy, heroic face and a voice with molasses and thunder in it. "What seems to be the trouble, Buster?"

"Jay Milton Mossman's the trouble."

"That upstart? That Sociocratic slug?" Elwood's laugh was rich with the disdain of the veteran campaigner for the untried novice. "Why, he's only thirty-two."

"Be that as it may," Buster Poole snarled, "he's been awake for the last three nights, talking to people around the clock. Tuesday, Hereford Creek. Wednesday Brompton's Falls. Last night at Indian Dune. All I can say, Elwood, is that you'd better shag your carcass back here and get busy. We've got eight weeks to election. If this upstart, as you call him, wins your Custodial seat, you know where you'll wind up."

"Hold on a second, Buster." Elwood clasped his hands behind his nightshirt, smoke wreathing his head. He frowned as though deliberating. Wisdom personified.

"Don't 'hold on' me, you old fool."

"Buster, that's hardly the tone to take with one who has served—"

"Yeah, but unless you serve the party a little better

than you've been serving it so far, Mr. Jay Milton Mossman's going to be state Custodian come January. And I repeat, if that happens to me, you know what happens to you."

A somewhat-undressed young woman peered imploringly into the scene behind Buster. "Not now, Dolly. Elwood, you shag yourself to the turboport. You've got a reservation on the noon Hustler direct to Indian Dune. You're going to debate with Mossman tonight."

"Debate?" Elwood's eyes popped in disbelief. "Tonight? Debate what?"

Buster opened a bag of peanuts and gobbled several with a bored sneer. " 'The Populist Stewardship And Why It Must Be Retained.' "

"I'm not prepared—"

"Shut up. Doc Radameyer's got the tapes ready."

A cadaverous, inward-turning sort of fellow floated into the screen, sucking on a pineapple drop. "That is correct," he said in a pale voice, and floated out again.

"Elwood, don't you have an inkling of the seriousness of the situation?" Buster asked.

With studied and theatrical elegance reminiscent of a Grander, Older Age, Elwood tapped an eighth-inch ash from the end of his glowing cigar. "You must be misinformed. Mossman could not possibly have remained awake three nights running. The public would smell a figurative rat, my boy, if it were true. Which is patently impossible, the laws being what they are."

"It's just a state commission decree, remember," Buster snarled. "Even if it is in all fifty-two."

"Are you certain about Mossman? Were you on the scene?"

"Elwood, don't sneer at me or I'll turn Radameyer loose on you."

From off-screen came a sepulchral voice: "Not just now, please." Plus the sucking of a pineapple drop and a shrill giggle.

Elwood frowned, then scowled—a perfect imitation of middlewestern moralism facing the decay of personal ethics. Buster Poole stood up. He began to pace in front of his lead-brick fireplace. The camera had trouble following him.

"Elwood, unless you're on that flight—"

"Three nights?" Elwood murmured. "Impossible."

"You've seen Mossman. He's young-looking. Vigorous."

"An appearance of boyish charm is no substitute for experience when it comes—"

"Oh, shut up, shut *up*. As I said, he's either a young man or—"

"An illegal model?" For the first time, Elwood sounded slightly alarmed. "That's—inconceivable. Have you checked? I mean, my boy, the commissioner—"

"I've talked enough, I'm sick of talking!" Buster shouted. "You be here today!"

"But I have my duty, Buster. This is the height of the Tourist Session, and—"

All at once Buster Poole's right hand seemed to leap out from his body, fisted, until it filled the screen. At the last second the camera pulled its zoomar. Buster's whole body shot into the background, miniaturizing to a spot. The screen blacked out.

For a long moment Elwood Everett Swigg did nothing but stare at the end of his cigar. Then he turned and pushed through the damp curtains to the tiny balcony overlooking the parking lot and Rock Creek Bridge. Against the dim hot dawn the traffic bullseyes stood out scarlet and green.

A sac in the corner of each of Elwood's eyes disgorged a glycerine tear. He picked up the hem of his nightshirt and dabbed at the gooey stuff. Then he turned and tottered back into his suite on spindly legs.

Much of what Buster Poole had told him had now begun to be absorbed into the cells of his sixty-year-old head. An expression of concern, even alarm, wrinkled his Olympian brow. This expression had not completely vanished when he bustled into the Shoreham lobby precisely at eight that morning, the solid silver head of his anachronistic walking stick winking richly.

Elwood wore his conventional costume—frock tunic, morning shorts and dickey with stickpin. All over the lobby young government clerks in various shades of gray shorts bustled to conferences with dispatch cases under their arms. Elwood tramped ahead briskly. He nodded to Murfree, the Sociocratic Custodian from Mississippi, who merely curled his fist more tightly about the bullwhip he always carried, and stalked on.

Near the lobby entrance a crowd of two dozen children in electric blue shorts, jumpers and beanies began to leap up and down and squeal. Two elderly women attempted to quiet them, uselessly. Several of the tots hoisted up a lopsided banner. It read:

>Illinois Powwow No 478
>Kiddee Kampers of America Says
>HELLO CUSTODIAN SWIGG!

Elwood stopped. He bowed formally, swept a palm over his mop of silver hair and flashed his famous smile.

"Good *morning,* Kiddee Kampers. Your Custodian welcomes you to Washington."

The two elderly ladies fumbled with lacy fichus at the collars of their sensible tunics. They nudged one another forward and introduced themselves as the leaders of the group, the Misses Teasdale and Hipp. Miss Hipp seemed unable to do much besides simper. But Miss Teasdale said it was simply thrilling for all the Kiddee Kampers to be able to view with their own tiny eyes the great legislative process taking place day and night on the floor of the Combined Congress.

"As your state Custodian," Elwood said, employing several theatrical gestures, "it is my pleasure to conduct you personally to the Illinois machine, which it is my privilege and duty, as your elected steward, to maintain and service in tiptop working order during my term as—"

"Pa says they ain't nothing but janitors," said a male Kiddee Kamper.

"Is your papa a Sociocrat, sonny?" Elwood said. Squeals of insane laughter convulsed the group, including Miss Hipp. Elwood's face instantly grew serious.

"Actually, sonny, one must not joke about the sacred responsibilities of the Custodians. Without their services the great and intelligent body which governs us would be unable to function effectively day and night, passing into the law of the land those rules which make this country a better place for one and all to live.

"(Step this way, kiddies. The chartered turbobus is waiting.) Of course, in our state—" (An indulgent glance at the Misses Teasdale and Hipp.) "—certain parties would have us believe that only youth can supply the knowledge and initiative to properly program our machine, whereas it is my deep and sincere conviction that only wisdom, garnered through four successful terms—"

The Kiddee Kampers continued to squeal and giggle as the group moiled out of the hotel and into the turbobus. Between the chilled temperature-control of the lobby and that of the bus Misses Teasdale and Hipp erupted into cascades of sweat. Elwood remained dry and cool, his silver-headed cane winking.

The turbobus shot up the causeway under the traffic bullseye. Elwood delivered his little lecture on the traditions of history which are the country's heritage, etc. etc., while gazing out the window at the busy scenes of early-morning Washington. A large Hustler travel poster shot by. It reminded him of Buster.

What should he do?

His head sorted the choices. Certainly he would not go back. He knew his duty. His duty had been taught to him most carefully, made a part of his very existence. He would not abandon it.

Thus, leonine and magnificent in the flashing sunlight, Elwood continued his lecture all the way to the Combined Congressional Building, grandly ignoring the few snide remarks and soft-drink envelopes thrown by Kiddee Kampers whose parents were obviously non-Populist.

It took two hours to conduct the group through just a fraction of the laboratories and control rooms buried beneath the Building, what with Elwood stopping every so often to pull open a wall panel and reveal miles of cable receding into the distance, or vast networks of pinpoint lights flashing on great boards behind thick glass walls. Since the Tourist Session was indeed at its peak, there were innumerable waits for lift tubes and floating stairways as other tourist delegations—Elks, Shriners, Girl Patriots, Non-Nuclearites, Birth Control Brigaders and the like —went through similar tours under the guidance of their own state Custodians. Shortly before eleven, however, the electric moment arrived.

With a finger to his lips and an expression of deep reverence on his face, Elwood turned his back on the Kiddee Kampers. He threw wide his arms and opened the double doors into the Chamber.

Dwarfed by the immense steel cases which towered three stories each, Elwood's group started down a long sloping walkway which, with the other walkways that were arranged like wheel-spokes, converged at the bottom of the bowl-like chamber before the dais where sat the Chairman-Printer.

"Ssssh!" Elwood breathed. "A bill has just been passed. See, it's coming out on the tape and going down the chute to the typesetter's. Let's see."

Elwood consulted one of the illuminated globes set at intervals along the walk. "P. L. Three-billion and nine, Retroactivity of Social Security Psycho-Happiness Credits During Odd Months. A most significant bill," he added, although the Kiddee Kampers were far too awestruck by the mammoth machines and the flickering lights to reply, facetiously or otherwise.

At last Elwood paused beside one of the larger machines. He placed his palm against its smoothly humming metallic side. Over his head a small engraved stainless steel plate read:

Illinois
(IBM)

"This is your computer, children. More perfect, more wise and fair than the most intelligent mortal representative could hope to be. It guarantees you perfect representation without emotion. Feel thankful, children, that you live in an America where the antiquated tradition of representation by human beings is recognized for what it is—disastrous, and impossible, I might add, in the light of the complexity of our world. However—" Elwood cleared his throat. "Under our democratic system we must, of course, guarantee representation to all. Therefore your parents have duly elected me State Custodian. I shall now give a brief demonstration of my duties."

The great chronometer at the north end of the chamber showed a few minutes past eleven. Elwood took out a silver key, unlocked a small panel in the computer's side and occupied himself for the next five minutes with the thoroughly spurious demonstration regularly given for tourists. He applied oil from an antique can to several false holes in the interior of a special non-functioning cavity in the computer's side. The oil can made little squirting sounds. These held the Kiddee Kampers, Misses Teasdale and Hipp spellbound, allowing Elwood to do a little electioneering:

"I have a message for you children before you leave. Next November, your parents will be asked to choose between Custodial experience and Custodial callowness, between—"

A pale figure stepped out from behind the Iowa computer, sucking a pineapple drop.

"I thought so," said Dr. Radameyer with a sigh. He was still rumpled from his quick Hustler trip from Starved Rock. Over the heads of the Kiddee Kampers Dr. Radameyer stared with highly magnified eyes at Elwood. "Oh Elwood."

"Yes? Who—Radameyer! Now Doctor, I made my position clear to Poole—"

"Phooey," said Radameyer tiredly. "I told him you wouldn't cooperate. Oh, well." Another pineapple drop. "Don't sit under the apple tree with anyone else but me."

Elwood collapsed against the side of the computer, his face screwed up in pain.

"Custodian Swigg!" shrieked Miss Teasdale. "Why are you clutching your side?"

Radameyer floated forward. He made a cursory examination of Elwood, who was now stretched out on the walkway, groaning horribly. "I'm afraid some elements have fused." Radameyer knelt down and turned up Elwood's eyelid, disclosing a milky pupil. "The rest of the tour will have to be canceled. Please wait in the rotunda for further word of the Custodian's condition."

Little faces no longer smiling, the Kiddee Kampers milled out of the Chamber. When the mammoth doors had swung shut Radameyer poked Elwood in the rib cage.

"Quick brown fox, Elwood old boy. Get up. We've forty minutes to make the Hustler."

Elwood blinked and followed the doctor up the aisle, all trace of pain gone from his face.

"Was that necessary, Doctor?"

Radameyer shrugged. "Poole wants the election. You're paying too much attention to your duty program. We'll have to have a checkup after the debate tonight." He patted a bulging pocket. "All the debate tapes are in here. We can feed them on the flight. A lot of interesting stuff, actually."

Radameyer guided Elwood toward the underground monorail entrance, used only by Custodians. The Kiddee Kampers would just have to stand waiting and wondering.

"Written by one of the best boxes in the business," Radameyer went on. "Normally does women's novels. When that last box of yours blew up from resistor fatique, we had to scratch. Luckily we hit it successful at the first auction. Come on, Elwood, pick up your feet. Do you want 'Don't sit—?'" Radameyer paused deliberately, unwrapping some new pineapple drops.

"No, no, I'll come along. I see it's serious now. I'll be glad to debate. Glad to, my boy, glad to, *glad* to."

"That sounds more encouraging," said Radameyer as they descended through the cool caverns to the whistling monorail track. "Maybe we won't have to re-program after all."

The Hustler pierced the sky in a burst of silent white flame. Within an hour Custodian Elwood Swigg and Dr. Radameyer were inside a sun-heated tent erected for the rally on the steep bluffs over the Mississippi, just outside the little lead-mining community of Indian Dune.

The tent swarmed with members of the Populist state committee. Tickers chattered. Pitchers of lemonade were constantly emptied and refilled. A corps of the Ladies Auxiliary was busy preparing pitch-pine torches. ("Not my idea," Buster Poole scowled, sweaty and in shirt-sleeves at a deal table behind a mound of memoranda. "Has something to do with one of the old Presidents that came from the state. Mossman thought of it. Or rather, that bastard Hawk. Pioneer spirit. Fresh blood. Etcetera. Makes me puke. Wait a sec, Elwood.")

Dr. Radameyer, holding firmly to Elwood's elbow, found himself overwhelmed at the collection of antique appurtenances freighted in for the rally—ancient telephones, for example. Buster Poole was talking into one, arranging for six turbobus-loads of rallyers. These would arrive, rally and demonstrate, one hundred a head, noisemakers and torches to be provided by the state committee.

Elwood picked up a handbill printed on a curious stuff. "Look at this."

Dr. Radameyer felt it. "My God. Real primitive paper."

Glancing down the list headed *Programme,* Elwood frowned.

"I wish I could talk to Buster a minute. This sounds like a program *I* should have arranged. Instead, I seem to have been forced to go along with what the opposition has set up." Immediately Elwood's tear sacs opened. He read the paper handbill aloud, large glycerine drops staining it like dark flowers: "Masson's Original Equestrian Troupe, Including Genuine Horses In Person. Lady Olivia on the Taut Wire. The Coal Valley Family Bell-Ringers."

"Bell-Ringers?" Radameyer grabbed the handbill. "Let me see that."

Buster Poole rushed up. "Know the speeches, Elwood?"

"Of course. Not precisely my style, but—"

"What a mess, what a miserable mess," Buster said vehemently. "Every act for miles is booked. We haven't got one lousy item on the program that says Courtesy State Populist Party. Oh, I tell you, Radameyer, this Mossman is a grand one. Youthful, healthy, vigorous."

"We'll have to do something about those bell-ringers, Buster," Radameyer said. "That's one trigger-error I've never been able to trace and correct."

"I know," Buster said. He shouted: "Charlie—remind me to memorize that Hawk crumb as soon as I get finished conferring with the Custodian."

He shoved Elwood, who was still dry and calm amidst the sweating crowds in the non-chilled tent, over to an entranceway. Buster lifted a corner of the moldy-smelling canvas. He pointed across to the edge of the bluff. Next to a pine-plank platform being hastily erected could be seen a small tent city, flag-festooned with the emblems of the Sociocrats. From the highest point of the biggest tent floated a huge dimensional styrene statue-balloon of the Sociocratic candidate, Jay Milton Mossman.

"You've got to turn on the charm, Elwood," Buster said. "You can get an idea of their organization. Out of nowhere, bang, they dig up this Mossman, and load him with gimmicks like this pioneer routine. Then they box us into accepting the debate, with only ten minutes' talk about ground rules. Next you waste half a day responding to your God damn duty program—" Poole waved aside Radameyer's mild protests that it wasn't really Elwood's fault. "—so now I'll lay it on the line to you, Custodian. You either get out there and win this crowd tonight, ooze them to death with your so-called charm, or you know what'll happen."

Elwood drew himself up to his full, rather regal height. "I know very well. You have taught me that most expressly."

"He can only do so much," Radameyer said.

"But he can do less than the most, if he wants," Buster snarled back.

"I revere and venerate my position as Custodian," Elwood said. "I shall give it full measure during the debate. However, I should like to ask one question. Have you ascertained anything about the nature of this Mossman? After all, it's quite a departure. Young. Handsome. Rather smart-alecky, if you wish my opinion."

"Times are changing," was all Buster would say. "In a minute, Charlie."

"Ah, yes, but when the computers replaced the representatives, and the non-humans subsequently replaced the human Custodians—experimentally at first, then on a permanent basis—it was thought psychologically correct to mold and model Custodial candidates in the fashion which would most perfectly appeal to the greatest number of voters."

As he spoke, Elwood did not respond emotionally to the fact that had been clearly taught him long ago: that non-humans were first employed in Custodial positions because the Custodial position was essentially a useless, harmless job. Except as it provided the voters with the satisfaction of electing somebody or something, once human beings became inadequate to fulfill legislative responsibilities. Further, the Custodial position kept the national party alive—perhaps the real reason non-humans had been tested and used first in this particular role. But Elwood's makeup didn't permit him to weep solely because he was useless. Though he knew, as a fact, that he was, he was so arranged as to act in the opposite fashion

—for the benefit of the people, especially during the Tourist Session. This sense of purpose rang in Elwood's voice as he went on:

"Window dressing, you call it. Yet I have seen the sparkle in the eyes of a crowd when I pass among them." There was no smile on Elwood's face as he said this. Only a great solemnity. He brushed at his heroic silver locks and took a firmer grip on the head of his cane. "In fact, we discussed this morning the state commission decrees which require non-humans to be cast in human mold—sleeping, eating and so forth, so as not to effect too rapid a transition that would psychically upset the populace. This raises the question of Mossman's—"

"I don't know, I just don't know yet," Buster Poole interrupted, wiping sweat. "You just hang around, Elwood. I may want to talk to you some more."

Buster dashed off: "Ready to memorize, Charlie? Right. To Andy Hawk, Sociocratic Headquarters. Subject—bell-ringers. The one weak point in our candidate's programming is an uncontrolled circuit closure triggered by a bell stimulus." Poole paced, sneering at the invisible recipient of the memo as he talked. "Out of consideration for the way in which you have managed to prearrange this debate—and out of simple decency—" Poole grinned at his own cleverness. "—I would appreciate it if the Coal Valley Family Bell-Ringers could be struck from the program. I repeat, Andy, the bells represent the one point of disorganization peculiar to our model. Rest assured, that should a situation arise in which any action of ours should produce a disorderly reaction in your candidate—(That ought to trap him into telling us about Mossman, one way or another, eh, Charlie?)—I would take quick steps to remove that stimulus. You well know that, due to the complexity of our candidates, we must be careful not to upset the delicate balance of factors on which the population depends for its emotional release in the politico-patriotic area of our national life." And Poole spat: "Sign it 'Cordially.' "

Turning aside, Elwood walked to a camp stool which a clerk had just vacated. He sat down and began to rehearse his debate material in a loud voice. A few minutes later he walked to the tent entrance and looked at the mammoth balloon-statue of Jay Milton Mossman floating above the Sociocratic tents. His sacs welled over with glycerine again. Still sucking pineapple drops. Dr. Radameyer guided him solicitously back to the camp stool, where the rehearsal continued through the remainder of the afternoon.

When the program began at eight in the evening five thousand pitch-pine torches had been lit, and the bluffs above the Mississippi flickered with tufts of orange fire that cast immense shadows inside the Populist tent. The tent was empty except for Buster Poole, Dr. Radameyer and Elwood. In the litter of papers and cigars and cashier's check stubs made out in advance to the paid rallyers, the three sat silently while twenty-five thousand throats made a thunderous roar. Lady Olivia was performing a sensational trick on the taut wire.

No word had been received from the Sociocratic tents about the bell-ringers. They were the next turn on the program, the fifth before the debate was scheduled to begin. Buster Poole's bald head was adrip with orange sweat. He held his ear cocked, one eye closed. But it was difficult if not impossible, for him to hear the tiny shouts of six turbobus-loads of his rallyers among the thousands of voices that cheered when Lady Olivia unzipped part of her costume and dropped it down into the crowd—a fancy pink bustle embroidered *Mossman*.

Suddenly the tent flap lifted.

Three men walked in. One, rolling ponderously, was Andy Hawk, a sow-bellied five-foot fighter from the southern coal regions. Hawk walked straight up to Buster Poole, all confidence and stinking sweat.

Elwood rose from his campstool. Back in the shadows the other two visitors waited. Elwood made out the handsome young face of Jay Milton Mossman, deeply tanned above his crisply-white but inexpensive tunic.

The third figure was so deeply in shadows that even the reflected firelight from the rally grounds did not reveal him. Buster Poole backed off a step. He wiped fog from his glasses, staring down at the quivering, smiling little fat man.

"Well, Hawk?"

"I got your memo."

"About time you answered, I think."

"We'll strike the bell-ringers. That is, unless your candidate wishes to withdraw for an uncontested election."

"Are you out of your God-damned mind?" Buster screamed.

"*Sir*—!" Elwood brandished his cane, the head winking and flashing with bright lights in the shifting red shadows. "As a patriotic Custodian who has served the sovereign state of Illinois with dignity and faithfulness and courage, I *protest* your—"

"Can't you shut him off?" Hawk asked.

Buster snapped his fingers. Dr. Radameyer said, "Drink Pop-A-Cola."

Elwood's mouth fell open, his enunciation complex electronically frozen. But he retained the capacity to move, and the stimulus-code did not affect his tear sacs, which began to well with glycerine. It ran in two greasy trickles down his cheeks.

Buster Poole's voice had acquired the dangerous, raspish quality of the growl of the tiger jabbed once too often by the trainer's stick: "Speak your piece, Hawk. You know I won't pull Elwood."

"Oh?" Hawk's cheerful face beamed malice and triumph. "You mentioned in your memo, I think, that all non-humans, because of their complexity, inevitably wind up with some disordered relays or what-ever-you-call-them. That, Buster my friend, is due to the fact that they've been made, by law, to resemble humans. But I can guarantee you that our boy doesn't have such a weak point." Hawk lumbered around. "Do you, Jay?"

The face of Jay Milton Mossman broke wide in a white grin that shone like ivory in the dark. His electronic voice said warmly, "No, Andy, that's right, I do not."

"You know as well as I, you conniving bastard, that anything but a human-model non-human is illegal," Buster snarled.

"Don't call me names," said Hawk, lightly but dangerously. "Although I guess I can't blame you, seeing as how you've already lost November. For your information, Buster, the law here in Illinois was changed three weeks ago. The new executive decree will be made public at a press conference. Tomorrow. You don't have any legal recourse, either. We may have made Jay contrary to what the law allowed—but he didn't start showing any of his little refinements publicly until *after* the new decree went into effect."

"Changed the law?" gasped Dr. Radameyer, surprised for perhaps the first time in his life. "*Changed?* Who changed it."

The third figure, tall, impeccably dressed, stirred out of the shadows.

"I did."

Buster Poole's face collapsed into disbelief and rage. "Wing!"

"It was my pleasure to sign the executive order, with the governor's approval," said Willis Wing, who was Illinois State Commissioner of Robots. "Illinois has always led the fight for progressive technology. Soon the other states will follow our precedent, I'm sure. The population is quite ready, psychologically, to accept a non-human who neither slecps, ingests or eliminates." A small, malicious smile curved the tonsured face. "And you might also be interested in knowing, Poole, that at noon tomorrow, following the press conference, I shall endorse the Custodial candidacy of Jay Milton Mossman."

"That is right," said Jay Milton Mossman with another jerk of the metallic musculature that pulled his artificial epidermis into a smile. "That's correct, he will."

Through it all the roar of voices from the rally-grounds had been growing to a thunder as Lady Olivia completed her act. Now searchlights wigwagged back and forth wildly along the taut wire. Lady Olivia took her bows. Then a raucous voice on the public address system tried to announce the next act. Elwood stood balancing his weight from one artificial foot to another, hearing everything that was said but unable to speak out. His tear-sacs had overflowed, coating his face with a grease of glycerine. Their tiny orifices still pumped, but no more fluid came.

Buster Poole looked at Radameyer. "We'll build another Elwood."

"That," said Radameyer, around a pineapple drop, "will take time."

"And the model you've got," said Hawk, "has to sleep seven hours every night. I saw the circuitry depositions in the state vaults, just to check."

"Those vaults are *secret*!" Buster howled at Willis Wing. "You cheap crook, I thought you weren't for sale."

Political Machine 49

Willis Wing paused in the act of lighting a cigar. His eyes resembled hard bits of Illinois coal. "Why, Mr. Poole, you never tried to buy."

"Elwood can't possibly keep up with the kind of campaign Jay here will wage," Hawk said. "That's why I thought I'd at least give you the opportunity to withdraw your candidate tonight."

Poole seized Radameyer's shoulder. "Can we re-program him non-human?"

"Impossible. We'd have to begin all over again. The principles are different."

"I realize this puts you in a bad position, Buster," Hawk said, suddenly solicitous. "Elwood will lose, of course, because he can't keep up. Can't possibly duplicate Jay's coverage of the state. Besides, people are growing tired of silver-headed canes and silver hair and golden voices. They want a machine that *acts* like a machine—that thinks quickly, works tirelessly. In four years we'll be able to take off Jay's epidermis and let him show his real skin. One of these days people may even decide the whole business of a Custodian in Washington is stupid—which it is. But until they decide that way, and as long as we keep having elections, I want my party to win. This time, it will."

"That's very true," said Jay Milton Mossman. "I believe it will."

Hawk turned, ready to leave. "Sorry, Buster. I know how the National Committee may treat you if you lose. Believe me, I treasure your friendship, but—" Hawk lifted one shoulder in a porcine shrug. "Politics."

"—*and now ladies and gentlemen,*" a hoarse amplified voice thundered through the flame-shadowed tent, "*the next stellar act on this stellar bill, all brought to you through the courtesy of your Sociocratic candidate for Custodian, Jay Milton Mossman—a group of stellar artists who come from our own native state, and who—*"

"The bell-ringers," said Radameyer, in a warning whisper.

Hawk moved toward a field phone on one of the deal tables. "I'll strike them."

Buster Poole looked at Elwood Everett Swigg with hatred and loathing.

"Forget it," he said. "Quick brown fox."

"My hands may not be clean," said Willis Wing, "but I will be very glad to see a man like you lose this election."

"Shut up," said Buster Poole, adding an obscenity. "Radameyer, we'll rebuild, and rebuild in time to beat—"

"Oh, we can't," Radameyer said listlessly. "We can't, we just can't."

"Don't say *can't*," Buster screamed. "God damn you, don't *say* that."

Over the amplification system the Coal Valley Family began to ring their bells, playing *Humoresque*.

Elwood Everett Swigg raised one arm. He brandished his cane. His eyes were full of flame and shadow, and his hair gleamed like molten silver.

"When in the course of human events," he said, his voice booming out above Buster Poole's hysterical pleas to Radameyer, "a government of the people by the people for the people provides for the common defense and protects against the Illinois computer which you now see before you—"

Walking out of the tent, Elwood Everett Swigg turned into the darkness. He walked proudly, his head high, his shoulders thrown back, his eyes glinting for battle. He walked decisively, with no waver in his step. He walked away from the crowds and the torches and the clatter of the bell-ringers, straight toward the lip of the bluff.

"I pledge allegiance to the flag," he said to the night wind, flinging wide his arms, "and to the demonstration of my vital position as Custodian, friends and neighbors, which I shall now proceed to render unto Caesar that which—"

He walked into air over the bright ribbon of the Mississippi under the moon. He sang *The Battle Hymn of the Republic* all the way down.

The Sellers of the Dream

This story is a dystopian vision about the eradication of choice and the domination of a society by advertising. Written along lines pioneered in science fiction by Frederik Pohl (who bought it from *Galaxy*) but still unique and non-derivative. We are sure you will think of it each year when the new automobile models are introduced.

I

His gaudy wristwatch showed thirty minutes past nine, sixth July. It was time. From here on it was do the job right or be ruined. If not physically, then professionally.

Finian Smith dug for tools in the pouches of his imitation stomach. The left eye of the watch's moon face gave a ludicrous wink to complete the time signal. Finian hated the watch. He'd got used to the confines of the camouflaged polymer leech clinging to the keel of the hydrofoiler. He'd got used to performing necessary bodily functions in intimate contact with the leech's servomechanisms for thirty-six hours. But the watch—never.

It was effete, like his clothes. Effeteness was big this year. Next year it would be hand-loomed woollens. But he wasn't being paid to inherit the soul of the man he was impersonating, after all. He applied the first of his meson torches to the thick hull. His long, pleasantly ugly face began to bead with perspiration.

He had precisely four minutes to cut through.

His face was half shadowed by the hull as he worked, half washed in flickering sunlight through anemone and brain coral. He defused a large U-shaped section and replaced the torch with a pistol unit fitted with a round cup at the muzzle. This cup he applied to the hull. A blue whine of power—he forced the hull inward far enough to accommodate entry to the fuel baffle chamber.

He set a small black box to blow the polymer leech off the hull in fifty seconds, glad that he'd spent a full twenty nights under the hypnolearner. The penetration plan was drummed so deeply into his skull he could operate like an automaton.

With a last tool he re-sealed the hull, touched a stud and watched the tool collapse to gritty pumice. Right now the leech should be quietly disintegrating, without so much as a murmur to disturb the TTIC spy radar. It took a lot of money to arrange this penetration, Finian thought. Knowing how much made him nervous.

Finian hurried up a lonely companionway. Before stepping to the yacht's deck he dusted his pleatless puce satin pantaloons and also made sure the precision camera, a combined effort of G/S dental technicians and optics men, was in place where his right front incisor had once been. The blade shutter's release was a knob on the tooth's inner surface, triggered by tongue pressure. Fake enamel would fly aside a micro-instant and TTIC secrets would be recorded for posterity, not to mention G/S market analysts.

On deck, Finian adjusted his identification badge.

Beneath his picture it said *Woodrow Howslip, Missoula, Mont., Upper North American Distributorship*. Finian hoped Woodrow Howslip was still lost in the Mojave Desert. If so, the only thing Finian had to worry over was his old enemy.

Every few yards along the deck armed TTIC security men stood at attention: TTIC seemed to have innumerable armed guards. So did G/S for that matter. Finian often wondered why. No one got angry any more, why have armed guards?

"Hi, there, I'm Woody Howslip."

"Morning, sir." The guard stared into the Pacific's cobalt swell.

"Say, fella. Last year when I came to see the new models innerduced, I ran into a hell of a swell person— Spool or Stool. Sure like to buy him a drink. Is he on board?"

"I don't believe so, sir."

"Oh, too bad. Maybe he'll show up. They always have the top dogs at these distributor shows. I hear Stool's a top dog. Chief of company spies or something."

The guard concealed irritation.

"*Sprool*, sir. Chief of industrial investigation."

Finian gigged the man's ribs. "Keeps those Goods/Services jerks hopping, huh? Well, sorry Sprool isn't around. Maybe later. See you in the videofunnies—"

Overdoing it, Finian thought as he hurried along. Still, it was reassuring to know the intelligence was correct: Sprool was in Bombay. Finian had run up against him most recently when TTIC tried to steal G/S designs for the mid-year hair-do changes during the 2004-5 season.

Finian joined a crowd of distributors hurrying into an auditorium beneath a banner reading:

WELCOME
Things to Come Incorporated
World Distributors
*"Last Year's Woman Is This
Year's Consumer"*

As he took a seat in the shadowy hall he listened to voices all around:

"It's rumoured she's of the Grecian mode," said the European Common Market distributor.

"What? Copy the tripe G/S peddled two years ago?" That was the White/Blue Nile man.

The Chinese distributor protested: "Last year, too severe. Humble per cent of market drop severely. Five thousand years in fields, China women do not desire box haircut, woollen socks."

"Hope it's a real smasher this time," said the British Empire distributor, a seedy fellow wearing Cologne. One rundown warehouse in Jamaica comprised the Empire any more. TTIC or G/S could buy or sell the Empire a thousand times. Or any other country. Finian was sweating. No wonder the stakes were so high.

On an austere platform up front sat three men. One was a florid old gentleman with dewlaps and blue, vaguely crossed eyes. Another—a spindly type with a flower at each cuff—rose and was introduced by a loudspeaker as Corporate Director of Sales, Northcote Hastings.

"Thank you, thank you. I won't waste time, gentlemen. You've travelled thousands of miles in secrecy and we appreciate it. We trust you also appreciate why we must maintain the mobility of our personality design center. One never knows when the—ah—competition might infiltrate a permanent site. They can't match our sales in new personalities, so they try to outfight us with punches below the belt."

He fingered his, of ermine, to illustrate. Finian joined the laughter, but meant his.

"After luncheon, gentlemen, you're scheduled for individual sessions with our designers, psychiatrists, plastic surgeons and sociability co-ordinators, not to mention apparel teams and accessory experts."

Hastings glanced at the old gentleman with the vaguely crossed eyes.

"Before we proceed, however, I should like to introduce TTIC's beloved chairman of the board, Mr. Alvah Loudermilk. Stand up, Mr. Loudermilk." The sales manager was plainly annoyed by having to make the introduction. The old dodderer took a step towards the podium. Hastings let a tolerant smile be seen by the distributors but did not relinquish the mike.

"You can talk with Mr. Loudermilk personally later, gentlemen."

The florid old gentleman sat down again, as though no one appreciated him. Smoothly Hastings continued, "Let me get on by bringing forward the great design chief of Things to Come Incorporated—" He flung out a hand. "Dr. Gerhard Krumm."

The famed Krumm, an obese toad with the inevitable disarrayed look of the corporate intellectual, walked to the podium. His apricot slippers, pantaloons and bolero jacket seemed to have come from a dustbin. Behind Krumm stage blowers whirred. They were readying curtains and screen.

Finian slid his tongue near his tooth.

"Gentlemen," Krumm said, "first the bad news."

At the unhappy grumble he held up his hand. "Next year—I promise!—TTIC will absolutely and without qualification be ready to introduce the concept of the obso-

The Sellers of the Dream

lescent male personality, exactly as we did in the female market ten years ago. I can only emphasize again the tremendous physical problems confronting us, and point to the lag in male fashion obsolescence that was not finally overcome until the late twentieth century, by the sheer weight of promotion. Men, unlike women, accept new decorative concepts slowly. TTIC has a lucrative share of the semi-annual male changeover, but we are years behind the female personality market. Next year we catch up."

"May we see what you have for the girls, old chap?" someone asked. "Then we'll decide whether we're happy."

"Very well." Krumm began to read from a promotion script: "This year we steal a leaf from yesterday's—uh—scented album." The lights dimmed artfully. Perfume sprayed the chamber from hidden ducts. A stereo orchestra swelled. The curtains parted. Finian's upper lip was rolled back as far as possible.

A nostalgic solido view of New York when it was once populated by people flashed on the screen. Violins throbbed thrillingly.

"Remember the sweet, charming girl of yesteryear? We capture her for you—warm, uncomplicated, revelling in —uh, let's see—sunlight and outdoor sports."

A series of solido slides, illustrating Krumm's points with shots of nuclear ski lifts or the Seine, merged one into another.

"Gone is the exaggerated IQ of this year, gone the modish clothing. A return of softness. A simple mind, clinging, sweet. The stuff of everyman's dreams. Gentlemen, I give you—"

Hidden kettledrums swelled. The name flashed on the screen:

DREAM DESIRE.

"Dream Desire! New Woman of the 2007-08 market year!"

Over enthusiastic applause Krumm continued: "At our thirty thousand personality alteration centers over the world, every woman will be able to change her body and mind, by means of surgical and psychological techniques of which TTIC is the acknowledged master, to become Dream Desire. Backed by the most intensive promotion program in history, we promise that more women will become Dream Desire than have ever become one of our previous models. Because, gentlemen, no woman could possibly resist becoming—this."

Sitting forward with tooth ready to shoot, Finian was unprepared for the shock that awaited him.

On the screen slid the naked figure of a girl. Only her back was exposed. Nothing could be seen of her face. Her hair was yellow, that was all. The flesh itself was tanned, in sharp contrast to the pale library look currently being merchandised. The proportions of the girl's buttocks had been surgically worked out to be almost the apex of voluptuousness. But what shook Finian to the soles of his mink slippers was a star-shaped raspberry mark on the new model's left rear.

That isn't Dream Desire, he thought wildly. *That's— that's—*

"We begin with the, uh, rear elevation," said Krumm. "In that colorful mark you see TTIC marketing genius. That mark will stamp the woman who buys this new personality as a genuine Dream Desire, not a shoddy G/S counterfeit. To be frank, adoption of this unique—ah —signature, was not planned. When we sought a girl for our prototype, we discovered the girl we chose was blessed with such a mark. It inspired serendipity. But this is just the beginning. See what we have done with the face."

Only just in time did Finian remember to trigger his tooth and take a shot of the rear elevation before the front view flashed on. The girl, naked and coy on a divan, had pink cheeks, red lips, china blue doll eyes. Pretty, in a cuddlesome, vapid way.

Quickly he exposed two more frames. He was falling apart, muffing the job. Krumm's voice became a drone detailing the surgical and analytical procedures necessary for a woman to buy the appearance and personality of Dream Desire. Finian didn't hear a thing about price schedules or what lower-priced models were contemplated. He photographed each slide mechanically, thinking of the raspberry mark.

It's not Dream Desire, he said to himself. *My God —it's Dolly Novotny.*

Not the face, not the breasts. But *there,* far down in

the eyes. They weren't even brown any more. But colored contacts could change eyes so easily.

Never had he been more profoundly shocked. His own sweet lost Dolly!

A heavy hand seized his shoulder.

"Here he is!"

Finian was dragged from his seat. A searing light flashed in his face.

"Well, well. Finian Smith. When you took hold of that rail coming into the hall, you should have recalled we have sweat prints for all you G/S boys. Give me the camera and come along quietly," finished Sprool.

II

"I thought you were in Bombay," said Finian. "I got bum information."

Sprool smiled somewhere in the depths of his almost colorless eyes. His pale, saturnine face, however, was devoid of humor.

"Never trust Lyman Pushkyn for information, Fin. Since when is an advertising man qualified to supervise an industrial investigation program?"

"You're right. I tried to get them to give me the post once."

"Did you? I didn't realize that. When?"

"Right after I was cashiered by the DOCs and finished my first case for G/S." He couldn't repress a smile. "The time I stole your men's changeover layouts by disguising myself as part of the lavatory wall. When you still had the design center on land, out in California."

Sprool chuckled flatly. "We've been friendly enemies quite a while, haven't we, Fin?"

"You never put one over on me like this, though."

"Shame you forgot sweat prints."

"My own damned fault." Finian thrust out his jaw. "I'll take what's coming. I was counting on this play to cut through all that stupid bureaucracy at the top of G/S and maybe net me the chief investigator's post." Finian scowled out of the office porthole to the heaving blue Pacific. Sprool smoothed thinning hair.

"Might as well give me the camera."

Finian made a show of dipping into his artificial paunch. He came up with a palm-sized micro 35 mm. and snapped open the case release. He pulled the leader on the cassette all the way out, exposing the film. Chuckling, Sprool picked up the cylinder.

"Very nice, Finian. May I now have the real camera?"

"Ah, you slick bastard," grumbled Finian. This time he took a piece of equipment from beneath his singlet. Sprool dropped it down a hissing disposal tube.

"You look positively vengeful, Fin."

"I could smash a few heads right now. That damn G/S Comptroller Central makes investigators do their own penetration work-ups. They're nickel-nursers besides. I *thought* of sweat prints. They said the corrective was too expensive. I wasn't positive you had the index on file, so—"

"Fin, please don't bristle. Remember we have telephotos on you at this very moment. In that bust of Loewy, for instance. His collar button is watching you. Don't fight me and you won't get hurt. TTIC is a business operation just like G/S. Firm but paternalistic. When we dispose of an irritant, we do it with flexibility and permanence, but no physical pain."

"That's nice to know, considering you'll probably ruin my career."

"Were you ever really cut out for business, Fin?"

"If I wasn't *what* the hell was I cut out for? Not the DOCs."

Sprool raised a chiding finger. "See? That burst of temper is all too typical of you. People simply don't rock the boat these days, Fin. Why, if either G/S or TTIC went for more than a 50 percent share of the renewal personality market—plus or minus the 2 percent gain or loss as a result of spying, design leaks and so forth—the U.N. would have its economic cycle theorists down on us instantly."

"God, Sprool, I try and try. I guess I just wasn't meant to be a twenty-first century man. I never had the proper education, like those reading primers written by the market boys from—where was it?—BBDO? I went to private school. On my Pop's knee."

"Then your attitudes are understandable. How can you expect to be anything but yourself when your father was a Galbraither? Perhaps the last of that persuasion allowed to teach economics in public universities? Your father was

The Sellers of the Dream

dead set against the kind of obsolescence practised by the corporations we both represent. The two largest corporations in the world!"

"Pop wanted consumer money spent on libraries, schools, highways, pretty green roadside picnic parks."

"None of which contributes very much to keeping the world plant running at top output. None of which provides the millions of jobs needed to give black and yellow and white alike ample opportunity for the good life. If you'd only understand yourself, how you fit the scheme of things."

"I don't. That's the trouble. What the hell am I supposed to do, join the prisoners in New York? I keep quiet about what I think. I call it well enough to be an operative for the Department of Obsolescence Control. I was doing all right until—"

Memory clouded his brow. He wriggled deep down in the foam of his chair. He wished he were free of this hellish interview, free to think on the problem of Dream Desire who was not Dream Desire at all but Dolly.

"Until what? I never really knew."

"Until I rocked the boat, God damn it! I was chief of the Indiana bureau. I tried to stop a car-smash rally a week before the new models came out. The district supervisor was there, making a speech. I thought I saw a kid inside one of the levacars the crowd was pushing into the Wabash River. I went to see, hold back the crowd. The district supervisor told me to stop. I hit him. *I hit him.* You know what happens when you hit an executive."

Finian pinched the bridge of his nose to shut out the ugly memory. At length he added, "In case you never heard the rest of the story either, a wreck crew examined the levacar afterwards. There was no kid inside. Only a big mechanical doll somebody had forgotten to take out before the smash."

"Very touching," said Sprool emptily.

"Come on, Sprool. Let's get this over."

"Of course. But let me make one more point. Do you know why I'm here, not in Bombay?"

"The mental riot at the TTIC nylon plant was a fake."

"Not at all. The rioters were manning the controls of the motorised strike gangs day and night, from their homes. The moment TTIC cabled agreement to their demand for two extra holidays, before and after Nehru's birthday, they gave up all their other requests—for free anti-cigarette immunization and the like. People are soft, Fin. They co-operate. It must be so, or the plant would stop functioning. How many billions do G/S and TTIC employ? Put those people out of work—disaster! Hunger, pestilence, *real* rioting. The people also have another role to fill, as consumers. If they're unhappy, they respond less adequately to advertising. The plant slows down. Why, until TTIC conceived the idea of introducing new female personalities every year, not just new clothes but complete new mental patterns, the world was headed for ruin. We ran out of new gadgets long ago."

"Don't kid me," Finian said cynically. "Personality obsolescence was thought up by Old Man Pharoh of G/S. His granddad told him a story about the Kennedy lady's mushroom hair changing the style overnight and it started him thinking."

"He had considerable help from Alvah Loudermilk."

"Who cares? All I say is, it's a hell of a shame the Triple Play War didn't end in something besides a stalemate. We wouldn't have had everybody palsy-walsy, black and white and yellow. And this damned population problem—the first rockets rusting on the moon and nobody interested in following them in person. Everybody's a consumer and a worker and—and damn it, soft as jello. And it's a miserable mess from top to bottom."

Sprool was genuinely shocked.

"Fin, are you seriously advocating periodic wars?"

Finian shielded his eyes from the sun falling through the port.

"Oh, no. I can't think of anything else, that's all. Fatness or fighting, fighting or fatness. In my book they're both lousy. I wish there were a third way. I can't think of one. Maybe if I were smart like you—" Finian stopped, bitterly.

Sprool dialled a magenta visorphone. "Really, Fin, this is becoming pointless temperament." Into the phone he said, "We're ready, Doctor." To Finian again: "Please don't try to reform our delicately balanced world, my friend. At least not until we scrub your mind clean of what you saw in the auditorium."

A shiver crawled on Finian's spine.

The Sellers of the Dream

"Scrub—?"

Too late. Pneumatic doors slid aside. Two unsavory specimens in white smocks bordered with lace wheeled a rubber-tired mechanism into the room. Before Finian could move they adjusted several wing nuts and lowered a bowl device over his head. He tried to stand up, cursing. He was quickly but painlessly pinioned by sleek tubular metal arms clasping him from the back of the chair.

"The worst damage you did was on film," Sprool said, striding back and forth, dry-washing his hands. "I naturally assume that in your heightened nervous state, what you saw with your eyes didn't make much of an impression. But we'll be sure. Give him a mild jolt to start, boys."

Several sinister cathode tubes began to hiss at various points on the machine. Finian felt a tingle on his scalp, similar to a healthful massage. He closed his eyes and tried to remember the rear elevation of Dream Desire.

He panicked.

Almost as though there were a mental vacuum cleaner in his head, certain synapses were blocked, certain memory receptors temporarily sucked dry. The technique was a portion of that employed in changing the female consumer's intelligence quotient from year to year to conform to the new personality design she purchased. It made Finian fume to think of them tampering with his skull. He was no rotten Metropolis wife merchandised into adopting the latest fashion trend. He writhed ferociously. Sprool looked on with disapproval.

Try as he might, Finian could not remember what— *good lord!* He'd forgotten the name!

What did she look like? *What?*

He had a blurry recollection of colors on a screen, little else. The laboratory cretins unhooded him. The chair relaxed. Sprool assisted him to his feet.

"Feeling better? Free of unpleasant memories?"

"You've no business tampering—"

Dolly Novotny had a raspberry mark.
So did Dream Desire.

"Yeah, Yeah, I'm okay."

It took all Finian's strength to keep from revealing that the mental dyke had just burst.

He wasn't really surprised. Dolly Novotny had once meant far more to him than assignment could. She would again, when he learned how and why she—

He laughed inwardly. Poor Sprool. He'd stolen a march. Two. Finian still had the tooth camera. And how could Sprool know Finian wanted to—*must*—remember Dolly Novotny, because she was the only creature he ever really loved?

Dolly was the girl to whom he'd been engaged, before her parents broke it off after he was cashiered from the DOCs. An ex-DOC who became an industrial investigator was little more than a low-life spy in their estimations. Finian had been away so much, on assignment. Dolly had tried to resist her parents, but they held the cash-box for a modelling career. She tried; she loved him. But one day when he came back to Bala Cynwyd she was gone. The whole family had moved.

Finian received one final letter. He thought from the words, or rather what was between them, really, that she still loved him. The words were obviously parentally ghosted.

Blinking at Sprool now, scratching his scalp to relieve the prickle, Finian realized anew the rather disheartening truth. He was a maverick. Pop had made him so, against his mother's shrill protests. So be it. Especially since someone—the system, maybe, he didn't know, cared less because a man couldn't really fight a system, not an ordinary man anyway—had corrupted the flesh he loved so well.

Finian was vaguely aware of Sprool, bland, pointing.

"Up that stairway, Fin. Directly to the vertijet takeoff stage. Spare you the embarrassment of going on deck." He extended his hand. "Luck, Fin. I hope the sacking isn't too bad."

Finian slipped the hand aside. He grinned. If you had to be a loony, why not enjoy it?

"Thanks for nothing, pal."

He marched defiantly up the stairs into sunlight.

Who had Sprool been kidding about paternalism? Three hours later the vertijet hovered six inches from Lyman Pushkyn's green front door, the lawn of Panpublix on the outskirts of the Eastern metropolis. Finian was rudely pushed out. The vertijet climbed a white column of vapor into the sky.

Finian picked fresh-cut grass from his pantaloons. Oh, that kind, gentle Sprool. On his instructions the vertijet pilot had beamed an anonymous message on the Panpublix band, announcing that Finian Smith was being returned to continental U.S. by a TTIC skycraft. Still, Finian had one ace to stave off financial disaster.

Five minutes later he lost it.

A squad of G/S industrial guards boiled on to the lawn and hustled Finian to a cold tile room in the personnel wing. There, he discovered two astonishing things. One, the corporation was not quite so paternalistic as it masked itself to appear. The policemen roughed him as they stripped him. Two, the vast G/S industrial police force was not the harmless, aimless body it looked to be from outside. Apparently the guards were paid so well because they had to move savagely if a bubble boiled up the bland surface of the world stew.

In fact, their professionalism with the see-rays in the personnel lab relieved him, howling and kicking and pummelling, of the precious tooth-camera, just before he was hustled to Pushkyn's floor.

III

Panpublix was the wholly owned internal advertising agency for G/S. The building loomed forty storys. Within its curtain-walls quite a few thousand communicators devoted themselves to the task of planning and executing campaigns to move the bodies, as the expression went. The fortieth, or solarium, floor belonged to the agency's executive officer, Pushkyn, into whose presence Finian was unceremoniously thrust.

"You miserable creep," Lyman said, as he shooed away his masseuse and beetled his thick Ukranian brows. "You bumbler, you! We heard all about your incredible performance from Sprool's agents. You're fired. Blackballed. Eradicated. *Kapoosht.*"

Finian had a hard light in his eyes. He sat down, tilted his feet to the chaise footrest and dialled the arm for a B-complex cocktail. "Lyman, those goonies of yours messed me up. I never knew they were more than window dressing. I didn't know they were supposed to fight."

Pudgy Pushkyn snapped the elastic of his old rose knickerbockers. His stomach, lumpy and white as the rest of him, hung out unglamorously.

"Rock the boat some more, creepnik. You'll find out how they can fight."

"Oh shut up. I delivered your pictures. Even if your men did take them by force."

Pushkyn turned his back. "Peddle it another place, jerk. You're through."

"You can't talk to me that way. If you hadn't chintzed about a lousy sweat-print job—"

Pushkyn squinted around. "So *that's* how. That Sprool, he's a regular fiend."

"Damn it, Lyman—"

Extending a trembling sausage finger Pushkyn breathed, "*You* we ought to have psyched, deep and permanent. What a fool I was to string along with you for years! A stumblebum private cop dignifying himself by calling himself an industrial investigator. Come in here storming, cursing—no wonder the DOCs kicked you out!"

Momentarily bewildered, Finian countered, "Lyman, your own guards—"

"Quiet! We'll get a nice fat rap in the public image when the investigator trade journals pick up the story of how G/S flopped."

Glowering, Finian stalked him. "Regardless of that, I delivered. I want my fee."

"I'll be damned if I—"

Conflict was temporarily forestalled by the arrival of a thin assistant art director, carrying a square item masked in grey silk. Finian stared moodily at the G/S model announcement layouts in the wall display racks. The tradename of the new G/S woman and her figure were greeked; but from the woodcut and steel-engraving technique of the gatefold and bleed comps, Finian suspected G/S was going to market a bit of nostalgia even older than the kind chosen by TTIC. Bustless, mandolins and stereopticons by gaslight? Finian had a prepossessing urge to throw up.

"Want to see this, chief?" said the assistant art director.

He whipped off the silk, revealing an oil panting in a platinum frame.

"What the rinkydink hell is that?" Pushkyn cried.

The art director blanched. "Why, chief it's R.R. Pharoh III!"

"Of course, of course, jerkola. You think I don't know? I haven't seen the old smeller in three years maybe, but think I don't know the chairman of my own bread and butter? Why the fancy-fancy oil treatment? You do it?"

"Spare time, only, chief," trembled the art director. "Got a memo. Salinghams—you know, the audiotonal effects veep—memoized Pharoh. Wanted a personal portrait of his leader. Pharoh memoized me, okaying having his picture done. I patched together this little work from the descriptive PR biog. There aren't any good portraits extant."

"Why bring it to me?"

"But chief! You memoized me when I memoized you that—"

"I did! Oh, yeah. Well, I'm busy. Take it to Salinghams."

The art director veiled his creation and disappeared down the tube. Pushkyn was about to speak to Finian when he noted the grey sweat patina on Finian's face. He demanded to know whether Finian was ill.

"Nothing, nothing's wrong," said Finian, shivering, wildly curious.

The image in the portrait burned into Finian's skull. It was that of a florid old gentleman with dewlaps and blue, vaguely crossed eyes.

Tightening his nerves, Finian said, "Pushkyn, let me lay it out. I got to have the fee. I need it to find the prototype of the TTIC girl. I used to know her."

A visorphone glowed. Pushkyn slapped the command button. A pale man danced up and down on the screen.

"Chief, chief, it's a breakthrough, a breakthrough! We turned up the TTIC pilot plant just an hour ago. Molecular triangulation. My God, sir, it's a miracle of deception. Manhattan! The prison! An old rundown distillery company building in the worst stews of—" He consulted a paper. "Parkave, that's the place."

Listening transfixed, Pushkyn started, slid his gaze to Finian and snarled at the screen, "Oh, boy, is *your* fat in the fire. Call me back." He shut off and squinted at Finian, whose mind churned. "You were talking?"

Finian swallowed hard. "Pushkyn, I must find out what's happened to the girl they made into the TTIC prototype. If they've changed her they've done wrong. She was sweet and desirable. They've made her all soft and disgusting. Like marshmallow."

"The new TTIC broad? You were hot for her once, that it?"

"That's it. I was only holding back the camera so you'd pay me. Give me a chance!"

"Think we run a snivelling charity?" Pushkyn's sweeping gesture encompassed the heavens and the pulsing, overpopulated smog blanks beneath. "We gotta keep the plant running! Create demand every minute! Off with the old woman! On with the new! The old woman, she smells, she's out of date! We got a crusade here at Panpublix! We got a holy mission! You want the plant wheels to stop like they put sand in them? While we take care of your *personal* problems? Don't be a jerkola. Like to argue about the fee? I'll call up the guards again."

Something akin to a cool rush of air swept Finian's brain.

"Then I'll find her without the fee, Lyman."

"Hah-hah, sure. Big independent operator, big millionaire. Go get psyched and lose those hostile tendencies. Don't rock the world, she don't rock so good. Everybody's happy, you be happy. Go grub and be happy."

"I'm not happy. All of a sudden I'm not happy, if people like you make the only girl I ever fell in love with obsolete."

"Get out, chummo. I don't like you any more. You're dangerous."

Finian Smith nodded crisply. "I could very well be." And left.

As Finian left the Panpublix building he heard a menacing hiss. He tried to dodge the rainbow spray. Too late.

His clothing was soon soaked with a noxious admixture of water, special nitrites and phosphorous compounds shot into the air by the underground sprinkler system.

At the levacar station he finally controlled his anger. How petty they could be, to order the lawns sprinkled just then.

Waiting passengers moved away and made rude remarks about his smell. Finian found himself sole occupant of the front car on the ride down the Philadelphia spur.

The enforced loneliness gave him a chance to organize his muddled thoughts and decide what course of action he had to pursue concerning Dolly Novotny.

Two facts he possessed. What they meant, he didn't know.

A likely place to find her was the TTIC pilot plant on Manhattan, the prison island. Still, he was certain to have a rough time getting on to the island and into the plant after that. With few resources at his disposal it might be better to pursue the other thread a bit.

Its significance left him even more muddled. Alvah Loudermilk, TTIC chairman, had appeared at the dealer presentation, somewhat to the annoyance of his inferiors. And R. R. Pharoh, top G/S executive, hadn't been acting quite sensibly either when he permitted an oil portrait of himself to be painted. Finian had never seen a public photo of either man. Both executives were practically legendary.

Then why in the name of Galbraith did they look so much like each other?

When Finian thought on it, one cold, unpleasant word gnawed his head. *Conspiracy*.

A moment later his professional memory dredged up a source of proving or disproving his odd theory. What he intended to do with evidence, if any existed, he couldn't say. But he had a vague desire to be armed with a little more certainty before he sought Dolly.

An achingly musical name. *Dolly, Dolly*—

He remembered her so well, from summer evenings on the back porch before Bala Cynwyd, like the other suburbs, was swallowed in the fester of the metropolis.

Her dark hair. Her gentle eyes. Her animated mouth. And the raspberry mark, one night during an electrical storm.

She'd tentatively shared Finian's inherited ideas about their constantly obsolete world, ideas long suppressed in him and now flooding back under the double stimulus of Sprool's lecture and Pushkyn's vindictive parsimony. Dolly hadn't exactly been sympathetic. The philosophy of enduring worth was too daring even then. (Today it was sheer lunacy.) But neither had she been as adamant as most citizens. As her parents, for example. They replaced their furniture monthly with the latest G/S fiberboard laminate imitation Finnish modern modes. Good consumers, both. Then came his dismissal from the DOCs, the enforced break-up—

The levacar slowed for Bala Cynwyd. In the abstract, remodelling a woman's mind to make her the pattern to which nearly all other women in the world could conform was acceptable to Finian. When it came to the specific of changing Dolly to the marshmallow-trumpery creature looming on the screen behind Krumm, that was too much.

As he stepped off at Bala Cynwyd, it began to rain. He hurried along beneath warped building fronts of chartreuse and electric blue extruded plastic. From a doorway a hapless bum in last year's pseudo-cotton sport clothes begged for three dollars for a tube of model cement to sniff. Finian shuddered and walked faster. He stopped at Abe Kane's Autosuiter, the last shop left open on the block, selected a few new clothes from the plastic catalogue sheets fastened to the walls, and fed his universal credit card into the slot after punching out his measurements.

A red lucite sign blinked on: *Credit N. G.*

Finian frowned, hit the cancel lever and tried again. The third time he tried his card was not returned.

Pushkyn! Damn the vindictive bastard.

He trudged on through the rain, never having felt so alone in his life. It was a queer sensation, the total absence of credit. Once, he remembered dimly, Pop had brought home a suit of clothes purchased with cash. It had caused a near-riot among Bala Cynwyd burghers.

Reaching his shabby apartment, Finian changed from the effete suit, scrubbed up as best he could, packed his few belongings into a satchel and walked back into the rain. He passed a crowd of workers from the local G/S visorphone plant. It specialized in treating receiver parts with reagents that would crack the plastic precisely eight months after installation.

A little smog had mixed with the rain, turning the street ghostly. At a corner booth Finian used his last few coins to make a toll call to the House of Sinatra in Los Angeles.

A sound truck rolled past, repeating over and over. *"Gee-ess, Gee-ess, don't guess, it's bess—Take free shuttle at Exit 5-6 to the G/S Plaza—Gee-ess, don't—"*

A dapper young man appeared on the screen, snapping his fingers. "Hiyah. What can this gasser of a full-service bank do for you, Clyde?"

Finian showed his bank identification card.

"I'd like to withdraw my balance."

The banker came back into view a moment later. "Get lost. Your balance is nonesville. Garnisheed at noon. Unperformance and non-fulfilling of verbal contract, with waiver of co-operation. You signed it, Charlie."

"Damn it, I performed—" Finian began.

The screen had already blacked.

He staggered into the drifting smog. So Pushkyn had gone that far. Just for the sake of meanness. Well, Finian Smith would show the whole rotten bunch. They had angered him now. He wasn't quite witless, not yet.

Gee-ess, Gee-ess, it's bess came a lonely bellow. The polluted smog made Finian cough. His eyes smarted as he turned his pockets inside out.

A dollar left. Enough for a cup of coffee. No transportation. Just a single walking man in a cloud of industrial fumes and a long, empty night for thinking of Dolly.

Resolutely Finian hefted his satchel and started out to walk to Missouri.

IV

Thirty-six days later Finian staggered into the National Record Office in Rolla. Thirty-six frightening, alarming, eye-opening, solitary, transfiguring days they had been, too.

Days of dodging robot levacars whose spot-beams hunted him in the shadows beneath the elevated turnpikes, seeking to arrest him for pedestrianship.

Days of remembering his Pop. And nights too. Especially nights, thinking as he lay under a berry bush half-starved and chilly, how Pop had enjoyed prize-fights, antisocial, uncooperative prize-fights. How young Finian had been dragged to lonely boxcars or dim garages where furtive men watched the sport before it was finally stamped out in the name of bland humanity.

The world too was one bland custard, blandly happy. Except not really, as Finian, horrified, discovered.

No plant could function at total efficiency, at complete peak year after year. A low percentage of chronic unemployment had never been whipped by the cyclid theorists. Strange wild caravans of men and wives and children, human wolves almost passed Finian occasionally on redleafed back-roads in Pennsylvania and Ohio. He almost fell into the hands of one such band. Thereupon he decided he must possess a weapon of self-defence at all costs. His belly he could protect by shovelling in wild berries and an occasional stolen chunk of honeycomb. But his life, against such a seething pack of wild creatures as he had fled from on that lonely road, needed more dependable protection.

Difficult problem. Under law, weapons were prohibited except upon special occasions. What necessity for weapons when all was pleasant co-operation.

Yet the G/S guards carried weapons. So did the TTIC internal force. Finian was beginning to believe he knew why that might be so. Too early to tell, however. And the other problem pressed him to concentration upon it.

Weapon-devotees were even more suspect than pedestrians in the lonely country between metropolises. Occasionally Finian glimpsed a wire compound, acres and acres, against the sunburnt horizon. Manhattan Prison was too far for local DOCs to send recalcitrant Hoosier or Buckeye anti-obsols, so they were thrown into smaller country compounds, together with those few madmen who settled disputes with fists. Such compound inmates were described as juves, Finian remembered, passing one such wire enclosure on a white moonlit night and shuddering. He didn't recognise the term juve, but it obviously meant the middle-aged or geriatric specimens huddled within the cages, a few defiantly wearing ancient gaudy jackets with mottoes stitched on them, forgotten anarchist slogans like Pfluger's Idle Hour Pin Barons.

On the outskirts of South Bend, Finian luckily came upon an obsolescence carnival.

Several thousand people swarmed across a treeless terrain in a housing project smash. Motorized workgangs stood at the development's fringe, waiting to set up new prefab Moorish Manors to replace obsolete Five-Bedroom Geneva Chateaux.

Finian infiltrated the wild carnival crowd, ripping draperies and smashing furniture with feigned laughter ringing from his lips. When the carnival wore itself out near dawn and the workgangs rolled in through clouds of soy-fuel smoke, Finian filched a shiny flick-blade knife from a Boy Scout chopping up a last slab of plastic plaster and lath.

The Scout shrieked for the DOCs on duty. Finian was away and running through a hydro-ponic cornfield before he could be caught.

Now, dressed in his only presentable suit, last year's G/S Nubby Oppenheimer, he flashed his personal identification card before the computer rid in the empty green marble rotunda of the National Record Office. Personal identity was one quantity Pushkyn couldn't revoke.

Finian felt his fingers tingle as the grid scanned the card.

"Investigator Smith, Bond Number PA-5006, you are recognized."

"Permission to examine ownership statements for corporations over one billion, please."

"What year?" buzzed the mechanical voice.

"Not certain," Finian replied. "Could be as far back as 1980 or even 1970."

"Second tier from lowest level. Tube nine, your left."

It gave Finian a weird sensation, plummeting in the airtube and realizing he was dropping eighty storys into the depths of the nation's largest insane asylum. But legal transactions had proliferated so in the past decades, as had neurotic behavior, that only a combined institution and record office was feasible for saving space and offering a less-than-fatal end for hopeless maniacs.

The reading room below ground smelled of mold. Grey block walls heightened the unpleasant mood. Finian sat at the call-out console. He manipulated the controls and spoke into the unit:

"Let me have the volume covering Goods/Service corporation for—ah—1974, please."

Several minutes passed. A door slid aside. A white

male, perhaps seventy, with yellow-rimmed lack-luster eyes and a lantern jaw, shuffled in and waited with docile manner. The creature wore a seedy twill uniform, anciently cut.

"What do you have on any asset transfers for Goods/Services, please?" Finian asked.

The elderly gentleman did not so much as blink. He hesitated only a moment as the index system in his sick skull, instilled by hypnolearning, turned over record after invisible record. Finally he said vacantly, "No asset transfers."

"Nothing in the way of stock, even?"

"No asset transfers, no asset transfers."

"Thank you, that's all."

But the man had already departed, needing no thanks. Finian turned to the console again wondering whether he could endure as many days as it might take:

"Let me have the volume covering Goods/Services corporation for 1975."

A total of eighteen hours went by, relieved only by three short naps above ground, Finian sleeping in a magnolia bush on Rolla's outskirts, before he found what he wanted.

He'd worked through Goods/Services from its 1969 inception to 1997, interviewing assorted madmen and women who shuffled in, reeled off figures and names or lack of them, then shuffled back out. Asset transfers exhausted itself as a lead. He tried register of directorship as well as deposition of tangible real-estate sale. Useless, useless. Only then did it slip back.

In some dim time in the past—Pushkyn had mentioned it once—public stock of G/S had been called off the market.

Once more he began with a different set of volumes, working his way down the years. In 1992, he located it: All certificates re-deemed.

The scent overpowered the must of the underground box like the smell of blood. He called out the volume covering Things to Come Incorporated for the same year. It was a naturalized Japanese weighing close to three hundred pounds.

One month after the G/S redemption came a callback

by the board of TTIC. Finian almost wished the poor Japanese could appreciate tea. He'd have bought him a bucket, had he the money.

Tensely his fingers flew to the console.

"Two volumes, please. For 1992 and 1993. Covering Flotations without tangible assets."

When 1992 arrived (a mulatto with his face fixed in a perpetual grin) Finian was disappointed. Nothing. The volume for 1993 (a strikingly voluptuous red-haired girl who had eyes that made him think hauntingly of Dolly) was another case entirely. Finian trembled:

"Give me what you have on holding companies, please."

The third was it, the redhead staring through him:

"Holders Limited. Ten thousand shares privately issued."

Finian was on his feet, sweating, his empty belly a-churn. "Officers, please."

"Chairman of the board, Alvah Pharoh."

"There must be some mistake. Uh—re-check, please. What is the name?"

"Full legal name Alvah Robert Loudermilk Pharoh."

A florid old gentleman with dewlaps and blue, vaguely crossed—by heaven!

Finian almost forgot to return the volume to its detention cell after he got the names of the other registered corporate executives, which meant nothing to him. But Alvah Robert Loudermilk Pharoh most certainly did.

Finian wondered, as he left the National Record building and turned his face east again, what had possessed the old man to think it safe to occasionally appear as head of both companies. Not that he appeared often, mind you. The painting *must* have been a slip. So too the appearance on the hydrofoiler, displeasing his underlings. Senility? Senility and a strength that had refused to completely drain away, as the dewlaps lengthened?

Hungry and tattered though he was, Finian felt renewed as he threw himself into the weary tramp back to Manhattan. The flick-blade knife armed him. So did the knowledge that even the most mighty, even those who kept the plant running at all costs, including the cost of sloth, could occasionally slip.

And they still had Dolly.

V

Ahead in the gloomy purple twilight, giant rats were squealing after blood.

Quickening his step, Finian unshipped the flick-knife. Making headway was hard. This particular section of the Hudson Bluffs National Dump was a miniature mountain range of discarded but eminently serviceable—except for the usual engineered-to-fail tubes and cracked cabinets—solido sets. To the east behind the rubble the towers of Manhattan Prison thrust into the darkening sky.

Finian walked rapidly away from the squee-squee of the rats. He'd glimpsed a pack of them earlier, down by the Tunnel at the far end of the hundred-thousand-acre junk tract. They were nearly three feet long from drinking the waste spewed out by the pharmaceutical factories upriver. Hoping to avoid a meeting with needly fangs, Finian was suddenly arrested by a fresh sound.

A human voice, in fright.

He doubled back in his tracks, cold sweat all over him. The vitaminized beasts were attacking a real person!

Finian rounded a solido heap. A little wisp-haired balloon of a man in a ragged grey smock was backed against a trash peak, trying vainly to swing at three of the rats, armed only with a plastic leg broken from a solido console. The man's left trouser leg was shredded, black-shining with blood. The blood maddened the rats. They danced and snapped and squee-squeed and made the little man even more pale.

Finian snatched up a solido cabinet and heaved. One of the rats yipped, turned and scuttled at Finian like a small furry tank. Shaking, Finian stood his ground. He tried to dodge the creature's leap but was not agile enough. Hellish teeth sank into his arm.

Finian jammed his flick-knife into the smelly hair at the base of the rat's brain. Squirting blood like a fountain, the rat flipped over in the air and gave a death-squee. Its comrades received solid whacks between the eyes from the other man. They turned tail and vanished.

"Let me see that arm," said the man, a filthy specter with moist, disappointed eyes. "Oh, not good at all. Come along. I'm a doctor. Humphrey Cove."

The Sellers of the Dream 75

Finian gaped as he was led along the bluff. "A doctor? In the National Dump?"

"I live here. Never mind, I'll explain later. I have a shack. Hurry, we don't want those rat toxins to run through you. I think I have immunization. Oh, I was really done for until you came along."

The small doctor giggled as he hustled Finian along. Finian was not too sure he approved of his would-be savior. In spite of Dr. Cove's rather pitiful mien, there was a certain unsteadiness in his wet eyes. He clucked and talked to himself as he led the way to a ramshackle structure nearly the size of a small private dwelling, constructed solely of panels from solido consoles jerry-rigged together with wire and other scrap materials.

"No one comes here. No humans. Only the littersweep convoys from up and down the coast, all mech-driven. The only people I ever talk with are the poor juves in the prison. What's your name? What are you doing here?"

At the hovel entrance Cove suddenly halted, stared at Finian and turned pale.

"Did you come to arrest—?"

Finian shook his head. "I came to get into Manhattan."

"Via the Dumps?" Cove blinked suspiciously. "There's the Tunnel."

"To use the Tunnel, you have to be a priest going in for last rites. Or a coroner or a psychiatry student. Or have a DOC pass. I watched the Tunnel three hours." Suddenly Finian had an impulse to trust this odd little person: "I have no pass. I'll be entering the prison illegally."

"Well, then! Come inside, do come inside!"

Names were exchanged again. Cove having forgotten he'd given his. From behind a triple stack of ancient medical texts Cove said he'd rescued from dump piles, the doctor produced a frowsy leather-plas diagnostic kit. He clamped the analyzer to Finian's upper arm and switched on the battery. A whir. A moment later the proper medication had been pressure-sprayed through Finian's epidermal cells.

Cove watched with proud glowing eyes, saying as he unstrapped the unit:

"A miracle I found this kit, I'll tell you. Three years

ago. The only persons who use it are the poor juves. No regular medical help for them, I'm afraid. So I've a skiff. Actually an old levacar inverted. I paddle across once a month after dark." He giggled. "The DOCs at the Tunnel post would psych me if I got caught. But I feel I'm doing my bit to keep the anti-obsols content in their unhappiness."

Through a rift in the wall Cove's moist eyes sought the darkening towers. His voice was quickly vengeful.

"I'd like to see those buildings fall to ash. Margarita, ah poor Margarita." He whipped his head around, eyes almost as vicious as those of the rats. "Who are you? If this is all a clever trap to smoke me out—"

"No trap," Finian assured him. "I'll tell you about it. But do you have any food?"

Cove nodded and fetched a brown gallon pharmaceutical bottle, instructing Finian to drink.

"Protein and vitamins. Distill it myself from the drug sludge in the river. After you drink I may or may not give you one of the soy bars I get from the juves. When their wives bear children, it's the only way they can pay, you know. They're very proud, always pay."

Cove squatted with difficulty, an oddly savage little man in the fading light.

"Whether I let you have a soy bar depends on your story. If you're an enemy, I can run away and leave you to wander the Dumps at night. You won't last long with the rats, being a stranger."

"There's a woman over on that island I have to find," said Finian and launched out.

As he recounted his tale, careful not to become too emotional about it, he noticed a growing excitement in Cove's damp eyes. Finally, when he had concluded, Cove leaped up.

"Capital, Smith, that's capital. Let me help. Let me ferry you across."

Finian smiled grudgingly. "Okay. I was prepared to swim it."

"The sludge would poison you before you got halfway."

"What's your stake in this, Cove? I mean, this food pays me back for the rats."

Cove's little eyes were miserable.

"Margarita. My wife. She died over there."

Painfully the story came out, dredged from an unhappy past:

Cove had been a plastic surgeon by speciality, in the employ of TTIC at its Bangor Personality Salon. But a quirk in his nature made him rebel against the work, permitted him to fall prey to dangerous Galbraither notions. His wife had informed on him.

Cove discovered it before the TTIC police could arrest him. He fled to the outskirts of Bangor, hiding there in the woods while a few reluctant friends supplied him with food. TTIC industrial police combed the woods wth talk-horns, threatening to psych his wife into anti-obsol attitudes if he didn't surrender.

"The filth!" Cove rocked on his haunches. "I thought it was a trick, a lever. I ran away. Margarita, poor thing, was on their side. She couldn't help what she did. She came of a respected family. TTIC middle management. But a year later I found out. They did it anyway. Oh, they smile and smile and treat the mob kindly. But underneath, when they're opposed—I learned Margarita had been sentenced to Manhattan. It took me another nine months to get here and find means of crossing. By that time she'd died of pneumonia. No antibiotics allowed the juves, you see. Juves are worthless. She died." Cove rocked and rocked, wild-eyed. "Died, died."

"Doctor Cove, will you help me get across?"

"Of course, of course. But to hunt that pilot plant, a knife won't be much good. The moment you're discovered they'll set on you like wild dogs."

"Then I'll need something else."

Finian's brain ran rapidly with his career with G/S. He recalled Leveranz, an unfortunate operative charged with a dangerous penetration of the TTIC Marketing Office in Beirut.

"I knew a man once who was bombed. Is there anything here—?" Finian's gesture swept the shack and dump beyond. "Do you remember enough, even if we could find an explosive source, to bomb me?"

The moist eyes of Cove widened with malicious delight. "Blow them up?"

Now Finian himself felt hard and cold.

"I just might, if they've hurt her."

"Possibly we could use the charger pack from an old

solido." Cove was warming to the challenge. "Yes, we very well might. Extremely miniaturized. I'd have to check the formula but I think I have a chem text in that pile. And a military medicine volume, too." He began to tear through the books. "No anesthesia, or precious little. Perhaps I could knock you out."

"What for a trigger?" Finian questioned. He showed his mouth. "I have this empty socket where I carried a camera once."

Chortling, Cove scuffled among his belongings and produced a cardboard carton full of ivory chips of all sizes.

"Why, that ought to work, Smith. The miserable juves aren't fluoridated either. I do quite a few extractions. Imagine a plastic surgeon doing extractions! Let's see, give me a minute to find the chem text . . ."

Dr. Humphrey Cove unearthed the text in two minutes. The rest took four days.

Finian suffered excruciatingly, especially during the operation. Cove kept smacking him on the head with a solido leg when the pain grew too hideous. Finian dug his nails into his palms and thought of murmurous summer evenings on the back porch in Bala Cynwyd, and vowed in his pain-streaked mind the hurt was worth it if only he had a means to strike at them if they'd hurt Dolly, his own Dolly.

When he was ready to enter the prison, his left foot flesh carried a small capsule that would detonate an explosive force when the yellowing tooth in his dead socket was turned a proper one-half turn in its clumsily hand-chiselled housing.

An old trick, bombing. A relic of the Triple Play War. But it gave Finian a little more courage to go hunting death.

In an unpleasant mist-clammy midnight, Dr. Cove paddled the improvised skiff through the sticky penicillin waste forming a crust on the Hudson, to the dilapidated pier that once belonged to the Cunard division of G/S. Off down black, ruined streets distant reddish lights pulsed. Cove shook his hand fervently. "I hope you kill them. I hope you don't co-operate and kill them all."

Then the skiff slithered away into the smelly broth. Finian shivered and walked.

Three blocks from the pier a ragged band of thirty-odd men and women, with a couple of malnourished youngsters hanging at the fringes, slipped out of an alley and closed around him.

They hissed and backed a terrified Finian against a polybrick wall. The leader of the juve pack, an oldster of eighty in tapered blue denim trousers and an antiquarian jacket spangled with fake platinum stars and buckles swaggered up and down, thumbs hooked in a six-inch belt.

"Sending DOCs into the streets these days, are they, sonny?"

"I'm no DOC." Finian searched the hostile eyes for succor. There was none.

"We eat DOCs alive in the prison. They step off the guard post, we swallow 'em up and chew 'em to pieces, sonnyboy."

"A DOC stew tonight! Oh, wunnerful!" piped a seven-year-old.

"Scream a little for us, will you please?" said the ageing juve with a smile, shuffling forward.

Finian thought of the flick-knife and whipped it out. Another sibilant hiss ran from mouth to mouth as the blade caught the distant red glow.

"Look, don't kill me. See this? It's a knife, a real knife. You people can recognize a genuine useful antique twentieth-century artifact, can't you? Non-obsolescent. Non-obsolescent, see? Still works?"

A touched stud and the blade retracted. Another touch and it sprang out.

"Would I be a DOC and carry this?"

The juve leader had an almost religious expression on his face. His hand shook as he extended it.

"Uh—could you—leave me see?"

Finian thrust it into his hand.

"Yours. Listen, take it." A dark, malicious streak forced out the next words. "Could you make more? Why don't you try? Now you have a pattern. Then you wouldn't have to wait for the DOCs to leave the guard post. Then a lot of you could pay them a visit."

Whispering over their icon, the juves melted into the night.

VI

Keeping to back streets, Finian crossed Bway several blocks above a strange complex of glittering red lights. Cove had told him it was the prison recreation area, a kind of open plaza known, unpronounceably, as Timesq. Hurrying on, he reached Parkave.

Several blocks south he saw a white chain working its way across the ruined thoroughfare. Approaching in the cover of shadows, he gazed up at a glistening glass structure with windows painted over. Then he looked down to the street again.

The white chain came apart into individual females, double-timing along between a cordon of TTIC industrial guards. One chain rushed west, another east, vanishing into the building. Finian skulked, grinning mirthlessly, estimating the time to be somewhere in the neighborhood of eleven at night. Protected, the pilot plant nursing staff was changing shift. Cove had told Finian about the nurses, and also what might be done. He hurried back towards Bway.

The recreation area was curiously deserted of juves at this hour. Finian wondered whether the flick-knife was really that much of a talisman. It must be, since he'd seen no juves after the first encounter. Cove said there were several hundred thousand on the island. Perhaps they'd gone underground to the ruined transportation tubes.

Timesq featured open shops subsidized out of national taxes as a sop to the theory of rehabilitation . . . antiques, genuine meatburgers, bizarre novelty stores where articles were actually displayed on open counters instead of behind automated windows. But the shops were actually intended to pander to the vices of the juves. Else why would Finian have been able to slip so easily into a deserted costumer's?

Half starved, his shanks frozen by wind whistling under the ancient white uniform and the musty grey wig prickling his ears, Finian dozed the daylight hours away in an alley, blearily on the alert for juves. He saw one large pack passing a block away, several hundred on the run. They didn't see him. Otherwise he was undisturbed until night fell again.

Midway between the hotel which apparently served as

nurses' quarters and the ruined liquor building, Finian ducked into one of the double-timing white chains as the eleven o'clock shift changed. He hoped his male shoes wouldn't be too noticeable. But the street was dark. The hundred or so nurses were on dangerous extra-pay duty from the way they rushed along between the guard cordons, not speaking, intent only on gaining the safety of the pilot plant.

As in all hospitals, lights burned low in the marble mausoleum of a lobby as the nurses fanned out to the various tube banks. Finian spied a rest room next to a boarded-up newsstand, slipped inside and waited half an hour out of sight.

Then he returned to the lobby. A late nurse was hurrying to the tubes. Outside, the TTIC guard cordons were no more. Finian ran up behind the nurse, thinking smugly that it had been easy so far. He'd remembered to touch no doors, in case there was a sweat-print check.

The nurse gave a frightened *kkk* sound as Finian looped his elbow around her neck.

"Where's the prototype kept, lady? Tell me or I'll crack you in half."

"Tw-twelve," came the panicky answer. "I can't breathe!"

"You won't ever again unless you take me up there."

"It's not my floor—"

"With lights out who'll know? There's the tube. Inside! Don't speak to anyone. Don't even raise an eyebrow, or I'll throttle you."

In the deserted tube the alarmed woman, elderly, eyed Finian's wig, all too obvious in the full illumination.

"What are you, some kind of degenerate?"

"Yes, but not the kind you think."

Finian laughed, feeling frightened and brave all at once.

On twelve, isolated pools of radiance interspersed vast islands of aseptic black. Three nurses clustered at a floor desk to the right. Finian's terrified victim led him to the left.

Double doors loomed at the far corridor end. Why was it so easy? Finian felt vague alarm as he shoved the old lady through the doors. The isolation, that must be it, he reasoned. The improbable isolation here on Manhattan where no investigator would dream of looking for a pilot plant.

Still, Pushkyn's people had discovered it by molecular-triangulation sonics. Were they penetrating even now?

In the chamber a white blur stretched naked in the warm, purified air. Finian held tight to the old nurse's arm and approached the dreaming girl. The raspberry mark stood out black in the faint gleam from the half-open door of an attached dispensary. There encephalographs and other equipment winked, chromed and cold.

"Dolly?" Finian's lips felt like shreds of paper, crinkled dry. "Dolly, hear me?"

A vacuous mewing sound came from the girl. She twisted deeper in silk coverlets. "Wake her," Finian ordered.

"You're a madman! I don't know how. I'm on six, neurosearch."

He shoved her rudely. "There must be a chart in the dispensary."

Finian had to threaten to cuff her several times before she tremblingly translated the medical Latin in the last twelve thick casebooks on the dispensary shelf. From the section marked *Emergency Antidotal Procedures* she read out the correct mix of ampoules from the wall-wide freezer.

Finian was acutely conscious of the silence of the great dark room, the whisper of Dolly's breathing from the bed, the rush of controlled air in and out of blowers. Time was moving inexorably. What he would do when and if he wakened Dolly he was not precisely sure. All he could tell was that he must talk to her. Talking to her once was what he had worked and tramped and almost died for.

The pressuredermic barrel gleamed in the light. Finian snatched it from the nurse.

"If you've tricked me—I don't take to hurting women, but I will!"

"I swear to Loudermilk I didn't. Only please don't hurt me."

"In there," Finian instructed. He latched the dispensary door behind her. There was no visorphone inside. He would be safe a moment longer.

With shaking hands he pressed the instilling cup near the raspberry mark, and plunged.

Slowly, slowly, the naked girl rolled over, lids fluttering drowsily. Finian crouched by the bed. His hand knotted up in the silken sheets. He'd turned up a rheostat to provide a gleam for judging her eyes. Doll-blue, they flew open—

Blank, unknowing.

"Why, hello there." The voice tormented him. It was so speaking, so silly. "Whatever are you doing in Dream's bedroo— Dream's bed—"

Like a broken mechanism the voice ran down. One of her voluptuous hands crept tentatively towards his. *"Finian?"*

"Oh, my God, my God, Dolly."

He buried his head on her shoulder, almost crying.

When he had controlled himself sufficiently to talk, he asked her what it was like.

"Not too terrible." Dolly's voice now, not her body but for the mark, only her voice trying painfully to re-form old associations. "When we moved . . . Well, it was luck and a little moral compromise that snared me a chance to be the prototype."

"Do you remember anything? I mean, when you're under?"

"A little. A very little. Far down in my head, like the bottom of a well. I won't in a week or two, so they say."

"It's wrong, Dolly! It's wrong for them to change you!"

She laughed tolerantly, not a little sadly.

"Those wild old ideas of yours again."

"I love you, Dolly. I want you the way you were."

"Impossible, Fin. My body's changed." One hand lifted the hem of the sheet. "It's part of the price for being the prototype. I nearly died when my parents made us move. I wasn't strong. I'm not much stronger now. This" —a gesture to the room—"when they're finished with me, in a week or two, I'll never be able to go back. The prototype can't. Other women can, the change isn't so deep when it's purchased. But in return I'll receive more money than most women ever see. I wish you hadn't come here, Fin. I'd nearly got over you."

"Take out the contacts, Dolly. Then tell me it's all over."

"Fin, I can't. They're permanent." She clutched his arm. "If you're caught here—"

Rapidly he told her of what he'd learned at the National Record Office. "Some kind of conspiracy, Dolly. Awful, awful. Hell, I'm not bright enough to fathom what it means. Maybe Pop could have. I'm just certain I want you out before this crazy doublecross blows right up."

Dolly hesitated. "I'm not sure. My mind's full of someone else—"

"Don't let him frighten you," said a voice. "He's done anyway."

Caught, heartbeat wild and racing, Finian turned as all the lights blazed up in the room. Dolly shrieked and burrowed under the sheet.

Outside the closing panel Finian glimpsed a phalanx of armed TTIC police. The three men inside moved swiftly towards him. Sprool and Pushkyn shoulder to shoulder, and shuffling behind, Alvah Robert Loudermilk Pharoh with his dewlaps jiggling and his blue, vaguely crossed eyes filled with fright.

"We should of killed the jerko," Pushkyn offered.

"Be quiet." Sprool breathed tightly, thinking hard.

"No one listens to me," Alvah Robert Loudermilk Pharoh whined. "No one listens any more even though I'm the chief executive of Holders."

"You simpleton!" Sprool spun on him, barely able to control his fury. "You incredible wreck! I wish Pushkyn and I had retired you to a senility farm long ago. If your addled brain could have understood it wasn't safe for you to go around making public appearances! Having your portrait painted!"

"Holders is my firm!"

"It *was*. Before your brains turned to mashed potatoes," said Pushkyn.

"You wouldn't have penetrated the pilot plant, would you, Pushkyn?" Finian was suddenly enraged, and beginning to understand. "Even though you knew where it was."

Pushkyn sneered. "Whaddya think, put sand in the wheels? Always the funny finko, huh? If it wasn't for me, Sprool and a few others on both sides, running the show while this old bonebag sits on the Holders board—"

"He means to say," Sprool put in, somewhat sadly,

"we have done our best to keep the plant running. You, Fin, have done your best to stop it."

"How did you find me?" Finian demanded.

Sprool shrugged. "See-ray."

"I never touched a doorknob anyplace!"

"There is a false socket in your head. Every person entering or leaving this plant is rayed for dental coding. Yours failed to check. It took a few minutes to collect Pushkyn. And the old man. I want him to see the fruits of his senility. We vertijetted."

"Ah, damn," said Finian, impotently.

"I very nearly admire you," Sprool told him. "In proper circumstances you might have filled a responsible position with Holders. Do you realize what a difficult and exciting enterprise it is to run this world, Fin?"

"I realize you sold everybody a bill of goods, kept them soft, sucked their guts out."

"Would you rather have howling millions out of work and rioting?"

"Yes! Yes. I mean, no. I don't want people to starve, but this way—I'd rather have some guts in life. Trouble and guts."

"Trouble we have, Finian," Sprool returned with a sigh. "Do you know what we saw as we came over the Tunnel in the vertijet? The DOC post in ruins. The juves are breaking out, Fin, actually breaking out. Most of them are dead, of course. But several hundred escaped. There's a pitched battle going on in Jersey this minute. The juves will die as soon as I give the mobilization order. A few may get away and start in other cities, inciting riot, pulling down what we've built so carefully to insure everyone a decent life. Both TTIC and G/S are alerting industrial guards trained for trouble such as this. We'll also have to apply considerable pressure for the DOCs to move. But we'll win. We gave up war long ago, Fin. We won't permit another to start."

"The creeps had knives!" Pushkyn bellowed. "Real knives! You stupid, did you—?"

"I think so," Finian looked up. "I hope so."

Again Sprool sighed, almost sympathetically.

"Fin, Fin. You seem to think we're evil men. We're not. We're *businessmen*. We didn't begin the system. We only inherited it. But you've never understood, have you? Always, I think, you resented us as a result of what your father taught you." Sprool was white now, impassioned. "We had no choice! Either we maintained calm or—"

"You changed Dolly! I don't understand your theories beyond that!"

Sprool outshouted him: "The alternative to a rocked boat is *chaos!*"

"There's got to be another way."

"Go to the guard post! See the mangled bodies and then say that."

"I don't *care*, Sprool! I'm taking Dolly off the island."

"Creep, you won't set one foot from here."

Finian peeled his lips back.

"Look at the tooth, Lyman. You know what was there before." He waggled his left foot. "I'm bombed. The tooth will set it off. Either instantaneously or on timed delay. Stop me from walking out with Dolly and find out."

"Salinghams wanted my portrait—" the florid old gentleman began.

"Bluffer! Lousy, rotten bluffer!" Screaming, Pushkyn rushed forward.

Sprool's hand flew up.

"Don't! I believe him."

For the first time Finian Smith saw Sprool perspiring.

"He's the kind to do it, Pushkyn. I don't want slaughter here, too. So you keep quiet and remember who's senior troubleshooter."

Cold, shrewd lights glittered in Sprool's eyes. "Fin, what guarantee can you offer if we release this woman to you, allow her to go with you under duress?"

"No."

Heads swung, startled. Dolly went on slowly:

"I think—I want—"

A disgusted sigh came from Sprool's lips. He controlled himself. "Very well, Fin. If we permit you to leave, what guarantees do you offer that you'll cause no further trouble? We'll have our hands full quelling the disturbances the juves will start. It hasn't got too far out of hand yet. But if I don't give the mobilization order, it could go nationwide. Even to other countries. I have to be around to stop it. It can be done, even though I don't much like removing the velvet glove."

"Guarantees?" said Finian. "My word. That's all."

Sprool walked quickly to the door and opened it. The threatening knot of industrial police still waited in the shadows. Finian bundled Dolly into the bedclothes and moved her towards the entrance as Sprool said, "Let him pass."

"I won't stand for it!" Pushkyn leaped forward and landed a solid one that rocked Finian on his heels. Then Sprool snapped his fingers. The TTIC police carried the foam-lipped Pushkyn into the dispensary.

Trembling, suddenly cold and trembling clear through, Finian made an effort to keep his face an inflexible mask as he guided Dolly through the aisle between the guards. He hoped she wouldn't question him, wouldn't relent until they were free. Sick fear engulfed him as he touched the tip of his tongue gingerly to the fake tooth while the tube shot down.

Dolly leaned on his shoulder, her hair warm. She made frightened mewing sounds. Finian shepherded her into the night, began the long, terrible walk to the Tunnel, hoping she wouldn't come to her senses until they reached the opposite shore. In time she'd be herself again. That much he could give her even if his search had been all for nothing.

The DOC post at the Tunnel entrance was afire. Juve corpses sprawled everywhere.

Midway along the empty tunnel Finian halted. A figure capered towards them.

"Capital, oh, marvellous!" Humphrey Cove trilled, stepping over a dead DOC's open-mouthed head. "Three hundred of them got out, running for their lives. I think it will spread this time. The local camps, the jobless—fullscale! There are so many really lovely pockets of resistance!"

"Shut up and walk." Finian pushed Cove back towards the Jersey side.

"What in heaven's name is wrong with you, Smith?"

"Armed." Finian whispered it so Dolly couldn't hear. "A guy hit me, I'm armed. Can't have more than half an hour before I blow. Cove, don't you say anything. When we're outside, you take care of this girl, understand? Watch out for her until she recovers. She's free of them, I bought her that much."

They passed a shrilling visorphone in a lighted kiosk at the far Tunnel mouth. A DOC alert was being scheduled for Philadelphia. Juve gangs were forming in the streets there, hand-made knives were appearing. The mask was off. Full mobilization of combined TTIC and G/S industrial police was being ordered by Sprool. Cove clapped his hands.

Rain was falling as Finian led Dolly out of the Tunnel. Three DOC vertijets from the south were homing on Manhattan, agleam with emergency lights. Dolly murmured. Finian lifted her chin and stared into the doll-blue eyes a moment, conscious of the bomb working, working towards detonation in the flesh of his foot. He couldn't even feel the death seed. Wasn't that a joke?

"Cove'll take care of you," Finian said. He kissed her. Bewildered, Dolly called for him as he turned and walked rapidly away, not seeing the rain or the littered bodies.

He had gone but a dozen steps when something felled him and brought the dark.

Pain, incredible pain was his first sensation.

Then a warmth of flesh. Dolly bending over him. Through a slatted section of solido panel he saw vertijets winking over Manhattan. Finian wriggled, then struggled up, screaming:

"My leg . . . *what happened?*"

Crying, Dolly pressed him down.

"Cove did it. Cove operated. He hates them, Fin. He hates TTIC. Something about his wife. He said you ought to live, even with—I wish my mind would straighten out. I can't say things all right yet."

Finian fought the terror, the dull-fire agony. "Where is he?"

Dolly shuddered. "He packed it in a valise and ran for the Tunnel."

In a burst of fire the centre of Manhattan Prison blew up.

When the reverberations and Dolly's screams had stopped, the two of them clung together, listening to the hysterical automatic sirens at both ends of the island wailing as they hadn't wailed since the Triple Play War. Confused, hurting, glad of life, guilty and fearsomely glad and yet sickened by the suddenly swarming sky full of vertijets, their flaring emergency lights promising violence across the land, violence maybe everywhere, Finian clutched the girl to his shoulder and stared at the inferno of the prison island.

"My God, I think I started a war, Dolly. Sprool said —I didn't mean to start—"

The words tore out of him, almost animal: *"Is this the only way?"*

Dolly sobbed. There wasn't any other answer, except the sirens multiplying all around in the disrupted night.

The Highest Form of Life

> Human beings are egotistical creatures. As the dominant life form on this planet we have a tendency to equate power with quality. Challenges to this point of view have provided the material for some of science fiction's most memorable stories, including the struggle between humans and insects, the only two life forms that are on the increase. However, as John Jakes shows us in this story, there can be more at stake than mere survival, and competition can take many forms.

In the lives of most men there are a very few, certain days on which they not only sense their purpose but know that a fraction of it may be accomplished. So it was with Dr. Robert Conn, when the alarm went off in the cottage in the hot Florida dawn. His mind said, *14 April,* and even his own breathing had a sound of music.

All the light had a crystal reality as he dressed in the uniform thoughtfully provided by Lt. Commander Spiegelglass, and ate all the breakfast his nerves could stand —three cups of chicory coffee. His wife and his two little boys were like sunlit ghosts. He could not reach or touch them in his excitement. Spinning the Volkswagen out of the drive for the ten mile run to the cobalt water of the Florida coast, he hoped that they understood.

He exceeded the speed limit all the way, roared through the checkstations with impossibly witty quips for each bored seaman at each check box, and braked with a stamp of his foot alongside the nuclear submarine *U. S. S. Sharkbait.* On the tower Sig Spiegelglass and Don Maddow were watching him. Neither man smiled or waved.

Conn wondered about the lack of smiles only for a moment. He found himself caught in the middle of a half dozen reporters.

"Is it true you're going to communicate with a fish this morning, Dr. Conn?"

"Not fish." Conn smiled and polished his glasses. *"Tursiops truncatus."*

"The press release says that means porpoise," said a grating female voice.

"I'm afraid the press release writer didn't look up the difference between the bottle-nose dolphin and the common porpoise," Conn replied, hoping he didn't sound too stuffy.

"You really think communication will be possible?"

Conn gestured to russet-haired Dr. Maddow watching impassively from the tower. "With Don's impulse translator—you should have the details in those releases—anyway, it was worked out by a team of engineers and philologists at Randco—"

Over a moving ballpoint a whisky voice said, "Maddow's the philologist on the team?"

"The best in the business," said Conn, raising his head. Maddow still wasn't smiling. "We think the combination of a language specialist and a neurophysiologist is ideal for trying to break through and translate what Bottle-nose may be saying."

Even as he spoke, Conn realized they couldn't possibly be as excited about it as he, because they reached excitement by different means. Special press runs, maybe. Names announced at a Pulitzer dinner. But for Conn it was impossible to ignore the sense of immeasurable awe, of reverence, which filled him whenever he thought of the small wonders the impulse translator might work before the sun went down over the green coast tonight. Patiently and lovingly Conn repeated most of the information in the press release: the cell count in dolphin brains; the forty percent greater brain size; the precocity shown by the biggest of the creatures in the learning experience; the unmistakable twenty sounds which made up their squawking, whistling alphabet.

"Since the cell counts are the same as the human brain per cubic centimeter," Conn said, "and the brains are bigger, and they have a language, we think we can communicate—make a first bridge between mammalian forms, as it were. It's taken us six years to perfect the translator."

"Would you consider this problem as difficult or important as the communication established last month by the Southwerk Mirrow with—" The reporter's voice hesitated and a couple of heads looked skyward. "—whatever is out there?"

Conn winced, enviously. Southwerk had scored a jump on the oceanographic team. Rather stiffly he said, "That was a marvelous achievement—the definite establishment of communication with a being or beings not of our Earth who have orderly, organized speech. Of course," he couldn't help adding, "Southwerk hasn't yet translated."

"Is that a case of interservice rivalry, Doctor?" someone asked in a barbed way.

Conn laughed. "I think I'd better get aboard." Amid Thank Yous, up he went, up the ladder, triumphant, up the steel sides toward the hot morning sky where the heads of Spiegelglass and Don Maddow floated like balloons. For an instant Conn felt totally like a god. Then he climbed into place beside them. He noticed that Maddow was staring emptily out over the gantry skeletons far across the yard.

"Ready to take her out, Sig?" Conn said.

"Why bother?" Maddow snarled. "We've been had."

"What's this?" Conn laughed nervously. "You guys trying to bug me?"

Sig Spiegelglass studied the cigar he was unwrapping. "I wish we were, Bob. Last night, around seven, Coast Detection picked up a sub out there."

"Then beam Washington and have it clear out," Conn said, a little irritated.

"Beam Red Square, you mean," said Maddow sourly.

Now the matchless, empty blue heavens had invisible clouds in them. Conn felt a chill wind through his blouse. "One of the regular line jobs?"

"Uh-uh." Maddow shook his head. "When the profile tape was developed it showed an unusual configuration. In fact they have only one like it."

"Oh, Christ."

Conn siezed the steel rail and stared down at the reporters drifting off. A tug hooted off the Florida coast in the lost cobalt distances, a dirty sound. Conn said:

"The *Nikolai Fernoyon?*"

Neither Maddow nor Sig answered when Conn pronounced the name of the almost legendary oceanographic vessel which carried three times the crew of the *Sharkbait*. For a long moment Conn hoped either of the men would answer in the negative. Neither did. Conn indulged himself in sixty seconds of the foulest language he knew.

Then he said, "I wish I had a knife. I wish I had a knife to castrate the dumb bastard in Washington who classifies Washington's birthday and lets our preliminary papers in every God damn Sunday supplement in the country."

"We're wasting time," Maddow said dispiritedly. "The *Fernoyon* has an instantaneous press transmitter. If they've made contact, they'll wait until we go out in the torpedo, and then Tass'll break the story they've already got set in type."

"Maybe they don't have a translator," Spiegelglass said hopefully.

"So maybe they'll tap in on us," Maddow snapped back. "And before we can transmit, they'll have the message in their sheets and how are we going to prove them liars?"

"If they don't have the dingus," Sig said, "you could screw them by not putting out in the torpedo."

Even though he had a sick, wasted feeling in his stomach, Robert Conn shook his head. "No, we have to go out. I don't care if they do tap us. I don't care whether some crummy witch doctor in Africa thinks the *Fernoyon* did it and we didn't, just so long as I'm there, just so long as I know." Conn's pale face burned like a coin hit by the sun. Spiegelglass picked up the tube and talked around his cigar:

"You gentlemen down there stand by. We are about to participate in another in the series of ever-popular U.S. propaganda defeats."

"Of all the lousy, crapping luck," Maddow said harshly. He spun on Conn. "And you stand there saying it doesn't matter."

"It doesn't," Conn said, trying to convince himself. "Once you get over acting like a six year old and realize that we aren't supermen in this country—that what we're doing, we're doing for everybody—" He seized Maddow's shoulders. Deep below the two men a faint fury from the reactors tingled up through the soles of shoes. "We've made contact wth something in space and now we're making contact with another mammalian life form, real contact, intelligible—"

"We think," Maddow sneered. "Bottle-nose probably speaks Ukrainian."

Conn was getting a little hysterical: "It's the human race doing it, man himself, Don. Don't you see, it's—"

"Unless you gentlemen would like to float to Jacksonville," Spiegelglass said around his cigar, "I would suggest we go below."

Maddow ducked down, preparatory to obeying, but could not resist a last thrust at Conn as his russet head vanished down into the artificial gloom: "Sorry, Bob, but I can't see it. I have an American flag tattooed on my buttocks, and when I'm flatulent I play patriotic airs. I'm funny that way."

"If you don't want any part of an experiment like this," Conn shouted furiously, starting down the ladder after him, "You should have put on your American Legion cap and gone home a long time a—"

"If you don't please get off my tower," said Sig Spiegelglass, "I'll kick you both in the ass. We're already forty-two seconds overdue."

Thus, with Conn and Maddow sulking on either side of the twenty-foot cylinder they called their torpedo, the *U. S. S. Sharkbait* moved slowly out between the gantries into the mercurial blue swell of the sea.

The intricate ritual of command, the soft blink of collored lights went on around them. Conn gazed furiously at the russet-haired Maddow, wondering why Maddow couldn't see the triumph of it, regardless of who won the propaganda advantage. Besides, the presence of the gigantic Russian oceanographic sub might be sheerest bluff.

Then, with a start, Conn recalled the intense personal feeling he had experienced upon waking that morning. What had happened to it? This was *his* mystery and miracle, his and Don's. Gradually the hastily-assumed attitude of the tower grew less strong.

A similar process was apparently taking place in Maddow's mind. After all, they were grown men. Before too many minutes had elapsed, they were speaking, though not laughing. For Conn, the personal mystery of it would not return, knowing as he did that he might not be alone in the victory now. All that was left for him, and for Maddow too, it seemed, was a kind of defeated gray calm, and a desperate clinging to the expressions of "doing it for all men" which Conn had so suddenly espoused in the heat of argument. But they were friends again.

On the color television a green hairline showed the Florida coast far behind.

"Take her down, please, Mr. Olufson," said Spiegelglass.

Then came the sensation of incredible power, the nonexistent yet palpably real surge and tingle that got inside Conn's bones when he watched the watery line sweep up and obliterate the sky on the screen. Cobalt shaded to emerald. And from out of a lucite panel on four stanchions, strange echoes began to bounce and sing. There was a low note and several higher ones. Every face in the mixed lighting—red, green and a bit of blue—showed that the low note was wrong.

"That's *Fernoyon*," said the conner, adjusting his earphones.

"Right in the middle of the school?" Maddow asked.

"Center, and not moving."

Maddow's face was the color of the sea outside. "So we do their work for them, Robert?"

"It is their work, in a way," Conn said, but the words felt hollow on his tongue.

"Philosophers I got to have," Spiegelglass said, his head floating blue in the half-lit maze of pipes and lights and bouncing eerie echoes. "Stop being such big social brains and climb into the torpedo. I'm carrying orders, you know. We're shooting you in twelve minutes. If something sticks out, it's not my fault."

The *Sharkbait* pulsed quietly, moving outward and downward through the plankton and the great pastel anemones, downward through whirling darts of phosphorescence brighter than stars in a liquefied cosmos of achingly beautiful green. As if to emphasize the importance of the coming contact, Spiegelglass activated all the annunciators throughout the sub. While Conn and Maddow peeled their uniforms and squeezed into the flexible black skin suits, there was not a sound on the entire submarine except for the low note counterpointing the steadily noisier higher ones that signalled the dolphin school.

Through the sealed plastic soles of the suit Conn felt the reactors under the plates like his own heartbeat intensified. Maddow, all business, slid back the double-hinged cover of the torpedo. Just under the curving forward plate in the narrow miniature sub, a row of green eyes like six eyes in a line gleamed on the ultra-simplified dials of the translator control. Maddow raised his hand in an Alphonse-and-Gaston gesture.

Conn's face, haloed in black plastic, shone with sweat. "I don't want to go."

"The Kremlin got you buffaloed, sport?"

"It's such a rotten shame, after so long—"

Maddow laughed. "I sang that chorus in the last set."

"I know, but—" Conn wiped his face, feeling faint. "All of a sudden—"

" 'It's man,' you said."

"No." Conn shook his head. "It's me, first."

"I suppose it's probably some of both," Maddow said, his voice surprisingly soft. "And that's probably why we make so many rotten mistakes. If—"

The annunciator squawked with the voice of Spiegelglass: "Will you both please cut out the penny philosophy and haul your pratts inside that thing? Four minutes." So there was no more time for Conn to wonder why he felt both triumphant and defeated, when nothing at all had happened.

He crawled up over the torpedo and wriggled out prone on the port side, facing the plate and the six green eyes in a line. Maddow came in after. On his back he took care of the gasketing while Conn snapped controls that closed the cover. With much cursing Maddow wriggled over on his belly. Beneath them an oiled track moved. Ahead of the plate a black hole opened like an iris to swallow them. Conn had never felt more afraid in his life.

"The talker," Maddow hissed in the humid, sweating dark.

Their only companion for the next two minutes was the voice of Sig Spiegelglass, counting steadily and tonelessly. The last whisper of his one-count was drowned in a whoosh and roar. The black burst open and became green,

The Highest Form of Life

white-streaked and furious, and they were launched in the deeps.

As the torpedo began to lose speed Maddow asked, "See anything?"

"Up ahead, I think," Conn replied. "But don't use the light. I wouldn't want to frighten them if we can help it."

"The vanes, at least."

Maddow raised on his elbows, his head jammed against the ceiling, and manipulated two of three rods with lucite handle-grips. The nose of the torpedo dropped a degree. Over the hiss of his own breathing Conn heard the light bubbling of the tiny reactor and the whispers of the controlled air system. He stared out into the miraculous green gloom of the undersea until he thought his eyeballs would burst. An instant before the image came permanently into his brain, his nerves felt it:

"There they are. Cut everything but the stabilization."

The bubbling dropped off. Maddow breathed, "Christ. They're beautiful."

And they were. Conn counted two dozen before giving up, long graceful shadows, some almost inky, others grayer, but all ghostly on their underbellies and the undersides of their jaws. Among them were giants Conn estimated to be well over the twelve foot average for the species. Some of them moved lazily, in a random pattern. Others, racing up for the surface, created a sort of basket-weave effect, lacing in and out among the big females swimming belly up for courtship. One flashed near. Conn thought he saw an eye gleam. At least he knew that the eye could be watching him, because the eye could see better than fifty feet, and if inside that bottle-shaped head lodged a brain that could interpret—

All of a sudden Conn remembered the *Nikolai Fernoyon*. But there was no sign of it. Of course there wouldn't be.

Maddow raised a tentative hand to the six green eyes.

"You ready?"

All Conn could think of saying was an inane, "Now or never."

Maddow threw on a switch. The circuits under the deck warmed for a millisecond. Then came the first faint sound, a mixture between a squeak and a drawn-out whistle.

It made Conn's spine crawl, transmitted as it was so perfectly through the exposed sound dishes on the torpedo's surface. In another second, as half a dozen of the huge creatures shot past their little craft, Conn heard the gabble intensify. He and Maddow were caught in the center of an underwater cocktail party, a kaffee klatch from unearthly voice boxes. Conn found himself reaching out for the switch which would activate the translator. His hand shook. He looked over at Maddow.

"You do it."

"Let's not be cornball," Maddow said, but his eyes were huge with wonder.

"All right. Count five."

"Five," said Maddow.

"We won't get anything," said Conn.

"Three," said Maddow.

"But if we do. Don—God—all my life—"

"One," said Maddow.

Before Conn's finger could hit the control a new sound blasted the speaker.

Conn's belly twisted within him. "What's that? The Russian sub?"

"I—don't know." Maddow sounded like a small boy, frightened.

They both listened for a full minute. An eerie, spiralling wail came down, it seemed, from above. Maddow switched off all the sound dishes except the dorsal and verified it.

"But the *Fernoyon* should be below us," he insisted, "and we're getting this from up above."

There was a dull thump. One of the dolphins had lashed itself against the torpedo. The whole school was moving, diving and shooting up in a senseless frenzy. Maddow cursed.

"They want to screw it up for us. They've done something in the sub—"

"That doesn't come from any sub," said Conn, pointing.

Through the plate they both saw it, an unbelievably bright and round column of bluish radiance which lanced down from overhead, straight through the school of dolphins, illuminating their slick darting bodies like a search-

The Highest Form of Life

light. The water began to churn and grow violent as the agitation of the school increased.

"The translator," Maddow said furiously. "Get it on, fast."

Helpless with confusion, Conn manipulated the controls automatically. A guttural, crackling sound came harshly into the tight confines of the torpedo. "That isn't Bottlenose."

"Then what is it?"

Conn indicated the blue beam which remained steady as it vanished downward to the impenetrable bottoms of the ocean floor.

"That."

Now the dolphin school had quieted. The huge mammals seemed to be circling the light in orderly, layered circles, four and then four above and then four more, on up toward the surface out of sight, each circle moving opposite of the one directly below and above. Conn imagined he was watching a ballet performed by human beings in elaborate costumes and wondered whether he was experiencing some unique underwater phenomenon never before mentioned in the texts on reaction and hallucination.

Abruptly impotent fury twisted Maddow's face. His hands flew on the lucite-handled levers. The torpedo nosedived, the bubbling grew louder.

Conn tore at his friend's arm. "Where are you going?"

"I'm going to ram hell out of those bastards on the *Fernoyon*."

"Why?"

"Because this is their foul-up, damn it, it's—"

The torpedo struck the shaft of bluish light and a huge indentation was hammered into the ceiling. Lazily the vehicle spun end over end, impossibly off course, impossibly out of control. Maddow and Conn tumbled like squirrels in a revolving cage. At last their frantic hands on the vane levers righted the craft. Now Conn felt overwhelming terror and confusion.

"We hit that light," he said. "No light on earth can—"

Both men looked at one another.

At last Conn swallowed, painfully. "Where's Bottlenose?"

"Not talking," Maddow said, as though he had wandered drunk and dirty into a church during an Easter service, and had wakened to find himself retching before the altar. "Not talking. *Listening.*"

Still the guttural crackling continued. Maddow suggested trying other frequencies. Like a madman Conn operated the controls. He caught a syllable, shouted aloud, lost the syllable in a too-hasty twist of the primary dial, regained it a moment later. The voice the two men heard was oddly slowed, like a one-hundred r.p.m. disc being played at sixteen. The accents could not be identified because they did not exist: it was a metal voice, an impulse funnelled through their translator and unscrambled into the sound-code their own minds could understand:

"*—picked up Southwerk. Wish no contact.*" A sharp, jittery whine of interference, followed by the words: "*—egocentric—pitiably brutal—*"

"There goes *Fernoyon*," Maddow shouted suddenly.

Rising up on foaming columns a great black bulk lurched surfaceward on the far side of the blue light. Now the dolphins had circled closer to the beam. More interference—the translation of the guttural voice was lost. As if linked together telepathically, Conn and Maddow began to work furiously over their instruments. The underwater world became a kaleidoscope of darting, spiralling dolphin shapes whirling upward near the beam. The torpedo broke surface.

Maddow hammered at the gasketing devices like a man possessed. He and Conn scrambled up and inflated their airpacks as the torpedo began to fill, forgotten. The sun blinded Conn, but he distinctly heard the squawk-and-buzz of the school before the amplifier submerged, and the squawk-and-buzz of the school had been translated to words, and the words were:

"*—we are the highest—you are the highest—we seek you—*"

The *U. S. S. Sharkbait* was surfacing thunderously. The *Nikolai Fernoyon* was already up, men in underwear pouring out of its tower, one, with a blond Georgian beard, waving his starred cap at the two men bobbing on the torpedo. Conn and Maddow clung, Conn with salt water and gall in his mouth. His face was so wet with the swell he could not taste his own tears.

He choked through mouthfuls of water: "They—neither

—they don't—" He swallowed more water, gagging. "—want us."

And indeed the dolphins did not, lancing up from the surface. They spiralled like beautiful glistening machines, around and around the blue beam of light, high toward the clouds, dots in the blueness of the sky now, riding the blue ladder of light, hundreds of them, a thousand of them from the floor of the ocean, riding up and rising toward the sun-hot circular blur of silver light that was the ship from beyond waiting to greet them.

One Race Show

Science fiction writers have explored nearly every aspect of mid-Twentieth Century society, including the art forms of today and the ways in which they are likely to change in the future. Notable works in this area include William Rotsler's PATRON OF THE ARTS, and the stories contained in the late James Blish's fine anthology NEW DREAMS THIS MORNING. In addition to exploring new art forms, sf also has important things to say about the nature of the creative process, as in this story about the struggle of a creative vision to break free.

I.

There are mornings and mornings. This was one of the latter. All rotten.

Isaac Nels Rhinelander knew very well the cause of the dark brown taste in his mouth the moment he awoke. In characteristic fashion he charged his happiness deficit to other accounts. For example:

The violent argument at breakfast with his brother-in-law Atwater Pope.

Ten minutes after it was over, Rhinelander couldn't even remember the topic. How cumulus clouds formed. The dimension of a gnat's wing. Some other equally inane subject from the filler slugs of the morning news sheet that unreeled from the printer in the breakfast atrium of Rhinelander's (actually his wife Iris's—*ugh*) villa.

Watty sat there cool and educated and superior, adjusting the chinstrap of his burnished steel crash helmet; he was flying his vertiracer in a rally at noon. To every argument which Rhineland put forth, Watty replied in metaphor and epigram and little rapier thrusts of logic. Finally Rhinelander just screamed. Lost the argument, of course. Watty chuckled, activated his sports-model personnel jets and went flying out of the atrium the winner. As always.

That was enough to make Rhinelander feel rotten through and through. But it wasn't the true cause of the rotten feeling. Rhinelander found still other events to blame. Such as:

The unaccountable breakdown of his Chrome De-luxe Executive Limoubus, whose magnetic pilot jumped the aerialway guidestrip on the two hundred and sixty mile trip from the suburbs into New York, and crashed in an undignified although harmless way into the thick foamex median. Other conveyances whizzed by. Their occupants cheerfully smoked or read morning tickers, unable to stop. Rhinelander had to trudge in the hot sun to a call box. He had to suffer the sneers of the mechanics who came, raised the forward deck of the Limoubus by means of magnetic cranes, and then took care of his difficulty.

Actually, it required only one mechanic to solve the trouble. He just reconnected a short spring which held two motor rods together in a most untechnical way. Rhinelander stumped from one foot to the other, beet red. He saw that the mechanics were exchanging sidelong glances of derision at his expense while they totalled up their bill. They let him go easily, however: eighty-five dollars. But that didn't relieve the mounting rottenness of the day.

As the Limoubus whisked on toward the slender gleaming pylons of the megalopolis eighty miles ahead, Rhinelander once more felt the sting of the true cause of his anger and frustration. Hot stabs of jealousy, of virulent envy, shot through him. He refused to acknowledge them, waiting, just *waiting*, for the next mess. That mess was not long in coming.

It happened ten seconds after he walked through the electronic doors of The Rhinelander Galleries, which occupied the entire first floor of The General Matter Building on Park Mall.

In the lift-tube up from the garage, Rhinelander had halfway composed himself. After all, he was about to enter his own personal domain, as he did on the three working days of each week. He pulled his corpulent frame up to its full height of five feet three. His cheeks stopped flapping. His protuberant blue eyes receded into their sockets. Like an emperor he breezed through the doors, rubbing his plump little hands.

And stopped.

Under the multicolored beams which bathed the central display pedestal in the gallery's marble foyer, several of his employees, including his assistant Phenley, were wringing their hands and gazing at a litter of striated coppershot stone on the floor. Phenley rushed forward.

"The workmen," he gargled. "Teamsters. Hook slippage during erection."

Gazing at the wreckage of Jan van der Maarsch's rendering of *The Culture of the Womb*, Rhinelander shrieked, "Get out of my sight, Phenley, before I kill you! Two hundred thousand I pay for that, and you let the boobs break it before we even get the critics in! Call the insurance people and stay away for two weeks or I won't answer for your safety!"

"Oh, sir, I'm so terribly sorry, so terribly sorry," Phenley kept saying. Then Phenley's voice was silenced by another sound. One of the gallery functionaries poked at a last piece of the sculpture teetering on the pedestal.

This piece, of course, crashed to the floor just a second before Rhinelander stepped into his private office.

By now his cheeks were flapping and bulging again. His eyes stuck out to amazing dimensions.

Groping for the spigot of the TrankwilSoda dispenser in the bottom drawer of his desk, Rhinelander heard the taped metallic voice of his automatic secretary:

"Please call Mr. Kuprin. Mr. Kuprin communicated at two minutes past nine, eight minutes past nine, fourteen minutes past nine, and twenty-eight min—"

"Ah, *God!*" breathed Rhinelander, slamming his hand on the stud that shut off the wretched voice. He swilled a tumbler of TrankwilSoda. It did no good whatever.

He buried his head on his arms and tried to shut off his mind. Impossible. Argument with Watty, wrecked Limoubus, smashed sculpture—all paled. He was face to face with the actual cause of his frustration.

He could not avoid getting in touch with Kuprin. The

ethics of the business demanded it. If he didn't there would be talk. Talk could hurt.

But perhaps the opening had flopped. Even as he reached for the hand microphone, he knew the opening had not flopped. He pressed the stud combination for Kuprin's studio. A section of desk-top lifted. A screen swam and blurred. Presently a thin, wild-haired man in a smock, his face smeared with daubs of ochre, appeared.

"Good morning, Nels . . . Seen the reviews?"

"No, I have not. You know I wouldn't concern myself with such trash. Who is this Caul anyhow? Who's heard of him?"

"The whole art world, by now," said Kuprin with a nasty little smile.

"Why are you badgering me? Just because I shaved the price on that lousy gesso item you flimflammed me into buying in August?"

"I merely thought you'd be interested in the opening of the Caul show!" Kuprin pulled some gobs of paint off his nose. "You really must see it, Nels."

"Go to Swallows'? I never go to other galleries."

"For this you must. The canvases—well, have you ever looked at hell?"

"Several good facsimilies," said Rhinelander, thinking of his wife and Watty.

"They're really remarkable. When the rest of us are polite, full of form and balance—" Kuprin swayed a little, weaving illusions with his paint-smeared hands. "—this man, whoever he is, wherever he is, has visions of nightmares. Ugly. Terrible. *Horrid*. No landscapes like his exist on earth anymore, with everything so beautiful and aseptic. But somewhere this Caul saw such scenes. I'm a little sick." From behind his immense spectacles, Kuprin glanced sidewise at Rhinelander through the screen. "Certainly this makes Swallows the preeminent gallery in the city, perhaps even in the world.

Jealousy wrenched Rhinelander's gut. "That good, eh?"

"Marvelous, marvelous."

"I haven't got time."

"Don't be petty, Nels. It's a shame you couldn't have snared Caul."

"Caul, who the hell is Caul?" Rhinelander shouted. "Whoever heard of him before?"

"Apparently Swallows did, one way or another. I understand there are even lines around the block. Can you imagine? Lines, for an exhibit of paintings! Well . . ." Kuprin waved in a vague way, "I suppose I might as well go back to work, although I doubt there'll be much market for my stuff in the next few months. Not at the best galleries, certainly. Swallows doesn't need me. I'll show you what I'm doing, when it's further along."

Kuprin promptly switched off, leaving Rhinelander to fume before the blank screen. He knew at last that he could no longer dodge the source of his feelings on this rottenest of all rotten mornings.

For weeks the art world had buzzed with rumors of the new show soon to open at Swallows'. Rhinelander, not wanting to believe, had tortured himself into believing. And it had all come true. But who was Joe Caul? Who'd ever *heard* of Joe Caul?"

Rhinelander sent for biographical tapes.

No painter named Joe Caul existed.

Then Rhinelander sent for the morning reviews.

They made him foam.

Rhinelander, finally, sent for his Limoubus. He would, to torture himself further, have a look at Joe Caul's hell.

II.

Let it be said in Rhinelander's favor that Joe Caul overwhelmed him.

A thin drizzle was falling when Rhinelander reached the ivory and platinum front of The Frederic Swallows Gallery. Doubtless the weather service felt it was time for a little rain, but the rain made Rhinelander mad, especially since he had to wait in a damp, shuffling line of customers that stretched half way around the square.

Most of the students in line had come with portable rain-deflectors. They were in a holiday mood, buzzing with talk about the Caul canvases which they would soon be privileged to view. Rhinelander felt his dignity violated by this forced mingling with members of the public. And then, just as his section of the line reached the great Swallows doors, the tower blowers came on and all the artificial rain clouds were swept away, leaving the streets gold and gleaming in the sun.

Feeling spongy, Rhinelander would have hated Michelangelo himself. So it was a strong reflection on Rhinelander's character and Joe Caul's brush technique when he was overwhelmed in spite of the fact that the gallery attendant hadn't even honored his trade courtesy card, but had made him pay admission just like anybody else.

Rhinelander was not only overwhelmed, he was awed and frightened too. Caul's canvases brought the stink of animal fear, raw as a piece of decomposing liver, into the refinement of Swallows' main hall.

Few spoke while viewing the Caul works. Swallows had, by design, reduced the lighting so that only the canvases themselves, huge panels a uniform twenty by ten, stood out against ebony drapes. Knots of art-lovers huddled together, soaked and struck dumb, under each of the five works. Their faces held none of the joy or exhilaration some sensitive souls show when gazing upon a new or revolutionary work. Instead, eyes gleamed wetly. Mouths hung loose and even a little moronically.

For in each of the five works, signed in block letters and black oil, *Joe Caul,* and labelled crudely *Pictur' 1, Pictur 2,* through *Pictur 5,* those who looked saw no heightened reality or beauty. They saw nothing they could measure by any customary yardstick. They saw instead, a heightening of sickness. They saw insanity made two-dimensional.

"Evil filth," Rhinelander whispered. But he couldn't tear his eyes away from Pictur 1 to gaze at Pictur 2, the first was so powerful.

Views of hell? Rhinelander knew the description was far too simple. Hell, as all the sophisticated spectators knew, was a fictitious place, like Amusement Land on the West Coast. The writhing purple and green and orange creatures, only dimly human, shrouded in pestilential vapors and frozen like hideous Laocoons, had a peculiar realism that made Rhinelander think to himself, *"This is ghastly;* then, *This is beautiful;* then *This is totally, utterly real—whatever it is.*

Under the spell of the canvases which seemed merely different views of the same subject (whatever *that* was, besides reality) Rhinelander found himself both repelled and fascinated. Repelled by the labyrinthine weaving of shape and color, suggesting ever so many indecent images. Fascinated by the sledgehammer realization that, although he didn't quite understand, he was face to face with total truth.

Let it further be said in Rhinelander's favor that he gazed at each of the pictures for at least twenty minutes without once feeling envy. At last, however, business concerns became too great. He tottered out of the exhibit hall, looking back as though expecting one of Caul's creatures to be roosting on his shoulder. Finally free of the grip of the paintings, he ended up in the office of Frederic Swallows, with Mr. Swallows on page by his autosecretary.

Fortunately Swallows' office was along an outer wall. Sunlight poured in and helped dispel the obscene guilt which Rhinelander had been feeling. It took only a moment for his regular nature to assert itself. He started pawing through papers and memoranda on top of Swallows' ornate desk, searching for a clue to the elusive Caul.

His cheeks puffed suddenly. He'd found something.

Caul, the slip said. Plus *Geneva Credit Depository. 43-1289-66*.

One of those numbered bank accounts? Rhinelander wondered. He heard footfalls in the outer corridor. Hastily he stuffed the slip back under a pile in its original place. He was lighting up a dollar Nirvanatella when Frederic Swallows whisked in like corn husks rustling on a stalk.

"I hardly expected you, Nels," Swallows said. His hair was white, his face still whiter, his hands laced with blue veins. He was ninety-six years old, kept alive by nutrient cosmetics and injections of hormones. Swallows drywashed his hands briskly and pursed his lips. "You are not noted for your magnanimity, old friend. One would have thought you would have stayed away."

"From—from that?" Rhinelander waved outward. "Impossible. All I've heard about Joe Caul is absolutely true. I congratulate you, Frederic."

Swallows nodded. "You're right, you're right. Once, in my youth, when I was taking drugs and painting in Tahiti, I saw one or two visions something like those pictures. I was so appalled I committed myself to a sanitarium. When I was cured, I thought about trying to recapture a little of what I'd seen. The prospect was so grisly that I remained drunk for three months. I've never had the impulse again."

Swallows began to bustle and pry among the papers

on the desktop. "Yes, I'm flattered that Caul, whoever he is, chose to send his paintings to me. He must have picked my name from the gallery directory. That was a lucky chance, eh, Nels?" From under the litter of memoranda, he drew out the slip at which Rhinelander had been peeking. "Excuse me."

Since Swallows' eyesight was so weak, he had to turn his back to the window and hold the paper to the tip of his nose, in the sun's beam. At that moment a window-washer's platform slid into view on the face of the building. The washer was scrubbing busily. He had an immense fan beard of red and wore a hearing apparatus. Rhinelander tried to remember when, if ever, he had seen a window-washer. When he was a child? Swallows forced the papers nearly against his eyeballs, then tittered.

"AH, yes, this is the one. Excuse me, excuse me."

The window-washer's platform vanished upward out of sight. Rhinelander was no longer paying attention, for his brains had suddenly fastened on a remark the old man had made a minute before. He watched Swallows waggle one foot in the air, make a few quick passes with his left hand, open the visual safe and pop the slip inside. *Casual, now*, Rhinelander thought. *Very casual.* He cleared his throat.

"Frederic, did you say you don't know this Caul personally?"

"I did, I did, old friend," said Swallows, meaning, *old enemy*.

"He selected your gallery at random?"

Swallows lifted a shoulderblade. "I suppose so. How else to explain the sudden arrival of five massive crates one day last month? A day later came a note, with ten cents' postage due. Ludicrously written. This Caul can barely spell. Witness 'pictur.' In his illiterate hand he informed me that something made him want to show his works, and if I deemed them of any value I should deposit funds in one of those secret Swiss bank accounts, whose number he conveniently provided. The numbers were so miserably written I had to try seven accounts before hitting the correct one. Some clever advisor has doubtless told this Caul, wherever and whoever he may be, about numbered accounts. His own hand—I had it analyzed—proves he's something above an imbecile, but only a little something. Very strange, very peculiar."

"Have you heard from Caul again?" Rhinelander asked. He felt better now, almost wolfish as his mind repeated, to fix it firm, *43–1289–66.*

"No, but I certainly hope I shall. If I never sell another canvas in my lifetime, Caul's five pictures will make me comfortable. I might even say wealthy." Swallows ruffled a few more paper and chits. "I do appreciate your stopping, Nels. Drop in again whenever you wish. But I have at least a hundred letters from various museums requesting chromostats of one or all of the Caul canvases, plus proofs of a critique I've just written, and—oh." Swallows blinked again, as though he had just remembered a formality of the profession. "How's your business?"

"Very brisk," Rhinelander said with a smile, hate boiling his guts. "Can't complain."

"Too bad you couldn't have gotten Caul. Pure chance, though. Well, good day."

"Yes, too bad," Rhinelander echoed. He shook the old man's spidery hand and passed out of the office thinking, *43–1289–66.*

With a shudder he walked beneath Pictures 1 through 5 and didn't look up. He didn't want to be unnerved again. He was feeling too rich, too hot-headed, too sure and exhilarated.

"Too bad," he said again as he shoved his way through the crowds still waiting outside. At the end of the building he paused, looked both ways, spat on the platinum gallery name-plate.

"Forty-three, twelve-eighty-nine, sixty-six, you old bastard. I haven't got him now. But I soon will have."

III.

At the evening dinner Rhinelander's wife Iris had one of her shrieking spells.

The meal began cordially enough. Artificial sunset filtered through the pergola that overlooked the pool where mechanical swans floated in geometric patterns. Iris, Rhinelander and Watty reclined on their couches, eating roast duckling with orange sauce.

Iris brought up the subject of a party she was giving in a few weeks. She planned to turn the entire house and estate, including Rhinelander's wing, into an extinct Asian commune. Watty, wearing only shorts and several bandages from the race, sucked on gobbets of duckling and appeared indifferent. Rhinelander struggled up from his couch to protest the party.

In the phony sunset light Iris looked disgusting to Rhinelander. No longer a young woman, she insisted on dyeing her hair a different shade each month. This month it was pea-green. She wore tight scarlet trousers woven with platinum threads and a blouse which revealed her large flabby bosom. Her nails were three inches long. Rhinelander cared for her only occasionally. Tonight was not one of the occasions.

"I won't have my house tricked out to resemble some socialistic experiment, Iris."

Iris clamped her sharp little teeth on her lower lip and tried to show patience. "Darling, can't you at least look at the clever plans?"

As if on signal, a young creature in pink drawers and a cosmetic suntan burst in at the pergola entrance. He began to unroll sheafs of brownprints. The sight of Yoggemeyer, Iris' personal decorator, infuriated Rhinelander even more.

"I *refuse* to look at them!" He kicked over a platter of duckling. Yoggemeyer minced aside, nearly getting his lacquered toes slopped up with orange sauce.

Watty chuckled, licking his fingers. "Obstinate tonight, aren't we, Nels?"

"You keep out of this, playboy!" Rhinelander snarled.

"Dear Nels," Watty said, propping up on one elbow. "I should love to do that. But you make it impossible. A moment ago you said you wouldn't have 'your' house redesigned to accommodate my sister's desires, but you really don't have much choice. Let's not have a scene. I had a hard day."

"Vertiracing?" Rhinelander sneered. "Pah. Playing games."

"Facing more reality that you possibly could," Watty said.

"Anyway," Rhinelander said, "we've gone this route before. The house and estate are registered in my name, and therefore—"

"Please," Yoggemeyer cooed, "if you'd just glance at these cunning plans—"

"Get the hell out of here!" Rhinelander threw half of the duckling at the decorator. Yoggemeyer squealed, his head covered with ooze and raisins, and disappeared sobbing behind the hedges.

This set Iris to flexing her claws. She paced back and forth, a raw ledge on her voice:

"Isaac Nels Rhinelander, we certainly have discussed the registration before, and need I remind you that it's *my* money, and my brother's, which enables you to live in such luxury? I'll decorate, and I'll decorate any way I damned *please!*"

"There," Watty chortled. "Now can you confront reality or not, dear Nels?"

For a moment Rhinelander's eyes threatened to explode out of his head. His cheeks worked like bellows. He glared at the pair with hate brimming inside him. He wanted to smash their heads. He wanted to kill. To shut them up. To kill. To kill. To *kill*—

But he managed to get control of his emotions. After all, he had Caul to consider. And the numbered bank account.

He lowered his sweating body back to the couch as Iris paced to the other side of the pergola, beating her fists against her thighs. Rather nonsensically, too, Rhinelander thought. Ah, things were calming down.

At that moment Watty noisily sucked some meat from a duckling leg. "You can't face reality, Nels. Really you can't. Few can. Care to debate?"

And, unreasonably, Rhinelander exploded again:

"Yes, God damn it, Watty. I'll debate with you, you smug wastrel."

"You see?" Watty pointed with the bone. "I, at least, know where I'm going. Nowhere. Whereas you, destined for the same goal, think you're going somewhere. That is precisely what I mean about reality. Take this morning.

"Two vertiracers collided at the rally. Bloody goo all over the firing pad. A crowd gathered, bug-eyed. Why? Because, Nels, no one could actually believe that two human beings had been jellied. The people stared at the remains until they convinced themselves of it. Then they went away. In an hour I'll wager every one of them was

One Race Show

certain again that *he* could never be jellied because those two wretches weren't jellied either—it was all some sort of dismal dream. The mind simply refuses to accept some things, and invents all sorts of clever excuses for not doing so. *Your* mind, for example, refuses to accept two basic facts. One, that you have flimsy artistic tastes. Two, that you have no real business instinct. Therefore your gallery is, and always will be, a monumental flop, sustained by the funds that Iris pours in."

"And do I pour them in!" Iris shrieked. "Oh, my God, *do* I!"

"I could kill you," Rhinelander said. "I could, Watty."

"Do you think it surprises me?"

Rhinelander stormed to his feet, bent toward Watty. "What if I admitted all you said? That so far I've never amounted to anything much? What if I said, all right, I know I exhibit second-rate items but now I'm on to something of quality. Now I'm going to fight and scheme until I get my hands on it?"

"Something of quality?" Watty was skeptical. "What might that be?"

"More paintings by Joe Caul."

Never before had Rhinelander seen Watty show astonishment. "I've heard of the Caul things. Are there more than five?"

"There may be, if I can unlock a numbered bank account in Switzerland."

"Impossible, Nels, old boy."

"All right," Rhinelander said tightly. "I agree. See, I'm realistic. But you have the right connections, Watty. And enough money. *You* could unlock the personnel dossier behind that account. If you wanted to do it badly enough. If you wanted to see whether or not I'd fail."

Rhinelander's eyes narrowed now as he tried to gauge the effectiveness of his goad, his dare.

"Would you like to gamble on my ineptitude, Watty? If you would, unlock the account. That's all I ask."

"It might be amusing to watch you fail."

"Take a chance, Watty?"

Watty threw back his head and laughed. "Give me the number in the morning."

A tide of relief swept over Rhinelander. "Thank you, Watty," he said as his mind ticked over a hundred cruel tortures he would enjoy inflicting on his brother-in-law in return for this particular bit of groveling. Emotions and luck had thrown Watty's help his way. Rhinelander felt a little stronger for having chanced and won.

But he was deeply ashamed, too, because his emotions had been laid bare.

Chewing on a piece of duckling as the rheostats began to fade out the sunsets, he heard Iris approach, her heels ticking on the paving. His eyes were large, wet, carefully empty of emotion.

"There will be a party, Nels," Iris said. "It's my money."

"There had better not be."

"There will be, there will be, there *will* be."

Rhinelander stuck his fingers in the pneumatic tubes of the sanitary unit next to his couch. Liquid jets and brushes cleaned off the duckling grease. He somehow felt a thousand miles away from this witch with green hair.

"I don't wish to talk about it any more."

But even as he promised himself that one day he would kill Iris and kill Watty, he also realized he could never have the courage to do it. *Small triumph only,* he thought. *Better than none, though. Watty thinks I'll fail. Reality? I can face it well enough. He'll see.* Still, the mixture of hate and doubt assailed him.

Iris went shrieking off to consult Yoggemeyer, Watty to shoot a game of dimensional billiards. As the last of the festering light died behind the lattices Rhinelander lay panting on the couch, rationalizing himself into believing that more Caul canvases would be worth what he had just suffered.

IV.

In the exalted orbits of leisure and finance in which Atwater Pope revolved, bribery was not bribery.

It was a cordial cocktail at a wheel lounge spinning in space five hundred miles above Cape Fear.

It was an exploratory luncheon at an inn among pine trees just outside Olde Manhattan Metropolis National Forest.

It was a process in which the briber (never *called* that, of course) made a polite request, and the bribee sent four or five dozen messages via the communications mirrors whizzing around Earth, then suggested certain discreet investments.

After a short interval, which allowed the bribee to get answers and the briber to gather up a small sinking fund of several millions, a yachting party was arranged in the ionosphere. Matters were brought to fruition over iced tonics on the infrared deck. Although the proceedings were wholly dishonest from start to finish, at least they were genteel.

It took Watty eight and a half weeks to unlock the secret of 43-1289-66.

And in those fifty-nine days the printing presses of the world hammered out matte finish reproductions of Picturs 1 through 5, in twelve colors, on press runs upwards of eighty million.

A news service ran a simulpix of a Tibetan monk examining a print of *Pictur 3* which had found its way into the crystal fastness on the back of a steel packass in the summer supply caravan. Aborigines (what few were left) and intelligent school boys (even fewer) carried Joe Caul prints around with them, dreadfully fascinated. Earth crowned a new god of canvas, one whose work it could not quite understand.

Editorials and clerical proclamations decried the veiled horror of the new messiah of art. But not a single voice denied the awful something that was the truth of the pictures, pictures which pirate lithograph houses had to spew out by the bale in order to keep up with the demand.

No one seemed to know the whereabouts of Joe Caul, at least publicly. This was due to the remarkable circumstance that no one, apparently, wished to find Joe Caul. If he were anything like his works, the unspoken feeling ran, best that he be left alone.

But in every six billion rational people there is bound to be at least one Isaac Nels Rhinelander.

He'd waited eight and a half weeks. He'd groveled before that. Now he was on the trail.

V.

The State of Industrial Jersey had an output amounting to one tenth of the GNP, and a resident population of twenty-eight. Rhinelander had to hire a low-paid ranger from the forestry service at Olde Central to lead him into the wilderness of towering automated factories, all alike except for their name signs and their products which went shooting, cased, to every land via underground pneumatic systems.

Industrial Jersey sprawled out beneath a depressing blanket of smog and drizzle. Even the ranger got lost twice in the empty cement canyons before he brought Rhinelander to Yummydinners Ltd.

The one clear, traceable name written by Joe Caul when he had filled out the personnel dossier for Geneva Credit Depository six months ago was the name Hubert Elk. This appeared in a column headed *Personal References*. Beside the name, Caul had scrawled: *lended me $ for paints*. Other vital sections—*Current Address, Current Employer, Current Cable Code*—Caul had left blank, shunning public attention. Well, now he had public attention, and Rhinelander had Hubert Elk, a portly man who shut off one lever marked *Broasted Gooselet in Artichokes Yummydinner* and yanked another stencilled *Tomato Surprise Under Glass Yummydinner*.

Fidgety with impatience—Elk refused to be hurried—Rhinelander watched the processes underway along the two-mile floor of the food works, six stories below the small bubble of an office. At one side of the vast cavern mammoth dump bins poured soya pods into funnels which led to hooded conveyors whose escape valves squirted occasional puffs of red steam. On the opposite side of the cavern, claw forks stacked bright cartons of Gooselet Yummydinners onto skids which were then blasted down distribution tubes with small rocket charges. When Elk switched from production of one Yummydinner to another the dump-bins continued to pour out soya pods but the packaged goods which emerged had become Tomato Surprises, plastic glass bells included.

"About Joe Caul—" Rhinelander dragged his gaze away from the belches of red steam which reminded him of Pictur 4. "You are the Hubert Elk with whom Joe Caul was once—ah—associated?"

"Right, that's me." Elk picked his teeth. "Owner and sole operator of Yummydinners. Caul used to work for me." He glanced at Rhinelander's enamelled card again. "Art dealer, huh? I heard something about Caul and his pictures. He used to paint around here, too. What's your interest, mister?"

"An an art dealer, I wish to develop—ah—greater public appreciation of his remarkable talents. I wish to locate him. So that I can purchase more of his pictures."

Elk guffawed. From behind a bank of instruments he dragged a small canvas whose subject was a water spaniel, done with syrupy realism in garish tones of yellow and rust. Rhinelander recoiled from its wetter-than-life tongue.

"Oh, come now, Mr. Elk. Caul didn't paint that."

"He certainly did, " Elk said testily. "I watched him do it. After all, he worked for me, didn't he? Plus eight or nine other factories."

"Not as an artist, surely?"

"Nope. Janitor. Swept out the office here." Elk waved at the clanking conveyors far below. "What else could he do in a place like this?"

"You seriously expect me to believe Joe Caul painted works of this sort?"

"If you don't believe me, here's the signature. You have to look close. Down in the corner. 'Joe Caul.' "

Aghast, Rhinelander saw that it was so.

Elk turned smug. "Didn't I tell you? He painted dogs, mostly. When it wasn't dogs, it was angels and martyrs. Caul wasn't too bright, you understand. How could a man be, and be a regular resident of this place? I haven't seen any of his pictures all the papers are talking about, except for one they ran in black and white. Didn't look like Joe Caul's stuff to me, at least not the Joe Caul I knew before the accident."

"Accident?" Rhinelander's cheeks quivered. "What sort of accident? When?"

"Sub-reactor on the synthesizer belt vibrated its shield bolts loose. Caul had swept up here and was on his way over to Blumenthal Better Ball Bearings to do the same. He got burned in the atom shower. Of course we rushed him to the autodoctor to get the charge neutralized. Only trouble was, I found out later the machine was due for overhaul that next week. Some of its tapes were a mite worn. Caul didn't seem bad off after the accident, but he had trouble sleeping nights. Slept like a top before. I was going to cash his compensation for him, send him to a clinic to check the work the autodoc had done—hell of a bother, but it's these Goddamn bureaucratic laws we got—but by then Caul was committed."

"Committed?" Rhinelander's eyes began to bulge. His nostrils grew big as dimes. You don't mean to some sort of therapeutic farm?"

"None other than Thlex," said Elk, with another smug nod.

"Narcotics? Caul was on narcotics?" (That would explain some of the visions. Some, but by no means all.) "How did you find this out?"

"Why, Caul told me. He had dreams, he said. Couldn't sleep, but he had dreams. Imagine that. So he robbed one of those robopushers always parked around the turnpike entrances, and got hooked. That was two years ago."

Elk rose and peered at a pressure gauge imbedded in a wall bank. "Hell, I was glad to see him leave Industrial Jersey. He wasn't the only one had insomnia. Soon as I brought him back from the autodoc I couldn't get more than two hours a night myself. Toss, turn, thinking of my inlaws, production problems, worry, worry, worry. Must of felt responsible for Caul's trouble. Anyway, when he committed himself to try and shake the habit, I began to sleep sound again. Shows you how the Goddamn spenders who run this country can make a man feel guilty if he doesn't wipe the nose of any stumblebum who sweeps up his shop. Caul's probably still in Thlex for all I know. Good riddance. After he was burned, I couldn't even stand to look at him." For a moment Elk's eyes looked far beyond Rhinelander to something ghastly. Then the mood passed.

"Excuse me now, mister. Time for the three o'clock changeover."

Rhinelander attempted to thank Elk but the latter was occupied with another lever labelled *Grape Aphrodisia Gelatin Yummydinner, With Extra Vine Leaves Included*. Rhinelander let himself out of the office bubble. He ran down the automatic stairs to the exit where the ranger was waiting for him in the rain.

As they walked along the ranger said, "Find what you were after?"

"I most certainly did." In his mind, Rhinelander saw himself delivering punches to Watty Pope's groin. "Let's hurry. I must catch a flight for Kentucky as soon as possible. I—good heavens! Look at that!"

On a corner between automated factories a man with a huge red beard was selling newssheets from a portable stand. Not actually selling them. Merely standing there holding an ear trumpet to the right side of his head while the rain turned the newssheets spongy. All at once the bearded man caught sight of Rhinelander and the ranger. He scuttled out of sight around the corner of a factory, kicking over his stand as he went.

The ranger shook his head. "Crazy. Who reads papers out here, I wonder?"

"These aren't even papers," Rhinelander said, stooping to pick up the top sheet. All the letters including the masthead were greeked. The reverse side of the page was blank. The bundle underneath was compressed excelsior. Rhinelander felt a shiver of fright chase down his spine. He looked around the corner. The red bearded man had vanished into the rain and the empty concrete distances.

VI.

The only staff professional at Thlex who had time to talk with Rhinelander was a Second Assistant Staff Recreationist named Dr. T. T. Wu. And he clearly demonstrated that he was none too happy about the assignment by reminding Rhinelander two seconds after they met that Thlex received a minimum of ten thousand patients a week. Rhinelander could well believe it.

At Central Administration in Lexington City he had made a generous donation of some of Iris' money. It had then taken him two hours by rotor to reach Dr. Wu's section, five counties away, because nearly three quarters of the state was occupied by the national narcotics hospital. The gently rolling landscape, all sunlit green hills and long grass, swarmed with thousands of figures in white gowns wandering to and fro like extras in some epic from Hollywood-on-the-Tiber.

Dr. Wu's irritation showed on his young, lemon-colored face. He and Rhinelander had to walk two miles before they found an unoccupied bench, where they could chat.

"I can give you only ten minutes, please, Mr. Rhinelander," Wu said. "At ten I am directing six hundred of our inmates in a Shakespearian therapy." Wu pinched his upper nose. "Going badly, too. Our lumber mill was supposed to have delivered the Birnam Wood costumes last Tuesday. All I get is excuses, excuses, excuses. Let's see."

Wu dug into his smock for a card. "Hmmm. Quite a substantial donation. I'm no public relations man, but I suppose I must cooperate."

Rhinelander said irritably, "I had hoped the donation might facilitate—"

"When we release a thousand patients a week only to get ten thousand?" Wu's little chestnut eyes snapped in the Kentucky sun. "God pity our staff if we ever have a depression, Mr. Rhinelander. Then we'll really be jammed. Now we have only the social cases. Those in the exurbs who try it for kicks and then—but time is wasting." Another glance at the card. "Caul, was it? Ah, yes, Caul, Caul. Low status, I recall. No education, no money, no children, no mistresses. No reason to become addicted. Here three weeks. Had to release him."

"Cured?" Rhinelander was disappointed. A confirmed addiction might explain the haunting, evil quality of the Pictures, but a reconstructed addiction—

Wu shook his head. "Totally hopeless. Besides, he caused riots."

Rhinelander's eyebrows shot up. "Riots?"

"Yes, riots. Among his village mates. When Caul arrived they began to complain of sleeplessness. As did Caul himself. Caul was completely uncooperative. Stayed up all night painting. Big, psychotic pictures. Three of them while he was here. One of our inmates looked at Caul's work and went into a screaming fit. '*I know what that is!*' he screamed. Two nights later he murdered three matrons and escaped over the Ohio. He drowned trying to swim to a roadside fix stand on the other side.

"The man had been partially cured, too," Wu added snappishly. "Well, I simply don't have time to stand for such regressive nonsense. So after the patients began to riot—the first riot broke out one night when Caul displayed his canvases after mess—I obtained an executive order. I crated his nightmarish work and shipped it, and Caul as well, to the place we send all our incurables."

Rhinelander batted away a bee which was buzzing and looping around his nose. His whole body erupted in perspiration. His heart jackhammered under layers of fat.

Dr. Wu fidgeted, stared at his sandals, at the sky, at his nails, at several inmates acting out their hostilities by playing freeway drivers in a nearby glade. Rhinelander thought: "What luck! A physician too idealistic by half, too caught up and concerned with his charges to know, even now, what a find he once had in the person and the paintings of Joe Caul. Carefully Rhinelander said:

"To what place do you send your incurables, Dr. Wu?"

Wu stood up. "Denver. The Monastery of Positive Thinking. It's for incipient and developed insanity. Caul reached the latter state shortly upon arrival. If you'll pardon me, I must check up on Birnam Wood. Your donation is appreciated, but it still hardly makes a dent. Send me a new lumber mill foreman instead." Off he went into the dappled sunlight falling through the magnolias.

Starting up a hillside toward the rotor park, Rhinelander got a jolt. Stencilled against the sky, an attendant wheeled an empty patient's chair. The attendant had something resembling a jeweler's loupe screwed into his left eye. His reddish beard flapped in the hot wind.

Rhinelander began to run. "Wait, you! Wait just a moment! Stand still, I tell you."

But the bearded man was younger and more agile than Rhinelander. He tipped over his chair, flung off his white smock and jackrabbited away over another hill. Rhinelander puffed after him, but got only as far as the chair whose wheel revolved lazily and caught the sun in chrome glints. He was panting too hard to run further.

Leaves stirred in the woods into which the figure had vanished. Rhinelander wished he were nearer an analytical lab that could, for a fee, get hold of the perspiration index left on the chair's handgrips. Who *was* that damned spook with the red beard?

Some flunky Watty had hired to check on the success or failure of Rhinelander's search?

Yes, that must be! Rhinelander mopped his face and pursed his lips in a little smile. He could feel his blood pressure mounting as he thought of Watty and Iris but he calmed himself by thinking:

DENVER. DENVER. When he shook a fist at the blue sky, it was the fist of a victor.

VII.

Rhinelander's sense of victory was so complete he couldn't resist sending Watty a message before he took off from Thlex. He reported his destination, reported that he had located Joe Caul, reported that within a day he would most certainly have Joe Caul signed to the exclusive management and representation of The Rhinelander Galleries. See how Watty liked that.

As the sonicliner whined down over Denver through a sundown sky all gold and royal purple, Rhinelander munched a Digest-o-tab provided by the stewardesses to help get rid of the sixteen courses of the flight meal. He reflected that soon he would prove once and for all that he was really a clever and resourceful person.

A short twelve miles by limoubus from Denver and he reached the sprawling onion towers of the Monastery of Positive Thinking. It was twilight. Motorized doves wheeled above the chapel. The carillon rang out the strains of *Smiles*.

As Rhinelander entered the gate he saw a platoon of the brothers marching briskly through a cloister. Barefoot, each wore impeccable flannel habilaments. Each was whistling in an optimistic way. Rhinelander had heard about the order. Its brethren were mainly hopelessly insane advertising executives. Their tranquility was achieved through the use of drugs. Nevertheless, the entire scene had a refreshing spiritual air which Rhinelander enjoyed.

A novice asked him to wait in the garden until Evening Plansboard was finished. Rhinelander sat on a marble bench in the piney mountain evening at the foot of a bronze statue of the great hospitaler himself, J. Walter Thorngate. The hands of the figure were widespread in a gesture of invitation to the figure of an ailing consumer lying at his feet.

Before he knew it Rhinelander was joined by a stately monk with a crew cut and horn-rims. He introduced himself in a cheerful way as Brother Buzz, the Vice President In Charge of Intravenous Equipment.

"Your inquiry isn't precisely in my bailiwick," said Brother Buzz with a warm smile, "but since we're a team here, all involved in caring for the incurable and so forth, I'm sure I can help put a little zing back in your swing."

"Thank you, thank you," Rhinelander replied. "I'd like to talk with one of your patients. I believe his name is Caul."

"Joe? A swell guy. But then they're all swell guys." Brother Buzz, however, could not suppress a gentle frown. "Unfortunately he's our unhappiest ward. Complains constantly that the fellows on the team think pure white thoughts. But of course we do." Brother Buzz laid his arm across Rhinelander's shoulders. "We've zeroed in on the great truths, my friend. When we send positive thinking up the flagpole, every man on the team salutes. Actually you won't be able to see Joe until after the morning meal. The patients have retired for the night."

"Oh. But he's here, isn't he?"

"Of course."

Now Rhinelander became very careful. "Brother Buzz, may I ask what may seem a question. Do you and your brothers have any contact with the outside world? That is to say, I mean specifically the world of art. You see, I'm an art dealer."

"The world of art? No, we're totally divorced from the world outside. We have no paintings here except for an original Rockwell in the narthex. However—" Brother Buzz shook his head. "I'm sorry you have made the trip for nothing, because that work is not for sale at any price."

Rhinelander suppressed a giggle. "All I want is to talk to Caul, please."

"Then you shall." Brother Buzz stood up and fished among the folds of his robe. "I'll show you where you can sleep. I regret the surroundings are modest, but our order believes that existence should be one single, harmonious ball of wax. In the meantime, you may be interested in this message. Our supply rotor dropped it along with our consignment of Gruel Yummydinners shortly after six."

Rhinelander did not unfold the slip until Brother Buzz had led him to the guest cell, and drawn Rhinelander's meal—Gruel Yummydinner—from the dumbwaiter. A beam of red sunlight came through the bars of the cell and lit up the letters of the message like flame:

GLAD TO LOCATE YOU IN TIME TO REPORT PARTY GOING SPLENDIDLY. YOUR PRIVATE POOL NOW PART OF SPLENDID RICE PADDY.

GOVERNOR STEMPLE HIMSELF APPEARING AS LEADER OF COMMUNE! CHAMPAGNE DELICIOUS. JUST HAD TWO BEFORE WIRING. WATTY RECEIVED YOUR MESSAGE. SAYS HE REFUSES TO BELIEVE UNTIL THE SIXTH PICTUR IS HUNG AT RHINELANDER'S. I'D BE WITH HIM, EXCEPT HAVING TOO DELIRIOUS A TIME COMMUNIZING TO THINK ABOUT IT. IRIS.

"God damn," Rhinelander said. Then more vehemently, "Oh, God *damn* her." The arrogant message triggered him like a bomb. He raged and stamped up and down his cell with his mind a turmoil of humiliation and rage.

Re-decorate his house, would she?

Against his wishes, would she?

Bitch! Flagrant, arrogant bitch.

Her money, her money, *her* money, he sneered to himself. *Oh yes—but not for long. Not when I sign Caul tomorrow*!

In a spasm of fury, Rhinelander kicked over the plastic wash stand with its metal bowl, towel, straight razor and bar of shaving soap. Then he stamped on the bowl until he bent it totally out of shape.

And Watty, he thought. Still thinks I'll fail. *Still, still, still.*

Rhinelander hurled the closed razor at the wall with a low scream of rage. Only the sound of the carillon pealing out *Happy Days Are Here Again* over the mountains prevented Rhinelander's noise from upsetting the entire monastery. At last, sobbing, he sank down on his pallet and blew out the single candle.

But he could not sleep.

He wanted to sleep. Something seemed to be sucking at his mind as he lay in the cool dark. Pulling and sucking and draining, until he could hardly move. He felt limp, exhausted. But his mind refused to accept this exhaustion. Instead, it conjured up tortures and indecencies and obscenities and cruelties committed upon the persons of Iris and Watty, tortures and indecencies and obscenities and cruelties of a magnitude which startled even Rhinelander's own soggy, hate-purpled self. At last, snuffling and weeping, he fell into a fitful light sleep.

Yet in that stage, foggy demons flew around inside his head.

"You," the voice was whispering. A wet, loose-lipped sound. "You, *you.*"

Rhinelander sat bolt upright. He was bathed in cold sweat.

Through the cell window a shaft of icy moonlight fell on the cell floor. Rhinelander tottered toward the door. There was a horrid crawling on his spine. His hand trembled as he reached for the latchstring. When Rhinelander opened the door and shrank back, his visitor shambled inside.

The visitor stood in the moonbeam, spittle gleaming on his lips. Rhinelander's legs turned to jelly.

The visitor was a bent, flaccid man in his middle forties, pale with a face like suet. He stood looking foolishly at Rhinelander. His big eyes seemed to have caverns behind them. His feet, sticking out of shabby gray work trousers, were dirty, as if he were too imbecilic to give himself good care. Then Rhinelander saw the fresh daubs of color on the toes, on the trousers, on the tattered shirt. Finally, he saw what the man held, as the man brought it forward like a Mongolian child displaying a bauble.

"Joe Caul," Rhinelander said.

"Thankee," said Joe Caul. "Ye helped me paint again. Many thanks."

And he showed the small canvas.

Rhinelander covered his face and fell shrieking against the cold stone wall.

"Turn it around, for Christ's sake. It's filthy."

Joe Caul blinked. "That's queer. A man calling himself dirt."

"What do you—no, don't come any closer! What do you mean?"

"I painted what I seed in your head tonight. I don't see things in the heads of them monks. They got pure white heads. Drugs or suthin'. What's wrong with a feller paintin' what he sees, huh?"

"What do you mean, you *saw* that?" Rhinelander howled.

Caul blinked innocently. "Why just like it always is, since the burn back when I was with Elk. I can't sleep no more. But when I close my eyes, I see. Finally I figured out what I seen. It must be inside heads. It *must* be,"

Caul repeated in his pleading whine. "Don't noplace in the world have crawly sights like that. One of the fellers at Thlex unnerstood. He unnerstood why I had to have drugs. Only way I know to get rid of this—" Caul wagged the picture again. Rhinelander retched.

"—only way's to paint it. Jesus—" Caul was nearly weeping in the steel-blue moonlight now, "—wisht I could paint a dog again. All I can see is this here. Awful. Take it!" Caul thrust the painting forward at Rhinelander. His voice shrilled up a note.

"Jesus, take it, mister. I don' wan't it, I can't *stand* it. That's why I sended the big ones to a name I seen in a directory book. The feller at Thlex, my friend, he said I could get money. I filled out some papers, he showed me how, except he was so high, I don't guess we did a very good job. Guess I got a bank somewhere. Don't know where, though. Money. I guess so, too. Except the feller unnerstood and swum all the way to Ohio and got killed hunting a new fix. He couldn't stand it either.

All at once Caul's mind ran down like a broken clock. He stood, just stood. His arms dangled. His lower lip made a plateau from which saliva dripped, evil and iridescent under the weird mountain moon.

"I see," Rhinelander choked, talking half to himself. "The burns—the incomplete treatment—you look inside heads—"

A stupid, pleading smile twitched Caul's lips.

"You unnerstand. You a friend?"

"No, I'm not your friend. Christ, *no!*"

"I can't he'p what I see," Caul mumbled. "I see it, I got to purge it out or I'd kill myself." Caul looked down at his most recent work. "Thankee. I wanted to paint again because some of what I seen was still inside my head, but—I guess—it takes a dirty head to get it really stirred again. Wasn't bad enough until you come. Just bad, not bad enough."

"A dirty head," Rhinelander said, with a moist, witless giggle. He could hardly speak. "You—that's why—the Pictures—they look so familiar, but—dirty heads. They're—all of us?"

"Please," said Caul, holding up the painting.

"Give me that thing," Rhinelander screamed. He snatched the canvas from Caul's hands, scrabbled on the stone floor, opened the razor and began to slash, crisscross, with great outraged strokes.

Slash, slash, slash. Anything to eradicate the putrescent vision of his own mind which Joe Caul had somehow seen tonight, seen and sucked out and transferred to virulent, shadowy life on his little scrap of canvas. *Slash, slash, slash*. Rhinelander struck back and forth like a demon.

"What you doin', mister?" Caul caught Rhinelander by the shoulder with one loose hand. "Hey, there, what—"

Unable to control himself, Rhinelander spun around. His arm whipped back and forth in a continuation of the hysterical attack upon the canvas. The razor gleamed cold as death and sliced clean through Joe Caul's jugular.

Caul screamed. He lurched into a corner of the cell, kneeling in his own bubbling blood. Something blue-white exploded from the corridor. Rhinelander grew conscious of a babble of voices he had heard for some time. Then a louder voice exclaimed:

"Awright, awright, how was I to know he'd kill him? I got the shot, you can go in now an'—quit shoving, dammit, I'm a representative of the press."

Rhinelander staggered to another corner, unable to look at the twitching, bleeding thing he had killed. Through his blurred eyesight swam the face of Brother Buzz. Then another face with a red fan beard. Monks were tussling with the intruder, who had a camera and was shouting about being manhandled:

"Sigma. Charley Sigma, Topflite Press Service. Legit? Sure I'm legit! Been following this bird for days. Mystery of Joe Caul. Got a tip in Geneva about a cracked numbered account. What a story. 'The cesspool of the human mind on canvas' . . . awright, awright, quit shoving. I know my constitutional rights. Where's the communication center in this dump?"

Mine, Rhinelander thought hideously. He had slashed the canvas but could not slash its image out of his thoughts. Purple, whirling, obscene. Mine, ah, God *mine*. Why did I ever want to find out?

"A little tranquility, brothers," said the voice of Brother Buzz with conference room authority. Rhinelander felt the blessed needle pierce his arm to bring the blessed dark.

VIII.

Rhinelander or Iris or Watty seldom went to the observatory in the villa because none of them were interested in astronomy. But the observatory sat upon the highest point of their property, overlooking a distant highway, so tonight the three of them stood by the balustrade, watching. Far off, lights by the thousands burned in a crawling pattern along the highway. Rhinelander turned his back, feeling chilly, although the evening temperature was over seventy.

He didn't care to watch. Iris had insisted, however. The psychomentalist who cleared Rhinelander of accidental homoslaughter at his hearing had also insisted.

Watty, never at a loss, chuckled.

"Did you see the sheets tonight, Nels old boy? Five hundred thousand copies of Professor Hatlo's new edition of *A Bioglossary of Great Artists* destroyed at the end of the press run? Poor Hatlo only finished revising it three weeks ago to include Joe Caul. And the reviews! What an about face."

"Vile," Iris breathed. "Those—pictures—" Her sticky lips twisted with loathing, "—couldn't come from any one of us."

"Oh, no?" Watty laughed again. He lifted his hand to indicate the moving chain of lights. "My dear, they're from all of us. Or were."

"When is Swallows' funeral?" Rhinelander asked. Swallows had hung himself.

"Tomorrow," said Watty.

"I must finish my paper," Rhinelander said vaguely. "Dewsimmon wants it for the next issue of *Palette*."

"What's it called?" Watty asked quietly.

" 'The False Aesthetics of the Caul Canvases.' "

All Watty would say was, "Ah. It certainly follows."

"What fools we were," Rhinelander said with another long shudder.

"Amen," Iris said. "For once we agree, darling."

"Oh, no," said Watty. "A week ago we weren't fools. We were sensitive men and women. Tonight we've become fools again. Incidentally, Nels. Although you did find your friend Caul, I still consider that you failed to win our little challenge. Nels? Ah, well."

Rhinelander stood rigid, smiling a little now. The procession of lights had come to a halt. A red smear leaked up on the horizon.

It grew redder and taller. Soon it revealed the fifty thousand who had marched out of the city to burn the five Picturs of Joe Caul.

Love Is A Punch in the Nose

> The pressure of modern life, with its success ethic, its jealousies and insecurities, and its bureaucracies and hierarchies, is familiar to all of us. These pressures build up frustrations and aggressions, which must find release. In American society sports and media violence are a major source of release—a safety valve for millions. The need for an outlet for aggressive behavior and the consequences of not having one are the subjects of this delightful little tale.

Those who marry, it seems, often puzzle over whether they do or do not truly love their spouses, and if not, why not? And if so, why? After the relatively short span of a year and four months of married life, I discovered, during a winter vacation to Hilton's Moon Lakes, just how deeply and meaningfully I loved my wife Shirley.

I discovered the reason I loved her also. It was because she made me feel happier (i.e., less unhappy) than I had ever felt before.

I discovered this when I knocked her down sixteen stairs.

At this point, I must deliver a message to the prurient: look elsewhere for your titillations. I am not, nor have I ever been, one of those warped souls who derive bizarre thrills from the act of striking someone. The act of injuring another person, repugnant to anyone with sensibilities, is especially so to a man in the legal profession. My first blow to Shirley's nose meant nothing; it was what it caused which meant everything.

Love Is a Punch in the Nose

On the day in question, our second-to-last at Moon Lakes, we were just about to board the airbus for the hotel's scenic tour of one of the satellite's natural wonders, Moriarity's Washboard. A hotel attendant rushed down the long flight of stairs from the hotel terrace, announcing loudly:

"Message for Mr. Charles Carter. Mr. Charles Carter, please."

"Here," I said, my nerves instantly taut.

Shirley's dear blue eyes clouded. "Oh, Charles. The promotion?"

"I expect so. Miss Lapsfogel promised to get in touch at the first news. Do you want to go back with me?"

"No, I'll wait here. But do hurry. I'm dying to see Moriarity's Washboard. And Charles—"

Her soft, warm hand touched my arm. She was as lovely, as sweet as ever, with her heart-shaped face, her stylishly blonde hair and blue eyes formed in such beautiful perfection that I often wondered why it was Charles Carter, nervous, 36, and balding, to whom she had chosen to speak casually that first day in the art gallery.

"Charles, don't let the news upset you if it's bad, dear. We'll weather it." Gently she kissed my cheek.

Hurrying back up the stairs, I forgot for a few seconds the terrible tension under which I had lived in the past months. Shortly after we were married, I lost two major cases, both of them involving defendants, my clients, who had ostensibly violated the space space of the two plaintiffs. This lowered my stock with the firm's senior partners.

A man reaches a certain point in his life at which he either begins to slip or go ahead emphatically, and I felt I had reached that point and begun to do the former. The evidence would come in when the senior partners of Fleeb, Hammerstroh & DePickeney made their annual choice of a man to be elevated to a senior partnership.

"Oh I'm so terribly sorry," were the first words from Miss Lapsfogel which I heard when I punched the *Receive* button in the lobby booth.

"Then Graham got the partnership?"

"Yes, sir, it was announced this morning."

"Thank you, Miss Lapsfogel," I said, for she was a polite, conscientious secretary, and terribly loyal. I de-

punched, sat staring at the booth wall, and my face twitched. "Oh, God damn it," I said in utter misery.

A tension-throbbing, of the kind that had driven me to snap and growl at Shirley with increasing frequency over the past months, began in my temples. As I left the booth, my hands were actually trembling. I felt spring-tight inside. Furious, enraged, boiling.

Such moods had possessed me often of late. I would, in the grip of one, abuse Shirley verbally, criticize her without reason (that is, I would decide later it was without reason; at the moment it happened it would seem perfectly justified), or sneer at her suggestion for what to do during an evening out. Frankly, prior to marriage, I had never imagined that any woman would put up with such vile temper, but Shirley did, with shy sweetness and sympathy. The only sign that she was ever the least upset might be a quiet retreat to the Family Recreation Space in our dome, where I would find her later, as I came to make my lame apologies, working at her little sonic ceramics kiln.

She was literally an angel; in moments of self-truth, the only fault I could reasonably find with our marriage was that we had been unable thus far to have an heir.

Leaving the lobby, I saw Shirley waiting at the top of the stairs leading down from the terrace. In the distance, the airbus was a diminishing speck against the gray-green loom of Earth far off. The airbus was whizzing across the lunar waste, already on its way.

As I approached Shirley, I felt my temples throb all the harder.

"Graham got the promotion," I said.

"Yes," Shirley said, "I saw it in your face. And we've missed the sightseeing tour, too."

There was absolutely no recrimination in her voice. She was merely stating fact. But I blew up: "What the hell difference does a miserable sightseeing tour make when Old Man Fleeb has marked me off as no longer a comer?"

"Would it hurt to think about changing firms, Charles?"

"So you think I'm a failure too!" I said, and let all my tension burst forth in the smashing blow I delivered right to her nose.

Love Is a Punch in the Nose   133

With a little moan, Shirley tumbled down sixteen of the stairs. "Oh my God," I whispered, and rushed to help her.

People stared. I did not care. Some kind of valve had opened within me, draining off every last drop of the accumulated frustration of the past few days, and, as I hurried to Shirley's aid, I realized dimly that I actually felt better. That is, less tense.

"Shirley, are you hurt? Darling, I'm sorry."

"No, I'm all right, Charles." She was already standing.

"Shirley dear, I'm terribly sorry. There was no excuse—"

Lamely I stopped. She had every right to castigate me. But in her blue eyes shone only love and compassion. Pushing back a wisp of soft blonde hair, she touched my cheek.

"Poor Charles. I understand the tension you've been under. I don't blame you for what you did. What I said was thoughtless. I would have done the same in your place. Look, the sightseeing tour doesn't matter. Why don't we go in and have a cocktail?"

Amazed, I clasped her in my arms. "You're wonderful, Shirley. Absolutely wonderful."

Against my shoulder she murmured, "No, I just understand how difficult it is for a man to make a go of it these days. Life's so complicated."

"Shirley, you do understand me. You really do."

But even as I embraced her, the first evil little seed was planted: because I realized that striking her, an act which had temporarily drained off all my inward hostilities and made me actually feel almost human again, had produced in her no reaction of anger (which might have checked future excesses), but rather only an outpouring of sympathy. I was both perversely pleased and dismayed when I analyzed the significance of her reaction.

The legal term for what had just happened is precedent.

Six weeks after our return to Earth from Moon Lakes, we were seated at dinner in our dome's Nutrition Space when Shirley stubbed her Kelp in an ashtray, then depressed the stud which brought the freezer silently out of the wall.

"Charles, I know you had a bad day—"

"That rotten Old Man Fleeb. I show him a brief to make him think I think he's a Solomon, not the dummy everybody knows he is, and he feels obliged to write all sorts of snide marginal notes as though I were some insignificant sixth-year law student! I tell you, Shirley, I think there's a plot afoot."

"Charles, you can't be serious."

"You're damn right I'm serious. They're all against me."

"No!"

"They want to get rid of me. It's a subtle campaign of harassment."

My temples were, naturally, throbbing, as they had done almost round the clock since our return from our vacation. Shirley nibbled her pretty pink lip, then pointed to the freezer.

"I just wanted to tell you that the electronochron broke down again today. I had to call the service people. Charles, I need some advice. That's the fourth breakdown in two weeks. I know you're watching our finances closely because you may want to change firms, but I was wondering whether we might consider looking at a new freezer to replace—"

"I don't need any insinuations about money on top of everything else," I said, feeling a mounting fury as I stood up.

"Charles, I wasn't insinuating anything."

"You certainly were. You were suggesting that what I make is inadequate."

"No, Charles, I was only trying to find out whether we had enough in the bank to—"

I slapped her full in the face.

Shirley fell off her stool. I glared down:

"I've had about enough of your sly, rotten little innuendoes! I refuse to be—"

Remorse swept over me. The tension throbbing ebbed. I bent down, helped her up, and for the next four days, I felt somewhat less tense.

Then, two weeks later, a Saturday evening, I kicked her in the hip as she relaxed on the bed in the Self-Restoration Space. All she had done was comment that the Bartmans, in the next dome, had just left for cocktails

Love Is a Punch in the Nose

down at the Riversides in the next quadrangle. I had been brooding over the cocktail thing ever since she'd told me early that same day that Marvis Riverside had snubbed her at the local IBM Foods, and also dropped the word that she and her husband were giving the party. I took Shirley's evening remark to indicate that I was, socially, the square peg whom everyone disliked. So I kicked her.

I need not dwell on the specifics of the pattern which developed. I think it is clear. I was in dire need of help— what kind I was not certain—because the tensions caused by daily living, and by not achieving the lofty personal goals I had set for myself in law school, left me angry and seething inside most of the time. My fatal discovery was that hitting or kicking Shirley drained off some of these bad feelings, enabling me to get through a few more days without a blowup down at the firm. Further, I had discovered that I now loved and depended upon Shirley as I never had at the start of our marriage. Consequently, I hit, kicked, slapped, pinched or otherwise assaulted her more and more often.

Why she took my mistreatment was a marvel and mystery, at least then. The fatal Thursday evening in October began, and ended, in one idle remark from Shirley as I stood at a counter in the Nutrition Space. I was still boiling with rage and resentment over a severe reprimand from Old Man Fleeb about a fee I'd set. I was bruising my fingers as a result of the pressure I was applying on the cordless vibroknife handle as I attempted to slice a synthetic lime for a stiff drink.

Shirley said, "Charles, Vivi Bartman told me today that *Ooops, It's My Husband!* is one of the funniest depthos she and Fred have ever seen. I checked the schedule. The last showing starts at 9:11. It's over at the Loew's Stadium. We haven't been to a deptho in so long, I thought perhaps—"

At that precise instant, the vibroknife slipped and sliced a chunk out of my thumb. Cursing and bleeding slightly, I turned.

"Look what you did, Shirley. I'm sick of your nagging about how miserable your life is."

"Charles, I wasn't nagging."

"By God I know nagging when I hear it!" I shouted.

"Please, Charles, don't let your temper—"

While saying those words, she raised her right hand. My enraged mind immediately signalled that she was going to slap me, a thought whose ludicrous proportions I only recognized later. In my tense, exhausted state, my reaction—and I might say more than a reaction; my dimly-felt yearning to open the valve because the precedent had been set—burst all bounds and I yelled a curse and leaped at her and drove the vibroknife into her breast.

An expression of pure fright crossed her beautiful face as she stared down at the humming haft sticking from her blouse.

"Oh, Charles, oh—you shouldn't have done that."

What I screamed, or babbled, I do not remember.

There was no blood coming out of the wound. None.

Hysterical, I ran for the visor. First I key-punched the hospital, then the authorities. I returned to the Nutrition Space, but she was gone. Shrieking her name, I ran through the house until I found her in the Family Recreation Space, the door to her little sonic kiln open. She lay on the carpet before it, pale, weak, and her blouse was stained by a few drops of liquid which had seeped out of the wound. The vibroknife was gone.

The drops on her blouse were a dark green

As anyone is certainly aware who has read the slanted and bloodthirsty copy written by the reporters, editors and sob-sisters who screamed for my neck and landed me in the situation in which I find myself, she (I still cannot think of her in any other way) had crawled to the Recreation Space to get the repair materials with which she had been provided. She kept the materials in our dome in the guise of ceramics hobby gear. But by accident, the vibroknife had severed four vital sections of tubing, and she could not save herself in time.

Nor could I, of course, for I was practically out of my mind with confusion and astonishment and—yes, I think I felt it even then—a sense of huge loss. She lay on the carpet while the authorities landed outside, the noise of rotors heavy in the air, and she looked at me with a complete, expressionless lack of feeling closed her blue eyes, rolled over and ceased to operate.

That I had known nothing of the plot, and had never

Love Is a Punch in the Nose 137

suspected her, so perfect were all details, did not aid my cause one whit.

While technically there was no statute under which I could be held for murder—how does one "murder" a non-human, laboratory-constructed thing?—false moral issues turned everyone against me.

Out on bail before the trial, I read the headlines with astonishment, then fear:

LAWYER INTIMATE WITH PLASTIC WOMAN!

I read the editorials:

STOP TIDE OF UNNATURALNESS—THE TIME IS NOW!

I read the interviews:

COM CHINS REFUSE EXTRADITIONS, SAYS JUSTICE DEPT. HEAD

Or:

WHY DR. HOOGASIAN CHOSE LAWYER

Dr. Hoogasian, of whom I had never heard (nor had most anyone else) until then, had fled by sonic liner to sanctuary in the Yellow Sphere the moment my arrest hit the headlines. The private detective who had apparently been shadowing me to provide Dr. Hoogasian with a report on my outward behavior likewise fled. The "why" article was of course deliberate journalistic misrepresentation, because in the one interview Hoogasian later granted from the sanctuary of his extradition-proof laboratory in some obscure city named Loo Foo, his answer about why he selected me was so simple as to infuriate the hypocritical public even further:

"Well, if you plan to save the world from itself, don't you have to start somewhere?"

What Dr. Hoogasian had started via me and the art gallery where Shirley lay in wait was a clinical field trial of the prototype of his answer to the Earth's ever-mounting problems of mental illness, tension, juvenile rioting, neuroticism, divorce, adultery, drinking, and virtually all the other evils which have plagued mankind with increasing frequency and virulence in these last decades of the century in which we and the Com Chins further polarized into two armed camps. Technology, plus Dr. Hoogasian's own damned, devilish brilliance as an inventor, had made it possible for each human being (as he envisioned it) to have at his disposal a personal safety valve for those inward torments which, unless harmlessly drained off, would further, in his view, poison society with billions of ever more anguished souls.

At the time of my conviction and disbarment, the papers resurrected 50-year-old lithographs of a fanciful small animal, the creation of a social cartoonist named Kapps or Cap; the fanciful animals had served the same purpose. But while Dr. Hoogasian's theories (like Kapps's) may have been eminently sound, their acceptance, and the acceptance of Dr. Hoogasian's practical implementation, by human beings was debatable—

As illustrated by my being sentenced to 48 years of corrective observation for Gross Immorality, Constitutional Lewdness, and Perverse Behavior.

Last month, after serving six years, I lost my last appeal.

I am under heavy sedation most of the time, and living, exacerbated by the prison conditions at Federal Corrective, is hell. Hitting the cell walls is no damn good, because they are resilient Saf-T-Foam and it is like striking marshmallows.

But what matters most now is not lost appeals but revenge. Revenge upon the hypocrites, the fools—a whole world full of Grahams and Old Man Fleebs—against me; so much against me that they had to railroad me to jail as their scapegoat. Revenge, revenge. It is the theme of my waking moments, of my nightmares. Even heavy sedation cannot dull its urgency.

Today, I learned Dr. Hoogasian is alive and has not given up. Indeed, I think he has been welcome and put to work by the Com Chins as an ally.

The turnkey on our floor at Federal Corrective is a fat, moralistic old woman who, like all present penological attendants, has nothing but a Ph.D. and looks like Everybody's Grandmother. Her name is Bessie. This morning she brought my usual tray of nutritional pills and shoved it through the aperture with her usual hissing sneer:

"Plastic-lover!"

I yearned to strike her. Unfortunately I could not reach her.

However, Bessie did not stand around for 15 or 20

minutes, as she customarily does, hurling obscene taunts and epithets. She left at once, sucking on a fllesh-colored bandage wrapped around her hammy right hand. I even heard her exchanging pleasantries with other corridor inmates whom she considers less leprous than I.

When I went for my daily interview with Dr. Phewster, I mentioned her altered attitude:

"That old harridan you've got on the floor actually seemed pleasant today. Rather, I should say less unpleasant."

"Yes, there has been a change in her manner," said Dr. Phewster. "Everybody's noticed. You wouldn't believe it, but Bessie has finally found a boyfriend."

"At her age? That's ridiculous."

"Well, I think so, but this young fellow is a refugee and freedom fighter from Japkor. Escaped through the Com Chin barricades in a packing crate. It was in the paper. Oh, that's right. You've given up on papers. Anyway, I'm sure he just wants to marry Bessie for her citizenship, but she thinks he loves her. As long as it moderates that vile disposition of hers, I suppose it can't do too much harm. Now, Mr. Carter, how were the dreams last night? Vibroknives in the Senate again?"

I could hardly speak. I kept seeing the bandage on Bessie's hand.

What had she done to her new love last night? Struck him on his chin of simulated skin? Splendid Dr. Hoogasian! Did I give a damn if he sent his creatures among us to undermine and show up the hypocrites, as will certainly happen eventually, in the guise of escapees from political tyranny? I certainly didn't.

Of course, the refugee might be a genuine, human refugee after all. But Dr Hoogasian, in the few accounts I remembered reading, had protested a shade too much when he stated that he was giving up his program to rid the world of mental illness via artificial scapegoats.

The one trouble with having my revenge is that, if Hoogasian is still at work, I won't have any hand in it.

But any is better than none.

Any is—

Where was I?

A world full of hypocrites, ghouls, enemies.

I wonder if Bessie might be persuaded to bring her new boyfriend around.

I probably could attack and strangle him a while before they pulled me off.

God, I miss my wife.

There's No Vinism
Like Chauvinism

> The inspiration for this story started one day at lunch, when John Jakes' companion, a colleague in the advertising business, came up with this title while under the influence and Jakes vowed that he would write a story to go with it. The result is another discussion of the future of an art form—that of war. It is an excellent blending of the real and perhaps real, a story worthy of Philip K. Dick at his best.

—1—

Union regulations did not make rising mandatory until reveille. Most of the troops were stirring by 0500, however. For Gregory Rooke, plagued by sleeplessness since an owl's hoot awoke him around 0315, this voluntary early rising of so many of the men bore out a certainty of his which had grown the past few days.

They had a happy army.

And once they finished the run, Rooke would be in a position to write his own contract for the next one. Not bad for a product of the East Hampton slums who only ten short years ago, after flunking out of Pharmacy H.S., had been toting a stingrifle in the rear rank of the Finger Lakes Freedom Fighters, the dusty summer that saw the culmination of the Napa Valley Campaign.

Yet he was just a bit fearful. And, as usual, the boots hurt his feet.

Rooke's vaguely Lincolnesque face, one of his decided assets, drew into thoughtful lines as he stood smoking at the flap of his small field geodesic. In five out of seven major campaigns, he had been fortunate to be on the winning side. And in all seven he had won distinction by giving the part more than it required, thus assuring himself a better part in each succeeding run.

Not all the hopefuls who entered this chancy business were so fortunate. Consequently he realized that when they had their final go today at the holdouts, the victory must be brought off with flourish. Like any man a bit on this side of forty, he was reasonably ambitious. He wanted the prestige that went with being able to demand, and get, a contract written his way.

Perhaps, then, the awareness of the stakes accounted for his nervousness. He stamped his field boots down hard in the sweet meadow grass to awaken himself, shake off the mood. Distressing, how the apprehensions wouldn't depart.

Or was his condition caused by something more direct and personal? He'd had several dreams about Mary Lu lately. Treacly, sympathetic dreams. Always upon awakening he was irritated.

In the HQ geodesic, the communications gear squawked. As Rooke watched two butterflies darting in the long grass down beside the gray-silver sheen of Lake Oconomowoc, a seductive female voice honeyed the sweet-smelling air of the May morning.

"Hi there, soldier. This is your old pal Frannie with some pleasant wake-up music for you fellows out there fighting, bleeding and dying for the dairy trusts. Bleeding and dying uselessly, I might remind you. But more about that later. Here's our first tune."

Rooke's thin lips turned sour. A group—Rooke thought it was the UBM combo—pumped a *bossa electronica* into the air.

Throughout the encampment on the lake shore, activity quickened. Extras, bits and principals rolled out of their sleeping bags. A clank and clatter of mess and makeup kits created a counterpoint to the whine from the ordinance pool where the FFs revved their generators and spun their treads. For a moment, Rooke's cynical professionalism, a hard-shell attitude produced by a decade as a working member of Fairness, melted. He was touched by something like a genuine loyalty to the troops, fifty thousand strong, and not a bad actor among them.

Well, not many.

Three hundred feet down the slope, a man in a trench cape beckoned inquiringly. Rooke hesitated. The man cocked his head. Why not? Rooke had no reason for uncertainty about the day's outcome since it had been programmed months ago by the big computers of Wm. Norris Industries/East, the government contractor for the creative part of this particular war. Still, his touch of doubt persisted.

Stage fright, pure and simple. Finale coming up. A trial run with the man standing down there beside the creepiepeepie would take the edge off.

Rooke was a figure of lonely, brooding splendor as he marched down the hillside, tapping his swagger stick against his leg. His epaulet stars gave off a dull glitter in the lightening gray air of morn. He passed the HQ geodesic and heard Fond du Lac Fran resume at the end of the musical selection:

"Gosh, fellows, are you really certain your heart's in this campaign? Think of your wives and kids, your moms and your sweethearts waiting back home—and worrying. Will you get home to them? Are you sure? You know our boys are ready to fight to the death. You know their battle cry. 'Better dead than the high-priced spread.' Do you really want to waste your lives, your young manhood, fighting against such dedicated veterans? Do you really want to oppose a cause you know deep in your hearts is just? What, after all, has made America great? The genius for the synthetic. Do you want to fight the tidal wave of history, fellows? Think about that, you soldiers of UDEF. Think about that while we play another—"

Among the UDEF troops past whose bivouacs Rooke walked now, there was understandably little interest in Fond du Lac Fran. Many of the men did have transistors going, but tuned to capture snippets of news from the area outside the Staging Zone. Only one here or there listened to Fran.

Rooke was one of the few higher-ups privy to the knowledge that Fond du Lac Fran, like her opposite number on the UDEF side, Kenosha Kate (not broadcasting as Milwaukee Marilyn since the Liberation) was non-human, a patch job of syllables and phrases culled and re-edited from hundreds of innocuous taped interviews with the most provocative-voiced actresses of past decades. The UDEF soldiers who listened to Fran did so to appraise her as they would any professional. The troops understood that the broadcasts by the propaganda girls were aimed at the general public outside the Staging Zone. Rooke's status was indicated by his knowledge that Fran and Marilyn/Kate were tape drums, nothing else.

"Thirty seconds, Pierre," said a sepulchral voice from the speaker grille in the side of the square metal creepie-peepie hovering above the ground on jets of air. The side of the creepie-peepie lens housing, as well as the cape and headphones of the man who had summoned Rooke, bore the logotype of the Government Broadcasting Company.

Pierre winked as Rooke came up. He answered the speaker grille:

"Right, Buster." Then, to his guest, "Morning, General."

"Hello, Pierre. What do you hear about the ratings?"

Pierre's blue eyes grew merry. "We're three points ahead of the Free BC and the Fee BC isn't even in the park."

"Terrific."

"Hold on. Okay, Buster, I read you."

Pierre switched off the grille speaker. He adjusted his ear button. "Stand by, General." He waited, fixing his wry and weary reportorial smile in place. Rooke shifted restlessly as Pierre got his signal.

"This is Pierre Pell, your GBC field correspondent, speaking to you from a lonely, embattled hillside on the shores of Lake Oconomowoc, less than two miles from the scene of some of the bloodiest fighting yet encountered in this campaign. Yesterday, in a lightning advance from Nashotah, soldiers of the United Dairy Expeditionary Forces pressed to within striking distance of the last major point of resistance of the AMMA irregulars, the headquarters of Burton Tanzy, former executive VP of AMMA. Casualties in the advance were heavy. To offer some comments on this climactic phase of the campaign, I have with me the commander of the UDEF striking force, Major General William ("Butterfat Bill") Smith."

The self-motorized creepie-peepie dollied back to include Rooke in a two shot. Pierre Pell continued smoothly:

"At the outset of the war five and a half months ago, the opposition had some caustic remarks about the nickname of General Smith, then newly elevated to the rank of chief field commander for UDEF. They've learned that General Smith's name was not bestowed lightly."

Rooke peered straight into the lens. "I certainly hope they've learned that, Pierre."

"To you—and to all these men fighting and dying out here, General—butterfat is not a joking word, am I correct?"

"Yes, Pierre. Butterfat is a way of life. The natural, wholesome way. And we're going to make the holdouts realize it, even if we have to jam the word butterfat down their throats with the point of the stingrifle."

"Then I take it, General, your orders from UDEF remain the same?"

Rooke's nod was brief. "Exactly the same as they were when we liberated Milwaukee three weeks ago and our batallions captured the AMMA executive offices. The only terms acceptable to UDEF—the only terms under which we will deal with the American Margarine Manufacturers Association—are the terms of unconditional surrender."

Rather good, Rooke thought to himself. Of course he had cribbed from the often-quoted unconditional surrender speech of the commander of the Finger Lakes Freedom Fighters, old Wesley Woodis, who was now retired at an Actor's Fairness Senior Citizen Ranch in Arizona. Wesley had stood in a light breeze in Golden Gate Park and vowed to the world that only the total surrender of the Napa Wine Cooperative, surrender terms to include a new contract with many binding East-of-the-Mississippi restraint of trade clauses, would be acceptable. Rooke had thrilled to Wesley Woodis' style, and never forgotten.

The war correspondent was talking again. "—perhaps you can give us some indication of the strategic situation this morning, General."

"Be happy to, Pierre."

The main studio in Washington cut in a visual. Rooke saw it on the monitor panel on the front of the creepie-peepie housing. It was a simplified map of the area. Pierre explained, voice-over:

"General, I might point out to our audience of three hundred million Americans that we are now looking at a map of the primary battle zone. This territory has literally been devastated by some of the most savage fighting in the history of modern commercial warfare. On your screen, viewers, you are looking at an area of roughly two hundred and fifty square miles, comprised of three counties, Jefferson County to screen left, Waukesha screen center and Milwaukee screen right."

Pell winked at Rooke to indicate they would be back on camera momentarily. The main studio zoomed in on a large Maltese cross, indicating the UDEF position, and a circle which marked the city of Oconomowoc just a short distance westward. Pell's sudden tired smile indicated they were back into the two shot.

"Can you outline the situation as it applies to Oconomowoc, General?"

"I can say this, Pierre. The AMMA forces would have saved themselves much bloodshed had they listened to the wiser heads on their executive board. The board members counselled unconditional surrender at the time we liberated Milwaukee and captured them. One recalcitrant holdout, however—Tanzy—"

"Excuse me, General, but let me clarify. The General is referring to J. Burton Tanzy, the president of the Golden-Glo Margarine Company, and former executive VP of the AMMA board. Please continue, General."

"Well, Pierre, as you know, Tanzy fled Milwaukee in a milk truck whose insignia had been forged to resemble that of the American Red Cross, which was in the process of delivering free processed milk tablets to men in the front lines on our side of Plankinton Avenue. Tanzy managed to slip beyond our perimeters and reach his plant in Oconomowoc. He has turned the town into a veritable stronghold of hysterical last-ditch resistance. The only men fighting with him, I might say, are misguided pseudo-patriots, escaped criminals and a large percentage of high-cholesterol degenerates. Barricaded inside the Golden-Glo factory, Tanzy has refused to surrender while still alive. Consequently we have moved westward from Milwaukee, suffering some heavy casualties from his guer-

There's No Vinism Like Chauvinism   147

illas, true, but determined to take Oconomowoc and bring Tanzy in." Rooke gave the lens his flintiest look. "Either alive or dead. The choice is his."

Now Pierre Pell had really warmed to the subject. "Just when do you anticipate taking Tanzy, General?"

Struggling to suppress a sudden thrust of shame at the hypocrisy of it all, Rooke put on a speculative, merciless expression. "By nightfall, Pierre."

"Let me clarify for the viewers," Pierre said in a hush. "You mean by nightfall today?"

"That is exactly what I mean, Pierre. We plan—"

The correspondent cut in abruptly, scowling: "This is Pierre Pell, on the battlefield in Waukesha County, where we have been talking to—this is Pierre Pell returning you to the Early News."

Angrily Pierre jerked off his headphones. He unscrewed his ear button, spat into it, "What the hell's the matter, Buster? Couldn't you for God's sake give me five seconds for a signoff before—oh. Yeah? No kidding."

Pierre turned to Rooke. The latter was already watching the peculiar scene which had appeared on the monitor. Flanked by another reporter in a GBC trench cape, a thin, peppery, white-haired little old man in fusty clothes was shown appearing in a doorway in a brick wall which bled all sides of the screen.

"Tanzy," said Rooke in surprise.

"Yeah, Greg—uh, General. That's why they cut in," Pierre said. "Sorry."

"What's that Tanzy has in his hand?"

Pierre peered. "Looks like a gun. My God—a real one."

"Quick! Can you get the audio?"

The correspondent rushed to the hovering creepie-peepie console. He began twisting dials and throwing switches. A small cluster of UDEF troops began to form around the two men. The soldiers wore khakis with the embroidered shoulder patches of the Elzie Division. They looked mainly puzzled. Pierre muttered several uncomplimentary things about the hamming of his professional rival on screen.

The GBC reporter was standing beside Tanzy, talking animatedly. The president of Golden-Glo Margarine watched something out of the frame. His glitter-eyed fanaticism came across even on the reduced framework of the monitor. Pierre's hands flew as he tried to adjust the controls and screw in his ear button at the same time.

"Can't get it amplified, General. Tanzy's hollering something about no surrender. I can hear a little in the earpiece. And I'm also picking up some net traffic at the same time. It's got them all in a flap back east. This was unexpected."

How unexpected, Pierre Pell certainly could not comprehend. In his role as UDEF field commander, Gregory Rooke was one of half a dozen persons who had been allowed to see the Master Warscript, and Eyes Only document. He recalled nothing whatsoever in the final pages of the outline that resembled this macabre interruption. His uneasiness had come home to roost.

Three men in guerilla coveralls entered the picture, hauling on a rope with obvious force.

Gradually the rope's far point of attachment became clear. A reluctant Guernsey was dragged into what was apparently the truck yard of the Golden-Glo plant.

Continuing to gesture wildly, Burton Tanzy advanced toward the cow. He paused for effect before putting the gun against the cow's unsuspecting skull and pulling the trigger.

Pierre Pell's cheeks were the color of oatmeal. "My God, he's gone crazy!"

"What the hell is happening?" Rooke said. "This isn't in the scr—"

He bit his lip before he uttered the damning word. The men around him were muttering uneasily. Abruptly Rooke shouldered a path out. He did not have to feign grimness or worry. For the first time in his acting career, he felt it.

The officers in the HQ geodesic were sweating. They stared stupefied at their blacked-out consoles of tiny lights. To Rooke's query, the baffled answer was:

"We just don't know, sir. Someone's cut the beams. We can't get a thing in or out of the producer's office in the Pentagon."

Somewhere to the west, Rooke heard gunfire.

The genuine kind.

—2—

Rooke said, "Keep trying the Pentagon. I'll—" The responsibility choked him up a moment. "—have to send one of you to find out who's doing that shooting."

One of the officers, a Major, carefully studied his nails. "Uh, sir?"

"Yes?"

"Isn't it true that all contracts of principals require no participation in actual hostilities except in the event of accidental direct confrontation?"

Damn stage lawyer! Rooke recalled the clause. In the unlikely event of pseudo-combatants actually coming to blows, accidental or otherwise, the job of investigating the altercation, and the implicit risk of doing same, fell to the CO. It was one of the penalties, if you wished to call it that, of the leading role.

Rooke felt a moment of hot hostility toward his fellow thespians. Then it passed. His belief in the principle of the union contract was too deep and abiding to allow for more than temporary anger. Loyalty did not prevent him from being frightened, though.

"Has anyone seen Colonel Greene?" he asked.

Eyebrows lifted. Another Major coughed. Nervously Rooke amended:

"That is, I meant to say, Aaron?"

"Think I saw him down at the Mess getting his morning injection, sir."

"Uh, thanks. I'll try to get back quickly with some intelligence."

Rooke rushed down the hill. He regretted his last slip in the HQ geodesic. It revealed the extreme state of his nerves to his co-workers of lesser billing.

Enlisted men were signed, processed and paid by serial number. Therefore they used their real names, except when called upon for character bits. But the officers, because they were more frequently dealing with press people like Pierre Pell, knew each other both by real names and role names assigned for the campaign. Which name a man employed depended upon his proximity to the representatives of the news media. An officer who slipped up and forgot his script name in a live interview, for example— he could not count upon his post-hyp block to help him since all the news people were aware of the realities and did not come under the heading "outsiders"—could be assured of never working in another commercial war again. So disconcerted was Rooke by what had happened that he had lapsed the other way. The lesser officers were probably wishing they had not auditioned for their parts.

Rooke entered the O-Mess geodesic and bypassed the short queue waiting for morning vitamin hypos administered by the medico-nutritionists. He searched the O-Mess for Aaron Peskin.

A first-generation descendant of a United Kingdom family, Peskin was a first rate mimic. As a result, he had won hands down in competition for the role of Rooke's aide, Colonel Googie Greene, a bespectacled, gumchewing, wisecracking officer from the borough of Brooklyn:

"—yeh, when I was just fourteen awreddy and loinin' about da boids and da bees from Shoiley—"

"Googie, may I see you right away?" said Rooke, beside the table where Peskin was having his morning breakfast cubes.

"Jeez, we godda fire boinin' or somepin', General?"

"Outside, please. Quickly."

Once into the light of the now-risen sun, Rooke explained the devastating developments of the last few minutes. Peskin's face lost its mugger's elasticity. When he spoke, the accent which he had been practicing in the O-Mess and which made him a favorite when he wisecracked with newsmen on the air, was gone, replaced by a light flavoring of his natural British:

"You mean, Greg old boy, we may have to expose ourselves to fire?"

"It's in my contract," Rooke said heavily. "And as my aide, in yours."

"Crikey! What happens to Operation Oconomowoc?"

"Issue orders to hold positions until we get back. Then meet me at the motor pool. And bring your sidearm."

Peskin's sandy eyebrows quirked. "What do we do for ammunition?"

"The only place they have ammunition is in Washington. But maybe whoever is doing the shooting doesn't know that."

Ten minutes later, Peskin came running across the pool yard. He hopped in the staff vehicle. He advanced the

There's No Vinism Like Chauvinism

knobbed levers and shot the car forward on short airbursts.

The vehicle hovered past a line of sentries. Rooke could see that the men were perturbed, uncertain. The cluster watching Pierre Pell's interview had doubtless passed the word that something unusual was happening. Rooke lounged uneasily in the tonneau while Peskin maneuvered the staff car through a clump of maple trees, then held it cautiously on the shoulder of a sunlit, four-lane, non-magnetized country road.

A light haze to the westward seemed to hang on the horizon, veiling the menace of inscrutable Oconomowoc from sight and comprehension.

"Not a thing stirring, old boy," Peskin said.

"Take it to the right. Slowly. We'll go half a mile and turn back. Unless we find something."

Rooke sincerely hoped they did not. The tight-mouthed, death-defying commander of the UDEF forces was a role only. An image projected to three hundred million Americans who, in their packed vertical cities, found release in the emotional catharsis of fierce partisanship with the armies on either side of the various commercial wars which had uncontrollably wracked the U.S. (so it was made to seem) for more than twenty years.

Out of three hundred million, perhaps one hundred and fifty thousand principals, bits, extras, scripters, producers, newsmen and members of ancillary service organizations such as The Combat Actor's Studio, were in on the secret of how the national sanity, at long last, was being precariously maintained. None of the hundred and fifty thousand odd, however, escaped the ministrations of the medico-hyp practitioners employed by the Pentagon before and after each run.

The technique was faultless. There had never been a single recorded case of a blabber who was able to talk about the realities to anyone clearly an outsider.

Naturally the commercial wars were excoriated in press and pulpit, and seemed ghastly happenings if you listened to the lip-service on the outside. Now, Rooke reflected as the air vehicle hissed along, this one was actually becoming ghastly, and he was on the inside.

"Bit of smoke curling up behind that ditch, old boy," Peskin murmured.

Glancing out of the bubble, Rooke saw it. The thin thread of black rose against the blue Wisconsin sky just beyond a deserted farmhouse. Civvies were always hastily evacuated at the eleventh hour to leave a Staging Zone clear. This action, billed as humane, was chiefly practical. No news ever left a Staging Zone except through authorized channels. The Pierre Pells checked in every six months for post-hypnos, too. Thus those who might carry unauthorized news outside by shank's mare were rushed from the battle's path by the airtruck-load at the start.

Cautiously Peskin geared down the staff vehicle. Rooke tensed to jump out and investigate. Suddenly he had a vision of Mary Lu's face. Delicately heart-shaped, cornflower-eyed, passion-lipped.

The words were comfortable, easy to call to mind because he had read them aloud, jeeringly, several times during the arguments about conflicting careers which had preceded the divorce. Her personal flacks had ghosted them for a handout. Ironically, Mary Lu had turned up as his opposite number in this campaign. She was the third woman ever to land such a major role. ("I can go to the top, Greg!" she had said. "I can! But not hitched to a quivering jealous baby like you. And once I do go to the top, I'll hamstring you, not to mention that ruthless, greedy union of yours!")

Rooke was glad that the Master Warscript had called for her surrender, as CO of the AMMA fighting forces, in the Battle of Plankinton Avenue. He hoped she was safe in her prisoner's compound back in Milwaukee. He realized he hadn't been so sentimental about her in quite a while. But today's situation had brought him back to essentials.

"Look at that, would you!" Peskin whistled.

A UDEF-marked FF lay upside down on its turret on the other side of the drainage ditch. The treads reflected the sun. Peskin and Rooke approached gingerly. The stench of a gasoline fire penetrated the grassy heat of the overgrown meadow. A redbird flew past above. Rooke extended his hand.

"Force field off?" Peskin said.

Rooke moved his hand ahead further, into empty air.

"Think so. Come on."

The two officers worked their way carefully through

milkweed and tall tasselled ryegrass, around to the far side of the smoldering FF. Rooke attempted to grasp one of the hand mounts to brace himself so he might peer up inside the gutted turret where a few flames still flickered. The metal was too hot to touch. Peskin let out a yell.

"Greg! They left one. Ours!"

Whirling, Rooke raced through the weeds. Peskin pressed a palm over his mouth. The sight was not pleasant.

Sprawled on his back over a rotted log lay a UDEF soldier costumed as a Tech Sergeant. A tiny blue plastic object was pinned to the corpse's blouse. Three messy, very final bullet holes had turned to black clotted spots up near his left breast pocket.

"What do you suppose happened to the other two on the patrol?" Peskin asked.

"Must have taken them along."

"But Greg—sweet Elizabeth! The patrols aren't warlike."

"Only from the air." Rooke unpinned the plastic object. "Only when the networks train their cameras from their newsplanes. Then the patrols look warlike. They—" Rooke stopped in mid-sentence.

The significance of the object in his hand registered. It was a soft poly trinket, molded into the shape of a certain kind of headgear once worn by farmers' wives. For the first time, some of Rooke's confusion was cut away by sheer anger.

"Recognize this, Aaron?"

"Weren't some of the margies wearing them on their berets in Milwaukee?"

"Yes. The Blubonnet Brigade."

Rooke shielded his eyes against the morning sun. He peered into the mysterious distance where Oconomowoc lay hidden.

"Aaron, it must be true. Tanzy has blown a fuse. Somehow, contact with the Pentagon producer has been blacked out and for one insane reason or another, this battle area has been turned into a real—"

A rising whroosh interrupted him. He and Peskin spun. "Some bloke's trying to steal the bus!" Peskin squalled. The men went running.

The thief, however, was clearly unskilled in the operation of an air vehicle. As their boots slapped the concrete,

Rooke and Peskin heard curses of frustrated confusion. A spiky-headed silhouette loomed inside the bubble.

"Take him on this side, Aaron, I'll get him from the other!" Rooke sprinted around the scooped cowl. The thief glanced up. As they pried up the bubble clamps, Rooke had the wild impression that they were about to lay hands on a scarecrow.

"Get the hell out of there, mate!" Peskin gave the would-be thief a biff in the ear. With a cry the man tumbled from the bubble, knocking Rooke to the pavement.

When Rooke recovered, Peskin was covering both of them with his empty sidearm, upon whose butt his hand looked shaky and untrained.

As he leaped up and took two paces back, Gregory Rooke had the eerie feeling that he had seen the thief before. The thief was elderly. He wore once-natty navy blue coveralls bearing the tag of a leading mail order firm, a matching light blue shirt and high-top work shoes. His hair was a wild, messy, grayed tangle.

The thief groaned, rolled over. Then his brown eyes popped wide behind his steel-rim spectacles.

"Greg! Aaron baby! Holy moley, are you a sight! I mean—it's me."

"Blooming spy for the AMMA doublecrossers—" Peskin began.

Rooke seized his arm. "No, hang on. It's our referee."

"That's right, that's right!" the thief exclaimed, on his feet and busy peeling gobs of putty from his cheeks.

Lumps of it came away from the side of his head, rendering his ears hairless. He stuffed his glasses, then his fright wig into the capacious coverall pockets. He stood before them twenty years younger, a thin, nervous man with hawk features and upset eyes.

"Charlie Ripallo, you remember me, I was in Milwaukee over that rehearsal time dispute." From another of his pockets, he fished first a transistor radio, then an embossed, forgeproof plastic card which stated that he was indeed *Chas. C. Ripallo, Authorized Referee, Actor's Fairness (Central Div.)*.

Rooke said, "Aaron, you can put up the gun."

"Dunno, old boy. Certainly it's our union. But what's he doing way out here?"

"I can explain that," Ripallo said. He fingered his cheeks, where several large bruises bloomed now the putty was off. "See these? I was out tramping the roads this morning in this damn rube get-up they handed me for this cornpone war, and three guys in an unmarked aircar jumped me and beat the hell out of me."

Rooke glowered, used his thumb. "The same kind who turned over our FF patrol, kidnapped two of our boys and shot a third one dead?"

"Shot!" Ripallo's sly Mediterranean face bleached. "Man, they're not playing Monopoly, are they? The guys who jumped me had themselves tricked up to look like some of Crazy Tanzy's guerillas. But I recognized two of them. Shep Swenson and Moe Gatch. Those names mean anything to you?"

Ransacking his memory, Rooke said, "Moe Gatch is chief referee for the other side, isn't he?"

Ripallo nodded. "He is to the union playing the AMMA crowd what I am to you fellas—the place you holler if something's not kosher in the contract. The only trouble is, those birds have altogether flipped. I heard 'em mumbling after they threw me out into a ditch—I was walking toward your camp when I saw the car standing empty, by the way. Anyway, I think those guys have got Crazy Tanzy hooked on some kind of stim juice back there in Oconomowoc. And they're stockpiling real guns and ammo fast as they can."

Peskin swallowed. "You mean, old boy, this is turning into a—a genuine war?"

"Looks that way."

"Bloody margies!"

"You still haven't got it yet," Ripallo said. "We aren't up against the AMMA crowd as such. That's a front. Their part. This is a union thing. Us—Actor's Fairness—against them, ACVA. The drift I get is, somebody has decided right in the middle of the run that ACVA has been on the losing side in too many of these commercial wars. They mean to call a halt. Some rabble-rouser who's big in their union escaped from Milwaukee and is over there in Oconomowoc stirring them up."

A cloud passed over the sun. Rooke had a premonition, scowled. "Do you happen to know the sex of this rabble-rouser, Charlie?"

"That's a funny thing. It's a female broad."

"She wouldn't have been one of the principals for AMMA, would she?"

In his turn, Ripallo tumbled. "You don't mean top dog in this gig? Yeah, I did hear that. Also that she really hates Fairness' insides. Bet it's the same one you're thinking about."

Wandering over to the shoulder, Rooke leaned in the shade of a huge elm. He shook his head, which throbbed.

"I should have heeded the warnings." He glanced up, noticed both men watching him, explained, "In addition to choice remarks about my acting inability, the lady of whom I'm thinking once treated me to several long lectures, the substance of which was, Actor's Fairness is an octopus swallowing all the goodies, while the poor American Congress of Variety Artists, of which she was a patriotic and reasonably powerful member, being the Philly area governor, always got handed the less choice roles. Now, apparently, she's decided to do something about it. I'm speaking of Mary Lu Beth, also operating in this campaign under the name of Major General Lynn ("Old Leatherboots") Lucky. The CO for AMMA."

Thinking of the corpse over in the ryegrass, he added in a glum tone, "Also my ex-wife."

—3—

In mufti and highly apprehensive, Rooke barely heard the reduction in the scream of the turbines. Scarcely ten minutes had passed since the commercial V-liner had risen from the Greater Milwaukee port. Now they were arriving.

That the situation was extraordinary was evidenced by a single fact. Rooke and Ripallo were the only passengers in all of the two hundred and forty cabin seats. High-ups in Fedair had lifted the customary ban on commercial traffic in or out of a Staging Zone so that the two men might attend the hastily-called bargaining session.

The Loop's two hundred story higher rises were coming into view below. Face pressed to the solex glass, Rooke wondered what the opposition hoped to gain by a meeting. Besides the chance to hurl insults, of course. In commercial war history, there was no precedent for what had occurred today.

Still, if they were talking, they would not be firing up near Oconomowoc. Firing, for God's sake! Live ammo! The notion was both ludicrous and terrifying.

On the air trip down from Greater Milwaukee, the horizon had been aglow with lights all the way. The Metromichigania Area as the media hustlers referred to it was populated by some fifty seven million people. Even far to the eastward, on the water, the little bungalows on their pilings in the aqurbs combined their many tiny window lamps to turn the midnight bright as noon.

The V-liner began to descend more rapidly.

Rooke felt slightly out of contact with reality. Things had simply happened too fast.

Shortly after they had returned from their scouting expedition, a message came through from the producer at the Pentagon. The AMMA—correction, ACVA—resistance had momentarily turned off whatever device had been concocted to block the beams, and the single transmission which got through was from the producer. The message requested two representatives of Actor's Fairness to attend the 12:30 A.M. negotiations; Fedair clearance was available for the emergency flight.

Rooke had left Peskin in what both men somewhat hysterically referred to as command. He had ordered Peskin to conceal the corpse which was resting under a tarp in the staff vehicle. Hiding the corpse was necessary to prevent panic from setting in. When Rooke and Ripallo left at sunset, an uneasy silence prevailed over camp and countryside. Since ACVA had called for the negotiations, presumably the union could keep its unhinged dupes such as Tanzy in check. But there was no guarantee.

Rooke shook Ripallo, who had a remarkable faculty for sleeping with his mouth open, even in trying times. A slender, coffee-skinned man carrying a brief bag was the only person waiting for them in the windy light of the V-port atop the one hundred and eighty fifth floor of the Merchandise Monolith. Southeast, a massed light cluster in Soldier's Square Mile indicated a partisan war rally in progress.

"Hello, Putney," Rooke said as he came down the ramp. "Are you the one on deck tonight?"

Putney George nodded. He seemed tired. "One senior counsel from each union was invited. Those are ACVA's terms, incidentally. They certainly must have some aces showing up north. They're being firm, even dictatorial about the ground rules. You should have seen the snide 'gram they sent to the exec producer."

"Gonna be someone here from the Pentagon?" Ripallo inquired sleepily.

The lawyer nodded again. "If it's any consolation, fellows, I gather Washington is more upset than you are about the possibility of real conflict."

"It's distinctly more than a possibility," Rooke said as they entered the tube. He described the corpse. Putney George listened in disbelief, then tactfully raised the issue of Rooke's ex-wife:

"Can you handle her, Greg? Cool her down some? She's being very vocal."

"I couldn't handle her when we were married. How can I now?"

Sounding annoyed, Ripallo said, "Well, you better think of a way."

Normal pedestrian traffic flowed on the third street level as they left the tube and entered an aircab which the lawyer had waiting. Even this late in the evening, vehicular traffic was stupendous. It took them twenty minutes to travel the few blocks to The Conrad Cloud House, in whose Pizzicato Room the bargaining session was to be held.

On one clotted street corner where they were slowed to a standstill, a fiery-cheeked partisan orator was haranguing a crowd of cheering, stamping, whistling, applauding margarine supporters:

"—and I ask you, I ask you, folks," came the orator's amplified roar, "what is the fifth freedom? Tell me!"

"Freedom from cholesterol!" came the thundering reply.

In an opposite lane, a sound truck with directional horns rolled past. It muffled the orator's speech with a special jingle in march tempo. Rooke felt a tingling but fleeting thrill of pride at the stirring music. He could hear little of the lyric, sung by a massed chorus, but he did catch the rhyming of "spoilers" with "corn-oilers" before the speaker incited his emotional audience to charge the sound truck, overturn it and set it afire.

No luckless driver scrambled from the cab, Rooke saw through the rear window. A drone unit, then. In the brief interval before traffic commenced moving again, Rooke watched the attackers fall back, then begin to drift listlessly away. Most were smiling.

The cathartic effect had prevailed again. It was precisely this effect which tended to keep marital hostility, preteen sex experimentation, job mobility psychoses and a thousand other social ills within the range of the manageable. It was this cathartic effect with which his darling ex-wife was tampering. Indeed, she was tampering with the precarious stability of the national good. The union struggle might obscure or even destroy the usefulness of commercial wars. Curse her parochial eyes!

They finally arrived. Passing under the marquee of The Conrad Cloud House, Rooke noticed a newsflash strip jerking its message along the facade of a building opposite.

—ALL COMMUNICATIONS WITH WISCONSIN BATTLE AREA STILL COMPLETELY CUT OFF.

*** YELLOWS SCORE IMPRESSIVE GAINS ON NEARLY ALL FRONTS FOR 15TH STRAIGHT WEEK. PEKING PREDICTS VICTORY.

*** SIEGE OF SAMARKAND ENTERS 958TH DAY WITH SPORADIC FIGHTING BOTH SIDES AS YELLOWS UNVEIL NEW SCHEME FOR GROWING VEGETABLES IN SAND, INSURING FOOD SUPPLY FOR CITY'S DEFENDERS.

*** FIELD MARSHAL NIKOL GRIMINSHOVICH KILLED AT AGE 37 IN KREMLIN FALL. FAMED "BATTLEFIELD BABY" BORN TWO MINUTES BEFORE OUTBREAK OF RED-YELLOW CONFLICT 37 YEARS AG—

Ripallo tugged his arm. Rooke followed the other men. Bemused, he had been watching the flasher stories without really seeing them. He was losing his alertness. He must make an effort to recover. Toughness, that was all Mary Lu venerated.

The men rode silently to the ninety second floor. Rooke tried to get his field commander image back in shape by scowling at the tube's closed semicylindrical door. An ominous-looking group awaited them inside the Pizzicato Room, to one side of a green-draped table.

A man seated at the head of the table rose, snuffing out a cigar in the table chute. "Gentlemen, good evening," said the man, as armed guards supplied by the Hotel Security Director slammed and barred the doors from the outside. "Was your flight, uh, pleasant?"

"We have no comment at the present time," said Putney George automatically.

The hostility in the meeting room was thicker than thick. Representing the American Congress of Variety Artists, and all glaring, were three persons. A mummified senior counsel. A slovenly, adder-eyed fat man, Moe Gatch. And in the center, slapping her riding crop lightly on the baize, Mary Lu.

As Rooke assumed his seat, he twitched the corners of his mouth to indicate that her showing up in her tight-fitting, star-shouldered battle jacket, battle trousers and battle boots, all of glossy black leather, was a bit much. No response. He might have been smiling at a pretty stranger, for all the expression on Mary Lu's—dammit, he had to admit it—poignantly remembered face.

After taking two capsules and screwing back the cap of the vial and giving a slight belch, the man at the head unfolded a blue-covered sheaf of papers. The mellow yet commanding voice which had made Desmond Cecil-Vidor Thatcher one of the most successful senior producers in the Pentagon now carried a faint quaver.

"Gentlemen and, uh, ladies, I have before me a brief prepared by senior counsel for the American Congress of Variety Artists in which certain demands are enumerated, together with a declaration that unless these demands are fully met by certain of us gathered here tonight, the contractual players currently engaged in Production Forty-Two, Sub-agreement Two, will foment and carry out armed hostilities against the contractual players represented by Sub-agreement One, the purpose being to force—"

Ripallo lunged up, glaring at Moe Gatch. "We already seen some of your rotten hostilities. We can play that game too!"

Gatch sniggered. "With that bunch of uniformed pansies you got? Pfaugh!"

"For God's sake, Charlie, sit down," whispered Putney George.

Ripallo, however, would not be silenced. "Mr. Producer, Greg Rooke here and I, we found this dead actor this afternoon, shot to death by some of these terrorist goons who are now pretending to sit down here like decent citizens—"

While Ripallo was orating, Rooke saw his ex-wife blink. Then she bent to whisper in Gatch's ear.

The obese man waved her question away as too ridiculous. Mary Lu slapped her crop on the table. The noise startled Ripallo. His mouth open in mid-defamation, he did not recover quickly enough. The stars on Mary Lu's epaulets caught the light from the ceiling panels as she rose and overrode Ripallo's feeble comeback with her smoky voice:

"Mr. Producer, ACVA categorically denies these ridiculous charges by the representative of Actor's Fairness."

This time Rooke himself felt prodded. "Listen here, Mary Lu—"

"My name," she said, "is Miss Beth to you."

"Your name is Mary Lu Wolowiczniski if you want to be painfully truthful about it!"

"You foul, absolute son of a—"

The ACVA counsel pounded the table. "Contempt citation! Contempt citation!"

"—and if you think you're so good at denying the evidence of your own damn eyes," Rooke was shouting, "then you come up to our camp and take a look at the dead man we've got there. Right now take a look at these marks on Charlie Ripallo's face which were inflicted in a beating by the same people, I don't doubt who shot that man of ours and kidnapped two others. I mean Mr. Gatch and his cronies."

Desmond C-V. Thatcher hammered for order. Mary Lu whispered to Gatch a second time. The latter bellowed, "I tol' you, babydoll, I was cooped up all afternoon with one of them little cuties from Tanzy's processing line. She was showing me her, uh, pat slicing mechanism."

The referee's lecherous leer substituted a lesser crime for a greater. Mary Lu bit her lip while the producer continued to plead for order.

Though she was a willful little twist, hot tempered and ambitious as hell, and though Rooke disliked her actively at the moment, yet deep within his heart he found himself harboring a trace of gooey sadness over their parting.

Mary Lu finally said, "The word of Mr. Gatch that

these accusations are false is sufficient evidence for me, Mr. Producer."

"This is the most outrageous travesty—" began Putney George.

"Oh go take a flying—" began Moe Gatch.

"Everyone, God damn it," Thatcher suddenly bawled, "calm *down*!"

Tense silence.

Thatcher brushed back his magnificent white hair with two palms, glanced from face to face reprovingly, said:

"I think this immature outburst on all your parts indicates that you fail to recognize the gravity of the situation. We are dealing not with partisan complaints, but with the very tissue of national mental health. I will not demean your intelligences—" His glare at Gatch indicated that that gentleman might be an exception. "—with a recitation of the difficult straits in which our nation—and remember, we are all Americans—found itself at the end of a decade of prolonged armed conflict between the Reds and the Yellows. We were at peace. We were prosperous. We were not involved directly in the major conflict. Yet our domestic problems, in this ostensibly idyllic time, became mountainous. I will not insult you with statistics on the rising crime rates, divorce rates, insanity rates, and the scores of other social difficulties which had to be forcefully met to prevent this nation from becoming a jungle."

Ignoring his notes, Thatcher continued fluently and with increasing emotion:

"We can all be proud that it was our profession, the theatrical profession, which offered the solution. We were the people both technically and temperamentally equipped to provide our restless, multiplying population with the kind of emotional diversion and release which thinkers more profound than I had reluctantly concluded was necessary to maintain the public order in our country. Your government and mine recognized this when it secretly called in the presidents of those two great corporations, The Dr. Landers Camera Company and Yellow Box, Ltd., and won their agreement to a limited, pre-planned conflict between rival work and sales forces."

Listening, Rooke once more felt a stir of patriotism. Probably to keep them mindful of the structure which unrestrained union feuding could so easily tear down, Thatch-

There's No Vinism Like Chauvinism 163

er sketched in the details of the evolution from street riots between actors disguised as photographic blue and white collar workers to battlefield combats between actors playing members of the private security forces hired by gigantic corporations and trade associations. Thatcher spoke with much verve and passion. Cynically, Rooke supposed he was eager to settle this because he was rumored about to step up to a cabinet post—either Secretary of Internal Well Being, the big one, or Secretary of News Management. Rooke watched his emotionless wife as he listened.

"—only a complex and super-secret alliance between the entertainment and communications industries, between the highest echelons of big business, the American College of Medico-hypnotists and your government, prevented the great population of America from becoming a neurotic, distracted, frustrated, purposeless—"

"Mr. Producer," Putney George interrupted. Thatcher glowered. "I respectfully suggest that we deal not with historical generalities but comtemporary specifics. Admittedly we have a critical and unprecedented situation here. As senior counsel for Actor's Fairness, I am empowered to suggest that the President, as a condition for negotiations, immediately neutralize the present Staging Zone by dispatching federal troops—"

Opposition counsel wheezed, "What federal troops?"

"Surely," Putney George said, "there must be some federal troops left in the United States. They can't all be assigned overseas."

"I'm afraid they are," Thatcher said. "As a representative of the Joint Chiefs of Production, I am in a position to know that, except for callow trainees, our entire military manpower is committed to perimeter defense of the Russo-Chinese conflict zone."

"The suggestion is ridiculous anyway," said Mary Lu. With a malevolent glance in Rooke's direction and an okaying nod from Gatch, she continued, "We don't need gobbledygook and government intervention. All we want is a fair shake."

"Like what?" Ripallo asked.

"A guaranteed agreement that members of ACVA will be on the winning side in all future commercial wars at least fifty percent of the time."

Rooke, Putney and Ripallo exchanged thunderstruck looks.

"We will never agree to that," said Putney with firmness.

"Then," said Mary Lu, slapping her riding crop against her leather breeches, "all we are doing here is wasting our damn time. Gentlemen?"

The ACVA delegation got up and walked out.

Producer Thatcher breathed, "Oh my God," called a ten minute recess after the fact, and swallowed another brace of pills for whatever other ills were contributing to the pained and horrified expression on his face.

—4—

Thatcher rushed around the table to Rooke's place.

"Greg, this ball is in your court. Can you go after her? She's leading them by the nose."

"I'm not so sure of that."

"What?"

"Did you notice how she seemed to be taking all her cues from that Gatch?"

"No, frankly I didn't. The point is, Greg, we must get them all back here. At least to sit down and finish the discussion so we know where we—"

Normally a fellow with the best of tempers, Putney George had been irritated in just the proper spot. He interrupted in a shout:

"Mr. Producer, Actor's Fairness will never, I repeat, never, submit to that ridiculous fifty-fifty proposal."

"Shouldn't you at least contact your president and your board before you make such a flat assertion?" Thatcher fired back.

"Mr. Producer!" Putney rushed on. "That Actor's Fairness is more often than not chosen to fulfill the winner's role is vivid testimony that we would be fools to negotiate on that point. Vivid testimony, I say, that ours is a craft union of professional artists, not floozy industrial show hoofers, jugglers, trampolinists, exotics and other mediocre talents unable to register any emotion save the stereotyped leer of the evil—"

"Now I kind of resent that, Putney," Rooke found himself interrupting in turn. "Mary Lu may have a nasty temper, but she's a good actress, not a floozy."

"Who's side ya on?" Ripallo cried.

Thatcher said, "We'll talk about it later. The problem now is to keep talking, period."

Hastily he summoned one of the armed guards. "Pick up your spyphone and peep those people who just walked out. I assume they haven't left the hotel. I want to know where they are."

The guard rushed from the room. Thatcher turned toward the three men, all arguing at the top of their lungs, and in a still louder voice demanded that they shut up. They did.

"Now, Greg," said the Pentagon representative puffily, "if they have not left the building, I'm putting it up to you to go after them, especially your wife, and bring them back to the bargaining table."

"Ah," Ripallo said, gesturing, "she's got those jerks brainwashed."

Gregory Rooke had a sudden impulse to punch Ripallo in the nose. He refrained, both because temper would not help, and because he suddenly felt compelled to learn who was actually in control of the ACVA delegation.

Mary Lu seemed the spokesman, true. Yet her whispered colloquy with Moe Gatch regarding the shot actor cast some doubt on her full awareness of what was happening. Rooke would have bet money Mary Lu had not been dissembling. He knew her well enough to know when she was performing, and when not.

He also felt a certain sudden and inexplicable urge to vindicate her.

Or himself?

Either way, he had thought enough of her at one time to propose. Ripallo and Putney George had already dumped her into a category with that oaf Gatch. He felt compelled to discover whether this was so, and the Mary Lu of yore no more. He hoped not. To Thatcher he promised:

"Mr. Producer, I'll do my best."

Shortly the armed guard buzzed. Thatcher lit up the panel for half a minute, then hustled back to the table, a tiredly hopeful smile on his face.

"Evidently it's as I suspected. The walkout was a bit of a bluff, gentlemen. All three adjourned to the cocktail bar on forty four. They're obviously waiting. It's our move. Go to it, Greg."

The tube ride downward seemed endless. Two commercial travellers off for a late flight were commenting about the mysterious shortage of war news from Wisconsin. Lest they recognize his face, Rooke quickly drew out his shades and donned them. Consequently, he could see virtually nothing when he stepped beneath the large sign suspended at the end of the arcade on the forty fourth floor. The sign's lettering, formed of glowing tubes, penetrated the green darkness produced by his glasses—*The Walt Bisbee Heirs present THE WONDERFUL WORLD OF LIBATIONS*—but for a moment nothing else did. He whipped off the shades again and peered around in the gloom.

That the bar concession was almost a huge hall had been cleverly disguised by a variety of divider panels and animation exhibits secluded in nooks and subtly lighted. As Rooke passed one such while searching the tables, an electronic Omar Khayyam with an Anglo-Saxon countenance rolled forward on casters, was hit with a spotlight and began to recite verses from *The Rubaiyat* to music. Rooke was so tense, he half swung to take a punch at an imagined adversary before he caught on.

"Why, it's the General. The General looks a little nervous, don't he, counsel?"

The voice issued from a dark cove booth. Rooke stepped closer. Moe Gatch had spoken, in an insulting tone. The attorney kept his peace. There was a third drinking globe hovering half an inch off the table, but Mary Lu was absent.

"I'll deal with Miss Beth, if you don't mind, Gatch."

"Suit yourself. Question is, will she deal with you?"

Rooke checked a sarcastic comment. Though Gatch might be a power in ACVA, he was clearly a hooligan. Baiting him would serve no purpose. Grubby gangster! He looked as untidy physically as he clearly was mentally. Beneath his sport cape Gatch wore an upper of a cheap, flashy lemon shade, fitting tightly around his neck where it appeared to darken to a deeper ring of the same hue. How did Mary Lu become involved with seedy sorts who didn't even bathe? Rooke wondered, facing around.

Just then Mary Lu emerged from beneath an electronic

wall figure representing Maude Frickert tippling from her cane; Maude's left hand held a sign animated by polarized light, bearing the legend *Gals*. Rooke was gratified to see that his ex-wife had had the good sense to don a mufti cape and shades. The cape was long enough to conceal all but the tips of her military boots. That was all they needed—recognition of General Lynn Lucky by the patrons.

As soon as Mary Lu saw him standing in her path to the table, she switched her course. She marched to the bar and took a stool beneath an animated wall display featuring an electronic figure with curly hair and pince nez. The figure periodically chanted a chorus of *The Maine Stein Song* through a megaphone.

The back of Mary Lu's cape remained snobbishly turned toward Rooke as the latter hitched himself onto the bucket chair beside hers. He adjusted the levarod so the air column lifted him a bit higher, to proper drinking position. He pressed a mixing stud. He slid a bill into the adjacent slot and waited until the highball revolved into serving position before he spoke.

"Am I allowed to buy you one, Mary Lu? Or are you just resting?"

As Rooke peeled the polyfilm from the top of his globe, Mary Lu swivelled around.

"I told you, Rooke. It's Miss Beth. I told you that. I am sitting here because you were so rude as to stand directly in my path."

Rooke looked rueful. "Miss Beth. God, that sounds ridiculous between people who have—well, anyway." A surreptitious glance. No one was within three stools. "How did you happen to pull that escape in Milwaukee? You could have gotten hurt."

"Listen to my ex faking worry, would you! Greg sweetest, you certainly weren't so solicitous when we were married. Your appeal is phony, dear. As always, your acting stinks. May I ask why you followed us?"

"Followed you," he corrected, his temper approaching the boil. "Gatch and that mummy lawyer you can have."

"Was it to softsoap us into more bargaining under impossible terms?"

"Why did you and your friends hang around here?" he

countered slyly. "To give our side the opportunity to grovel while we persuaded you to come back?"

Mary Lu bit her lip. "Well, the strategy wasn't my idea. Gatch's. He's so obvious. I was prepared to walk all the way out."

"Mr. Gatch, along with some friends, beat up Charlie Ripallo and possibly shot and killed at least one member of Actor's Fairness."

The actress guffawed in ladylike fashion behind her hand. "Oh, stop."

"Mary L—Miss Beth, I mean it. A man is dead."

"But Gatch swore—" She depressed a stud. "I believe I will have a drink. But I'll pay for it myself. Greg, you're lying in your teeth, just the way you lied about that canteen chippy when we were married and you were a looie in Romley's Raiders in the Invasion of Detroit. You stood on your flat feet—how are your flat feet, by the way?"

Morosely he drank his thiamine-laced highball. "Still flat. They still hurt like hades in combat boots. Concerning that so-called canteen chippy, I did not lie and she was no chippy, she was geriatric, practically. You'll refuse to believe this too, but I was worried about you when I heard you had escaped."

"I'll bet you were! You admit I'm a real threat!"

"Not that way, dammit. Worried you might—get hurt. How did you manage it?"

Briskly Mary Lu downed her drink in a nonstop gulp. Rooke was tempted to say something about living the part of the colorful lady commander, refrained. "That, my bucko," she told him finally, "is my little secret. But I'll be glad to tell you the why. I was enraged by the behavior of those Milwaukee compound guards. All, I might point out, members of Actor's Fairness."

"Heck, you know either union accumulates some scum among the extras, Mary Lu."

No eruption anent the name. He felt he was getting through. More astonishing, he was oddly gratified that he was. His suspicious side cautioned care, wariness, and tried to mentally catalogue all the fierce differences leading to the divorce filing. Somehow, his face inches from hers at the noisy musical bar, the catalogue would not fall together.

There's No Vinism Like Chauvinism

Mary Lu's ripe lower lip was quivering.

"You should have seen this fat swine of a guard, Greg. Immediately he discovered I was a district governor of ACVA, do you know what he did? He and a bunch of plug-ugly pals surrounded me. They began buzzing me with their stim prods. Not enough to hurt, not then. This leading swine reached into his credit case, pulled out his Actor's Fairness membership card and made me kiss it. Kiss it! The plastic tasted horrible. You know I've always felt you people in Fairness believed you were so damn superior, and that one callous act by that brute in Milwaukee showed me. Frankly, it set me off."

Now Rooke sympathized, his own anger directed parallel to hers. "Callous isn't the word for an act like that. What you should have done was screamed for the union referee."

"But darling, I knew the union referee, Moe Gatch, would be getting ready for the finale out around Oconomowoc, don't you see?"

"Of course! Naturally you'd read the—" He lowered his voice. "—Warscript."

"Yes, and seen the same humiliating role forced upon ACVA people one more time. When I told that porkjowled guard that I wanted him to 'gram the referee, he laughed. I tell you, there's a lot that goes on behind the back of the stuffed shirts in the Washington front office."

"I can certainly see that." Rooke nodded. "Something ought to be done."

"Exactly. I did it. I won't tell you details, because that would incriminate some people on your side. But it seems there's a tidy little under-the-ledge trade in special favors going on. You know the type of situation. A family emergency arises but the contract says you can't leave until the engagement ends on such and such a date. Well, doors can be opened. They were for me, in return for a perfectly barbarous percent of some residuals. But I made it to Oconomowoc, right enough—was within a mile of your campsite once, too. I filed my complaint with Gatch, which is all I intended to do before giving myself up. And then, Gatch flabbergasted me."

"How so?"

"He said he too was fed up with ACVA getting second choice all the time, and why didn't we do a bit of impromptu scriptwriting? At firsht—" Mary Lu was not all martinet; the one drink she had swigged was beginning to render her speech slurry now and then. "—I had some, you know, patriotic reservations. Then I thought—oh, what the hell? Fairness has rubbed our noses in it long enough. Mr. Gatch is not as dense as he might look or act, Gregory. He opened his portfolio and showed us some schematics for a contraption to neutralize the outside communications beams, seal off the area while we made our demands. And he had a decanter full of stim juice, one drop of which would make that old hothead, Tanzy, putty. It certainly did. Gatch was the one who called for these negotiations, too. But undersatnd." Stiff upper lip, determined glance. "I was all for it. He seemed to have several friends with him, all equally enthusiastic about the cause, and before very long, we were rewriting the script."

Over his shoulder, Rooke noticed with some slight alarm that the ACVA counsel still sat with his drink, but Gatch had left the booth and disappeared.

"Whose idea was it to have Tanzy shoot the cow?" Rooke asked.

"Gatch's. I thought it was coarse and cruel myself. But effective."

"Then you actually haven't engineered what has happened, Mary Lu, Gatch has?"

"Well, I guess you could shay—say—" She flicked at the collar of her cape, struggling to maintain an air of composure. "Damn you, Gregory, I haven't had a drop shince —since I went into the field. And no dinner tonight, either. Here you've gone and gotten me all gooey and plastered, made me tell—"

The sudden appearance of two bleached spots in Mary Lu's cheeks caused Rooke to stiffen. Mary Lu's pretty eyes attempted to focus somewhere past his shoulder. He spun his bucket just as Moe Gatch popped out from behind an ornamental pillar across the aisle, reaching for Mary Lu's throat region:

"I heard a few things, General. I think you're talking too damn mu—what's wrong with you, Rooke, ya chump?"

Cold in his middle, Rooke pointed.

"The question is, Gatch, what's wrong with you?"

The shaking tip of Rooke's index finger indicated the place where, by virtue of Gatch's energetic lean and reach as he attempted to throttle Mary Lu, the collar of his lemon-colored upper pulled away from his throat, exposing again the saffron-colored ring Rooke had noticed earlier. This time, however, there was no trick play of lights and reflections to account for it.

Blundering back, Gatch whipped his left hand up to his collar. He checked the move too late. "Who are you?" Rooke shouted, and leaped.

His fingers dug in savagely at Gatch's collar line, ripped—

A heartbeat later, strips of something like human flesh and hair hung from Rooke's right hand. Disbelieving, he turned the microthin molded material over. He saw the true nature of the stuff on the obverse—it was an undyed, undoctored off-white color, with a fine pattern of tiny trademarks in parallel lines. The pattern was unbroken except for the breathing apertures and other openings.

Whipping the material up to his eyes, Rooke read one of the trademarks:

PLIO-MA-KUP®
*A Mondanto Chemical
Substance*
(Max Vector Division)

"God in heaven!" came Mary Lu's breathy voice. "Greg, he, he's a—"

The apparition in front of them whipped out a genuine pistol from somewhere beneath its cape. The half of the apparition's face yet unpeeled belonged to Moe Gatch.

The other, authentic half, totally hairless and of a deep saffron hue, belonged to a high-cheeked, glittering-eyed and sinister Oriental.

"You will pay for your addled behavior, Miss Beth," hissed the apparition, grabbing Mary Lu by the arm and wrenching her to his side.

Stupefied, Rooke swung a fist. A bar steward rushing from among the tables to investigate the nature of the fuss inadvertently ran between Rooke and the Oriental just as the latter's gun went off. The steward reeled, shot to death. Only the man's accidental intervention saved Rooke's life.

Dragging Mary Lu and scattering tables and glassware behind, the Oriental ran into the arcade and disappeared into a tube. In pursuit, Rooke slammed back from the tube's semicylindrical door as it rotated shut. He shook with shock. He had almost had his hands clipped off at the wrists by the shutting door.

"I don't understand this," came the voice of the ACVA counsel who had chased Rooke into the arcade. "Who was that? Where is the real Mr. Gatch?"

"Probably dead. Keep quiet." Rooke bowled past him, back into the lounge. He indexed the button for the Hotel Security Staff, next put in a call to the civil police. Then he and the unstrung counsel took the tube back up to the Pizzicatto Room.

As there were no indicator lights above the entrances to the tubes, Rooke did not know whether the Oriental had gone up or down. He did not know where to begin looking for the Oriental and Mary Lu either. The Security Staff would know the hotel better anyway. But he was deathly afraid for Mary Lu's safety, which now, inexplicably, mattered very, very much. He prayed the Staff would get their licensed spyphones to work peeping promptly.

In an hour a representative of the Staff dolefully announced that the missing pair was nowhere in The Conrad Cloud House. Thatcher sent for a multi-channel set which was installed in a corner of the site of the aborted negotiations, and the group spent the remaining hours of the night sucking on caffeine cubes and waiting for ominous Bulletins.

None came.

At four, the civil police reported that the pair had evidently escaped the city. Thatcher used his influence to contact Fedair's top echelon. Yes, an unidentified V-craft had slipped out of the Chicago pattern at approximately 2:48 A.M., heading northwest.

"Oconomowoc!" said Rooke in a ghastly whisper.

"—expose at last the rotten hypocrisy of your own leaders, from first-hand, personal experience in—"

Blear-eyed, Rooke turned toward the noise. On the top left monitor of the panel of nine screens, a bizarre scene was unfolding. A wild-eyed, disarrayed man on a soapbox was haranguing a crowd on a street. Thatcher frantically fooled with the gain until he got the volume so that he, Rooke, Putney George, Ripallo and the ACVA attorney who had been weeping intermittently for several hours, might hear.

"I know that face," Thatcher was saying as he watched the scarecrow image on the monitor. "I'm sure I know that face."

"Which channel is carrying that?" Rooke said. "Where does it come from?"

"This is the hotel's own internal ID channel, Greg. The camera is trained on the main entrance, street level."

"Get him down, get him down, you people!" a civil policeman at the fringe of the pictured crowd was crying.

"Push him off the box! Push him off!" other voices chorused.

"—know what I'm talking about!" the orator exclaimed, windmilling his arms in excitement. "I've been there! It's all a fraud, a sham, these commercial wars. Nothing but fakery!"

The man had the same coked-up look of runaway insanity as the man himself had observed on the screened face of J. Burton Tanzy at dawn. Rooke's mind reeled under the impact of this latest turn of events.

The screaming muckraker on the soapbox was Pierre Pell.

—5—

Gregory Rooke gripped the gasketing at the hatchway edges and held on, arms throbbing, to keep from being blown out. A chron dial high on the control panel and seen at the oblique through his shatterproof goggles showed the time as 09:17. An adjacent indicator registered the chopper's altitude at nine hundred and fifty feet and dropping.

A quartet of smokestacks, the construction-grade high-impact material carefully scored and soot-sprayed to give a quaint and charming effect of ancient brick, seemed to rush at the chopper with frightening speed. Permanently radiating vertical letters on each stack spelled out identical messages:

G
o
l
d
e
n
G
l
o

The cheery yellow signs somehow lent a sinister cast to the wide, innocent blue arc of Wisconsin sky beyond.

Rooke was surviving on sheer tension energy alone. His belly hurt fiercely. He was totally unskilled in matters of this kind. Of course he was willing, considering Mary Lu's plight.

Thatcher and Putney George had V-linered back to Lake Oconomowoc with Rooke and Ripallo shortly after sunrise. Thatcher had consulted the battlefield computers and received a printout which indicated that a quick, guerilla-type strike was the only means of saving the situation. The others had drawn lots.

Rooke had merely watched. He had already volunteered to lead the party, following a short, but hot-tempered hassle with Thatcher in which the Pentagon producer had ultimately promised triple time wages and, most important, full death benefits from the Fairness pension fund to be paid to Mary Lu regardless of their divorced status in the event Rooke did not survive.

Below, howling, fist-shaking clots of ACVA-AMMA irregulars jammed the streets of Oconomowoc over which they were passing rapidly. The holdouts were clearly surprised by this non-scripted appearance of the huge chopper. Noting their fury, Rooke grew more and more tense.

He moved his left leg gingerly as he squatted in the chopper's open hatch. The holstered press of one of the genuine, loaded, nontheatrical sidearms commandeered by Thatcher God knew where unnerved him. He kept fearing the thing would go off and remove part of his leg.

The chopper pilot began adjusting levers.

"Stand by, gents. It's gonna be a helluva bump."

Thus far the pebbled roof of the Golden-Glo plant, nestled among several other suitably antiqued factory structures, was unoccupied. Behind Rooke, Aaron Peskin shoved his goggles up in place. In his Colonel Googie Greene voice he kept reminding himself aloud:

"It's a perfoimance, nuttin' else. Bluff is half da battle. A perfoimance."

The actor who had drawn the second lot to fill out the trio, a spindly bit player, had fainted when he lost, or won, depending on how you looked at it. Consequently Putney George had volunteered. George, Rooke had reflected, was truly a loyal Fairness man. He had had no reason for returning to the Staging Zone with the others, except patriotism. The same went for his volunteering. Putney George apparently felt Fairness had been stabbed in the back.

Rooke wasn't all that loyal about it. He was concerned about his ex-wife. Had he not been, he would have been unable to maintain even a semblance of the flint-eyed, stern-jawed expression of a fearless CO. They were, after all, actors going against international assassins.

The chopper dropped down and down. Above the rotor clangor, the vocal fury of the holdouts could now be heard as they ran every which way in the streets below. To Rooke it appeared that the chopper would smash into the cornice of the Golden-Glo plant. The pilot cursed, much perspiration on his face. Rooke gripped the hatchway edges all the harder, prepared to jump out at impact.

A courier had been dispatched to the Pentagon by Thatcher, informing the President and Joint Chiefs of Production that, with their major war going successfully at last, the commanders of the Peking bloc had evidently seen fit to release and assign espionage agents to infiltrate the ranks of U.S. commercial war players, with the dimly-guessed purpose of exposing the whole fabric of the trickery and dealing a shatter-blow to U.S. morale.

Perhaps the U.S. was Peking's next target if the anti-Russ campaign went well, as it had been for the past months. Perhaps this blow to morale was but the first stage of the softening process. How the Yellow spies had penetrated the secret of the commercial wars was unknown at the moment, but since that side warred in earnest, it was assumed by Thatcher that their intelligence agents knew all the tricks. There was no doubt that the Yellows had discovered a means of overturning post-hyp blocks. But of course the devils had always been experts at that type of cerebral tampering.

Vivid testimony to their expertise was the appearance of Pierre Pell. Shortly after the scene witnessed on the monitor in the hotel by Rooke and the others, Pell had leaped from the soapbox and fled into the disconcerted crowd. Pell was still at large somewhere in Greater Chicagoland.

Clearly Pierre Pell had been kidnapped. He had vanished from the UDEF bivouac at about the time Peskin and Rooke discovered the burned-out FF yesterday. He had probably been un-blocked and shipped out of the Staging Zone—or perhaps fetched along by the false Gatch and then released—to spread his message of dissension. Anyway, it was plain that Pierre Pell no longer had any mental barriers to prevent him from speaking about the great fiction to people not directly connected with commercial wars. Rather than worry about Pell, however, Thatcher and the Pentagon had agreed that a strike must be made at the heart of the conspiracy, Oconomowoc.

During the last few seconds the chopper had descended practically to the roof of the Golden-Glo plant. In the factory's truck yard directly below, Rooke saw hundreds of ACVA-AMMA troops queued up outside a bay from which they were being issued firearms. Putney George craned over Rooke's shoulder, howled above the roar:

"Bet those are bandoliers of live stuff. Bet they airdropped it from drone planes coming in over Canada."

A throaty ker-*chow*, a puff of smoke, and the chopper reeled under a metallic whang. Horrified, Rooke looked out through a small circle in the fuselage into blue sky. The tiny circle was a scant inch or two above his hard-gripping left glove.

A few more shots were fired from the yard, and several sections of a margarine packing crate were hurled fruitlessly upward, only to fall short. Then the chopper was past the cornice, its skids hitting the pebbled roof and dragging along, slewing the craft around.

"Out, out!" The pilot's voice rose to a squeak. "I ain't taking any more bullets. Lotsa luck."

Rooke leaped to the roof. Aaron Peskin followed. Putney George had hardly begun his deplaning when the pilot, a civilian mercenary, gunned hard. The upward jerk of the chopper spilled Putney combat boots over shock helmet. He managed to pull the big twine-tied, paper-wrapped bale out with him, however. It landed with a clump.

Rooke peered through the anti-glare lenses. Carefully he withdrew his sidearm and pointed the muzzle at a small house-like structure between two of the smokestacks.

"That looks like a stairway."

The chopper whirled away up into the blue sky, leaving the trio alone but fortunately out of sight of the cursing, shouting men in the truck yard below. Among the profanities and obscenities which drifted up to them, Rooke heard cries of, "On the roof, the roof!"

Putney George shuddered visibly. "I've never heard actors so furious before."

"Well," Peskin said, "da bums loined—ah, shove that, I'm so blighty scared I can't keep it up. Guess they've hated Fairness' guts a long time. They finally got a chance to do—"

"The—the—door—"

Rooke's gauntlet was flung out, pointing. Why, oh why, hadn't he finished Pharmacy H.S.? He was as brave as the next, but the next was not very brave, not in Fairness.

Peskin and Putney George had their backs toward the door panel in the small roofhouse. That door panel now displayed a tiny but widening vertical crack of black between edge and jamb. Putney and Peskin continued to exchange remarks designed to reassure one another. Rooke grabbed the shoulders of their combat jackets to spin them around.

"The door's opening. Get your guns out!"

Putney and Peskin managed to whirl as the door crashed backward. Carrying a large, round-muzzled portable riot cannon, the sinister Oriental whom Rooke had unmasked in the cocktail bar lunged into the light. From the neck downward he was still costumed, though rather grubbily and showing the wrinkles, as Moe Gatch. He had, however, peeled the remaining half of his phony face off in the interim.

"Put up your guns, Americans!" The agent's saffron pate glowed in the sunlight. Behind, thrusting up from the stairwell, came a tough-looking cadre of half a dozen younger Orientals who made no pretense; they were garbed in the flimsy gray disposable paper jackets and pantaloons of the People's Army.

"Tell them to stop shoving in the rear," the leader said over his shoulder.

"It is the plant president, honorable one," said a Sergeant just emerging.

"I instructed you to keep that imbecile in his office, with the girl."

"But he went into a frenzy upon learning we had captured butter trusters, honorable one."

Muzzle to muzzle, the thespian trio faced the fully armed hard core of the Chinese espionage team on the sunlit roof. Tense seconds passed while no one fired. The Orientals refrained, Rooke felt, because they knew they had already won, and could take their time. Rooke refrained out of a firm conviction that he would be finished if he pulled the trigger, since he would probably miss but the Orientals would not.

One lucky thing. The passing reference to a girl indicated that Mary Lu might be safe. Somehow, that made all the fright knotting his belly and the perspiration steaming up his goggles worth it.

A raucous voice gave a bleat, a curse, from the dark stairwell. The leader swung his head a bit more. His fierce yellow nose was in profile as he hissed, "I do not want that unruly, witless dupe fumbling out here to spoil—"

Too late. Against the growing shrieks, screams, catcalls and curses from the ACVA-AMMA troops in the yard below, a more strident voice broke through:

"Where are they? Where are the unprintable cow-lovers?"

And, nearly knocking the Oriental leader off balance, J. Burton Tanzy, wing collar askew, hair flying, fought his way onto the roof.

There's No Vinism Like Chauvinism 179

Lurching along rubber-legged, Tanzy dug his left hand into his clothing. He drew out a polished flask, took a hasty swig. Shoulder to shoulder with Rooke, Peskin whispered against the former's helmet, "They're feeding him stim juice, right enough. The UK ought never have pulled out of the China Trade. That liquid hell has proved worse than the poppy."

The Oriental leader chewed his thin lower lip, then adjusted what Rooke was afraid was a cocking mechanism on his riot cannon. He swung the muzzle slightly to the oblique so that it pointed at the wobbling back of the margarine magnate who was tottering toward the trio, his right hand outstretched. The Oriental's eyes grew even more narrow as he sighted.

Tanzy came on, coked and giggling maniacally. Extended before him on the palm of his hand was a glistening yellow pound brick of Golden-Glo.

"Now, you devils! Burton Tanzy is going to have his revenge. Burton Tanzy is going to watch each of you swallow some of this—" He hiccoughed violently.

"Tanzy, be careful!" Rooke said. "They're going to shoot you in the back."

"—swallow some of this superior, refined, emulsified vegetable oil. Hah! Won't that flay the butter trusters? Their own toadies forced to down a vegetable oil product? I'm sick of the restrictions!" Tanzy shrieked, his mind unhinged, all knowledge evidently gone that AMMA participation in the commercial war had been wholly voluntary and worked out at cordial bargaining sessions. "The high-priced spread, the high-priced spread! Why can't we just come out and tell the truth, the truth about that rotten but—"

There was a *blam*.

Watching the Oriental's trigger finger, Rooke had had a slight warning. He had seen the knuckle flesh pale perceptibly. In that desperate second, when all his cerebral processes broke down and fear and adrenalin took over, Rooke brought his right boot flying up, hoping to kick poor Tanzy out of the path of death as the riot cannon went off.

His boot-tip caught Tanzy's outstretched hand. The margarine manufacturer flailed and fell, an instant after the margarine block, kicked from below like a football, shot up into the air.

The riot cannon chattered again. Rooke and his companions fell flat from instinct. An equally powerful instinct was at work on the other side. Pairs of startled human eyes followed the upward path of the kicked margarine for a fraction of a second. Rooke—he never knew how or why, later—reacted. Perhaps professionalism ran deeper than fear after all:

"Charge!"

Sidearms spitting, the counsel and Aaron Peskin followed Rooke's headlong lunge. Once you got the hang of it, the sidearm was remarkably easy to fire. The noise was thunderous.

The espionage agents in their paper uniforms managed a few return efforts. But having glanced upward collectively at the margarine was their undoing. Rooke's bullets mowed down three. Peskin and Putney George accounted for another four between them. Then only the leader remained, scarcely feet from the charging Rooke now. But fully in control as he swung the riot cannon around to remove Rooke's head with a single blast.

The trio's attack and the exchange of fire had taken less than seconds. From out of the sun, the brick of Golden-Glo completed its flight path and splattered soundly against the leader's shaved pate.

"Aieeee!"

The Oriental jerked the riot cannon trigger as sunny yellow table spread oozed down around his ears. The light blow on the head threw him off balance just enough, however. The cannon projectile puffed past Rooke to smash blocks from the cornice behind. Rooke had the presence of mind to realize that someone might wish to question the chief spy later. He thrust his sidearm against the Oriental's left leg and fired.

He disarmed the chief spy after he fell. Laughing uproariously in surprise and disbelief, Peskin and Putney George rushed among the other agents, disarming them also. No more Chinese appeared on the stairwell.

"Kill the cow-lovers! Kill the cow-lovers! Kill the cow-lovers!"

The chant, unnoticed by Rooke during the shooting, now beat on his ears with fresh force and menace. Putney

George rushed to the cornice, turned back. "My God! They're coming up the walls after us!"

As if it were a cue, a grappling hook, then another, caught the cornice with solid chunks. Rooke hurried in that direction.

Directly below the first hook, a member of ACVA, a genuine sidearm gripped in his teeth, was climbing a flexible ladder. Anti-Fairness hostility shone in his eyes.

"We're finished, Greg," Putney George shuddered. "They'll tear us apart."

Rooke had to admit it looked that way. Desperately he scanned the roof. Then he saw it.

"The bale! You forgot the bale!"

The men seemed all thumbs getting the twine and wrapping off. But at last, just as the scalp of the first ACVA performer rose above the cornice, Rooke and the others unwrapped the leaflets. They were jerry-printed, the ink still smeary on the front cover where the numerals 50/50 blazed forth in 36-point fluorescent green ink. In his right hand Rooke carried the one other object from the bale as Putney George and Peskin began raining handfuls of leaflets down onto the hundreds in the truck yard.

The actor who had climbed all the way up already had a leg over and resting on the cornice. He was aiming his sidearm at Rooke's forehead.

"Take a leaflet, a leaflet!" Rooke waved one and prepared to dodge another bullet if necessary. "Actor's Fairness agrees! Fifty-fifty split on the winning roles from now on!"

"It's a trick," snarled the cornice gunman.

"No it isn't, here! The President of Fairness is waiting to talk to anyone of you, any spokesman! You can talk to him if you want. Here, the dial's set for the Vegas band. Just get someone to turn off whatever machine is scrambling the beam signals and you'll be able to talk to him." Rooke held the tiny transmitter inches from the quavering muzzle of the ACVA professional. In rather superior fashion Rooke managed to feel that the man was obviously as inexperienced with firearms. Correction, had been.

The brows of the actor on the cornice beetled briefly. In order to take the transmitter, he had to put away his sidearm. Mercifully, he did.

In minutes, it was all over.

The scrambler was located, turned off and discreetly smashed. The mellow voice of Frankie Clan III, amplified to blare out over the yard, assured the ACVA members that the offer was genuine. The sidearms disappeared.

Putney George found the room where the two UDEF soldiers, kidnapped while on patrol, had been kept prisoner. In Burton Tanzy's executive office—the margarine magnate tried to block Rooke's entrance by madly running a motorized pallet-load of cartoned Golden-Glo down the corridor: he was carried out frothing—Rooke found Mary Lu, shaken, alarmed, but unbruised. The Oriental leader had been on the point of administering a punishment with some bamboo slivers when the unexpected chopper arrived.

To Rooke's surprise and delight, Mary Lu actually hugged him.

Next came a hasty script conference, with Rooke acting for Fairness, Mary Lu for ACVA. Rooke pointed out that despite the new agreement, to alter the outcome of the current engagement would not be playing by the rules. Delighted by the copy of the leaflet she was reading, Mary Lu offered no objection whatever.

So, at 11:02, the UDEF banner was raised from the Golden-Glo flagpole, per script. The flag fluttered out, rich blue satin and crested with two smiling tots with tumblers of milk rampant upon a field of milking machines and udders.

Even the ACVA-AMMA troops, fingers messy with the green ink of the leaflets, waved and cheered. A new day of concord was at hand. The correspondent from the Fee BC was the first to reach Oconomowoc and flash the word to a breathless nation.

The one clear and present danger still remaining was the deranged, unblocked Pell, at large somewhere in Greater Chicagoland and armed with a catastrophic weapon which could undo them all.

The truth.

—6—

Eastward from the esplanade, lamps in the aqurb bungalows glowed like cheerful fireflies in the twilight. Behind, the Greater Chicagoland skyline reared impressively.

There's No Vinism Like Chauvinism

A news flimsy went skittering past, left by some pedestrian who had abandoned the strollways to the nippy autumn wind. Part of a headline proclaimed that the Reds were on the advance, the Yellows had suffered a series of calamitous setbacks.

A large, new Unioncarb Preferred Paste stone on Mary Lu's third finger caught a random beam from the sinking sun. The new ring glittered as she snuggled close beside Rooke, eagerly waiting for him to open the cover page of the Master Warscript which had been flown out to them Saturday by the assigned producer.

"Who is it, darling?" Mary Lu said before the opening cover had quite revealed it.

Seated on the right, Rooke had the advantage: "Wow! PanEastern against the Harold Hughes, Junior, Airfleet." Rooke glanced into his new, yet comfortingly familiar, wife's face. "Sonic dogfights! This looks like a dandy."

"I've never flown a plane," Mary Lu said.

"Neither have I. The stunters'll do the actual flying. We'll just appear on the cut-in cameras. Think of the great process effects. There we'll be, in the studio cockpit, and it'll look just like—"

"Two dollars for a cuppa java for a vet, mister?"

The bum's whine interrupted their excited talk. Against the dim twilight radiance in the sky, the bum was a sorry, decrepit figure in a filthy cape, with unclipped hair and untrimmed fingernails. He extended a palsied hand. Rooke goggled.

"Pierre!"

The bum blinked. "You know me?"

"Of course! You're Pierre Pell, former GBC correspondent. Nobody's seen you for months! Where have you been?"

"I don' know you," the bum said, with suspicion. "How about two dollars for a cuppa java, mac?"

Mary Lu shivered. "Oh, the poor creature."

Rooke leaped up. "Pierre, let us find a doctor for you."

" 'G'wan!" The derelict flailed loose, almost savagely. "'M okay. Gotta mission. Gotta tell people—wars 'r phony. Being tricked. Been wandering streets days 'n days. Nobody'll listen. They laugh. Throw rocks. Beat me up. Won' listen. They won' listen 'r believe." Large crocodile tears began to trickle down his cheeks, glistening in the fall sunset.

"Help him, darling," Mary Lu whispered, warm against Rooke's side.

"Yes, he needs—" Rooke stiffened. Pierre licked his lips. He seemed to peer right through them at nowhere. *Sotto voce*, Rooke said, "His collar."

Mary Lu looked, stifled a gasp. Pierre seemed oblivious. A telltale saffron ring was briefly visible. Rooke pressed his lips against her ear so the bum would not hear:

"Probably realizes he's failed his mission and it's driven him mad."

"Casualties," the false Pierre was saying with a sweeping gesture at the skyline. "Three hunner million casualties of th' wars of d'ception. Gotta tell the truth. Tell 'm they're all casualties."

"God," Rooke breathed with a shudder, "war is hell. Even our kind."

"War's a lozzy phony deal," Pierre exclaimed.

With only the briefest twinge of conscience Rooke said, "War is also, unfortunately, necessary. That's where you people made your mistake. You still expend your energies in real killing. We've learned." He indicated the skyline. "They've learned too, even though they don't suspect a thing. That's why nobody would listen. That's why the government gave up looking for you a long time ago. Now get out of here."

"No money for a cuppa java for a vet?"

"No."

Pseudo-Pierre shrugged, blinked, burped. "Well, thas' showbiz," he said vaguely, as he turned and tottered away into the failing light.

Recidivism Preferred

> Here is an example of two science fiction cliches in the hands of a talented writer: (1) all utopias have their price; and (2) a new form of social control. It may remind you of a scene from ONE FLEW OVER THE CUCKOO'S NEST.

Randolf Mellors ("rhymes with cellars," the newsmagazine *Tempis* in its cover story three weeks before declaring bankruptcy) was the world's greatest thief. His only difficulty as a subject for scrutiny here is that circumstances beyond his control had made him completely uninteresting. That is to say, dull.

But if you had asked the passengers in the long, mighty and black Excalibur Special Touring Saloon roaring down County Highway #2 one hellish hot day during state fair season whether Randolf Mellors was unworthy of study, all three, including that small, mummified, pink-scalped one in the immense tonneau, would have exchanged sly sneers which implied that if you thought Randolf Mellors was dull, you just didn't understand the workings of free-wheeling capitalism.

Still, Randolf Mellors was a soulless hulk of his former conniving self.

Oh, the looks were there. He had aged somewhat. The sleek hair was a trifle gray. But the willowy frame remained. And the inscrutable mouth, the long jaw, the cadaverous frame. But suavity is a difficult item to merchandise while selling turnip greens, baking soda, peanuts, baby bottle brushes and bunion remedies from behind a counter of pine planks in a crossroads store.

Where oh where, was the Raffles-like glory of yesteryear?

Who cared? Certainly, not the inhabitants of Pineville. To them Randolf Mellors was only a slightly suspicious (because strange) outlander who had come shuffling through the gumtrees one spring morning. An outlander who had gradually oriented himself to Pineville community life or what passed for it around eight shanties, two stores and a gas pump. He kept his mouth shut and made no mistakes when totalling up purchases in Larry Lumpkin's Emporium.

Larry Lumpkin liked to show dogs, hunt possum and play checkers. Hiring a clerk gave him the time, now he was getting along. (Of course that wasn't any accident either. His psychic readiness to employ a clerk had been thoroughly researched.)

But other than the relaxing Larry Lumpkin, who, in all honesty, cared a hang about Randolf Mellors? Certainly not Vinnie Mudgerock, for whom Randolf was just now wrapping up a bolt of muslin and a pack of disposable diapers. Outside on the pine sidewalk Vinnie Mudgerock's wee month-old infant reposed in a broken-down perambulator, sucking eagerly on a nutritionally deficient peppermint stick.

"That be all, Miz Mudgerock?" inquired Randolf, wiping his hands on his apron. Randolf had always been a consumate actor. In Pineville he had managed to acquire a trace of the local dialect, which demonstrated conclusively that no matter how hard bureaucracy tried, bureaucracy could not win every hand. (As the three assorted inhabitants of the Excalibur Special Touring Saloon, a quarter of a mile out of town now, engine snarling, were hell-bent to prove.)

When Miz Mudgerock said that would be all, Randolf said, "Leave me carry this bundle out to the car for you."

"Why, thank you, Mr. Mellors." Miz Mudgerock gave him a yeasty smile.

Randolf Mellors, of course, found it impossible to smile. He did not know why. He also had a violent dislike of anyone who looked at him straight in the eye. He did not know why about this either, except that it made him want to start running. Further, he had periodic dreams in which he saw only one thing, a vast signboard in the rain, painted with three-foot letters reading:

Acme Lead Works.

Even including these three idiosyncrasies, however, the dullness of Randolf Mellors was reasonably total.

Distantly down County Highway #2 boiled fuming clouds of tan dust. Pineville dozed. The sky stretched blue and bright all the way to the state fairgrounds where Larry Lumpkin was doubtless engaged right now in a checker game, having left Randolf to mind the store. Randolf put the paper sack into the rear seat of Miz Mudgerock's dust-yellow flivver. Then he walked over to where the lady was picking up her infant from amongst gooey blankets.

While burping the smeared tot, Miz Mudgerock's mouth dropped open.

"Why, Mr. Mellors, you have the funniest look on your face."

"I do?" said a surprised Randolf.

"You sure do. What you lookin' at? That silly ole candy stick?"

"I guess I was," said Randolf, suddenly extremely nervous.

"You hongry or suthin? You looked like you wanted to chew up that ole peppermint sick just to bits."

"Hon . . . uh, hungry? No, er, not in the least." With a real feeling of terror Randolf Mellors said, most truthfully, "I loathe . . . er . . . don't like candy."

"You *are* a puzzler," said Miz Mudgerock. "Where'd you ever come from, to a place like this, anyhow?"

"Up north," Randolf, mortally terrified now. It was the best answer he could give, considering he didn't know the correct one.

The roar of the Excalibur Saloon grew thunderous. The dust cloud bloomed. A yellow hound narrowly avoided being jellied beneath the tires of the highway monster. Randolf Mellors wiped his hands furiously on his apron, as though he'd done something unsanitary. A view of the Acme Lead Works sign flashed on and off and in his head, for no apparent reason.

"Excuse me, Miz Mudgerock."

He quivered and plunged like a scared hare back into the cracker gloom of Larry Lumpkin's store. He stood with his back to the fly-specked plate glass in the diffused sunlight which filtered through it until he heard the flivver putt off up into the rolling hills. Once again he was face to face with the dreadful enigma of himself. The sensation was akin to staring at a newly wiped blackboard of the dimensions of the Great Wall of China. Only the deafening peal of Larry Lumpkin's jangling store bell prevented Randolf from plunging further into a morass of futile introspection.

The trio from the Excalibur Special Touring Saloon were certainly a sight.

The first tapped one mummified spat-clad foot and peered at Randolf from out small ratty eyes. The old gentleman wore an old-fashioned high collar and eye glasses on a black string, plus a pin stripe suit which even Randolf Mellors—somehow—knew was out of style. The small old gentleman's companions, however, were startling studies in what could either be termed the seedy or the raffish. Or worse.

There was a fat one, three hundred pounds, in a suit the size of a tent, that sported egg stains on its lapels. He had a tangled brown beard the size of a spade and a mass of wooly brown hair to match. His novelty was further heightened by the suggestion of alien life within this hairy mass.

His companion, an epicene youth hardly old enough to vote but possessing a head too big for the rest of him, appeared to stare inside himself, if that were possible, from behind like plate glass window spectacles. He looked as though he might unveil a hatchet from somewhere within his obviously rented chauffeur's uniform and go totally berserk any minute.

The little old mummy advanced. He studied the store, but had no time to speak before the behemoth with the brown beard pulled a whisky flask from his pocket, tilting back his head, and proceeding to pour booze down his throat while orgiastic shudders seized his immense person.

With surprising agility old mummyface danced across the store and slapped the flask out of the fat man's hands.

"All right, Dr. Kloog, that is sufficient. I warned you."

"But—my God—" gasped Dr. Kloog. "Seven hundred

miles cold turkey. Banner, you fiend, I've got to have a drink—"

"Which do you need most?" hissed mummyface. "Hooch or a paycheck?"

"Someday," Kloog threatened, "someday some college'll take me back and—(belch)." Dr. Kloog lowered his bovine head. "You win."

The cretinish prodigy in chauffeur's garb sniggered at his companions expense. The little addressed as Banner spun around on one of his patent leather toes and pointed a finger.

"As for you, Dr. Rumsgate, you're no better off than he is."

"It's just that the attitudes on vivisection in this country—" purred Dr. Rumsgate.

"That," said Banner with steel in his tone, "will be all."

Returning toward the counter and making a gesture which included the stupefied Mellors, he continued, "If you gentlemen will bear in mind that we're in a public place, and stop making exhibitions of yourselves, I'll proceed with my purchase." Glancing up at the shelves, he said, "Good morning, sir. I wonder if you could tell me how far it is to the state capital."

"State capital?" Randolf repeated. "That's a hundred miles west."

"Dear me," said Banner. "A wrong turn. I wonder, could you sell me a pack of cigarettes? Do you have Status? Ivory-tipped, if you please."

"No Status, no, sir," said Randolf, running his eyes over the shelves. "How about Board Chairmans? Wolfbaits? Big Cities? Sexos?"

"A pack of Board Chairmans will do." Randolf handed him the brightly lithographed cardboard container, accepted the twenty dollar bill without taking his eyes off the register, rang the sale and held out the change. Randolf blinked. Banner had already broken open his pack, turned his back, and was passing out the door, lighting a Board Chairman while his two flunkies flanked him.

Randolf stared for ten seconds at the nineteen dollars and fifty cents resting in his palm. The Acme Lead Works flashed behind his eyes, three feet high in the rain. Suddenly Randolf felt as though a sledge had knocked him in the head.

"Excuse me sir, but you forgot your change."

The expression on the mummified face of the little old man as he turned back into the store was maniacal. For a long moment he seemed frozen in a beam of sunlight, giggling and leering at his two scientific mates. He nudged each one in the ribs. Dr. Kloog snuffled like an elephant about to charge. Dr. Rumsgate rolled his eyes. Somewhere within Banner's shrunken ribcage a peculiar sound was building, a sound of crackling paper that passed for hysterical mirth. It came bursting from his scissors lips and he began to caper up and down.

"He's the one," Banner cackled. "Oh, mercy, yes, he is the one."

"Don't let's waste time," said Dr. Rumsgate, as though sadistically titillated.

"Grab him," said Dr. Kloog in a pant.

"Wait a minute, gentlemen—" Randolf began. "You're making a —"

Dr. Klogg, Dr. Rumsgate and Banner, all three, looked Randolf straight in the eye.

Something wild, like a whip, cracked in Randolf's head. He put one hand on the counter and vaulted.

He came down like a cat on the balls of its feet, perfectly poised, as though going off balconies and second stories were old stuff. One lithe hand whipped out. A silver gleam caught sunlight. Randolf crouched in the shadows near the magazine rack. He made small wicked circles in the air with the blade of the carving knife he'd ripped from a faded point of sale card.

"Stay back! I—I don't want any part of you three."

Dr. Rumsgate sniggered. "Automatic reaction. Partial breakthrough."

"Weak conditioning," nodded Dr. Kloog. "It'll be a cinch."

"Ah, God, to have the chance again," exclaimed Rumsgate, "after being de-licensed—"

"Keep quiet!" Banner snarled. They did. Banner tried to assume an ingratiating air before the tigerish man crouching beside a display of the July issue of *Hollywood Love Thrills and Confessions*. "My dear Mr. Mellors—"

"How do you know my name?"

"Never mind, Mr. Mellors, we know it. I want to assure you that—"

"Get out of this store before I do some carving."

"You're being extremely uncooperative. If you only knew—"

"Leave me alone," Randolf shouted suddenly, an odd, desperate sort of pleading note in his voice. Almost like a child he yelled, "I haven't done anything!"

"But my dear man," shrieked Banner, "that is precisely the trouble."

"*Get him!*" exclaimed Dr. Kloog, and launched himself through space.

The ambition of Dr. Kloog was considerably more elevated than his trajectory. One supple spring to the top of a cracker barrel by Randolf and Dr. Kloog found himself tangled in the magazine rack, *Hollywood Love Thrills and Confessions* raining down upon him in profusion. Dr. Rumsgate, apparently had an aversion for the physical. He hopped back and forth from one foot to the other, clapping his palms together as if he could not contain his excitement. Banner couldn't contain his excitement either, except that it achieved a somewhat more lethal nature. Its release took the form of curses, then physical blows rained upon the persons of the two scientists. By that time Randolf Mellors, raising his forearms to shield his head, had gone through the plate glass window of Larry Lumpkin's Emporium in one magnificent crashing leap.

"Oh, you wretched *bunglers*—!" Banner howled.

A smooth muffled roar filled the store. The gas pump disappared in a cloud of saffron dust. The Excalibur Special Touring Saloon began to weave up County Highway #2 at something near seventy, its course a continuous S-curve, as though a mortally terrified man were at the wheel. Which happened to be the case.

Dr. Kloog, peering through the fractured shards of glass, did a double take and caught hold of Banner's arm.

"Banner, hang on. Banner, don't punch me that way. He took the bus."

"—vile, unspeakable, bungling, wretched—"

"Ah, *ah!*" shrieked Dr. Rumsgate. "Yes, *yes*. Banner, the remote, the *remote!*"

"—unprintable, censorable, bowlderized *fools*, you'll never—"

Banner's eye blink rate suddenly accelerated. His breath hissed between his two thousand dollar New York City teeth. Then he let out a queer little chuckle.

"The remote! Why, of course! Poor Mellors. Been out of the city too long." From the inner breast pocket of his suit, he pulled a small electronic pack housed in plastic and covered with knobs, similar to the units used in a less advanced day to tune televisions across a room.

Unaware of the manipulations about to be committed, Randolf Mellors drove like hell over, around and through the execrable chuckholes and corduroy strips of the county road. Behind him a volcano of dust obscured the crossroads in the mirror, which was just as well. The horrid vision of staring eyes in the store's musky interior haunted him and brought unbearably cold sweat to every point on his body.

Next to him on the seat shone the fierce, naked brightness of the carving knife. Glancing at it, Randolf experienced a mysterious shudder of revulsion. He quickly rolled down the Excalibur's side window, steering with one hand and flung the weapon off into the pines.

A moment later he wondered just why he had thrown away his only means of defense.

His wonderment was transitory. The window began to roll itself up.

Randolf tried to crank it down manually. No go. He felt the Excalibur Special Touring Saloon begin to decelerate. He crushed the floor pedal all the way down. He swung the steering wheel in a full circle. It did not object. The Saloon, however, was now running in a perfectly straight line, corduroy and all, at slightly less than thirty miles per hour.

Next thing Randolf knew, the car nosed itself into a side road, threw itself into reverse and started to cruise placidly straight back toward the crossroads where three figures and a gas pump stood waiting.

Randolf flung himself to the other side of the car. But every exit including those in the tonneau, had been remotely locked. Helpless, sweat popping out all over his face, Randolf sat under the wheel and watched like a man hypnotized as the Touring Saloon rolled inexorably back to Lumpkin's store.

The brakes gave a faint squeak as it stopped in the dust. The three stranger surrounded the vehicle, whose doors now popped unlocked. Banner opened the one on the driver's side. He motioned in a most gentlemanly way for Randolf to climb out.

Terrified, Randolf asked: "W—what—please tell me what I've done."

"Nothing," said Banner, false teeth gleaming. "You're an unfortunate victim."

"The process," rumbled Dr. Kloog as he rummaged in the tonneau, "is called Socialization. You're social, that's all. Now where are my instruments?"

"Actually," came the voice of Dr. Rumsgate, from somewhere behind Mellors, "you'll really thank us after we—"

After? After *what?*

After the gleaming needle slid into the musculature of his shoulderblade, which was after he screwed his head around to stare at Dr. Rumsgate, who had sneaked up on him by opening the door directly to the rear of the driver's seat. Now Randolf's horrified gaze locked with the slightly mad eyes behind the window glass of spectacles. Randolf felt himself consumed by that gaze, swallowed by it. He tried to crawl from the vehicle. Somehow or other that devil Rumsgate had injected simple syrup into his veins.

And the simple syrup was spreading. His legs turned into it. Then his arms. When he tried to move, flee, escape, all he could do was ooze. He had no power left.

Most amazingly, it was raining inside the Excalibur Special Touring Saloon. Raining on Dr. Rumsgate's big head.

No, Randolf thought to himself, bemused now, gripped by a pleasant twilight lassitude, he doesn't have a head at all. On Rumsgate's shoulders sat the sign over the main gate of the Acme Lead Works, the Acme Lead Works in the rain in Sep . . .

In Septe . . .
In Septem . . .
September!

It burst from the back of the whirl of his mind: *September . . .*

Seven hundred and fifty thousand dollars stashed in a three-wheel ice cream truck labelled Yum-O FreezieTreats.

Pedalling away down the rainy road...

Ding-a-linging his bell in triumph.

Roadblock.

Federal men.

Vendor back from vacation, but too late, tri-wheeler stolen, too late to alter plan...

Worked anyway...

Greatest coup...

Until...

Pedalling, pedalling...

No reverse gears on FreezieTreats wagons...

Manacles...

Dark rooms...

Guilt, shouting guilt:

Yes (Randolf heard himself crying in that rainy September in the darkness of his mind) *yes, you sons of bitches, I foxed you again!*

Too bad (whispered ghost voices). *Too bad. So colorful.*

One of the last (went the whispering voices blowing through his dimming head). *The last, the last. The last of the great.*

Penological triumph (keened a ghost-choir). *Break down the walls. Rebuild the personality. Disassociate. Assimilate. Integrate.*

SOCIALIZE.

—reporting from geographical selector, chief (CHIEFCHIEFCHIEFCHIEF went the dark black echo down the fast-failing electrical paths of his reworked, muddled, tired head) *and we find* (FINDFINDFINDFIND) *ideal—readjustment—environment—Pine* (PINEPINEPINEPINE)—

For one virtually unbearable fraction of time Randolf Mellors stared again into the looming erudite eyes of the psychosocializer who had leaned over him in a room tiled in green and lowered the face mask for the submerging.

The eyes... *the eyes*...

Guilt.

Guilt.

GUILT!

They just couldn't make the eyes benevolent. Writhing (they had strapped him, he remembered in a roman candle burst of remembering) he saw the eyes blaze guilt which already, as the hormones and the enzymes and the catalyzers bubbled through him in the first moments of social metamorphosis, already he had come to loathe.

Guilt; he loathed guilt.

But you sonsofbitches (he shrieked before they gassed him all the way into being somebody else entirely) *you're making me so damn dull* (LL . . . LL . . . LL) . . .

At sundown, a great red sundown suggestive of far places waiting beyond the pine hills, the Excalibur Special Touring Saloon was parked on a bluff overlooking Lumpkin's crossroads store, but concealed behind a sufficient quantity of trees so that observation could be carried on discreetly. A panel in the rear fin had been opened, from which a spring steel trellis shot forth a powerful optical tube. Through this instrument Harlow B. C. Banner was now observing the interior of the store.

Distantly through the still, crisp air came the putt of a flivver. Banner clicked his false teeth in exultation.

"What's he doing now?" asked Dr. Kloog. In point of fact, Dr. Kloog actually said, "Wuzzydoonow?", as a result of the reward given him by Banner following the surreptitious re-direction of personality that took four hours. This reward was a fifth of premium Scotch whisky. Insatiable and triumphant, Dr. Kloog had also consumed a pint of rubbing alcohol out of the medical supplies. He was even now suggestively eyeing the tin of canned heat bubbling over which their dinner cooked.

"Writing a note," Chuckling, Banner screwed the lens adjustment so that he could peer more effectively inside Lumpkin's. "Wait, I'll be able to read in a minute—"

"Delicious," came the piping cry of Dr. Rumsgate somewhere within the tonneau of the vehicle. Dr. Rumsgate had not bothered to convert the tonneau back from an electronic operating pad into conventional seats. In fact it was his particular reward to be able to leave the pad up a while, and conduct some sort of procedure which Banner didn't care to inquire about.

"Just as I thought!" Banner exclaimed. "He's writing a farewell note to Lumpkin. Now he's coming out. Locking the store, and—oh-oh. Car pulling up. Blasted woman. Getting her buggy out, too."

"Bassids," belched Dr. Kloog, in reference to his former faculty colleagues. He gestured flamboyantly with his empty pint of spirits. "All bassids. Jus' because man geds delicen don' mean he don' know how 'just personality . . ."

"Don't pat yourself on the back," sneered Banner, furiously adjusting the eyepiece. "He was easy. After all, he had strong antisocial drives."

"Has," Kloog corrected with several lurches. " 'Z goddam bag."

Banner refused to pay further attention to his disreputable comrades. The scene captured within the circle of the lens fascinated him. Randolf Mellors had emerged from Lumpkin's Emporium just as Miz Mudgerock wheeled her perambulator up the sidewalk and kicked on the footbrake. Mellors was standing in the winy red sunlight, one thumb hooked rakishly in his belt, his other index finger through the eyelet of his coat, the coat over his shoulder.

Whatever the woman desired in the store, Mellors told her to get it herself, with an insolent jerk of his thumb. She scuttled out of sight. Glancing in all directions, Randolf Mellors leaned over the pram. In a twinkling he darted back popping half a peppermint stick into his mouth.

Even from high on the bluff Harlow B. C. Banner could hear a faint squall of protest. Mellors stepped off the sidewalk into the dust. He turned beside the gas pump and thumbed his nose at Lumpkin's. Then, swinging his coat and whistling, he walked up County Highway #2 into the sunset.

"He *smiled!*" Banner shrieked joyfully. "He actually *smiled!* Ah, in a month, maybe less, the crimes—the delicious crimes."

Banner snapped his fingers.

"All right, Kloog, Rumsgate—pack up! On to the next town. We've got that sex degenerate. I'll teach those bureaucrats!" Righteously, Banner shook his fist at the reddening pines. "Try to stamp out crime, will they? Try to adjust criminals into goodie-goodies, will they? Illegal or not, I'll show them they can't tamper with free enterprise—destroy what I built!"

"Wunnerful," said Dr. Kloog. "Wunnerful for me, wunnerful for you."

"You bet it's wonderful!" cried the little old mummy. "After ten years of bureaucracy—near bankruptcy—" He clamped hands on the oversized Kloog and his whole larcenous face was illumined. "—finally, *finally*, Banner Newspapers will once again have some news that's fit to print!"

Here Is Thy Sting

This may well be the finest science fiction story to come from John Jakes' typewriter. It is a successful attempt to use sf to deal with a most serious theme—that of death. Jakes worked on the story for more than two years, receiving suggestions from Joseph Elder and Damon Knight along the way. The interpretation of death in the story is theological: as with the phenomena of pain and evil, death is a purposeful stimulus to human endeavor. The fact that this subject is treated both intellectually and humorously is testimony to the writer's skill.

> *Sometimes, too, warmed by the fire, Shakespeare stayed downstairs all night . . .*
> *"Rest, rest, don't fight so," Judith whispered to him once.*
> *"I can't rest," he answered, "while the black beast waits for me."*
> —Robert Payne, *The Roaring Boys*

I

His brother came home from the Moon in an economy coffin, on a night when the meteorological bureau decided on rain. Something went wrong, as it frequently did. The April mist turned to a black, blinding downpour.

Through the shed's thick windows all peppered with rain, Cassius could just discern the vertical pillars of fire that grew thinner, thinner still, then flamed out. Rain hummed and slashed. It was a foul night for such a painful, intensely personal errand.

As the transport rocket settled into its concrete bed far

Here Is Thy Sting

out there, a dozen haul trucks raced from all directions toward its unfolding ramps. Then there seemed to be a collision. Headlamps tilted crazily. Men ran this way and that. A controller wigwagged his glowing red wands hysterically.

"Wild buncha cowboys," grumbled the Freight Customs official. "Next? Hey, you."

Parcels, crates, cylinders, drums were spilling down a dozen chutes from the rocket. Which was Timothy? Cassius turned from the window as the official called out again. He stepped up to the booth. The official's uniform was damp, wool-stinking. His expression was cross. Cassius recalled hearing the man ahead of him argue loudly with the official. He felt he should have chosen another queue, but it was too late.

"Okay, buddy, what's yours?"

"I'm picking up my brother," Cassius said.

The official mugged his disgust. "Oh for Christ's—the next shed is passenger, mister."

Cassius said, "You don't understand. My brother was —that is, he's dead. His body is on the rocket."

"Oh." The official blinked. "Name?"

"Cassius Andrews. Here's my News Guild card and my personal digit card if you need identification."

"His name, *his* name."

"The Reverend Timothy Andrews." Cassius tried to scan the upside-down manifest on the counter. "Maybe the shipment is listed under the Ecumenical Brothers. They paid his stipend at the Moon camp. He was stabbed trying to break up a knife fight between two miners, and the Brothers arranged to ship his—"

Reading down the lines, the official waved his hand to cut off the talk. Cassius felt sheepish. What did the man care about details of a family death? Nothing, of course.

When at last the official had ticked off the proper box with a checkmark and raised his dull eyes to stare through the wicket, he was no longer merely bored. He was plainly resentful. Of my mentioning dead people on such a miserable night? Cassius wondered.

"Mister," said the official, almost triumphantly, "whoever prepaid the body at Moonramp made a mistake. Underweighed by thirty-six pounds. There's extra duty due. Dozen point five credits."

Cassius fumbled inside his raincloak. "I'll be glad to pay it."

"You gotta see the adjustments manager. Three doors down. Next!"

The dismissal was so peremptory that Cassius, ordinarily a mild-tempered man, flushed. He was about to make a nasty retort. Then he recalled his own recurring dream. It tormented him twice or three times a week, regularly. He sighed and took the punched card from the official's hand.

Nobody liked to be bothered with death. Especially not in such rotten, depressing weather. Cassius could understand how the official felt.

Out another window he noticed that the haul truck tangle had been straightened out. The various crates, parcels and containers were being picked up by vehicles operated by the big and small land freight companies. Cassius had made no arrangements for transportation. But he'd been told that an on-the-spot haul service was for hire. He intended to send Timothy's body directly to the headquarters of the Brothers, where they had a chapel.

After the memorial service due all missionaries who died violent deaths—and many still did, in the lonely, rotgut-happy camps on the Moon and around Marsville Basin—Timothy would be interred with their mother and father in the family plot in Virginia. Timothy would have been, let's see, two years younger than Cassius, who was forty-two.

The adjustments manager had another client. Cassius lingered in the hall. He tried to restrain his impatience, then his anger. He had the eerie feeling that official stupidity was conspiring against him to delay the obligatory reunion with his brother.

After spending twenty minutes in the corridor, Cassius finally got to see the adjustments manager. The idiot didn't have the appropriate rate book at hand. That took another five minutes. Cassius paid the excess duty, watched while the manager thumbed his Hilton Bank card into a machine along with a triplicate invoice. At last he was given a pass to the pickup area.

He walked across the concrete in the slashing rain. He had already decided that he'd damn well write an exposé

Here Is Thy Sting

of the mismanagement at Dulles Interplanetary and file it with the feature editor. God, there was enough bumbling bureaucracy here for ten exposés.

But the idea passed quickly.

Long ago Cassius had recognized and accepted his limitations. He seldom dreamed any more of writing *the* news story or series that would catapult him to fame.

There were eight hundred reporters on the *Capitol World Truth*. Out of these, a top dozen received around eighteen thousand credits per annum. They wrote all the exposé pieces of the type Cassius was imagining. Cassius himself earned a meager twelve two, almost the Guild minimum. Years ago he'd been slotted by Hughgenine, his editor, as a competent man to handle a section of the vast Alexandria suburban news beat. The Parent and Teaching Machine Association was his bailiwick. Well, he said to himself, the exposé was a good thought, anyway.

Dread came then.

The rain-soaked handler blinked at the receipt. "I seen it here a while ago, okay. But there ain't many items left and I don't see it now."

Cassius stared around the open shed. "I was delayed in the terminal. It must be here. It's a coffin."

"I know, I seen it. We had a real mess out here tonight, mister. Some jerky new driver rammed into a couple of the other pickup rigs. Maybe Elmo knows. Hey, Elmo?"

Elmo was fat and officious. "Sure, I seen it. The driver picked it up."

"What driver?" Cassius snapped.

"Just who the hell are you, mister?"

"The man's brother."

"Oh, okay. Keep your pants on." Elmo thumbed his flash. He riffled his tickets. Then he extended the packet, less blustery. "Ain't that the nuts? The part of the ticket showin' the name of the carrier is torn off. Oh boy, things are sure screwed up tonight, man, oh man."

Cassius raged and fumed and promised official vengeance for a full fifteen minutes. He turned out half the minor bureaucracy of the receiving department, to no good end. The coffin was gone.

Someone had stolen his brother's corpse.

"It's crazy!" he sputtered. Cowlike faces ringed him.

"Who would steal a preacher's body? It's absolutely senseless."

No one answered. Cassius looked past the rain-lashed men. They were strangely nervous. Perhaps because of a theft; the rain; the accident and mix-ups and their obliviousness to the pickup driver. Or perhaps they were quiet because the situation had been further complicated by death.

Out beyond the concrete beds where the Sino-Russian Line was preparing to launch its evening shipment, Cassius saw the multileveled tangle of roads leading from the field, rising to merge with the ten broad lanes of the Washington Belt. Up one of those ramps and onto that highway had gone an unknown truck, carrying a stolen corpse.

"Crazy," Cassius said again. "You'll hear about this." He stalked off in the rain.

What indecent maniac would take such elaborate pains to pilfer the corpse of a man of God from a public place? Cassius was at once afraid he'd come in contact with some sinister group of madmen. Only later, when hindsight began to operate, did he analyze his reaction more deeply. He knew later that what had really troubled him was the fear that those who'd stolen the body were not crazy but perfectly, if esoterically, sane.

Lurching along in the rain, Cassius didn't know what he was going to do about the theft. But he was positive he was going to do something.

II

The trip to his apartment in Alexandria would require the better part of an hour. Cassius decided to put the time to use.

After he jockeyed his Ford Aircoupe to the hook-on with the magnetic strip, he dialed the tinted shell. The shell closed around the seat blister, shutting out the dazzle of thousands of headlamps in the oncoming lanes. Cassius rang up the headquarters of the Ecumenical Brothers in downtown Washington. The paper had paid for installing the minimum-screen visor in his car.

Presently a sleepy, clerical-collared face appeared.

"This is Reverend Tooker speaking. Yes?"

"I'm sorry to disturb you, Reverend."

Here Is Thy Sting

"Quite all right. Tonight's my shift in the B-complex free kitchen. How can I help you?"

The cleric was unfamiliar. But so was Timothy's whole life, practically. Cassius hadn't seen his brother in twelve years. That didn't lessen his sense of duty and outrage:

"Reverend, I'm Cassius Andrews. I just came from Dulles where I planned to pick up Timothy's body. There seems to have been a mixup. Did you by any chance send a hauler from your building to fetch it?"

"No, Mr. Andrews. We understood you wished to take delivery. Wasn't our departed brother on the rocket?"

"He was. But somebody stole the coffin."

Reverend Tooker at once launched into theologically tinged commiseration. Cassius listened politely. But he knew he'd get no help from the white-haired divine. Most of Tooker's sincere and sympathetic talk about Timothy's service on the Moon, his dying a violent death in the service of the Creator and His Son, to Cassius was neither here nor there. Long ago he'd abandoned any concern with religion.

While the Reverend eulogized Timothy, Cassius drifted off into other realms. Timothy had been a shy, dreamy boy in their childhood. He had been passionately religious, in contrast to Cassius who was passionately secular. For no special reason, Cassius was stung with somber recollections of his boyhood dreams of becoming a famous newsman and correspondent.

"—can only suggest you contact the police," Reverend Tooker concluded.

"Yes, I planned to do that next."

"Please come into the chapel at any time if we can be of help in your hour of trial," the Reverend said.

"Yes, I'll do that too, thanks." That was a lie. Cassius rang off. There was no point in telling the gentle, simple old fellow that he was becoming convinced Timothy's body had been pilfered by some sort of sex ghoul cult. A cult which—God help his brother—must be massively organized.

The Ford Aircoupe whizzed along on its thin pillars of air, halfway to Alexandria now. Cassius dialed the central police switchboard.

They were officially receptive, properly angry. Somehow, though, the conversation seemed routine. Cassius doubted the police would learn anything new when their operatives visited the freight sheds. The rain, the accident caused by the inexperienced driver, the resulting confusion, all had worked together to effectively blot out the trail of the body snatchers.

The Aircoupe was on the less crowded feeder belt over the polluted Potomac. The hour was growing late. In spite of that, Cassius dialed another number. He didn't want to be completely alone tonight. He found that Joy was home.

"That's terrible, Cassius," she said. He thought she was sincere. Joy was nearing forty, rather chubby-faced and a little ferret-eyed in the wrong light. Basically she was pretty, if grown stocky now that she'd given up hope of marriage and settled on a career. "Would you like me to come over?"

Rain hammered black, lonely, on the Aircoupe bubble.

"Could you, Joy? It'll take you an hour, I know. I really would like company. I can cook some eggs. You can stay the night."

"I wish I might, sweets. But the piece I'm working on is due tomorrow. I've unearthed some positively fantabulous little gimmicks in re what to do with leftover paper undies. They make the cutest buffers for a dusting robot and—oh dear. Forgive me. This is a terrible time to talk shop."

"That's all right." He forgave her. One of Joy's failings was a kind of compulsion to seek editorial paydirt in any situation, even lovemaking. Once in the middle of the night Joy had suddenly interrupted everything, sat up and jotted down some notes on a simply fantabulous position a housewife might use to relax her calf muscles. He added, "You don't have to stay the night, then."

"I can't, dear. As I say, this little piece is due. Cassius!"

"What, Joy?"

"You don't suppose there's anything in this theft, do you? Oh, I realize the moment is very trying for you. But could we make anything out of it?"

"I doubt that it's Joy de Veever's cup of tea," he replied. "Nor mine either. I also have a sinking feeling the cops are going to get nowhere. To tell the truth, Joy, this business has some nasty overtones. I'm not sure I want to pursue it myself."

The screened face grew bright-eyed. He might have

been irritated if he hadn't understood that her query sprang from her compulsive professionalism. But only in part. He knew from their years of pleasant liaison that she was, at bottom, kindly.

"But you will pursue it, won't you, Cassius?"

"Yes, I suppose I must. Provided I can figure out where to turn next."

"We'll think of something. See you in an hour, sweets." And the screen blurred out.

Cassius occupied a one-room flat on the eighty-seventh floor of one of fifteen cluster buildings in a small Alexandria development. Decelerating for the hook-off, Cassius saw a familiar sprawl of towers just this side of his own project. The towers dwarfed the other units in the district. They were the local project of the Securo Corporation.

Securo, a private firm started ten years ago by a contractor and a professor of psychology, provided co-op living for young marrieds but added a fillip: all conceivable services, including mortgage, burial and educational insurance were included in one payment for the benefit of the occupants, who signed a lifetime contract. All across the country and everywhere abroad, Securo was building similar projects, but not fast enough for the demand.

Down at the paper, the boys, fancying themselves rather independent souls, referred to a Securo flat as a womb to tomb room, since many young parents were already willing their living space to their infants, to provide them maximum protection against the buffetings of fate.

Now, riding in the dark rain, Cassius shuddered a little as the lights of the Securo tract flashed past. There was something to be said for knowing you were protected, especially on unpleasant nights like this. And the newsmen weren't all that independent, either. The last Guild negotiations had lasted eighteen weeks, because management initially refused to include podiatry benefits in the package. Everyone wanted to be safe. Sometimes Cassius clucked his tongue, but sometimes too he sympathized.

Unlike Securo, Cassius's landlords offered only the standard auto, theft and major medical insurance with their flats. Cassius's place was a litter of books and the other paraphernalia of bachelor untidiness.

He opened two packages of Birdseye Brawny Breakfasts, watched while the fried eggs and bacon began to mushroom from the tiny white capsules. Joy wouldn't be arriving for a while yet. He drew the curtain around the cook unit and went to the bookcase to get his diary.

Faithfully he recorded the events of the evening. As a younger man he'd imagined he might be a latter-day Pepys. Now he wrote in the book out of habit more than anything, though occasionally he admitted to himself that what he was doing was hoping with words and phrases that a third-rate newspaperman could gain a slim remembrance after he died.

Someone might come across the diary among his effects, for instance. Recognize the burning perceptiveness and, lo! long after he was buried, elevate the name of Cassius Andrews to the heights of—

Rats. He knew it was idle foolishness. The prose was clear but mundane. It in no sense burned. Still, he wrote in the diary every night.

Joy de Veever arrived within an hour. Her evening wig, slightly awry, was an exotic purple to match her lip rouge. She hugged him briefly. They sat down to eat, Joy rather noisily and untidily. It was comforting to have her present.

Her real name was Joy Gollchuk. The editors believed, probably rightly, that Joy de Veever was the sort of byline housewives preferred in a helpful hints column. She shared a cell at the *Capitol World Truth* with a pert sixty-year-old grandmother named Mrs. Swartzmore, who reviewed films under the name Ma Cine.

"Really (munch munch), Cassius (swallow), this is the most despicable type thing I've ever (swallow) heard of. Stealing a body indeed! A Holy Joe's body, too."

"I don't get mad about the minister part so much as over the fact that he was my brother. I feel an obligation not to let the whole thing pass."

"Maybe (swallow) it's some sort of obscene ring operating."

"I've wondered that. It's actually the reason I'm slightly leery of pushing too far. But I know in the long run I can't let the possibility stop me."

"Tell me again what the police said."

"That they'll do their best. I don't doubt it. But I was there tonight, Joy. The handlers felt sorry about it, sure. Things were obviously in such a confused state that they could do nothing beyond what they did. Which was, admit someone drove in, picked up Timothy's coffin with false papers, then drove away again."

Joy's eyes glittered. She leaned near. "Did you ask for police cooperation?"

"Didn't I just tell you?"

"Not about that, silly. I mean cooperation in case there's a juicy story behind—oh. You're offended."

"No I'm not."

"Juicy was a bad word. I'm sorry, sweets. But there might be a piece in it for you, Cassius. Sort of a memorial to your brother, you might say," hastily justifying herself. "After all, dear, let's face it. You're not the world's hottest reporter. You could use some self-promotion."

"Joy, after a while a man knows what he is and isn't."

"Oh come on, Cassius! Don't you have any drive to assert yourself?"

He thought of the diary. He glanced at a collection of file card holders on the self-suspending bookshelves. He frowned.

"Of course. But it doesn't come out in trying to make hay from what's happened to Timothy."

Joy crunched a last morsel of bacon. "Well, you certainly won't do yourself any good with that silly biography you've been working on for six years. The poor man's been written about in eleven different volumes."

"Twelve," Cassius corrected. "As you know, I've discovered some new angles which might—"

"Enshrine you with posterity?" Joy smiled. "Cassius, really."

"I wasn't going to say that."

"It's what you meant, though."

"Joy, I like working on the book," he said. "How did we get on this subject?"

For a moment anger sparked in his rather downturning brown eyes. He controlled the anger. Not a major effort at all. He gripped her hand across the fold-up table.

"Joy, if I didn't know so well that you can't help hunting for angles any more than a cat can help chasing a mouse, I'd get damned mad at you sometimes."

"Yes, you do understand me," she said gently. "Which is more than I do for you most of the time, I must confess."

He squeezed her hand. "Thanks for coming tonight."

"I apologize for calling your book silly, dear."

"I don't mind. So long as you realize I'll keep right on working on it."

For a moment Joy's eyes were shadowed. "Still have the dream?"

"Yes."

"That's the reason for the book, isn't it?"

"Um, partly, I guess."

"I don't have any dreams like that, Cassius. But I suppose I run after stories for the same reason too."

"Yes."

Suddenly she snapped her fingers. The cocktail zircon on her right hand flashed back the rays of the solar panels which lit the room. "I just had the most marvelous idea. If you get no satisfaction from the police, why don't you go right to the W.B.I?"

"Are you out of your mind? I don't know anybody down there."

"What difference does that make? Go straight to the director himself! If you ask me, Cassius, this theft sounds downright sinister. Maybe the Neo-Leninists are making a comeback."

"And you suggest I waltz right in and state my case to Flange himself?"

"That's not as impossible as it sounds. I was talking to Charlie Pelz yesterday over morning vitamins."

"Charlie Pelz?"

"Oh, you know. He does those Black Museum pieces on Sundays for the true-crime nuts. Charlie said he was down to the W.B.I. Building last week and it's practically turned into an old people's home. Offices empty. Men sitting around doing nothing. He asked whether he could see Flange's assistant a moment, to get a comment on a story he was writing, and he almost dropped over when the secretary said Flange had no appointments all day, why didn't Charlie talk to him? So you try him. Maybe this unstable world peace is more stable than we think."

Cassius chewed his lip. "I don't know who could set it up for me."

"I tell you, Charlie Pelz said no one had to set it up! Flange was so *un*busy even a bootboy could get in to see him."

Although he rejected the idea as slightly ludicrous, Cassius nevertheless filed it away. He and Joy finished their caffeine water with a rehash of the mysterious events out at Dulles. It got them nowhere. She kissed him neatly and rather moistly on the cheek, squeezed his arm, and he ushered her to the door.

"Must run, sweets, but I do hope you sleep well. Try not to fret over what's happened."

"I have to find out what happened to Timothy, Joy. I must."

"Of course. Take my suggestion, though. Thinking about the W.B.I. And Cassius—" Again the eyes, rimmed in purple mascara, glittered. Consolation went out the window, replaced by professionalism. "—if there is anything in it, a hot tidbit either one of us could use—oh, I know I sound terribly crass, but after all, you have only one life to live and you have to make the best of it."

"That's right," Cassius said, hiding laughter. "Good night, Joy. And thanks."

Poor girl, he thought when she'd gone. Imagines one day *the* story will fall into her lap. He'd never had the courage to tell her, as she repeatedly told him, that her talent was small.

Oh, she could do a major story, all right. But the material for the story would have to drop from heaven. She'd never find it picking around among new uses for paper undies in the home. Perhaps he'd continued their liaison so long because, unlike Joy, he had realized his personal limits and therefore could feel gently, privately superior.

After a vigorous rubdown with a pre-wetted shower cloth he pulled a switch. His bed rose from the floor. He awoke an hour later, snuffling and breathing violently, an ache in his chest.

The dream had returned.

III

It was a dream of himself running, mile after slow-motion mile, while the dog snapped at his heels.

The dog was twice as long as a man. Its claws were like sharp iron files. Its fangs were like white spikes. Its yellow eyes were the only two blazes of color in the gray waste where he was pursued.

He'd dreamed the dream regularly for about six years.

It had begun about the time he had first noticed at cocktail parties that people were talking with low voices and embarrassed laughter about how short all the days seemed, how rapidly they flew. People his own age. He knew what the dog represented.

Knowing, however, didn't relieve the after-effects of the nightmare. It only intensified them.

Hastily Cassius threw back the coverlet. He turned on the lights and started to work cross-indexing notes and snippets for his book. The project was probably futile, as Joy maintained. Twelve books had been published on the same subject already.

The book was to be a biography of Colonel Robin Delyev. He was the officer responsible for leading the combined American-Russian shock forces which repelled the initial invasion of Puerto Rico by the Chinese, sixty years ago. All Delyev and his thousand troops had to work with was a storehouse full of antiquated U.S. personal missile launchers.

Poring and poking at the National Archives, Cassius had stumbled across some new materials. They had been misfiled: seven hitherto unpublished letters, four long, three no more than notes but revealing nonetheless, written by Delyev to the Pentagon just before the Colonel's death. Headily Cassius had realized that none of the other twelve biographers had included the letters. And they added fresh insights into Delyev's brilliant deployment of his meager forces.

The majority of the book Cassius planned to draw from the secondary sources, re-slanting it to his own rather scholarly, restrained style of writing. The volume would contain most of the anecdotes already available, such as the one about the night in the Chinese consulate in Chicago, before the war, when Delyev drank too much and made the epigrammatic speech which earned him the nickname "Old Rattling Rockets." But the book, his book alone, would also contain the seven letters. Provided he finished the draft fairly soon, and got it submitted to a publisher.

Cassius knew that even when the volume was published, if it ever was, it would be relatively obscure in the crowded market; read only by those faithful who would always buy one more work on a subject that interested them. Cassius had no illusions. But he did believe that the fresh insights contained in the letters might add one small grain of truth to the world's accumulation as it related to the dead Delyev.

Besides, the book almost demanded to be written, worthy or not. It demanded writing especially in the lonely hours after he dreamed about the slavering dog who ran so slowly, yet so remorselessly, at his heels.

He labored on, a lonely figure in his small box of an apartment, alone in the night, alone in the rain, ignored but uncaring, until he finally crawled back to bed around four and slept untroubled until dawn.

Next day, he conferred personally with the Washington police.

They were investigating, yes, certainly. But to be honest, they'd interviewed several dozen people at Dulles and gotten nowhere. They would certainly keep trying, yes. There might be something decidedly sinister behind the theft. They would call him.

At lunch in the newspaper mess, Joy reminded him about the W.B.I. Cassius felt a little silly. But the obvious impending failure of the local police angered him. He took the afternoon off and rode the belts over.

As Charlie Pelz had promised, he was admitted to the Director's office without question or hesitancy. And to fulfill the rest of the prophecy, Cassius actually felt exactly like falling over on his face in utter surprise.

Not over getting in. Over what he saw after he got there.

IV

R. Ripley Flange, the mastiff-chinned Director of the World Bureau of Investigation, was sitting at his broad desk, feet up, throwing darts.

One whizzed perilously close to Cassius's head as he closed the door. Cassius flinched. The iron spike of the dart thudded into the door. On it a paper bull's-eye had been nailed, the large nails carelessly driven into the lustrous patina of the obviously antique and priceless wood. Even the newly-refurbished White House had been pannelled in polystyrene. For a genuine wood door to be pocked with thousands of dart and nail holes amounted to desecration.

"Sorry," Flange said. He grinned in a sleepy way. "I'm

rather on the track of a big one. Fourteen bull's-eyes this morning. Best yet."

Edgily, Cassius sat down. The Director sighed, laid aside his dart case and tented his hands. He tried to frown with interest. Cassius had the uncanny feeling that the Director was peering straight through him, as though he were one of those model-kit men, wholly transparent.

"What can I do for you, sir? Care to apply for a position as a special operative? We have dozens of openings." The heavy lips, which had once sneered so heroically out of simulcast screens during the lectures on Chinese subversion in the bedding industry, now pursed out in what Cassius could only describe as a careless, thoroughly lazy way.

"No, sir, I didn't come about a job."

"Some crime then, I'll bet." Flange sounded unhappy. "Isn't that it?"

"I hate to bother you, sir. The local police seem so overburdened, and unable to make any headway. You see, sir, my brother's body has disappeared."

"Pity." Flange was restlessly eyeing a wall bookcase in which stood nearly a hundred copies of the inexpensive five-credit polybound edition of Flange's magnum opus, *Alert! The Yellow Underground Is Attacking*. "I'm certain we can help you. Many more resources open these days. Laboratories, so forth. International crime, I take it?"

"I'm not sure what it is, sir. Perhaps I should talk to someone else in the Bureau."

"No, no, I'll handle it." Flange frowned. "I suppose it is my responsibility, after all. Now where are those damned forms?"

And he grumbled and rumbled through his desk, his hands shaking in a palsied way. Cassius fidgeted. He felt hot, embarrassed. There was something wrong with the old fellow. Where was the lion's roar for justice, the eagle's scream for watchfulness? Gone was the ferocity that had made Flange a legend, whether you cared for his style of operation or not.

At last the Director produced a paper, incredibly frayed.

"Well, I found one report form, anyway. I'd send you to someone else, except my deputy director has gone to

Here Is Thy Sting

Las Vegas and I haven't heard from him in four months. That's all right, though. He needed a rest."

Cassius had an urge to bolt and run. Had the W.B.I. turned into a rest home for its obviously mentally infirm chief?

"Something about a brother's body, wasn't it?" said Flange.

The peculiar situation would have been laughable had Cassius not suspected there was something unpleasant lurking just under the surface. Flange's weird mood made it impossible for him to generate very much righteous rage as he rattled off a bare sketch of the mixup at Dulles Interplanetary, the theft of Timothy's remains. Once in a while Flange's pen jerked, marking appropriate box or space.

"Distressing," Flange said at the end, with patent insincerity. "Yes, I see. Body theft."

"I thought it might possibly have some international implications. That's why I came to you. Of course I'm also anxious personally to make whoever did it pay up."

"Naturally. We'll put our best men on it right away. What's your office digit?"

Cassius repeated the eighteen numerals which included his extension. While Flange wrote down the figures with his right hand, his left strayed like a spider over to the dart case, then drummed on the edge. Cassius rose abruptly. He couldn't stand any more. The old man was senile and no one had the heart to remove him from office, that was it.

Also, Cassius felt with a certainty that stoked his determination to a new height, that R. Ripley Flange had no intention of putting his best men on it. Or maybe even any men, period. The Washington police wanted to try but were overworked. Flange simply didn't care.

"Visor you as soon as we have anything. Get right on it, yes we will." Flange was slumped in his throne chair like a punctured balloon. His hand drummed on the dart case, drummed.

"Don't you want any more details? I only gave you the essentials a minute ago." Flange, though obviously sick, was beginning to infuriate him.

"We have enough, we have plenty, best men. Visor you."

After several weeks Cassius even gave up hoping. He discussed it over vitamins with Charlie Pelz one afternoon. Charlie agreed that things were sure strange at the W.B.I. The place appeared understaffed. Moribund. He could offer no explanation other than the one Cassius had already come up with—Flange was such a fixture that the government was almost conscience-bound to await his death with something like unquestioning reverence.

Cassius agreed. He thought privately that it was distressing to watch the disintegration of a person's drive as old age crept in.

But Cassius didn't badger Flange or the W.B.I. Indeed, he forgot them. At the end of the fourth week following Timothy's disappearance, a few other curious things had pushed their way into his mind. They had no bearing on Timothy, probably. But they were the kinds of things which he, on the paper, was in a position to pursue a bit without the aid of sad old men who were once mighty tigers but who were now all gums and no guts.

What first put Cassius on the trail was the peculiar and shocking concert of Madame Kagle.

V

By intermission the shock was profound. Cassius noted its beginnings in the unusual amount of head-turning while Madame Kagle ran through *The Joint M.I.T. Faculty Sonata,* never missing a note but missing the fire of it altogether.

No one was so impolite as to gasp during the second selection, Oodner's *Peripheral Stimuli.* But Cassius saw mouths hanging open all up and down his row. No music critic, Cassius had nevertheless seen plenty of photos of the celebrated Kagle attack. At its best it was a savagely bow-shaped posture above the keyboard of the harpsivac. It emphasized the woman's boniness and made her resemble, some said, a fairy-tale witch maniacally searching for the touchstone in a casketful of junk beads. Out of such agonized personal involvement, great music was wrenched.

Except this evening.

Madame Wanda Kagle sat perfectly straight. She was watching the one hundred thirty-six keys, all right. But she was glass-eyed. Her mouth, like many in the audience, hung open in a peculiar slack-lipped indifference. The applause at the end of the first half of the program was thin.

Stumbling and shoving up the aisle for a quick smoke, Cassius and Joy heard all around them whispered comments such as: "Unbelievable." "Lackluster." "Crushingly disappointing." They pushed out into the vast foyer of the Sports Dome. The roof was rolled back to the stars and warm night breezes. Joy waited for her smoke to pop fire, inhaled and said:

"The old babe must be close on sixty. Wonder if she's slipping. Maybe she has to key up with amphets, and forgot."

"That's a bad pun," Cassius said. "I'd guess she was loaded with booze if it wasn't common knowledge that she very nearly lives like a saint. I read somewhere that she's even tried hypnotism to push everything out of her mind but her music."

"She certainly succeeded," Joy answered. "That was pure claptrap in there. She couldn't have been less interested."

"This puts a little different complexion on going to the reception afterward," Cassius mused. "Ordinarily I wouldn't be much interested in using those chits Greeheim gave you along with the tickets. I don't know beans about music. Or about how to get along with musical coteries, either."

Joy's eyes glittered. "For God's sake, Cassius, you can pretend, can't you? You could even make 'em think you're the regular critic. Fake it a little. Just sneer. Greeheim isn't that well known yet. He's only been with the paper a few months. I certainly don't want to insult him when he gets over his illness by telling him we used the tickets but not the party passes."

The crowd was beginning to stir, pushing back to the entrance ramps for the second half. "You won't have to tell him," Cassius grinned. "In the light of that first half, I wouldn't miss seeing Madame K. close-up for anything. Maybe we'll get a hint of what's wrong with her."

"Now you're talking!" Joy said, eyes sharp as awls.

As they fought the aisle battle on the way to their seats, Cassius considered telling Joy the real reason for his curiosity. She was on one of her imaginary scents again, hoping she'd unearth some hot exclusive. While Cassius, on the other hand, had stared at Madame Kagle and seen something else entirely—

A ghostly twin image of the vast, weary indifference of R. Ripley Flange.

Lights dimmed. Madame Kagle appeared from the wings. She seemed to stumble. Like a sleepwalker she approached the bench of the harpsivac. She sat down. She dry-washed her hands, as if warming them. Joy was noisily rippling the pages of the program, twisting it to get light. She hissed, "Oh boy, this'll be fantabulous. *The Algebraic Suite.* It's one of my favorites."

But there was to be no *Algebraic Suite.* Madame Kagle seemed frozen at the console. A look of supreme sorrow came onto her aging features. It was immediately replaced by a sly, mocking smile. Moving with the painful lethargy of the arthritic—which she definitely was not—Madame Kagle rose. She circled the harpsivac and yanked the plug from the floor socket. The thousands of tiny multicolored lights on the banked tonal computers simultaneously went black.

Madame Kagle cast a tired glance at the shocked audience. She lifted her right shoulder in the smallest shrug. She sauntered off the stage.

Once the curtain dropped and the impossible became a fact, the crowd was as silent as mourners entering a mortuary. There were hushed little speculations about narcotics, insanity, sex, religion, gall bladder, dropsy, thrombosis, poor investment counseling and so forth. People seemed reluctant to move from the foyer onto the broad piazza outside the Sports Dome. Only a few drifted from the piazza toward the parking docks.

"Wow," Joy whispered, "I can't wait to get the dirt at the reception."

Cassius was about to speak when the annunciator horn of a newsvend machine rolling through the crowd blared that everyone mustn't forget that next Monday was D-Day, and that details on the free city-wide immunizations against scaling scalp could be had by inserting a coin in the slot. The contraption dinned the fact that its papers contained a full list of the twenty-two hundred dispensaries which would be set up to distribute the free capsules to inoculate the populace against the dread scourge. The drive was the latest work of the ancient March of Quarters Foundation. Details, details inside—

Blaring, the machine trundled on. Rubbing his ear, Cassius answered Joy by saying, "Suppose we don't find out. Suppose Madame Kagle doesn't show up. Perhaps she's ill."

"Somebody'll be there who knows the score. Come on, Cassius, get the car."

As they wormed through the stunned throng on the piazza, voices rippled suddenly in excitement. Cassius and Joy craned around. Down the performer's ramp a sleek, expensive Rolls-Fujica air limousine was gliding, fast. People were crossing the ramp now. The chauffeur was forced to apply the brakes. That was when the yellow-cheeked bootboy, probably the son of some Chinese war refugee, fell off the piazza balustrade.

The lad had been up there brushes in hand, chanting in a singsong about shining the dress boots of gentlemen. Somehow he slipped, just as the Rolls-Fujica came to a halt.

"He's dead," a woman cried. The crowd, herd-like, shifted. Joy couldn't resist. Cassius was dragged along.

For a moment the scene was very vivid to him. The drop from the balustrade to the main ramp was twenty feet or more. By some twist of fate the bootboy had hit skull first on the prestressed poly. He lay with his red and gray brains smashed out. Meantime the Rolls-Fujica had started up.

The performer's ramp crossed the main one, on which the bootboy lay, at the piazza corner. A blur of motion in the aircar tonneau caught Cassius's eye. He saw Madame Kagle order her chauffeur to stop again. Her face strained to the window. Of all the curious who were gasping and oh-ing over the accident, she alone seemed truly moved.

The Rolls-Fujica sped on. Cassius shuddered. The woman's eyes had mirrored some pure hell even he couldn't see.

"Wonder if there's a human interest bit in it," Joy said.

"Joy, for God's sake don't be so callous."

She smiled. "It is one of my failings, isn't it, sweets? All right, first things first. But let's hurry. We don't want to miss the reception."

The reception, they discovered, was already going full blast in one of the larger private function halls of The Hotel of the Three Presidents. Passing under an arch decorated with a bust of one member of the trio—they were entering the Edward Room—Joy grabbed his arm.

"Cassius, look! The old girl's here. And drunker than a hoot owl, it seems."

"I don't like this a damn bit," he muttered.

"Oh, for heaven's sake, why not?"

"It just seems like a wake before you have a dead body."

"Don't be so squeamish. I wouldn't miss it for anything."

Joy pulled and tugged until they were past the coat robot, through the champagne line and lurking at the fringe of a small crowd surrounding Madame Kagle. The lady virtuoso was indeed pretty well gone. She staggered around like a scarecrow off its pole. Nobody was laughing, though. Not the socialites, not the critics. The mood was one of acute embarrassment.

Madame Kagle seemed to be centering most of her remarks on a ruddy-faced priest of middle years. Joy whispered that the priest was a well-known expert on sacred music. Madame Kagle was waving her champagne glass back and forth under the priest's long-suffering nose. Each wave threatened to douse him.

"—and I say you still haven't answered my question, Father Bleu."

"Haven't I, dear lady? I thought I stated that death is merely the beginning of—"

"No, no, *no!*" Her voice was high as a harpy's. "Don't go all gooey and metaphysical. I mean to ask, what is death the act, the situation, the moment?"

She watched him foxily. The priest in turn struggled to remain polite. "Madame, I'm not positive I follow."

"Let me say it another way. Most people are afraid of dying, yes?"

"I disagree. Not those who find mystical union with the body of Christ in—"

"Oh, come off it!" Madame Kagle shrilled. "People are frightened of it, Father Bleu. Frightened and screaming their fear silently every hour of every day they live. Now I put it to you. Of what are they afraid? Are they afraid of the end of consciousness? The ultimate blackout, so to speak? Or are they afraid of another aspect of death? The one which they can't begin to foresee or understand?"

"What aspect is that, Madame Kagle?"

"The pain." She glared. "The pain, Father. Possibly sudden. Possibly horrible. Waiting, always waiting somewhere ahead, at an unguessable junction of time and place. Like that bootboy tonight. How it must have hurt. One blinding instant when his head hit, eh? I suggest, Father Bleu, *that* is what we're afraid of, *that* is the wholly unknowable part of dying—the screaming, hurting how, of which the when is only a lesser part. The how is the part we never know. Unless we experience it."

She slurped champagne in the silence. She eyed him defiantly.

"Well, Father? What have you got to say?"

Discreetly Father Bleu coughed into his closed fist. "Theologically, Madame, I find the attempt to separate the mystical act of dying into neat little compartments rather a matter of hairsplitting. And furthermore—"

"If that's how you feel," she interrupted, "you're just not thinking it out."

"My good woman!" said Father Bleu gently.

"Pay attention to me!" Madame Wanda Kagle glared furiously. "I say you pay attention! Because you have never stopped to think about it, have you? If death resembles going to sleep, why, that's an idea your mind can get hold of. Isn't it? You may be afraid of it, yes. Afraid of the end of everything. But at least you can get hold of some notion of something of what it's like. Sleep. But can you get hold of anything of what it must feel like to experience the most agonizing of deaths? Your head popping open like that bootboy's tonight, say? A thousand worms of pain inside every part of you for a second long as eternity? Can you grasp *that*? No, you can't, Father Bleu. And that's what death is at its worst—the unknown, the possibly harrowing pain ahead."

She clamped her lips together smugly. She held out her champagne glass for a refill. A woman in furs clapped a hand over her fashionably green lips and rushed from the group. Though puzzled, Joy was still all eyes and ears.

"Even your blessed St. Paul bears me out, Father."

The priest glanced up, startled. "What?"

"The first letter to the Corinthians, if I remember. The grave has a victory, all right. But it's death that has the sting."

In the pause the furnace doors behind her eyes opened wide, and hell shone out.

"I know what I'm talking about, Father. I've been there."

Slowly she closed her fingers, crushing the champagne glass in her hand. Weeping, blood drooling from her palm down her frail veined arms, she had to be carried out.

The party broke up at once.

The gloom was even deeper than at the Dome. "Wait'll Greeheim gets a load of this dirty linen!" Joy whispered as they left.

Later, when Cassius escorted Joy to the door of her flat, she held out her cheek for a routine buss. But her mind was elsewhere. "I certainly wonder what Greeheim will make of that nutty harangue. Artistic temperament?"

"It's an interesting notion, anyway."

"What is?"

"Oh, there being two elements in death. The sleep and the pain. I wonder which one you really do fear most. I never thought about it before."

She patted his cheek. "And because you never think about really sensational story material like funeral rackets or sewage control graft, Cassius my love, you'll never get anywhere in our particular little rat-race. But that's all right. I like you just the same. Good night. Thanks for a fantabulous evening."

Waiting for the tube to take him down, Cassius was struck again by an eerie feeling. It wasn't so much the peculiarity of Madame Kagle's statements. They were pretty obtuse, after all. It was the queer resemblance he saw, or thought he saw, between her attitude and that of R. Ripley Flange. Somehow his mind wanted to equate the jerked plug with the dart case. It was almost as though the pair of them had had exactly the same lunatic vision, whatever it might be.

But the matter really had no relation to the problem

Here Is Thy Sting

still nagging him, he realized. The problem of Timothy's disappearance.

I've been there. The woman's words stayed in his mind the rest of the evening. What could they possibly mean?

Dutifully he recorded the unusual affair in his diary, then put in some time on the notes for his book. The dream of the dog at his heels was even more intense than usual. He awoke near dawn, wringing with sweat. Three cups of caffeine water were required before he was fully awake and free of the grip of the nightmare.

As he went to work he remembered once having read something about Madame Kagle's brother. Later in the day he had to go to the paper's morgue on another story. He looked up the Kagle name just out of curiosity. In addition to much material on Madame Wanda, there were several clips on her younger brother. The last of them stated that Dr. Frederic Kagle, a renowned neurosurgeon, had resigned from the World Institutes of Health to enter private practice. The clip was three years old.

Maybe, Cassius laughed to himself, the poor old woman had been put through the wringer by her brother in the cause of science. He laughed again, envisioning the usual horrific collection of apparatus, electrodes and blue lightnings that leapt from point to point while the demon doctor looked on and tittered.

The wool-gathering did have one solid result, surprisingly. It got Cassius to speculating again about a new angle on Timothy's fate.

Originally Cassius had wondered whether the body had been purloined by some unspeakable sex ring. Now he had another notion, no doubt equally off base but at least remotely possible. There was no connection with Dr. Frederic Kagle. It was only that Kagle's obscurity suggested scientists who, for one reason or another, were forced to work in absolute anonymity.

A third time Cassius laughed at himself in the gray loneliness of the morgue's reading cubicle. The medical body-snatcher bit in this day and age? Ridiculous.

Or was it?

Was the government, for instance, preparing some new superweapon in fear of possible disintegration of the tenuous Sino-Caucasian Peace? Something compelled him to take down the morgue index book. He leafed through until he located the proper heading. *Disappearances, Unsolved.*

He used the keyboard to code the paper tape. The tape vanished down a slot. A humming. Cassius was startled when not one but three microfilm spools popped from the tube.

There was always a routine number of unexplained disappearances within any given period. Distraught offspring. Erring husbands. Crimes that never saw the light of day. So he expected one spool at the most. He fed the first spool into the view box.

He did find that customary expected number of accounts of vanishing humanity. He also found thirteen instances of the disappearance of dead bodies within the last twenty-four months.

His brother Timothy was the last of the thirteen. He was represented by his obit and a two-paragraph item in the *Capitol World Truth*. The item covered the jetport incident, Cassius had seen it several times.

He double-checked each spool again. He hadn't misread. The thirteen who were gone had died in a uniform way.

By violence.

VI

Almost one year to the day after the theft of Timothy Andrew's body, the sovereign and somewhat backward state of New York prepared to let Butcher Balk have five hundred thousand volts. Cassius was waiting.

He was waiting in the prison burial ground on the Hudson bluffs, hunched down in his Ford Aircoupe. The vehicle was parked in a growth of budding maples to one side of a small service road. The time was 10:05 P.M.

Theoretically, Butcher Balk had been dead five minutes. April snow swirled, a quaint effect, courtesy of the weather bureau. Cassius was glad for the white scatter. It would afford him extra concealment in the dark, he hoped.

In order to be here this evening Cassius had been forced to lie both to Joy and his editor Hughgenine. He complained of a spell of male post-equinoctial depression, a common burden of urban life anymore. Three other times in the year that had just passed he had also gone off following his elusive suspicions. On those occasions he had pleaded acute hangover, g.i. distress and bucket-seat hip, respectively.

Each time he'd figured that at last he was right. Each time he had been wrong. Worse, there was nothing to suggest tonight would be different.

But he refused to give up.

The first time, he'd traveled all night to reach Watkins Glen. The Continental driving star Baron von Pfalz had smashed up his Sonic Special in the Grand Prix, dying in a multi-car wreck on the chicane. Cassius had felt like a ghoul loitering around the little chapel where the other racers and mechanics held a memorial for the Baron. A sobbing woman, three children in tow, took von Pfalz's corpse away in a hearse. Cassius drove home keenly disappointed.

The following week the sports section of the *Capitol World Truth* carried a photo of the little family beside the Baron's grave plot. The woman and children, then, had not been actors.

So it went twice more: complete failure in outguessing them. Whoever *they* were.

The second occasion, no one tried to snatch the corpse of Dolly Sue Wei, the first non-American ever to register at the University of Levittown. She entered her first class flanked by the drawn pistols of U.N. marshals. Cassius had been sure the situation would produce violence. It did. Next night someone threw a sharp rock and Dolly died of brain damage.

But she was buried in a routine way in a free cemetery in Manhattan's Oriental ghetto. Cassius was there.

He had also rushed to a mortuary in New Jersey just last February. The Great Rococo, a stage magician, had died with the back of his head shot off while performing the bullet catch before a convention of Moose. Buried without incident in Tenafly.

The three blind alleys might have led another man to abandon the search. But Cassius had access to the paper's morgue. There he convinced himself he wasn't a lunatic.

In the interval during which he'd guessed wrong and gone on fruitless chases, the bodies of five other men—a film star, a slum pastor, an insurance salesman pushing his car to two hundred on the Interstate, a hunter after possum in Kentucky, a suicide in Cleveland—had all disappeared before interment.

Now, in the snowy night, Cassius brooded over his lack of success in outguessing *them*. Yet he was certain *they* were still in operation, and it was merely a matter of time before—

Thinking, he failed to see the drop of the translucent gray force wall of Ossining's new Bartlow Martin wing. He saw the headlights, though. They threw yellow up the hillside. The burial gang was on its way.

The outer wall shimmered up into place again, hiding a ghostly flag on the nine-hole therapy course. Speedy and efficient, the corpse handlers parked the truck on the other side of a low knoll. The rolled the gravedigger from the truck. They lowered the plain poly coffin containing the remains of Butcher Balk into the pre-dug hole. They turned on the digger and stood back while it went to work pitching on earth, its eight metal arms wigwagging black across a spotlight on the truck's cowl.

Unobserved, Cassius spied from his Aircoupe. He'd selected Butcher Balk as a likely target because the killer had received so much publicity. Of course, that might frighten *them* away. But the publicity said Butcher Balk had no living relatives. And that was another part of the pattern Cassius thought he'd discovered.

In six instances the disappearing dead people had also been survivorless. In other cases Cassius couldn't tell; no mention was made in the printed obits, but since they were wire service items, that didn't necessarily rule out the possibility of no relatives.

Snow swirled. The gravedigger flashed its green light and retracted its arms. Butcher Balk was a safecracker who had been rehabilitated after his first manslaughter conviction. His adjusted personality had been imperfect, had cracked, had resulted in a berserk massacre of ten men, women and children one Sunday afternoon in a hamlet on the St. Lawrence. Hence the seldom-given maximum penalty. Now Butcher Balk was only a faint mound among other mounds under the fresh snow.

The prison wall field sank. The truck vanished. The wall went up. Silence and the snow claimed the ghostly Hudson cliffs.

"If Joy could see me," Cassius said aloud, to keep himself company, "she'd think I was completely gone."

The hours passed. Eleven o'clock. Twelve. One. One-thirty. Cassius was convinced he'd made another wrong guess. He was ready to abandon the whole project. He took out the laminated card embossed with his personal digit, poised it over the ignition slot.

Two red-dusky eyes opened below.

He knuckled the weariness out of his eyesockets, looking again. The eyes were headlamps, large ones. But with reddish lenses for snow- and rain-probing radar.

Instantly Cassius began to sweat and gnaw his lip. The murky red circles would be invisible from the prison. He had difficulty seeing them himself. Radar lamps indicated a very costly vehicle. Something with a lot of equipment inside, like the mobile surgery and consultation rooms so many personal-injury lawyers drove. Gently Cassius levered up the vent in the Aircoupe blister.

He thought he heard voices. He certainly heard the gutter and clank of a machine. They'd brought their own gravedigger.

Twice its black arms flashed across the circles of the red radar lenses, illusory, quick as a blink. Cassius was now desperately afraid the thieves were vicious mobsters, revanchist foreign agents or something equally deadly. He slipped the card into the slot, heard the compressors begin to whoosh. Gently, gently, he levered the Aircoupe out of parking contact with the ground, ready to race in pursuit.

The thieves took twice as long as the prison detail. From this Cassius inferred they had dug up the coffin, then replaced the earth so their work would go undetected. As the thoroughness of their operation hit him, he found himself suddenly pumped full of adrenalin and rage. When the radar lenses vanished, indicating the truck's departure, he was ready.

He jerked the Aircoupe into forward. He picked them up on the feeder leaving the burial ground.

Apparently because of the snow or the solitude of the countryside or both, they never suspected he was roughly a mile behind them on the long trip over the state line into Westport, one of the cancerous slums affixed to the body of Greater Manhattan.

The truck whizzing along on its air jets finally slowed on a seamy street. It pulled into the side drive of a ramshackle funeral parlor and disappeared in the rear. Under a lonely mercury light a sign reading COMMUTER'S REST MORTUARY CHAPEL stood on the unkempt, snow-patched lawn.

Cassius cruised half a block down, parked and waited.

The truck never came out.

The windows of the place were black. Painted over? There was absolutely no sign of life. As false dawn broke, Cassius got away from there. He relaxed only when he was on the Washington Belt North. He licked his lips, fought his tiredness, struggled with what he must do next.

The police?

Yes, that was the sensible answer. But something in him rebelled.

After all, he'd invested nearly a year on the chase, which was now hotting up considerably. Had Timothy not been involved, he'd have reported to the authorities at once. But the authorities hadn't done much of anything for him the first time. He still resented it.

Had he the guts to carry it one step more and see what happened?

Well, maybe he hadn't the guts. But he had the will. Months of frustration had developed it.

Once back in his flat, he was bothered again. He was the only person who knew the location from which the ring operated. Whom could he tell? Joy?

He warned himself off. Fond as he was of Joy, he knew his lady-love would try to convert the dross of a personal cause into the gold of self-promotion via a hot story. Tell her, and half Washington would know before he reached the Commuter's Rest Mortuary Chapel again.

As he pondered alone in his littered room, his eye struck the boxes of notes for his book. All at once the project seemed trivial.

What if—just *supposing*—he uncovered some sensational facts over there in Connecticut? Some monstrous conspiracy? He assumed he was the only one who knew anything about the underground organization, whatever its purpose. Certainly he was the only reporter. Opportunity beckoned. So did faint greed, he admitted.

Greed was unfamiliar to him—but probably only because of lack of opportunities. Hell, what harm would it do to write the exposé himself, if there was one to be written? Why shouldn't he get the credit for doing all the work and taking all the risks?

First, though, he must protect himself.

Next morning, instead of taking the usual vitamin break, he said to Joy, "I have to go out for a few minutes."

Joy folded up the edition of the paper she'd been studying. The front page carried a simulphoto of two cabinet members, the Secretary of Social Security and the Secretary of Fringe Benefits, cutting ribbons to open the new Birth Defects Insurance Administration Center.

"What're you after, love?" Joy asked. "Another dusty book that mentions your favorite colonel in small type in the appendix?"

"I need a new diary."

"Oh, that. You're a great one."

"Why do you say that?"

She pinched his arm, oblivious to the others in the newspaper mess. "I prefer my reflections printed in public, sweets, with my name above them, ten point or better. Cash in the bank is what I'm after."

Cassius grinned. "How do you know my diary won't make me famous one day?"

"That's what all diary-writers think. How many make it?"

Admitting she was right, and promising to meet her for lunch, Cassius left. He hurried down to an arcade on the fourth sub-level of the newspaper building. He bought an expensive diary at a stationery shop. The diary in which he'd been writing lately wasn't filled. But it was just a plain lockless diary. The one he purchased had a sonic lock: the first nine notes of the old folk song *Mister Clean*, whistled. The lock was tamperproof.

That night, after dinner with Joy, he went home and wrote down the events at the Ossining burial ground, as well as the location of the headquarters of the ring. Then he locked the new diary and went to bed, and dreamed the dog dream vividly.

The next night he set out for Connecticut.

He was unarmed. He was rather frightened. But he went.

He parked the Aircoupe down the block and walked.

The moon was full. A gusty wind blew. Even here in the stews, where one tumbledown split-level housed a dozen squealing, fighting families, there was a sense and tang of earth's annual renewal. The wind carried the sweet breath of life. Turning up the mortuary walk, Cassius was suddenly conscious that he was approaching the age when men had instantly mortal coronaries.

He stopped on the walk, his uplifted face moon-bathed, almost sad. The black dog seemed somewhere near.

He knocked quietly. He'd decided he wasn't the type to wave a gun or kick at locks. But his jaw fell when the door opened promptly.

Under a weak light stood a tall, rather soft man with receding hair, rimless glasses and brilliant blue eyes. The man wore grimy clothing. He looked slightly familiar.

"See here, my name is Cassius Andrews—"

"Of course," the man cut in. He smiled understandingly. "There's no need to take that tone. I've almost expected you to show up one day."

He held out his hand. "Come in, come in! Incidentally, my name is Kagle. Dr. Frederic."

VII

Before budging from the stoop, Cassius had to still his suspicions. "I mean to say, Kagle, what I came about is my brother. I want to know what happened to his body."

"Of course," the other repeated, as if it were only natural. "I'll be glad to tell you everything, Andrews. Not here on the doorstep, though. Come in and—oh." Frederic Kagle's eyes were intense and unwavering as blue gas flames. They took in Cassius's nervous glance at the dingy shadows in the hall. Dr. Kagle's manner became wry. "I see now. You expected something else. You still do. The latter-day Mafia or its equivalent. This is a perfectly legitimate research establishment."

And he reached around Cassius to grasp the door with a left hand whose ring finger bore the faint red ghost of a removed wedding band. He kept talking.

"We're a little under cover, I must admit. But we have our problems. I think you'll appreciate them once I explain. That is, if you've got the stomach to hear it all." A challenging glance. "Being a newsman, dedicated to truth in principle if not always in practice—I'm only speaking

Here Is Thy Sting

generically, of course—you should have an open mind if anyone does."

A small, confident smile played on Kagle's mouth. Cassius noted, however, that he secured the night chain on the door.

"I have to take your word that this operation is legitimate," Cassius said defensively. Kagle spun, peering hard. Cassius felt uncomfortable, as though he'd been tested and found wanting.

"Legitimate by my lights, is what I meant," Kagle said. "Some—my ex-wife among others—don't agree. I'll leave it up to your sense of fairness."

Cassius was fully aware of what Kagle was doing: using soft soap. But he was disarmed, temporarily anyway. Kagle led the way down the corridor which plainly hadn't been greatly renovated since the days when the place served as the final rest of thrombosis-stricken executives. Through two different doors jumbles of laboratory equipment winked faintly in the dark.

A third door was open, lighted. Kagle closed it quickly. He frowned, as over a minor annoyance. But not before Cassius had glimpsed more glass and metalware, and two men in spotted white coats.

One had been bending over sympathetically. The other had been seated on a stool, head on his forearms on a lucite bench, crying.

"Our work does have its personal problems too," Kagle said. He rolled back scrolled oak double doors. "Even dedicated people get shaky over the moral aspects now and then." He stood aside, waiting for Cassius to pass. Cassius caught the renewed flicker of blue intensity in the man's eye. The calm fire said that Kagle, a dedicated man, was not to be lumped with those who wallowed in shakiness.

Kagle rolled the doors shut again behind them.

The room was large, full of cheap, sharp-angled metal office furniture. A solar tube had been jerry-rigged in the wall. It shed a white, uncompromising light over all. The only signs of the room's former function were thick, threadbare carpeting, rose-petal wallpaper peeled in many places and an ancient framed motto, *I Am the Light of the World,* under which someone had taped a photo of some sort of molecular model.

Kagle circled the desk. He sat down, indicated Cassius's place.

"I think I'd better stand," Cassius said. "I didn't come here to be social."

"My dear Mr. Andrews," Kagle said gently, "you have every right to feel as you do. We should never have selected your brother. It was a mistake."

"Yes, it was. For you."

The scientist ignored the feigned toughness. "Ordinarily we try to choose people with no survivors. Last year, however, I had a fellow working for me." The blue-flame eyes brightened merrily. "My, shall we say, traffic manager? He proved to be an idiot. But he was all I could get. Now I handle that end myself. And have, ever since he slipped up a couple of times. One of his worst slipups was your brother the Reverend. It meant thirty hours' worth of work in a day instead of my usual twenty-six. But that's all right."

Cassius didn't do Kagle the favor of smiling even a little. "I want to know what you did with him."

Kagle didn't seem worried, just more amused. "So you can report us to the authorities?"

"Maybe. Well?"

Kagle pursed his lips. "Mr. Andrews, are you really tough enough to stand the truth?"

"I'm a newspaperman. I guess that qualifies me a little."

"Provided I tell you everything about your brother—which will mean in turn telling you everything about what we do here, and why I'm reduced to crawling out at night like some roach just so I can conduct a perfectly legitimate scientific study—will you promise in return not to write one word about what I say?"

Abruptly Cassius sat down. He fought to keep a straight face. A moment ago he'd been cowed by the man's assured, almost jocular manner. Now it was his turn to feel like laughing.

If the man was indeed a scientist, he was the stereotype: foolish, naive, unworldly beneath his veneer of hard-lipped dedication. What a hell of a stupid offer! Did Kagle honestly think he would pass up a chance for an exposé now that he had the material practically in his hands? He had to write what he learned. For Timothy's sake.

And for his own, too. He'd seen a glimmer of a real chance to improve his lot. Such a chance hadn't come his way in longer than he could remember. He'd almost believed he was no longer interested in opportunities. Sitting across from Kagle, he discovered otherwise.

Carefully, softly, he lied, "All right, Dr. Kagle. If that's your price, I promise."

The sap fell for it at once. "Thank you."

Why were the blue eyes merry a moment? Or was it a trick of the light? Kagle tented his fingers, leaned across the desk.

"First tell me how you found me."

"No harm in that, I guess." Cassius described his speculations, starting with those initiated the night he heard Madame Wanda Kagle ranting. "I'll admit I didn't dream she really had any connection with you. Or with Timothy. It was just sort of a—well, trigger."

Kagle shook his head. "Poor sis. She badgered me until I showed her."

A trickle of sweat, unbidden, rolled down Cassius's cheek. "Showed her what?"

"The results of our research here into the nature of death."

"The nature of—?" Cassius's eyes bugged.

Dr. Kagle leaned back, chuckling. His pink forehead shone. "There it is again. You imagine we're a bunch of necrophiles, don't you? Nothing so debased, Mr. Andrews, though in certain quarters we're certainly regarded in that light. What we're doing is simply probing the experience of dying from a qualitative standpoint. I could give you a long lecture on the theory. But in plainest terms, our work is this. I'm a neurosurgeon by training. What I do with all the dead bodies I'm forced to steal is analogous to what a man in a darkroom does when he develops film. He brings forth the latent image. A photo's latent image is both there and not there, in the silver. It awaits the right combination of chemicals before it becomes visible. So with the—" Dr. Kagle hesitated a second, as if gauging Cassius's nerve again. "—call it the latent image of death. Or images. The sensory record of the last microseconds before the mind blacks out. All the pain. All the smells, tactile sensations. The blurred sights. When I was killing time as just another white-coated bureaucrat with the

Institutes of Health, I worked out techniques which would parallel the first formulation of the proper photochemicals. And that's why I need the bodies, Mr. Andrews. What good is a darkroom technician without exposed film?"

Kagle paused. "Do you want me to go into the surgical and electronic techniques more deeply?"

"No. Let me get this straight." Cassius was sweating hard. "You're able to take someone's—corpse—and from it get a record of what it felt like for that person to die?"

"That is more or less it, yes. The process involves a great deal of painstaking surgery, much work with computers and video tape and sound-recording equipment. I tried to get the Institutes to underwrite the initial study. Naturally they wouldn't, they didn't dare. You're too young—and so am I, though perhaps I don't look it—to remember the DNA Riots when Gadsbury finally created one single cell in his lab. I'm sure you've read about the riots often. Old illusions die hard, Mr. Andrews. Some of mine died, too, when I first took up this field. I wanted to work legally. Obtain legitimate corpses in the manner of a private medical school."

"Couldn't you?"

The blue-flame eyes brightened. "A court order obtained by a committee of certain members of the clergy in this country frustrated my efforts. I decided it was prudent to go underground, so to speak. To steal the bodies I needed. After all, I'm convinced in my own mind that the work is necessary, important. And honest. Men have been martyred before. I'm prepared to be martyred myself, though of course I prefer to avoid it."

More amusement suddenly. "And I've discovered it won't be necessary, either, Mr. Andrews."

"Isn't this very expensive research?"

"Frightfully."

"Then where—?"

Kagle shrugged. "Patents. Three big ones, several small ones. Neurosurgical apparatus. The royalties are more than ample."

Cassius said, "But I don't really understand why you chose to work in this particular field."

Kagle sounded sad. "After I stumbled across the fundamental technique, it wasn't a matter of choosing."

"Your reason is—?"

"To know. What else?"

"I can see why the clergy would stand in your way."

"Franky," Kagle snapped, "I can't. I'm not in any way tampering with their precious concepts of immortality. Of course I am in a position to state that, as far as sentient experience goes, there is no immortality after the act of death. The neural latent images are feeble at best by the time I'm through scrounging for the bodies. And they quickly go altogether. Yet even though I resent the opposition, I've tried to be circumspect. Picked subjects who fit my requirements—a violent death, for maximum image strength—but have no relatives or family. I've done this partly out of vestigal moral considerations, partly from a practical wish to avert discovery and continue my studies as long as possible. With your brother, as I stated, the fool I had working for me slipped up. You were shrewd enough to locate me. Therefore I'll hide nothing, Mr. Andrews. I'm no criminal."

Cassius frowned. "Are you sure? What you're doing touches on realms other than the purely scientific."

Kagle sighed. "Metaphysics? I'm only concerned about that as it relates to the people—the clerics—who prate about it and therefore act because of it. I don't want to be dragged into a lot of messy court trials. Which is exactly what would happen if this work became public. Trials, more trials, publicity and, eventually, other harmful effects, evidences of which you saw in my sister's behavior. I'm really going to have to do something about her soon."

Cassius felt as if he should draw back, flee. But he was oddly unable.

"About my brother's body. Where is it?"

"Ruined, I'm afraid. Gone. The techniques we use are destructive. That's why there mustn't be relatives."

"What happens to your so-called latent images?"

"We record them. Five separate tracks which can be projected simultaneously for a viewer. Though viewing is a dull, limited term for the experience."

"So a person—knows how it feels to die?"

"Yes. By violence. The most painful deaths possible. Raises some interesting speculations, doesn't it? I think you intimated that Wanda was mouthing some of them. Quite apart from the empiric achievement of translating and recording a dying body's sensory images, the research opened up whole new areas of less tangible results. I only began to think about some of the related questions after the work was well under way. Namely, do people fear the *what* of death, or do they fear the *how* and its lesser partner, the *when?*"

"For myself," Cassius said slowly, "I—I'm afraid of the end. The blankness. The finality."

"Are you? I assure you there is evidence to the contrary. Death must be a little like sleep. Before you sleep, what is going to happen while you sleep is rationally graspable. The sleep of death is permanent. So you can't reconcile yourself to it wholly. But you can begin to reconcile yourself to it, if only slightly. While I don't think you can reconcile yourself to the other part reasonably. To the pain. The anguish. The lifetime of hells in one instant, one instant waiting, always waiting up there ahead. It's my contention that, because of innumerable variables not present in the sleep aspect, the pain of death can only be known when it happens. And the variables only increase the terror."

"The theory won't hold up," Cassius said. "Death, the absolute end—that's the fearful part."

"Ah, you assume that because everybody's always assumed it. I assumed so too. All I can say is, my work has revealed evidence to the contrary. Evidence no open-minded person can deny. Which is why I made you promise not to write a word."

Abruptly Cassius felt the thrust of ambition, possibilities, chances like gold. He tried to fix the lines of his face and sound demanding:

"Look, Kagle. So far all you've given me is a lot of talk. If you've recorded these so-called latent images, then they ought to be available for someone to see, right?"

"See is another poor word. Experience would be more correct."

"All right, experience, see, view, you name it. But I want it demonstrated."

"You have more courage than I thought."

"Listen, Kagle, you can't scare me. What about it?"

"If you'll hold to your promise not to write—"

"I will, yes," Cassius lied, feeling very foxy and, incidentally, very righteous.

Weren't those gas-jet eyes laughing at him all at once again?

He was puzzled. Kagle was a naive fool. Maybe Cassius only saw laughter in the eyes. The man wasn't mad, Cassius was positive of that much. Yet his confidence ebbed quickly. He had the feeling he oughtn't to go through with what he himself had suggested.

But the copy possibilities—! My God! Staggering.

"Since you volunteer, Mr. Andrews, let's step down the hall." Dr. Kagle rose, smoothing his thin hair. "I'll show you as little or as much as you find you're able to stand. This way, please."

VIII

The chamber at the rear of the funeral home had been renovated with theater seats to resemble a private projection room minus the screen. Cassius took a place in the front row center. Dr. Kagle wheeled over a cart on which were mounted several odd-looking instruments. From the instruments dangled fifteen or twenty wires which ended in assorted pads and needles.

"It'll take me a few minutes to get you wired up properly," Dr. Kagle said, snapping a leather cuff around Cassius's bare left forearm. There was unmistakable pride in his eyes as he worked. "I apologize in advance for the needle pricks, but they're necessary."

Cassius was sweating harder. He was fearful but determined to go through with it. He pointed beyond his boot.

"What's that for?"

"The pedal?" It was corrugated iron, painted red. "Just put your left foot on it. There, perfect. If at any point you want to stop, press down. All five tracks will come to a halt simultaneously. Which people do you want?"

"I don't care. Butcher—" Cassius gasped as a needle went home in his thigh. "Butcher Balk? He was the one really responsible for my being here. And Timothy, if that's possible."

"Certainly. I'll also show you one or two others for the sake of contrast. Are you quite sure you're up to it, though?"

"Hell yes," Cassius said, with more conviction than he felt.

"Very well." Dr. Kagle kept working, presently stood

back. "Got you trussed up, eh? Any of the pads chafe too much? Good. I'll be leaving. The console is in the next room. There's no need to close your eyes. The lights will dim. Then you won't see a thing in here. You'll be—But explanations are inadequate. Remember the pedal, Mr. Andrews. I won't be offended if you use it."

A door chunked shut. Cassius peered through the crisscross of wires padded to his temples. He blinked. His vision was failing.

No, it was only the dimming of solar sheets across the ceiling. Dimming fast, from pearl to ebony to nothing. Must adjust the boot on the pedal, he thought, in case it's so harrowing I—

Blur-and-whine.

A light bulb way up there. Weak, shaded with a scrap of tin.

He shifted his head. The rusted springs of the rickety cot squeaked. Suthin needs fixin with the furnace. About this time at night I got to fix the furnace but I can't remember what it is needs fixing. Suthin's wrong.

A slow, labored turn of his head. Difficulty seeing because a film of water was on the eyes. Blinking didn't help. A monster old metal furnace hulked in a corner of the musty storeroom. He could barely read the nameplate. EUREKA *E-Z Draught No. 22.* EUREKA COMFORT WORKS, *Eureka, Iowa.*

In his chest he felt the annoying, clotted little pain.

Ah Momma I can see your face right now. I been havin trouble sleepin lately Momma. Little pains in the middle. I can see you Momma, I can hear you singin and playin the piano Momma like you did on Sundays.

In his throat the breath caught. He lifted himself, blinked the eye-water back. He saw a faded, patched quilt over his chest, hands on top of it, shaking. They were ancient, wrinkled hands with thickened blue veins standing out.

The Doc don't make me work so hard these days because of the pains but the furnace needs fixin and I wonder what's wrong with m—Momma my God I'm dyin that's what's wrong.

He remembered forgotten music, *The Old Rugged Cross,*

with the bass hand beaten out in Sunday-morning rhythm, *thrummm, thrummm, thrummm.*

Fearful, he tried to cry aloud for help. He couldn't make a sound. The clotting pain, a small hurting ball inside him, widened. It troubled and troubled him. Not the pain itself, which wasn't so bad. Knowing what the pain meant.

Momma I'm goin to be seein you. I don't want it to happen like this I—

The Eureka furnace sank into darkness and sucked all the light after it.

Blur-and-whine.

"Brucie? Brucie? Oh God Brucie, don't!" his wife was screaming.

Against his palms, under his boots, the pebbled poly of the hotel wall and ledge. On his lips a queer saltiness, blood he'd drawn biting down, getting up the guts to do it.

The wind was blowing hard. It whistled and smelled of the pollution of Lake Erie. Ten stories below a crowd had collected in the Public Square. For miles he could see the lights of Cleveland, warm whites and yellows.

They were snares and delusions. The lights were behind doors of understanding, friendship, love, shut to him, shut to him every one—

"Officer, officer!" his wife screamed. "Don't let Brucie do it! Go out and get him. The poor children—"

He jumped.

The wind tugged at his palms, his cheeks. The lights blurred. His bowels loosened. Vertical rows of lights blurred and became a single strip as he hurtled down. Wind hammered his eardrums. He was falling fast, faster—

The hit was explosion. Body's total scream. Coalescing of sensation into one enormous burst of pain—

PAIN PAIN PAIN PAIN PAIN PA—

Blur-and-whine.

Behind the effin glass in the visitor's gallery the effin newsmen were already talkin on their effin portable visors.

He ran his tongue over his rough, dry lips. His scalp

felt prickly where they'd wiped it bare with that effin aerosol. Under his strapped arms the porcelain chair was cold.

Somewhere behind, footsteps, as the last effin attendant shuffled out. A door closed.

The room had a funny smell. It was prolly cause of the green walls, so effin clean an sanitary like a hospital, like a place for killin bugs. Well he wasn't no bug.

He bunched his face muscles to show he had guts. One of the effin newsmen, a fairy with ringlets, was watchin him and talkin in the visor. He was sure he saw the effer's mouth make the words, "Butcher Balk is now sitting in the chair ladies and gentlemen."

All at once, without wanting to, he was pulling against the cuffs and leg straps. They hurt. "Oh no, oh no, please Jesus, I—"

Something whacked softly like a toggle jamming between contacts. Lights dimmed. Eyes?

Pain was beginning. A stiff, ghastly tickling that instantly doubled, tripled, quadrupled, multiplying, multiplying, a rising blast of dreadful murdering pain—

PAIN PAIN PAIN PAIN PA—

Blur-and-whine.

"—outa this! You stay out or ge' killed," de Diego chanted. "You watch it, Christer, I'm warnin' you."

Tipsy, back and forth, faces in the cheap bar swung. His hands were ineffectual, soft, untrained for struggle. He tried to hold both the right shoulder of de Diego, the left shoulder of Ratface Lats. The three of them struggled, roiling the amphet vapors thick in the bar.

"Watch out Revrun Tim," one of the whores cried. "He gotta knife."

"I tell you you must not take each other's life," he shouted, fighting between them, vocal cords nearly raw.

Something jerked at his left shoulder. Spun him fast. De Diego's drug-swollen eyes loomed. Silver flashed in his hand.

"I warn you din I Christer?" was the scream, and suddenly a hole was in him, and tears tasting on his lips.

The hole widened in his stomach. He could feel de Diego actually wrenching and driving the knife into him, down into his bowels to the bottom, bringing in one un-

foreseen torrent a dimming of his eyes, and no time even to think a prayer as he tottered, everything blurred beneath pain—
PAIN PAIN PAIN PA—

Crash, crash, like a madman Cassius hammered his boot on the pedal, where was it, it must be there, *crash, crash.*
Drool was on his lips. His head was thrown back, wrenching, the eyes shut. Wires snapped as he wrenched, his leg going up and down like a mad thing, *crash, crash, crash—*
"Stop it! Stop it! Stop it! Stop it! Stop it!"

IX

Limp, drained, Cassius leaned one arm on the ledge of the Aircoupe blister. His left leg hadn't yet stopped trembling.

The moon sailed high and round over the Westport slums. A shadow disengaged from the night, leaned close to the little car. For a moment Cassius had trouble recognizing or remembering.

Then everything washed back. His hands clawed on the blister ledge. He strained up, thrashing at impossible terror all around.

"There, there, take it easy," said Kagle. The grip on his arm steadied him. Cassius sank back down in the bucket seat.

"How did I get out here?"

"I carried you after I unstrapped you. You fainted. I'm sorry about that last sequence. But you did specifically ask for it. I have a bottle of brandy in my office. It might help. Do you want to go back inside?"

Cassius buried his face in his hands. "Christ, no. Christ."

After several seconds he raised his head again. At last he was gaining control. "Kagle, you're a goddamn monster, that's what you are. What you have in there—it—it's—" He shivered. No one word could encompass it.

Cynical tolerance tinged Kagle's lips in the moonlight. "No, Andrews. You're wrong. It's only the truth. Death as it really is."

Cassius swiped at his moist upper lip. "Who was that first one? That smelly old man?"

Dr. Kagle looked quite interested. "Why do you ask?"

"Because—it wasn't as bad as the rest."

"Interesting. I found that to be the case myself. That was old Peckham. He used to be the janitor here. I kept him on to do odd jobs. He was eighty-six and nearly senile when he died in the middle of the night one night, of simple old age."

"That was—just an ordinary death?"

"Yes. Did you find it painful?"

"A little. Not as bad as—the others. Not nearly as bad."

Dr. Kagle went, "Um. After I'd begun my work, it occurred to me to look into at least one natural, quiet death by way of contrast. Peckham's latent images were quite weak. But they surprised me. I've done a couple of similar analyses since. The so-called quiet, ordinary death has a minimum of pain associated with it, but it's all quite bearable. So you see, Mr. Andrews, I think that what we really fear is the awful pain of a violent end." Kagle paused. He peered down sharply. "Or don't you grasp the significance?"

Hardly hearing, Cassius blurted, "I'll write about this. Expose this dirty business."

"Mr. Andrews, I don't think you will."

"There's something indecent about—what did you say? Oh. My promise. Well, I lied to you."

"I know you did."

Cassius stared.

"But that's all right, Andrews. I let you lie to make it seem you were putting something over on me. That you were fooling me into permitting you to see the tracks. When Flange and his toughs came here right after the court order business, he also threatened me, Mr. Andrews. Arrest. A treason trial. You name it. I appeared to be frightened, pliant. I explained my work. I told him I'd let him judge for himself, and if he thought I was a criminal, I would submit to arrest. I let him sit in the same chair you occupied. And then his men, one at a time. Flange hasn't bothered me since. That's why I let you see, Andrews. In a way, you and Flange and Wanda are part of the surprising evidence that's begun to come in. Evidence that it isn't the long sleep we fear after all but the how that's our lash and spur. The unknown, potentially horrible *how*. There is some reason to fear it if we die in

Here Is Thy Sting

bed, but monumental reason if our death turns out to be violent. As you saw."

Cassius's mind was still slow. It grabbed at phrases: "Flange? He came here? You bastard."

Kagle nodded. "Yes. I must say he and his men bore up rather well. So did my sister Wanda. They all endured the tracks to the end."

"Trying to say I'm a coward?" Cassius choked. "Trying to say—"

"Don't be belligerent," Kagle cut in gently. "The only reason you reacted so violently back inside was because of the intensely personal connection. Your brother was dying, not some stranger. The human body, mind, are surprisingly resilient. The endurance is remarkable." Kagle seemed sad. "Yet isn't it strange how men and women don't know their own strength? Think they must protect themselves? Make themselves safe, secure?"

Cassius glowered. "Quit it, Kagle. Weepy expressions don't fool me. You don't give a God damn for anybody else."

Kagle seemed to muse over this. "In a sense perhaps that's true. Else I wouldn't be in this peculiar work. Or intending to go ahead with it, as I am. But I am rather sorry for you, Mr. Andrews."

The "Hah!" from Cassius was short, cackling, grotesque.

"Oh, I realize you don't believe me, but I truly am sorry in my own way. I shouldn't have put you through it. I should have been aware of the personal element. Also, I should have avoided it because I'm beginning to see the pattern which I hinted about. In the aftereffects, I mean."

Suddenly Kagle leaned close to the Aircoupe again. For the first time there was raw, fundamental emotion on his face:

"If it became widely known that I could arrange such experiences I'd have no peace. No, I can't let you write, Mr. Andrews. For if they came after me *en masse*, there'd be no end. Don't you see what I could offer them? That is to say—" Eyes haunted now. "—if I would, which I won't, because I know where it would lead?"

"No," Cassius said, low. "I don't see."

"I could say to them, come to me, steel yourself, prepare to endure five minutes of the most agonizing pain on this earth. Live through the most anguished of deaths, the most violent. Then you'll be free the rest of your life. Free because the worst will be over. Free because, satistically, don't you see, you and millions like you wont ever die so violently. You'll die the lesser death of a Peckham, with only a bit of eminently endurable pain. Nothing near the kind of pain which, say, that criminal endured."

Cassius snickered. "Who'd fall for that?"

"Many, Mr. Andrews. In fact I believe most. I won't pretend it's a riskless proposition, I'd have to say to them. You might, just might, be one of the few in ten millions who will die violently one day. But the risk is infinitesimal. While the reward—well, I could say, if you go through the ultimate, the worst now, think of the years ahead. The years of not having to fear, always fear the unknowable. Dying a Peckham's death then would be child's play, don't you see? And should you lose the gamble—die a violent death after all, I would say—why, then even it might be a whit less terrible. Of course the real benefit, I would say, lies in the years free of fear. If that sounds like a foolish offer, Mr. Andrews, five minutes of hell in exchange for a lifetime of release from the terror dying holds—if it sounds illogical that anyone would accept—if you believe people wouldn't clamor for it—then I submit, Andrews, that you don't know a damn thing about the nature of the world you're living in."

"No one would want—" Cassius began, unsure.

"Wouldn't they? Are you aware of the temper of men's minds over the past eighty years? What do most people desire of life anymore, Mr. Andrews? To be secure against the harms of life. Don't ask me why. Perhaps we'll never understand all the complicated reasons lost back in the years. But people want it. The price keeps rising, but they still want it. I could give it to them. At the price of being Butcher Balk for five short minutes. And they can stand it. Wanda stood it. Flange stood it. Afterward, there'd be *nothing left to fear*. The world is peopled with Peckhams, not Butcher Balks, Mr. Andrews."

Then, slowly, Kagle sighed. "But I'll never say any of that, Mr. Andrews. I'll never say I could pull fear's fangs, simply because I know they'd want it. They wouldn't be satisfied with less than everything once they heard. Not until they learned the real price. Not until it was too late. Not until the world's engine stopped."

"Yours hasn't stopped," Cassius snarled.

"No," Kagle said, almost sad again. "But then I've never permitted myself to experience more than two senses of any subject at any one time."

His pale hand lifted, in the general direction of the moon high above the world, as if to say the subject was at last exhausted. Flickering on his face were the expressions of two men, one the god, one the assassin of everything.

The god could have slain the assassin by surrendering his godhood in suicide. Being a god, he couldn't quite. No, said the gas-blue eyes, he couldn't quite, ever.

"Good night, Mr. Andrews," Dr. Kagle definitely sounded weary. "I know it's been too harrowing. But you did ask me about your brother. What choice did I have?"

Muttering all the obscenities he knew, Cassius jammed his card into the ignition slot and rammed the Aircoupe away from the vicinity of the funeral parlor, leaving the blister open so he could shout back, "You rotten bastard, I'll tell the world about this, I'll let them know—"

X

The Etaoin Pub was located on the fourth sub-level of the Capitol World Truth Building.

The pneumodoor went *hush-hush* open, then closed. Cassius heard it dimly. He was slumped over the bar, looking at his globe of Old Kentuckye Woodesman 120 Proof Sippin' Sauce.

He heard footsteps. He continued to peer into the amber infinity of the booze. Who the hell cared about footsteps?

"Cassius? It is you! Good God in heaven, sweets, what's happened?"

The barkeep ambled over. "Friend of yours, lady?"

"You're new around here."

"Yeah. Hired on two weeks ago."

"This man works on the paper upstairs."

The barkeep sniggered. "When?"

"What?"

"Lady, this guy's been campin' here since the day I started."

Fuzzily Cassius recognized the voice of Joy de Veever. His body felt weighted with bags of lead shot. It was an effort merely to turn and blink his red eyes slowly, like an owl.

Joy had something clasped in her arms. Her glance was alternately indignant and sympathetic.

"I should have thought of coming to this bar sooner, Cassius. But you're not the drinking type."

"Every time some of the boys from the paper come in," said the barkeep, "he goes to the john. First time, when he didn't come out for a while, I thought he was sick. Went back there myself. He was just standing. Told me to leave him alone. I did. When the boys left after lunch, he came out. Same routine in the evening, too. Sometimes he leaves but he always comes back. Wonder where he goes at ni—"

"Thanks for your help," Joy cut in. "I'll take over. Cassius?"

"Lee me lone," he said, finding it like climbing Everest to gesture.

"Cassius, what in God's name is the trouble?"

Getting no answer, Joy pulled up the next stool. She told the barkeep she wanted nothing to drink. The tone clearly instructed him to leave. He did. Cassius blinked at the object in Joy's hand. Some sort of book with a tricky shining clasp.

"Cassius love, I've been searching for you ever since I got back yesterday. It's apparent that I shouldn't have spent that week and a half in Bonn at the Floorwax Institute trade show." She sounded affronted. "In the interval it seems you've completely lost your mind."

"Perfly all right." His tongue was oh so heavy. "Perfly."

"Perfectly my eye! I just talked to Hughgenine upstairs."

"Bothrin me. Come in here and bother me. I didn't make it to the men's in time."

"Bothering! I should hope so! After all, when you don't show up to work for sixteen days straight, it's natural for him to bother. Cassius—darling—" And the tears were genuine all at once, rolling down over her rouged cheeks. "Are you in trouble? Hughgenine said he lost his temper. He's sorry he fired you on the spot. He'll take you back if only you'll tell somebody what's wrong. Cassius? Wake up and listen to me! You're being horrid. You don't know the agony I've been through. Last night I nearly had your floor super thinking you'd suffered a heart attack and must

Here Is Thy Sting

be lying dead inside your flat. What hit that place? Your books were all torn apart."

"So wat?" he inquired. "So wat, so wat? Joy lee me lone."

"I will not leave you alone! I'll get you to a doctor. Do something! Are you having a nervous breakdown, sweetheart? To destroy your things that way—all the notes for the biography of that colonel strewn all over in pieces—"

"Stupid book. Useless goddam wase time."

"Are you in trouble with some woman, Cassius?"

He giggled, but it had a dull sound.

"Cassius, I must say it again. You're treating me very unkindly. After all, you do mean something to me, you know. Please, please, please tell me what's wrong."

"Oh nothin. I just got a tase for booze, 's all."

"Obviously." Joy couldn't help sounding smug. "And obviously you're in no shape to help anybody who wishes to help you, whether it's Hughgenine or me or anyone. That's why I brought this. I figured if the answer can't be gotten from you, it can be gotten from this. Unless you've lost your mind so thoroughly you've broken every single habit you ever had."

She was extending the object in her hand. The clasp looked vaguely familiar. Why did he feel alarmed?

"I found your other diary too, Cassius. In pieces. This one was intact."

"Too tough," he muttered. "Too dam tough tear up. Hey." Again he blinked. "Snoopin?"

"Yes, snooping. I admit it. I had to find some explanation for the peculiar, awful way you're behaving. Now you tell me how to open this lock, Cassius. Either that or you tell me what's the matter with you. Else I'll go to the stationer's where you bought it. See, the name's stamped in gold on the back. It's right on this level. I'll force them to disclose the code."

"Gimme tha," he said, lifting his eighty-pound hand, trying to thrust it through the gloomy darkness of the bar.

The effort cracked away some of his lethargy. He felt he must have the diary in his possession. Then he knew that the last entry mentioned the Commuter's Rest Mortuary Chapel by name. Didn't it?

He wasn't positive. He thought so. Warning bells, so faint he barely heard them.

"I will not." Joy held the book miles away. "I will not give it to you."

"I said gimme—!" he cried, standing. He toppled on his face.

From afar, Joy said to the barkeep, "You watch him. This man's sick. I'm going to get this book opened and then we'll take him to a hospital. You just watch him a few minutes. No, you shut up, do as I say! Want to lose your job? The paper owns this building, leases this space, or aren't you aware of that? Here, Cassius. Stand up."

As he fumbled his way back to the stool with her help, he managed to perceive what it meant. Joy, poor old Joy. Sure she wanted to help. Sure. The locked diary tantalized her. Anything that might harbor a scrap of something hot tantalized her.

Paper leased the space? For the stationer's too, probably. They'd come across with the code under threat. He made one more abortive lunge for the book.

He grabbed the poly bar rim to keep from falling. He could see it now. He didn't actually care but he felt he should. The book would open to a tune whose notes and name he couldn't recall. Then Joy's curious eyes. They'd glitter, running down the entries.

Then showing it to Hughgenine. Then the trail to Kagle. Joy's hot one, the big hot one in reach at last. Plus her sense of avenging him. As if that mattered.

Christ. What Kagle had said was true, true. First one person would have—he shuddered and knuckled his eyes and moaned a little—those experiences. Then the next would have to see what the experience was. Then the next after that. Then someone would see how it could pull the fangs of fear. Go through the worst, the very worst, and your imagination won't have anything to gnaw on, year after year. Wanda Kagle put it right. *I've been there.*

Christ, the government and the do-gooders would probably seize everything. The public good. Uplift. You can stand five minutes of Butcher Balk to be free, can't you? Take a chance, you're bound to die like Peckham. Think of the peace. *I've been there.*

Dimly he recalled the thousands on the waiting lists of the Securo Corporation. They'd want it. Everyone would want it but a few who, like Kagle, might see the threat.

Here Is Thy Sting

They would cry out. Their cries would be lost in the howls of happiness. *Get it over. Nothing so bad ever again.*

I've been there.

Did they know what it would do? Did they care? No, they wouldn't care, they'd weep for joy as it multiplied, on, on, to the ends of the earth—

But though he knew these things in a dim way, he couldn't put them all into words. It took too much effort.

"Worl's engine," Cassius whimpered. "Joy don, worl's engine."

Or had he said it aloud at all? He wasn't sure. He'd made the effort in his skull. Whether the effort had stirred his voice box, lips, tongue, he couldn't say. He felt so immeasurably tired. He crawled back up on the stool. Even his sense of urgency, alarm, had aborted. No longer could he be sure why he'd spoken. It certainly couldn't have been for any good reason. He didn't have any good reasons.

Still, something made him squeak it once more, "Worl's engine."

The barkeep clucked his tongue. "Mister? The lady can't hear you."

A feeble whisper, dying: "Worl's engine."

"Mister, you're dreaming. The lady left."

That roused him a little. "Use have a dream. This dog. Chasin me. Not anymore. No dreams since—"

The sentence dribbled off. It didn't seem worth finishing. Only the drink. His hand crawled out. Only the drink seemed worth finishing. And he wasn't even certain about that, really.

A JOHN JAKES BIBLIOGRAPHY

BOOKS—SCIENCE FICTION AND FANTASY

The Asylum World, 1969, 171 pp. Paperback Library.
Black in Time, 1970, 171 pp. Paperback Library.
Brak the Barbarian, 1968, 173 pp. Avon.
Brak the Barbarian Versus the Mark of the Demons, 1969, 159 pp. Paperback Library.
Brak the Barbarian Versus the Sorceress, 1969, 160 pp. Paperback Library.
Conquest of the Planet of the Apes (novelization of the screenplay by Paul Dehn) 1974, 187 pp. Award Books.
The Hybrid, 1969, 157 pp. Paperback Library.
The Last Magicians, 1969, 190 pp. Signet Books.
Mask of Chaos, 1970, 134 pp. Ace.
Master of the Dark Gate, 1970, 219 pp. Lancer Books.
Mention My Name in Atlantis, 1972, 142 pp. DAW Books.
Monte Cristo #99, 1970, 176 pp. Curtis Books.
On Wheels, 1973, 174 pp. Warner Paperback Library.
The Planet Wizard, 1969, 159 pp. Ace.
Secrets of Stardeep, 1969, 192 pp. Westminster Press.
Six-gun Planet, 1970, 174 pp. Paperback Library.
Time Gate, 1972, 174 pp. Westminster Press. Junior Literary Guild, 1972.
Tonight We Steal the Stars, 1969, 173 pp. Ace.
When the Star Kings Die, 1967, 160 pp. Ace.
Witch of the Dark Gate, 1972, 175 pp. Lancer Books.

SHORTER FICTION

"And the Monsters Walk"
Fantastic Adventures, July, 1952.
"The Android Kill"
Planet Stories, January, 1952.
"The Beast"
If, May, 1952.

"Blizzard Brain" (by Darius John Granger)
  Space Travel, July, 1958.
"Buggaratz"
  Worlds of Tomorrow, January, 1966.
"A Cabbage Named Sam"
  Fantastic, October, 1961.
"Checkmate Morning"
  Avon Science Fiction and Fantasy, January, 1953.
"Coffin to Mars"
  Fantastic Adventures, September, 1952.
"Crack-Up"
  Fantasy and Science Fiction, September, 1954.
"The Cybernetic Kid"
  Fantastic Universe, February, 1956.
"Deadly Mission" (by Alexander Blade)
  Space Travel, September, 1958.
"Death Has Green Eyes"
  Fantastic Adventures, March, 1951.
"The Devil Spins a Sun-Dream"
  Space Science Fiction, Spring, 1957.
"Devils in the Walls" (Brak)
  Fantastic, May, 1963.
  (revised) *Swords Against Tomorrow*, (Hoskins, ed.), NAL, 1970.
"Dirge for the Sane"
  Fantastic Universe, September, 1954.
"Doom Jungle"
  Fantastic Adventures, October, 1952.
  Fantastic Adventures Yearbook, 1970.
"The Dreaming Trees"
  Fantastic Adventures, November, 1950.
  Thrilling Science Fiction Adventures, Summer, 1970.
"Earth Can Be Fun"
  Imagination, May, 1953.
"Feed Me, Mr. Wodgett"
  Monster Parade, September, 1958.
"The Fiends in the Bedroom"
  Cosmos Science Fiction and Fantasy, September, 1953.
"The Fire Magicians"
  Amazing Stories, February, 1952.
"Forever Is So Long"
  Avon Science Fiction and Fantasy, April, 1953.
"Frozen Hell"
  Planet Stories, July, 1952.
"Ghoul's Garden" (Brak)
  Flashing Swords, No. 2, (Lin Carter, ed.), Dell, 1974.
  Flashing Swords, No. 2, (Lin Carter, ed.), Nelson Doubleday, 1975.

SHORTER FICTION (continued)

"The Girl in the Gem" (Brak)
   Fantastic, January, 1965.
   The Fantastic Swordsmen, (de Camp, ed.), Pyramid, 1967.

"Half-past Fear"
   Super Science Stories, August, 1955.

"Here Is Thy Sting"
   Orbit 3, (Knight, ed.), Putnam's, 1968.
   Orbit 3, (Knight, ed.), Berkeley, 1969.

"Hero at Work"
   Venture, January, 1957.

"The Highest Form of Life"
   Amazing Stories, August, 1961.
   The Most Thrilling Science Fiction Ever Told, Fall, 1967.

"Hunt the Red Roe" (by Alan Payne)
   Avon Science Fiction and Fantasy, April, 1953.

"Idiot Command"
   Amazing Stories, October, 1952.

"In the Days of King Arsgrat"
   Fantastic, January, 1963.

"The Long Love-In"
   Broadside, March, 1968.

"Love Is a Punch in the Nose"
   Bizarre, January, 1966.

"Machine"
   Fantasy and Science Fiction, April, 1952.

"The Man Who Wanted to Be in the Movies"
   The Hollywood Nightmare, (Haining, ed.), Taplinger, 1970.

"Merry Christmas, Post/Gute"
   Amazing Stories, January, 1970.

"Miranda"
   Fantastic, May, 1965.

"The Mirror of Wizardry" (Brak)
   Worlds of Fantasy, vol. 1, no. 1, 1968.

"Miss Impossible" (by C. H. Thames)
   Imagination, October, 1958.

"The Most Horrible Story"
   Imagination, January, 1952.
   Playboy, February, 1955.

"My Brother on the Highway"
   Infinity, October, 1956.

"Night of the Robots" (by Allen Wilder)
   The Original Science Fiction, July, 1959.

"Nine Shadows at Doomsday" (by S. M. Tenneshaw)
   Space Travel, November, 1958.

"No Dark Gallows for Me"
   Fantastic Adventures, January, 1951.
   The Strangest Stories Ever Told, Summer, 1970.

"No Vinism Like Chauvinism"
  Amazing Stories, April, 1965.
"Old Spacemen Never Die"
  Amazing Stories, October, 1951.
"One Race Show"
  Galaxy, August, 1962.
"The Opener of the Crypt" (2-part)
  Fantastic, November, December, 1952.
"The Pillars of Chambalor" (Brak)
  Fantastic, March, 1965.
  Sword and Sorcery Annual, 1975.
"Political Machine"
  Amazing Stories, March, 1961.
"The Protector"
  Amazing Stories, May, 1962.
  Science Fiction Greats, Summer, 1969.
"Ranging"
  The Farthest Reaches, (Elder, ed.), Trident Press, 1968.
  Pocket Books, 1969.
"Recidivism Preferred"
  Amazing Stories, February, 1962.
  Great Science Fiction, Fall, 1967.
"The Revenge of Edwin Mudd"
  Amazing Stories, 1954.
"The Running Hounds"
  If, November, 1952.
"The Screams of the Wergs" (by Jay Scotland)
  Fantastic, May, 1963.
"Secret of the Burning Finger"
  Amazing Stories, March, 1951.
"Seedling from the Stars"
  Worlds of Tomorrow, Winter, 1970.
"The Sellers of the Dream"
  Galaxy, June, 1963.
  Spectrum IV, (Amis, ed.), Conquest, Harcourt, Brace and World, 1965.
  Berkley, 1965.
  The Far-out People, (Hoskins, ed.), NAL, 1971.
  Tomorrow, Inc. (Greenberg and Olander, eds.), Taplinger, 1976.
"Shango"
  If, February, 1956.
"The Silk of Shaitan" (Brak)
  Fantastic, April, 1965.
"Skin Game"
  Imagination, October, 1952.
"Space Opera"
  Imagination, March, 1952.

SHORTER FICTION (continued)

"Stranger with Roses" (1-act play) (short story version: Half-past Fear")
   Acting version: Dramatic Publishing Co., 1972.
   Reading version: *Infinity 4*, (Hoskins, ed.), Lancer, 1976.
                        6 Science-Fiction Plays, (Elwood, ed.), Pocket Books, 1976.

"Survey"
   Cosmos Science Fiction and Fantasy, March, 1954.

"The Taint"
   Science Fiction Quarterly, August, 1955.

"The Treasure"
   Pittsburgh Courier (magazine), July 10, 1954.

"Underfollow"
   Fantasy and Science Fiction, May, 1963.

"War Drums of Mercury Lost"
   Planet Stories, January, 1953.

"When the Idols Walked" (2-part)   (Brak)
   Fantastic, August, September, 1964.

"Witch of the Four Winds" (2-part)   (Brak)
   Fantastic, November, December, 1963.

"With Intent to Kill"
   Cosmos Science Fiction and Fantasy, November, 1953.

"With Wings"
   Space Science Fiction, September, 1952.
   British edition: *Space Science Fiction*, 1953.

"Your Number Is Up"
   Amazing Stories, December, 1950.
   Science Fantasy, Winter, 1971.

ANDRE NORTON
in DAW BOOKS editions

☐ **MERLIN'S MIRROR.** A brand-new novel, written for DAW, of science-lore versus Arthurian legendry.
(#UW1340—$1.50)

☐ **SPELL OF THE WITCH WORLD.** A DAW exclusive, continuing the famous Witch World stories, and not available elsewhere.
(#UY1179—$1.25)

☐ **THE CRYSTAL GRYPHON.** The latest in the beloved Witch World novels, it is an outstanding other-world adventure.
(#UY1187—$1.25)

☐ **HERE ABIDE MONSTERS.** Trapped in a parallel world, just off Earth's own map and right out of legend.
(#UY1134—$1.25)

☐ **GARAN THE ETERNAL.** An epic adventure in lost worlds and unmeasured time—never before in paperbacks.
(#UY1186—$1.25)

☐ **THE BOOK OF ANDRE NORTON.** Novelettes, short stories, articles, and a bibliography make this a treat for Norton's millions of readers.
(#UW1341—$1.50)

☐ **PERILOUS DREAMS.** Tamisen crosses four worlds in her quest for reality ... a DAW exclusive.
(#UY1237—$1.25)

DAW BOOKS are represented by the publishers of Signet and Mentor Books, **THE NEW AMERICAN LIBRARY, INC.**

THE NEW AMERICAN LIBRARY, INC.,
P.O. Box 999, Bergenfield, New Jersey 07621

Please send me the DAW BOOKS I have checked above. I am enclosing
$_____(check or money order—no currency or C.O.D.'s).
Please include the list price plus 35¢ a copy to cover mailing costs.

Name_____

Address_____

City_____ State_____ Zip Code_____
Please allow at least 4 weeks for delivery

Presenting JOHN NORMAN in DAW editions . . .

☐ **SLAVE GIRL OF GOR.** The eleventh novel of Earth's orbital counterpart makes an Earth girl a puppet of vast conflicting forces. The 1977 Gor novel. (#UJ1285—$1.95)

☐ **TRIBESMEN OF GOR.** The tenth novel of Tarl Cabot takes him face to face with the Others' most dangerous plot—in the vast Tahari desert with its warring tribes.
(#UE1296—$1.75)

☐ **HUNTERS OF GOR.** The saga of Tarl Cabot on Earth's orbital counterpart reaches a climax as Tarl seeks his lost Talena among the outlaws and panther women of the wilderness. (#UE1294—$1.75)

☐ **MARAUDERS OF GOR.** The ninth novel of Tarl Cabot's adventures takes him to the northland of transplanted Vikings and into direct confrontation with the enemies of two worlds. (#UE1295—$1.75)

☐ **TIME SLAVE.** The creator of Gor brings back the days of the caveman in a vivid lusty new novel of time travel and human destiny. (#UW1204—$1.50)

☐ **IMAGINATIVE SEX.** A study of the sexuality of male and female which leads to a new revelation of sensual liberation. (#UJ1146—$1.95)

DAW BOOKS are represented by the publishers of Signet and Mentor Books, THE NEW AMERICAN LIBRARY, INC.

THE NEW AMERICAN LIBRARY, INC.,
P.O. Box 999, Bergenfield, New Jersey 07621

Please send me the DAW BOOKS I have checked above. I am enclosing
$_____(check or money order—no currency or C.O.D.'s).
Please include the list price plus 35¢ a copy to cover mailing costs.

Name_____

Address_____

City_____State_____Zip Code_____

Please allow at least 4 weeks for delivery

☐ **THE 1977 ANNUAL WORLD'S BEST SF.** Featuring Asimov, Tiptree, Aldiss, Coney, and a galaxy of great ones. An SFBC Selection. (#UE1297—$1.75)

☐ **THE 1976 ANNUAL WORLD'S BEST SF.** A winner with Fritz Leiber, Brunner, Cowper, Vinge, and more. An SFBC Selection. (#UW1232—$1.50)

☐ **THE 1975 ANNUAL WORLD'S BEST SF.** The authentic "World's Best" featuring Bester, Dickson, Martin, Asimov, etc. (#UW1170—$1.50)

☐ **THE DAW SCIENCE FICTION READER.** The unique anthology with a full novel by Andre Norton and tales by Akers, Dickson, Bradley, Stableford, and Tanith Lee. (#UW1242—$1.50)

☐ **THE YEAR'S BEST FANTASY STORIES: 2.** The only annual of its kind, edited by Lin Carter, and starring DeCamp, Davidson, Swann, Leiber, and many more. (#UY1248—$1.25)

☐ **THE YEAR'S BEST HORROR STORIES: SERIES IV.** Another great DAW service volume, this one has Hal Clement, Lafferty, Lumley, Leiber, and other favorites. (#UY1263—$1.25)

DAW BOOKS are represented by the publishers of Signet and Mentor Books, THE NEW AMERICAN LIBRARY, INC.

THE NEW AMERICAN LIBRARY, INC.,
P.O. Box 999, Bergenfield, New Jersey 07621

Please send me the DAW BOOKS I have checked above. I am enclosing $_____ (check or money order—no currency or C.O.D.'s). Please include the list price plus 35¢ a copy to cover mailing costs.

Name_____

Address_____

City_____ State_____ Zip Code_____
Please allow at least 4 weeks for delivery

☐ **ELRIC OF MELNIBONE by Michael Moorcook.** The first of the great sagas of the Eternal Champion—back in print in a new and corrected edition. (#UY1259—$1.25)

☐ **THE SAILOR ON THE SEAS OF FATE by Michael Moorcock.** The second Elric novel—now first published in America. (#UY1270—$1.25)

☐ **LEGENDS FROM THE END OF TIME by Michael Moorcock.** Strange and diverting adventures of the last decadents on Earth. (#UY1281—$1.25)

☐ **THE JEWEL IN THE SKULL by Michael Moorcock.** The First Book in the History of the Runestaff. (#UY1276—$1.25)

☐ **THE WEIRD OF THE WHITE WOLF by Michael Moorcock.** The third novel of the saga of Elric of Melnibone. (#UY1286—$1.25)

☐ **THE MAD GOD'S AMULET by Michael Moorcock.** The second Book in the History of the Runestaff. (#UY1289—$1.25)

☐ **THE LAND LEVIATHAN by Michael Moorcock.** High adventure in an alternate past and an alternate future. (#UY1214—$1.25)

DAW BOOKS are represented by the publishers of Signet and Mentor Books, THE NEW AMERICAN LIBRARY, INC.

THE NEW AMERICAN LIBRARY, INC.,
P.O. Box 999, Bergenfield, New Jersey 07621

Please send me the DAW BOOKS I have checked above. I am enclosing
$_____(check or money order—no currency or C.O.D.'s).
Please include the list price plus 35¢ a copy to cover mailing costs.

Name_____

Address_____

City_____State_____Zip Code_____
Please allow at least 4 weeks for delivery